THE SISTERHOOD OF THE BLACK DRAGONFLY

Timothy Reynolds

cometcatcher
press

Cover Art & Design by Timothy Reynolds.
Front Cover Background Image: egal: iStock/Getty Images.
Author photo: Cometcatcher Media

First Edition: 2019

Library and Archives Canada Cataloguing in Publication

Reynolds, Timothy G. M. 1960-
The Sisterhood of the Black Dragonfly/
        Timothy G.M. Reynolds

ISBN: 978-0-9939631-5-5

1. Fantasy .2. Fairy. I. Title. II.
Title: The Sisterhood of the Black Dragonfly

Cometcatcher Press
Calgary, Alberta. Canada.

Also from Timothy Reynolds

Waking Anastasia

The Death of God & Other Stories

The Broken Shield

the Cynglish beat

Stand Up & Succeed

www.tgmreynolds.com

For

My Wonderful, Dancing Fairy of a Granddaughter,
Cadence Allyson Hope,

&

The wonderful, unknown artists who created these
beautiful, inspiring ladies who, to me, are
The Sisterhood of the Black Dragonfly;
(I contacted the company - www.NemesisNow.com -
and they said they were "designed in-house")

&

The fabulous women in my life who inspired the
personalities behind the Sisterhood...
V, B, J, C, S, & N

Special Thanks to

Adrienne Greenwood-Cruise
Jennifer Rahn
Katherine Salter
Shannon Allen

&

David B. Coe & my fellow
When Words Collide Workshoppers:
Marie Banville
Anna Bortolotto
Kathy Briant
June Carr
Brent Nichols

&

ShaunaLee Curwin
Naomi Davis
Stacey Kondla
Suzy Vadori
Virginia O'Dine
Sue Campbell

Chapter One

The old, one-eyed troll squeezed himself into the dark recesses of the cave. Deadly sunlight punched hard and fast through a fissure in the cave's roof and sliced a bright beam of death much too close to his massive, knobby, hairy foot. Torby the gnome and his grandson hung back, lest they be stepped on or eaten. Their liege, Lord Orrin—a faery not much taller than the troll's ankle or Torby's waist—hovered in the sunlight and laughed. Two faery guards hovered close by.

"Don't worry, troll. The sunlight doesn't reach farther than that." The Lord brushed at a huge cobweb on his once-spotless sleeve, but the web was well and truly latched onto the nap of the dark green velvet doublet. He turned quickly in the air to face the gnomes. "Cast the bones, Old Timer! I need to know!"

Torby towered over his liege, but dared not look him in the eye. "I have done so."

"You *did* them for yourself and gave me a second-hand account. Throw them now for *me*, and hope the results are not the same." He jabbed a finger at Dillweed, Torby's grandson. "And you, Dimwit, make certain your grandfather tells the truth or you'll set off the truth-or-pain spell. I cast it on *you* so it won't affect the veracity of the old one's bone rolling."

"Yes, m…m…milord." Dillweed sighed. "Roll them, Grandfather, please. I just want us to go home." He hung his head.

Torby's old gut went icy with the shame he'd gotten them both into this mess. "Aye. Our own hearth would be welcome about now, even with your grandmother's nagging."

The faery lord coughed a cough more full of menace than phlegm. Torby reached into the enchanted, worn, suede pouch at his belt and came out with a delicate handful of tiny bones. When Torby inherited them, his own grandfather told him they were bones of an infant dark-sprite. He'd never had reason to doubt the tale, but just this once he wished they were merely enchantment-free hummingbird bones so he could manipulate and read whatever he wished into them. He tossed the handful of fine, bleached remains into the copper flat-bottomed bowl Dillweed held out, and accepted the bowl. He closed his eyes and swirled the bowl, causing the little bones to spin around the inside. He gave the bowl a twist and the bones flipped gracefully into the air, arcing to land back in the bowl with thin metallic pings.

Dillweed held the lantern close and the two of them bent over the casting. Torby shook his head, sadly. He had to speak the truth or pain would burn through his only grandson like a wildfire. "Two full moons from tonight, your sister, Lady Orlaith, will inherit your lands, uncontested." Orrin and his dark sister had been subtly poking at each other with sharp sticks both literal and figurative on and off for eons, and Torby had a horrid feeling deep in his gut that his casting was going to send his liege over the edge to do something reckless. Many faery folk could die on both sides of the borders.

"Nothing has changed, then? Is there *nothing* I can do to alter this path? What if I send an assassin to my dear sister's court?"

Old Torby swirled the bowl of bones around thrice, widdershins, and tossed them with a quick, practiced flick of his wrist. They landed firmly and stuck. The truth lay before him in the bones and he could do naught but read them. "Send assassin after assassin and they will all fail. You have a hope, though. You must marry a willing faery lass who has not yet bonded with her Life Tree."

"Easily done. I'll simply take a *dozen* unbound lasses."

The gnome examined the cast bones again, pulling Dillweed's lamp closer. "The bones are quite specific, my Lord. She must be *willing*."

"This is nonsense! My sister cannot simply inherit my lands. Not only will *I* not permit it, but neither will The King."

"King Oberon will have no choice, milord." He continued to read the portent. "On the second new moon you will be nowhere to be found in Faerie. He will declare you dead a fortnight later and Lady Orlaith will assume all you now have."

Lord Orrin fluttered up and into Torby's wrinkled face, likely looking for any sign Torby lied. "None of what you say makes any sense. Your dark bones say I will be gone from Faerie and King Oberon himself will be unable to find me?" He hovered over to face young Dillweed. "Does he lie?"

"Ev...ev...every word he spoke was the truth, milord."

"Bah!" He flitted away, then spun back. "I should cut both your throats right here and let Rock-Eye suck the marrow from your stumpy bones."

At the sound of his name the troll swung his big head around and growled. Dillweed whimpered and scuttled behind Torby, who ignored him and looked Orrin directly in the eye.

"You'll do with us what you will, milord, but that'll not change the casting. The bones do not lie and neither do I. You can remain on this path or you can take this second one. Few are offered a choice in life. And if you feed us to Rock-Eye, here, you will never know when you are safe. You'll have no castings to show when you have stepped firmly off the path of your doom. You need the dark-sprite bones, the bones need me, and I need Dillweed."

"Maybe so, but I suspect neither of you need all of your fingers and toes to do what I need you to do. Maybe Rock-Eye likes fingers roasted, with a hint of garlic and rosemary."

Torby and Dillweed both squinted at the grinning, nodding troll, and swallowed hard in unison. Lord Orrin flicked Torby's blue hat off with his tiny sabre.

"So, you will live, at my whim. If your castings are so accurate, then maybe it's time I paid more attention. Do your curséd bones say where will I'm to meet an unbound lass I haven't already had?"

From the shadows opposite Rock-Eye stepped another faery, dressed more conservatively in royal livery. "There *is* your sister's Mid-Summer Ball this very night, milord. As is traditional, the unbound lasses will all be there for the official launch of the Bonding Season."

Orrin sheathed his sword slowly. "Did I receive an invitation?"

"No, sire. Lady Orlaith finally gave up inviting you. You haven't accepted in over a hundred seasons."

"Are you suggesting we drop in on my sister's party, uninvited, Gilroy?"

"Does the idea offend you, milord?"

"Not in the least. I can kill two witches with one stone— finding a lass, *and* seriously upsetting my dear sister's cherished party." He flew to face the troll. "I'm suddenly in a much better mood. You want help finding your missing great-granddaughter. My spies tell me my sister has taken the troll pup captive, along with a dozen others from different tribes."

The huge troll growled, "Winsome. Baby is Winsome."

"Well, whatever her name is, if you want to get her back, *that* tunnel..." he pointed down a low-ceilinged, dark passage to Torby's left. "...will take you under the river and into Orlaith's lands. Have at her. Go save your kin."

With a furious roar, the troll dropped to all fours and charged headfirst into the dank, root-strung tunnel. Rock-Eye's crashing, growling, and mashing filled the chamber long after he was out of sight.

Orrin huffed to his steward as if Torby and Dillweed were no longer present. "The beasts I have to deal with in order to get a simple job done, nauseate me. When I'm firmly on my sister's seat, I think a petition to Oberon to banish the lesser species from court might be in order. Now, let's get out of this rancid hole and make ready for a party." With a flick of his wings, their liege soared out through the fissure in the cave's roof. Gilroy the steward and the two guardsmen trailed after. Torby breathed a quiet sigh of relief.

Dillweed flashed a bent, two-finger Gnomish hand-talk sign at his grandfather and Torby answered in kind, with an upward half-curl to invite the youngster to continue.

You didn't tell him everything! Dillweed flashed.

But I didn't lie, and neither did you, otherwise the spell would have been triggered and you would have been harmed.

We will die horribly, fed to the troll one finger at a time!

Nonsense, lad. That royal dung beetle wouldn't have believed me regardless of a half-truth or a full one. He'd have killed us for trying to play him as a fool. He tapped the bowl twice and the tiny bones fell loose and slid into the enchanted pouch, which protected them from everything up to and including a rock giant's bite.

Dillweed held the now-empty bowl loosely, flashing finger signs against its curve. *And who could blame him? You left out 'or a faery maiden who is not a faery, with wings of man's and a fae heart, will bring him down, and tear him apart.'*

As I said, it makes less sense than his vanishing from Faerie. But if not speaking of it saves the life of one single faerie maiden, then the weight of the omission is easily borne by the likes of us.

I hope you're right and true, Grandfather, because I don't think I could hold up well under torture. Even the threat of it has nearly loosened my bowels.

Torby smiled. *Let's try to save that mess until we get home.* He tucked the bone bag away in his jerkin and started off into the beckoning sunlight, in the opposite direction from the hungry, angry troll.

Nyla swung open the round window in the flank of the family oak tree, high above the ground, but stopped it just before it banged noisily into the shutters. "Go go go!" She whispered. "Get to the meadow and let the others know I'll be along right behind you." She gave a hand up to her younger sister as Kara swung her leg over the wide sill. "Careful now. Get a good grip on Oak's bark and take it slowly. I've bound your wings, but they're not padded."

"I know what I'm doing, Ny. I climb out my window all the time. I'm not some clumsy ogre." Kara ducked her head and maneuvered her way out onto the exterior of their home.

"True, but my window is higher than yours, and you can break a leg any other day but today." Their parents would sell them both off for harvesting labour if Kara got hurt before this evening's Midsummer's Eve's Ball. They shouldn't be going out at all, but with all the pressure and preparation leading up to the year's biggest stupid social event for young faeries, Nyla was simply ready to explode. Fancy dancing and silly ancient music while being stared at by lads, parents, and even their liege, Lady Orlaith, made her want to throw up. She needed to feel the forest floor under her feet, breathe clean, perfume-free air with maybe a hint of forbidden wood smoke. Most of all she needed to be free of hearing her mother nattering in her ear about rules and propriety and who in the court was important, and who wasn't.

"Fine. I'll see you there. Don't be long."

"Right behind you. Now *go!* Before it gets too late." She gave Kara a quick kiss on the end of her nose, then Kara scrambled down the outer bark of the Rainsong home and departed.

Nyla quietly closed and latched the window, turned back to face her black-silk-decorated room, and took a deep breath. The morning nearly gone, she drew in her Monarch butterfly wings and quickly wrapped a wide band of dark green silk around her chest and wings, binding them close to her back. Scrunching her shoulder blades a smidgen more, she gave another tug, then wiggled to test the wrap. Her strong hands expertly spun the two ends of silk together into a knot that would hold until she told it to do otherwise. All faeries were brilliant knotters, but Nyla was the champion, three seasons running.

A quick twirl in front of the dewdrop mirror hanging in the corner and she was ready to brave the darkness lurking beyond her 'cage', out in the oak tree's main chamber. With a gentle pull, she swung the round portal open. She'd taken three silent steps across the polished floor of the high-ceilinged Great Room before the alarm sounded.

"Mother! Nyla's gone and bound her wings again!"

Nyla took two more steps toward the main portal, ignoring her twin brother, Cray—hovering somewhere up over her left shoulder from the sounds of it—and hoping she could make it outside before the second wave of the assault came. A rapid flutter approaching from up the interior of the trunk, along the heartwood path, snatched away her hope, but she kept walking, determined not to panic. Four more steps to go. Three more. Two more...

"Nyla *Rainsong*, where do you think you're going, hobbled like that! Unbind your wings this instant!"

"She's a *stump*, Mother! She wants to walk like a pixie. They're *all* stumps, her whole stupid *sisterhood*! She's even got Kara wanting to be a stump." Cray sprang from his roost up near the house-spider's web and hummed to a landing between his sister and the wide portal. He drew his wide, masculine, bumblebee wings in a bit to protect them, and folded his arms across his chest.

Her brother was almost twice her size so Nyla stopped, but she held her ground. "My name is *Nightshade*, and the only stump in this family is *you*, Cray. You have the imagination of an earwig and the grace of a one-legged dwarf." Wings fluttered behind her, and small feet thumped softly on the floor. A hand grabbed her silk binding and pulled. Nyla spun around fast as a bumblebee and pushed her mother's hand away, careful not to actually strike her. To embarrass her mother was a *social* crime, but to strike an elder faery was a *criminal* offense. They'd haul her up before the Council and sentence her to a whole year of honey harvesting or pollen sweeping if she didn't take care.

"I said to unbind your wings, now, Nyla! No daughter of mine is going to humiliate me any further by walking around the meadow where everyone can see you and laugh at us. You are a member of Clan Rainsong and you will behave *accordingly*." Tears flowed freely down her mother's pale lavender cheeks, but Nyla knew they were an act. Mock tears were her mother's stupid 'gift'. She was famous for them.

"You will frolic and fly, Nyla, and stop being such a... a *stump*, like Cray said. I hate that word, but lately you've been behaving like one. Do you want the whole world to think you're a complete miscreant? To think you don't fit in? The Midsummer's Eve Ball is tonight and your bonding is in a fortnight. Once you've bonded with a tree, you'll be needing to find a mate and the Ball is where you make a good impression with the other clans. No lad is going to want to marry a lass who binds her wings and—"

"And comes home smelling like *wood smoke*." Cray pushed his luck, but Nyla wouldn't lay a hand on him with their mother there. He was strong but compared to either of his sisters Cray was sluggishly slow and not quite as smart. He'd wake up with nettles in his bed or worse, but he knew he wouldn't get slugged in front of an elder faery.

"*Wood smoke*?! Oh, Nyla, you haven't! Faeries making true fire is... simply forbidden! We're *faeries,* living in harmony with the world. Just because you haven't bonded yet, doesn't mean The Oath doesn't apply to you."

"We're not *starting* fires, Mother." She sighed. "It was a lightning strike. We just sat around with some local pixies and watched the flames flicker. We were going to put it out, but Willowmina said to leave it. She explained that the poor cedar's spirit had already moved on and his ashes would feed the soil. It's part of the natural process, she said."

"There is nothing natural about watching fire, young lady. You're not behaving like a stump, you're behaving like a *human*."

Nyla gasped. She'd never heard her mother use the 'h' word, ever. Not even her father used it, at least not at home. Maybe with his fellow Council Members in jest, but not here, in the meadow. She heard Cray suck in a shocked breath behind her. Enough! The Sisterhood waited and the morning was theirs before the burring ball later that day. Nyla turned away from her mother, slipped past her still stunned brother and left Rainsong

Oak, sliding down the ivy to the meadow floor. The soil and grass under her bare feet calmed her soul, but she still fought back genuine tears as she walked off to meet her younger sister and the four other members of the Sisterhood of the Black Dragonfly.

Chapter Two

Trinn absently tipped the rare, Lesser Buttercup toward his mouth, and caught the thin stream of potent butter-juice on his tongue. It was his third drink of the morning, but unlike most faeries, juice woke him up and helped him to think clearly — or so he believed. As the lukewarm, viscous plant juice slid past the dangling thing at the back of his teeth and down his throat toward his belly, a solution to the problem vexing him all morning popped into his head, like a bursting milkweed pod.

"Yes, yes, and — hiccup — *another* yes!" He hopped off his pebble stool and skipped over to the small natural pool bubbling in one corner of his workshop, flapping his stunted wings as he went. He brushed his bangs out of his eyes and squinted into the shallow, bright green pool at the assortment of gears, wheels, screws, nuts, and bolts. "There you *are*! He reached his bare arm into the pool and snatched up a cog. "No. Not *you*. Dumb pool." He dropped the cog back in and slipped his hand in more slowly this time, watching the desired gear closely as the mischievous spirit of the pool tried to move it away from his grasp. The pool spirit wasn't particularly bright, just extremely playful, so it didn't take much effort for Trinn to outsmart it and come up with the hand-sized gear he needed.

"Gotcha!" He dried the gear off with a moss towel, careful to get in between the teeth and the centre hole. The pool enchanted the iron so it could be handled within the faery realm without danger, but it didn't keep the metal from rusting. Trinn marched the part over to the mechanical wings taking shape on his stump workbench in his secret little glade. The purpose of gears, struts, springs, and pistons wouldn't make sense to anyone else, but to Trinn they were as simple as the parts of a flower.

He removed a larger, heavier gear, adjusted a setting pin, then slipped the new gear over the axle-pin and tried to snug it into place. A finger-width too wide, it didn't fit. He needed a smaller one. He returned to the pool and peered intently into the rippling clearness, but he didn't see what he wanted. He reached in and stirred the parts up, hoping the little twelve-tooth beauty he needed hid under something else. Nothing. "I think it's time I made another visit for parts." With a few turns before dark, he took a final sip of butter-juice and curled up next to his tree stump bench.

"Mother called you a *what*?" Kara held her delicate, mouse-whisker paintbrush an inch from her own hip.

"A *human*." Sitting on a rock, Nyla tapped her finger impatiently on a drum she'd made of an acorn shell. "It's all about how her friends around the meadow and the other Council Wives will see her. She doesn't give a burr about us, or what we think. She would *scream* if she knew we were this far from home with chores undone."

Kara put the finishing touches on a delicate henna dragonfly high enough on her leg that it wouldn't be visible beneath the gown she would be wearing this evening. She was the last of the Sisterhood to be so adorned, having painted her five Sisters first. "I'll wager that Cray stood with Mother."

"He's the one who called me out, just before I escaped from Oak. I was so mad I almost hit Mother and then clobbered him."

Another drum tap to Nyla's right drew her gaze. "He'd have crushed you like a fruit fly, and then the Council would have had their turn." Twilly flipped her own acorn drum in the air and tapped the leaf-head twice, lightning-fast, before catching it with her bare feet. A lock of her long, mahogany-dark hair fell over her face. She blew it off to the side where it hung for a moment, then it dropped back to tickle her eyelashes. She brushed it back with her hand and tucked it under her braid. "They don't appreciate our genius. They just want us to be lasses, right Hemlock?"

"They don't give a burr about us and I couldn't give a flying burr about them. They can lick dung for all I care. Stupid little beetle farmers."

"'Lick dung'? That's disgusting, Hem."

"Burr, yah it is. But that's what they say about *you* playing a drum. 'Drums are for lads, flutes are for lasses.'"

"Faeries fly, they don't walk!" Kara giggled.

"Your name is Fiona, not Cassava!" Fiona growled in imitation of her strict father.

"You're Twilly, not Acacia! Silly lass!"

"Poisonous plants, Nyla?" Nyla squeaked. "Why name yourselves after poisonous plants? That's so *human*!"

All six lasses collapsed in laughter in the grass. They only stopped when they ran out of breath. When a ladybug landed on Fiona's head, looking far too much like one of Lady Orlaith's bizarre headpieces, the laughter started up again. Eventually Fiona lifted the ladybug off her head, kissed its 'nose' and placed it on the ground where it scampered over to Brigid and climbed up into her lap.

"You're a *stump*, Acacia!"

"No, *you're* a stump, Nightshade!"

"No, my sister's a stump, I'm a *human*!"

"Stump!"

"Human!"

"Human stumps!"

"Stumpy humans!"

"Humpy stumans!"

Uncomfortable silence fell into the space after Fiona's twist on the words.

"Humpy stumans? Now you're just being silly, Cassava."

"Yup! I'm a silly, humpy stuman! A rebel, a nonconformist, and a proud, founding member of the Sisterhood..." She lowered her voice, trying to sound both ominous and mysterious.

The others joined in. "*... of the Black Dragonfly.*"

Rock-Eye stayed in the tunnels long after he cleared the river, but he was hungry, and furious at the child-stealing noble. A side tunnel opened into the shadows beneath a rocky overhang next to a stream, and he took out his frustration and fury on the first living thing he came across in this duchy. The great elk stag had no warning. Massive hands darted out of the dark tunnel and tore his head off as he sipped the cool water in the shadows. Rock-Eye crushed and chewed and tore asunder the magnificent lord of the glade, then snapped off an antler point and used it to pick the raw meat from his teeth. When he finished, he tossed the remains out into the sunlit glade and went back to the safety of the deeper caves.

"...and then the Mist Eater plucked the old brownie right off his daffodil and ate him in one teeth-flashing bite!"

"But you said no one's ever seen a Mist Eater and lived to tell about it. How do we know they even *have* teeth, Fi?"

Fiona adjusted her ever-present red calla lily hat and draped her long white braid over her shoulder. "Because, Rainn, they found his left foot... and it had teeth marks!"

Rainn huffed in disbelief. "You could grow mushrooms in the tales you spin. If Mist Eaters are even *half* the size you claim they are, they would swallow a brownie whole. There would be no foot, teeth marks or not." She tightened the silk bindings keeping her oak-leaf-shaped wings contained, then executed a perfect back flip, landing on the moss-shaggy branch hanging over the six of them. The others applauded her flip and she bowed. "Fiona, you should be at court, spinning tales for Lady Orlaith. She would pay you handsomely and you could get your pick of the suitors."

"Or maybe *you* could be her court jester, flipping and dancing and giggling."

Rainn twirled, but lost her balance and nearly tumbled off the branch. She caught herself and plopped down to sit on the branch's cool moss, which changed colour three times as she wiggled to get comfortable. "I have no designs on a court life. I prefer the perfume of fresh air, the towers of ancient oaks, the dancing of dandelion seeds on the breeze, and the courting rituals of thrushes."

Nyla nodded. "I wouldn't mind court if there weren't so many rules about *everything*. 'Don't gorge on cream'. 'Honeysuckle is *never* eaten out of season'. 'Dancing is saved for *after* a meal'. 'Periwinkle blue is only worn during a solstice'. Life there would bind our *souls*. The Sisterhood is about being ourselves, not about who our parents and the courts say."

"Hear hear!"

"Exactly!" Kara clapped her hands twice and hopped, then she clapped three times and hopped twice. Each hop moved her a little further around her sister, Nyla, standing in the centre. She repeated the pattern and after a moment, Fiona, Brigid, and Twilly joined in. They each matched their Black Dragonfly Sister's rhythm, but improvised their own steps. Brigid's moves were more of a wiggle or two followed by a couple of hops, Twilly skipped and flipped, Fiona pirouetted perfectly and flung her long braid around like a lash. When an opening passed beneath the branch, Rainn flipped off and down into her spot, adding a shimmy, a shake, and two wiggling hops to the mix. Nyla nodded her head to the beat then slowly and deliberately stepped into her place in the dancing circle.

The Sisterhood of faeries hopped, bopped, gyrated, clapped, and snapped around their ring; and magic rose from the ground in silver and gold sparkles. Each step produced bluebells and buttercups, and bloom-by-bloom the air shimmered a little more. With each increase in shimmer and sparkle, the lasses' dance steps became wilder and more flamboyant until Nyla broke off from the formation and started marching out of the grove of trees and across the meadow. "Off to the smoking stump, before the burring ball tonight!"

Even during daytime in Faerie Trinn had a good idea when night fell in the human realm. The temperature of the water in his realm-spanning pool cooled, just a tad. It was the larger of the two pools in his home glade: nearly thrice as wide as the magic pool with his brass and iron gears and other parts. He'd heard some passages into other realms took the form of doorways or holes under rocks, but this one, shown to him by his uncle when he was young, was a watery tunnel leading from his subterranean pool to a pond in a garden in a human city. He still needed to1 carry his charm to pass through, but he enjoyed the swim. He tucked a large pouch in his jerkin and laced it tight, then made his way to the cave to check the temperature of the portal pool.

Sixteen-year-old Sally leaned on the windowsill, not caring that the ever-present soot from Glasgow's Saracen Foundry clung to her nightgown's sleeves, or that the cold wind off the River Clyde raised gooseflesh on her arms. She sat like this most nights, waiting and hoping he would come. With the moon nearly full and the clouds few and far between, when one of the Royal Scottish Airships crossed slowly between the moon and the Stuart's middling-sized garden, everything between the walls and the two-story house plunged into darkness. Everything, except the spring-fed pond.

The pond, a mere two-yards square, glowed a soft gold. Without the great airship's shadow, Sally might have missed spotting the glow altogether. "He's here." She whispered. Then she leaned over and shook her eight-year-old brother, Malcolm, who slept soundly in his bed in their shared room.

Malcolm snorted and opened his eyes. "Where?"

"The pond. Look. I always put the small sack of watch parts from Father's shop to the left, beneath the old bench."

"I don't see a thing, and I'm cold, Sally. I know you're making fibs and I'm gonna tell… *I see him!*"

Sally clapped her hand over her brother's mouth to silence him. "Shut your trap, Colm!" she hissed in his ear. Something caused the surface of the tiny pond to ripple, then a small, glowing, man-shape climbed up next to the lilies.

Malcolm pulled Sally's hand away from his mouth and whispered. "He's a wee one. No bigger than one of your old dolls."

"Trinn's a *faery*, you numptie. Faeries are wee, but they're busting out with magic."

"Magic? *Now* who's a numptie, Silly Sally?"

"He *is* magic. Shut your gob and watch."

"He's no faery. Even *I* know faeries have wings. He's got none."

"He says he was born that way."

"He comes from the water. Is he a kelpy?"

"He's a faery, you idiot!" Sometimes she wanted to swap her brother for Trinn. A faery would be so much more fun than her brother.

She watched Trinn stand up on the flat rocks bordering the pond, untie a cord running around his waist and back into the pond. He placed a small stone atop the cord, shook himself off like a puppy, looked up at the window and waved. Then, in two blinks of an eye, he ran widdershins around the pond, skipping, leaping, twirling and touching each and every flower. As he tapped each bud with his fingertips, a tiny shower of gold sparks burst from the buds, before settling back down and dimming. The airship's shadow cleared the walled garden, once again freeing the moonlight, overwhelming the golden sparks.

"Trinnean is why our flowers grow so much grander than everyone else on the lane."

"He's brilliant! I wonder if our faery can make me grow bigger, so I can stand up to Auntie and stop her from hurting us. I'd give *her* a slap in the ear, I would."

"You'll not be slapping anyone's ear, and Trinn is not *our* faery, he's *my* faery. And hopefully after tonight, we won't be having to worry about Auntie hurting us ever again."

"He's gonna knock her in the head and take her away forever?"

"No. Now shut yer gob and keep a close eye."

Trinn, the wingless faery, reached into his jerkin, withdrew two small packets, and tucked them under the bench. He looked back up at Sally, and when she gave him a thumbs-up, he laughed the sound of tiny bells, and returned the raised thumb. He retrieved the end of his cord and disappeared under the bench.

After a moment he re-emerged into the moonlight, dragging the sack of discarded clock parts on the end of the cord.

A sliver of light speared across the yard as Mary, the housekeeper, opened the back door to let out the family Skye Terrier, Bobby. A sharp bark of alarm pierced night.

"It's Bobby! He'll *kill* Trinn!"

The faery jumped straight up in the air with a squeak, but when he landed he quickly blew Sally a kiss and saluted Malcolm with all seriousness. He then gave the cord a good hard tug up from the pond, released his grip, and let the cord pull the sack across the rocks, off the edge, and into the pond, where it sank out of sight. A closer bark startled Trinn again, and in a flash of gold he dove into the pond, without making so much as a ripple.

"Keep an eye while I grab Bobby and fetch the charms."

"The what?"

"The charms of protection, you numptie. Trinnean promised he'd bring them this visit. No more beatings from Auntie."

Chapter Three

Trinn emerged from the water into the near dark of his cave. As dark as it was, it was far from quiet. The clockwork winch clicked and whirred away, rewinding the cord up out of the well. The mechanical sounds thundered off the damp rock walls. If he'd had anyone to talk to, they wouldn't have been able to hear him. There was a heavy clunk of metal on metal, followed by a horrible grinding sound, and Trinn leaped to shut the device off. As soon as it stopped reeling the cord in, it started to unwind again, and the weight of the sack pulled it back down into the well. He jumped at the cord and grabbed it with both hands, bracing his feet against the jutting rocks of the well's lip.

"Oh, no, you don't!" He began hauling on the line, pulling it up, hand over hand. Progress was slow, but he was determined not to let the sack fall back through the portal to the human realm. Pull by pull, he made progress, until finally, the top of the sack broke the surface of the well. Trinn braced himself and with a two-handed heave, had the sack up and out of the water. "Oh, thank the Old Ones. This load will—" A wave of nausea slammed into him and he swooned. "Oh no. Too much iron at once." He stumbled back to the cave wall and edged his way around to the narrow tunnel. Once there, he made his way out into faery daylight. "Burr me, that was close."

"Faster, Twilly! Faster, faster, faster! The smoke will be gone before we get there!" Brigid skipped and twirled around Twilly, who had stepped off the narrow log across Dewtickle Creek, having trouble with the silk binding her wings.

"They just want to get loose. The stupid knots won't hold! I've tripped twice already." She stopped in the shade of a milkweed and fidgeted with the knot, undoing it and trying to redo it. "I can't remember if it's over and under, or under and over. Stupid stumping knots. I can't wait until we bond with a tree and I can do stronger spells than a stink-nose."

Nyla stepped out of the grasses and placed a steady hand gently on Twilly's frustrated fumbling ones. "Let me. I'll give you knots you can't shake by accident now, and show you again how to do them yourself when we get home."

"Thanks, Ny. You're the best. I'm just so burring clumsy."

"We all have our gifts. You're the only one I know who can harvest spider silk without getting bitten at least twice."

Twilly giggled. "What can I say? Our house spider has a crush on me."

Kara leaped up and over a dandelion and landed lightly beside them. "*All* buggies have a crush on you, Twill. A huge chafer bug has been following you since we left the grove." She pointed at the elm overhanging the slender path behind them. A big, oval, brown beetle sat on a low branch, looking at Twilly, its antennae twitching.

"Silly Juney bug." Twilly shook her head. "Go home. I don't need a hat today." Juney chittered softly and spread its wings just a little. "No hat?" she asked.

"Mother will be furious if she finds you missing. This would be the *one* day she wants to wear you. Go home, Juney." The beetle didn't budge.

Twilly threw her arms up in frustration. "No hat! Now go home! Shoo! Shoo! Shoo!" Startled, Juney skittered along the branch and disappeared behind the elm's trunk.

"Don't be rude, Twill. Juney just wanted to hang out with us."

"Chafer bugs are so five seasons ago. There's a good reason my mother hasn't worn Juney out since your cousin's bonding ceremony—she'd be laughed at." She straightened the tiny cameo-pinned scarf around her neck and ran off along the trail. "Last one to the smoke is a stump!"

Brigid, Kara, Fiona, Rainn, and Nyla ran after her, but Rainn couldn't help herself from asking the obvious question. "If we're in such a hurry, why aren't we flying?"

"Flying is what our parents would do!" Nyla called out. "It's what they would want *us* to do! The Sisterhood doesn't follow the rules! That's our only rule!" She laughed at her own joke and her Sisters laughed along with her. "I can hear the creek. Not far to the smoke, now!"

A horrified scream ripped through the day and silenced the Forest around them.

Twilly stood next to a pool of blood big enough for a sprite half her size to swim in. Nyla nearly slammed into her when she charged out of the long grass ahead of her Sisters, but twisted deftly to the left and avoided both Twilly and the blood. "Careful! Don't rush in!" she shouted back over her shoulder. She hoped they heard her, but her biggest concern was Twilly. The taller faery didn't move. She stared, unblinking, across the grisly pool. Nyla gently, cautiously, touched her friend's shoulder with her fingertips. "Twilly. Sweetie. It's okay. I'm here. You're safe."

"It's... Lady Orlaith's stag."

Nyla's gaze rose to the object of Twilly's horror. Partially hidden by long grass, the stag's great head and massive antler rack towered above them like a winter-stripped tree. "Oh, burr! Not Torinstag!" She ran around the edge of the small clearing, careful to avoid stepping in the blood. Behind her, Kara started to scream but silenced abruptly. Nyla turned back to her little sister. Fiona had her hand clamped over Kara's mouth. She leaned in and whispered something to Kara, who nodded in understanding. The two of them slipped back into the higher grasses. Nyla nodded thanks at Fiona and continued on to the ruins of the stag. From the other direction, Brigid and Rainn crept up, keeping their heads low while avoiding the blood. Rainn wept as she walked, twisting her coppery hair around her finger and glancing about.

Nyla put her fingers to her lips and waved the two of them closer. "Something ripped Torinstag in half. What could have the power to do such a thing?"

"A hill giant?" Brigid suggested.

"A Mist Eater!" Rainn spit out. "There's a Mist Eater here!"

Brigid guffawed softly. "This is *not* the work of a Mist Eater."

"How can you be so certain? Torinstag's head is torn clean off."

"Because Mist Eaters don't exis—". Brigid stopped mid-word. "I think you're right. Nothing else could have done this. We need to get back and warn Lady Orlaith."

"No, we need to discover where it's going." Nyla looked around for a trail. "We can follow it. Anything capable of doing this to Torinstag is too big to hide its tracks. I'll find them and we'll start off."

"Absolutely *not*! We have to warn the others, and we have to get Twilly back home. She looks like she's been hit with a stun spell." They all turned to their Sister, whose eyes darted back and forth as if she were searching the woods for an invisible attacker. Her lower lip trembled and a single tear tracked down her cheek.

Nyla relented. "Of course. We'll take her home, but give me three blinks and a shake to ask if anyone saw anything."

"Three blinks and a shake?" Fiona held Twilly's hand.

"Maybe two shakes, but no more. Just lead her away from

this horror, and keep out of sight. I'll catch up." She took off at a run, trusting her Sisters to care for Twilly while she asked around.

She first stopped at a dally of daisies not far from the blood pool, but each and every flower-head closed up tight and turned away from the scene. "Ladies, please. It's me. I won't hurt you." She stroked one leafless stem and a quiver ran up from her touch to the closed flower-head. The daisy opened just a smidgeon, paused, and clamped shut again, shaking 'no'.

"*Please.*"

Another negative shake, echoed by the other dozen in the dally.

"Very well. I'm sorry. We'll send someone soon." She spied a line of leaf-cutter ants trudging across a flat rock and disappearing into the timothy grass. She bolted over to intercept them, hopping right into their path, but they steadfastly detoured around her feet and kept on marching past.

"Really? You won't even stop to talk with *me*?" She looked closely at the parade, trying to recognize any of them. "If that's the way you wish it, you leave me no choice." She spotted a familiar pair of antennae and gently snatched the ant up and placed her on her open palm. "You, Honeyfinder, talk to me."

Honeyfinder made to leap away, but Nyla held her firmly.

"Honey, what did you see? Help me to help the Forest."

The ant sat abruptly and sighed. She chittered softly and Nyla had to lift her closer to her ear to hear her. "We *saw* nothing. None of us. But we *heard*. We heard Torinstag's scream, we heard his flesh tearing, we heard his life water flow into the grass and down into the tunnels. And we heard crunching and snapping, like sticks and stones, but antlers and bones. Big. Huge. Bigger even than Torinstag."

The faery maid felt nauseous. "A Mist Eater?"

"Or a troll. The air tasted like troll. Leader took us to the edge of the lake of spilled life-water, then turned us back to home. We are nest-bound with the news, and to get new orders. Maybe we will clean the tunnels, or maybe tend to poor Torinstag. Not our decision. The Queen will decide." She glanced down as the last ant in the parade passed by. "Be safe," she chittered, before leaping off of Nyla's palm and onto the soil, where she quickly caught up with his brethren.

Nyla looked around for other possible witnesses, but she knew deep in her heart the only place she would find the answers she sought. She took a deep breath and sprinted through the high grasses, around the milkweeds, leaping over the poisonous red-and-white forest mushrooms, and finally arrived at Torinstag's massive head. Blood tainted everything—in puddles, in splashes, and congealed in mid-drop from violets, dill weed, crocuses, and dandelions alike. Covered from wingtips to tail, a pale yellow vestal moth lay drowned in Torinstag's 'life-water' as the ants called blood. Nyla took a long, slow breath through the makeshift filter of her hands, because she didn't have time to be squeamish, she had to *hurry*. Not only did the Sisters need to get Twilly back home, but also the memories of the woodlands were notoriously short. If she didn't make her inquiries now, by the time Lady Orlaith's people arrived, Torinstag's murder would be a non-event, forgotten forever.

The stench overwhelming her. Tendrils of a nearby corpse-willow were already reaching up and spreading out over the great elk's remains, absorbing blood quickly, and solid matter more slowly. Nyla doubted Lady Orlaith's men would arrive in time to even examine the remains of poor Torinstag. A beetle scrambled past, or at least it tried to. The faery maid hopped in front of her.

"Rosie, my dear sweet beetlette." Beetles adored flattery. "Your carapace is looking ever so marvelous! It must be the sage in your diet. I have never seen such vibrant green and dark pink stripes! And your rows and rows of dimples—I would kill to have even *two* dimples."

"Hello Nyla Wingbinder." Rosie chittered much louder than Honeyfinder, so Nyla didn't need to hold the beetle ear-high. "Such deliciously welcome words, especially with such a dark taint in the air. Poor Torinstag."

"That's what I'm here about, Rosie. Did you taste anything at all?"

"About what? Taste what?"

Nyla cursed to herself hearing Rosie's memory of the event already getting spotty and fading fast. "Torinstag's murder. Did you taste anything?"

"Oh. Torinstag. Poor thing. He shouldn't have confronted a Mist Eater."

"A Mist Eater?"

"Must have been, dear. Nothing else could grab him in the shadows and do such horrors to poor Torinstag."

"Are you certain?"

"Of course not. My senses aren't what yours are. Why don't

you ask the troll, though. He probably saw the entire thing."

"A troll?" A troll would make more sense than a Mist Eater. She'd even met a troll once.

"Yes, dear. He nearly stepped on me. I walked in a drop of his drool." She lifted her slender legs, one at a time to prove it. "I don't think I will *ever* get the stench off."

Nyla lifted Rosie closer and took a tentative sniff. She flinched at the odour. Definitely something rancidly trollish stuck to Rosie's feet. "Could the troll have murdered Torinstag?"

"Oh, don't be silly dear. Why in Faerie would a troll do something so ghastly? They may be big and lumbering and will eat anything living or dead put in front of them, but this sort of business reeks of Mist Eater mischief." Rosie leaned over and bit a chunk off a nearby leaf, chewing loudly. She seemed to have forgotten she had company.

"Have you ever seen one?"

"Oh. Hello, dear. Seen one what?"

"A Mist Eater." Nyla held back her frustrated scream.

"Oh mercy no, dear. I saw an Icebane once — half-elf, half-salamander, all flame, but never a Mist Eater. Why do you ask?"

"Because I…" Oh, this is useless, she thought. The beetle had a worse attention span and shorter memory than a pansy. She gently placed the leaf-beetle back on the ground. "Thank you for your help, Rosie. I'd best get back and report Torinstag's murder."

"Oh, yes. Of course, dear. Poor Torinstag." She turned her attention to a fallen leaf and Nyla left her to it.

With a whispered word, the faery released the silk bindings on her wings, tucked the silk in her bodice, and launched herself up into the air, beating her butterfly wings hard, to make haste. She cleared the long grasses, soared high up over Torinstag's once-magnificent antlers, and surged off to where she'd last seen her Sisters. As she flew over the congealed pool of blood, she wept silently for the great beast. Mist Eater or troll, whatever butchered Torinstag could still be near and she had to get her Sisters out of the area.

Fiona and the others must have thought the same about the killer beast and were moving with extra stealth, because she couldn't find any trace of them. She let out a high-pitched trill like a Cedar Waxwing, and a moment later heard an answering trill off to her right. She leaned, dropped a wing tip ever so slightly, and changed course. A second whistled trill was answered even faster and Brigid stepped out from under a sparkling pink middling fern and waved. Nyla waved back and Brigid slipped back under the fern. Nyla came in so quickly that she needed to tuck and roll twice before she could pop back up on her feet under the fern.

Brigid held a slender finger to her lips, so Nyla leaned in for an explanation.

"We heard something big," Brigid whispered in Nyla's delicately pointed ear.

"Then unbind your wings and let's get Twilly home."

"We would love to, but she's not flying anywhere and we can hardly carry her."

"Fine. Let's start you walking. You and Fiona walk with Twilly, while Rainn and Kara get word to home that you're coming. Maybe you can flag down a Sky Patrol airship. I'll fly straight to Lady Orlaith at the Lake."

"Did you learn anything?"

Nyla shook her head. "Nothing we didn't already suspect. Maybe a Mist Eater, but more likely a troll. We have to hurry, or any traceable magic will be gone before we bring back help."

Brigid leaned in close to Rainn, quickly tugged the knot binding the other faery's silk. Rainn stretched her red oak leaf-shaped wings to get the kinks out, stepped out from under the fern, and took to the air slowly, turning to survey the forest around them. Brigid whispered to and unbound Kara as well, and Kara joined Rainn above. Nyla gave Brigid and Fiona hugs and launched up and into the canopy of green, keen on getting word to Lady Orlaith while the others made their way home.

Quiet settled on the meadow, but not preternaturally so. The shock of the attack on Torinstag wore off quickly, and life in the meadow drifted back to normal. A herd of white Glider butterflies popped up from a bed of clover and clumsily raced each other all the way over to the patch of giant thistles where they flitted about, teasing and chasing. Nyla flew away as fast as her wings would carry her.

Chapter Four

Rock-Eye squirmed deeper into the loose soil of the freshly dug alcove in the old tunnel. Once upon a time when he could sleep for weeks with sunlight no more than a paw's-breadth away, but not lately. Between his fury at the royal lady who stole his great-granddaughter, and the longer days of sunlight as they reached mid-summer, he found sleep worm-riddled and rotten.

He started counting backwards by threes, as his son once taught him. "100…97…94…91…88…" He tumbled into a restless sleep before he reached seventy.

The slight illumination in the cave came from a patch of glow-buttons—what the dwarves called 'chlorophos fungi'—carpeting one wall.

"We have a problem." Liadán the pixie paced, careful not to smite her head on the elbow of George, the crouched troll towering above her. Always naked, mottled, scrawny twin brownies—Kevan and Kieron, Tristan the stubby gnome, and an elder faery listened respectfully. The troll—the group's counterpoint voice—make objections in order to bring attention to both sides of all discussions.

"Always problems. It is what we do." George leaned back and scratched an itch on a rock sharp enough to cut most people in two, but just perfect for getting the spot between a troll's itchy shoulder blades. "Always problems, Liadán."

Liadán stopped pacing and turned to face the troll. "This problem is of particular interest to you, George. A troll just tore the head off of Lady Orlaith's precious Torinstag. With *her* temper, this could start a war."

"Hmmm…yes. Maybe so." George nodded, and freshly tunneled soil rained down from his shaggy head, barely missing Liadán.

The brownies stepped forward and spoke in perfect unison, but their voices were harmonized, not identical. "Are we certain it is a troll?"

Liadán frowned. "The forest says either a troll, or a Mist Eater."

The twins laughed at the joke and it sounded like water tumbling over rocks. "Well, since we Betweeners invented the legend of the Mist Eaters, then it must be a troll. Or an ogre."

"Well, I'll vouch for Brother Braden." The gnome slapped a nearby fungus and delicate spores drifted up to land on his welcoming sleeve. "He was rather fond of Torinstag, which is an odd thing for an ogre, unless elk is on the menu."

A distinguished faery stepped out of the darker shadows and gently picked a glowing spore from his long grey braid draped over his shoulder. "Brigid and her little 'Sisterhood' have wandered afield quite a bit as of late. Knowing my granddaughter, she was nearby. Trouble follows those six like a curse. She could be a brilliant Betweener if I could ever separate her from her friends long enough to finish her training."

George chuckled. "How far you got with favourite little faery miss?"

"She's well-versed in the locations of the six open gates to the human realm and she's found all but three of the twenty closed ones. Some day she might even be able to create her own."

"Truly? Few have *that* gift." The twins liked Brigid and even called her by her Sisterhood name of Hemlock. "Maybe she is indeed ready to join us, Cathaoir."

"Yes, and no. She's a natural Betweener, and she's very keen to help guard the gates between realms. She's talented, even gifted, but I have concerns about her maturity. Brigid and her friends have some silly ideas, which have brought them some unwanted attention from both the Council and Lady Orlaith herself. Five of the lasses are being introduced at the ball tonight, because this is their season to bond, but some days I have my doubts if they're even ready for that."

Her decision made, Liadán crossed her arms and spoke up. "Then continue with her training as you see fit. We trust your judgment on this, though I'll admit I have the same concerns after hearing they were enjoying the smoke from a lightning strike."

"My granddaughter is simply bored, as are her friends. They're all very bright, but they find everyday faery life to be tedious, much like *we* did at their age. They simply want something more."

"Well, if Orlaith makes war with my people, trolls and faeries *all* get something more." George sat.

Cathaoir turned back to Liadán. "Where was Torinstag killed?"

"Not far from Wigglehop Meadow; and the Forest indeed reports Brigid's little Sisterhood of the Black Dragonfly came upon the scene. My sources also tell me they've separated, with one flying straight back to Lady Orlaith at Laughing Elf Lake, two back home to summon aid, and three on foot, heading in the same direction."

"On foot?!" The brownies couldn't imagine anyone walking when they could fly.

"The details are fuzzy. My report came from a magpie."

"A magpie?"

"I know. I'm hoping to get a more reliable report soon. In the meantime, everyone be careful. If there's a rampaging troll, then none of us are safe. Tristan, please tell Braden, and I'll get word to the other groves. The Betweeners have remained a secret society of protectors for this long, so let's do our best to keep it that way while preventing a war."

George stood up, preparing to disappear down his tunnel. "If lone troll rampaging, be sure someone else helped. We like peace too much. There be something greater here than just rogue with bad temper."

Liadán frowned, though only George would be able to see it clearly in the dark. "Then we have work to do. The Midsummer Ball is tonight and we all remember last year's ball."

The twins giggled. "A human almost got through a gate from her world and crashed into the party."

"A *human*. That will *not* happen again. Not while the Betweeners are on guard."

A flurry of activity filled the long but low cabin built into the gnomes' earth berm as Torby and Dillweed rushed back and forth, gathering supplies. His wife, Winnie, stepped into Torby's path and forced him to stop in his tracks.

"Torby Tewilliger Pondbottom—I am *not* leaving the comfort of my home without more than a 'you are in danger, woman!' I want an explanation, and I want it *now*, or I'll take all of your hats in two sizes and you'll be forced to go bareheaded this Midsummer's Eve."

Torby made to step around Winnie, but she stopped him with a thick finger jabbed at the tip of his big nose. Before he could swat her hand away, however, Dillweed intervened.

"Grandmother, Lord Orrin has spelled us and forced Grandfather to do dire castings. The bones foretold disaster and we just want you all away before our liege blames the entire family." He stuffed an armful of socks into a sack.

"Orrin?" She spun on Dillweed, a head shorter but twice his girth. "*Lord* Orrin himself? You're burring with me, young gnome. I'll drink rancid butter-juice before I'll believe His Grace will have anything to do with the likes of you two."

Dillweed's mother and three older sisters all came in from their parts of the cabin. The young gnome continued. "It's true. Lord Orrin heard about the casting a fortnight ago, corralled us, and took us to a troll cave. He cast a truth-or-pain spell on Grandfather, but directed the pain to me."

His grandmother raised an eyebrow in doubt, but his oldest sister, Sina, cuffed the back of his head, knocking his favourite hat to the floor. "You *liar!*"

Dillweed bent and picked up his hat, but wrung it in his hands rather than return it to his head. "Grandfather, we have to show them, otherwise they won't believe us and they won't leave."

The old gnome's anger dissipated. Did his grandson truly know what he asked for? "You're certain, lad? It won't be pleasant, to say the least."

"I don't care if it kills me if it saves my family."

Sina cuffed him again. "You two are full of burr and twice as sour!"

Her brother looked back at her. "That doesn't even make sense." To his grandfather he nodded. "Just a small one."

Torby nodded back, then addressed his wife while Dillweed lay down on the floor. "Give me a lie to tell. Something we all know is false." He turned to Sina. "Get a pillow for your brother's head."

Sina folded her arms and held her ground. "I will *not* pamper his lazy—"

"NOW!" Torby never raised his voice. Ever. But he had no choice now. His granddaughter ran off for a pillow, her shocked, hurt sobs loud in the silence.

"A lie?" Winnie whispered. She finally seemed to be taking the problem seriously.

"A small one. We don't want to kill the lad just to prove we're honest men to the only people who shouldn't doubt us."

"I'm sorry."

"A lie. *Now.* We'll get this over with and you will go to your second cousin's daughter at Leaftop Hill in Lady Orlaith's duchy. Your brother can get you across the river."

Sina returned with her own perfect, hand-picked-straw-filled pillow and gently slipped it under her little brother's head. Her tears had stopped, but her eyes were still moist and her nose dripped.

"A lie." Torby demanded, growing impatient.

"Um, your name is Gregarius Rocknose Blossompants."

"Your brother-in-law? Hmm. Too big. A smaller lie. A shape or color that isn't."

Winnie pointed at his cobalt blue hat. "Your hat is red."

"Perfect." He looked at each of the five women. "Believe. And never doubt Dillweed again. He does this for *you*." With a final sad look of sympathy and thanks down at his grandson, Torby took a deep breath and simply stated: "The hat on my head is... red."

As if the last word were a white-hot sword piercing his side, Dillweed arched impossibly up, screamed loud and long, and then he threw up on himself. His family all clamped their stubby hands over their ears and fell to their knees in horror. It ended as suddenly as it began, but they each wept at what Dillweed had just voluntarily suffered. His grandmother forced herself to her feet and his mother scooted over and pulled him close and cradled him.

Winnie Pondbottom wiped her tears away with her sleeve, straightened her back and growled. "Get your brother a towel, a clean jerkin, and a mug of cider. We'll take only what we can carry. The more valuable, the better. Each of us takes a weapon we can use. We'll pack all we can on the three goats, as well. We leave immediately. Go!"

Gnome feet padded off in all directions. Torby's daughter—Dillweed's mother—placed his barely conscious head back on the pillow, leaned in and kissed his forehead, then she pushed up from the floor and jogged off after her daughters without a word.

"I'll prepare the goats." Torby went off to the small barn.

Dillweed shook his head to clear it and tried to sit up, but his grandmother knelt beside him and pushed him lovingly back down. "Rest. *We* can do this. Save your energy. I suspect you two are not finished with our unroyal burr of a lord, and I need you to protect your grandfather." Dillweed sniffed the air and looked down at the vomit down his front. Winnie smiled. "I have clean clothes coming. No one here will *ever* mock you for this, or doubt you again."

A smile of his own curled Dillweed's lips. "I would have doubted me, too. It's not like I haven't spun a tale or two over the years."

"True enough, I suppose."

"But no more."

"No more. But, quickly, tell me about this bone casting, please."

His youngest sister, Lita, arrived with a fresh jerkin and a towel. Sina came in with the cider, and then they both rushed off to gather what they needed. Dillweed took a long draught to rid his mouth of the taste of supper come up, and then he changed his clothes. While he did so, he told his grandmother everything, especially about Orrin's threat to cut off their fingers and toes and feed them to the troll.

The five Pondbottom women started off for Uncle Hubble's riverside farm not long after, leaving their two brave men to deal with the faery lord and see the bone casting through to its dark end.

Rainsong Grove was closer than Dewtickle Pond, so Kara and Rainn went straight there, finding Kara and Nyla's mother in the middle of the grove, giving the bluebells a stern talking-to. The lasses dropped down in the grass, out of breath and unable to speak for a moment.

"I expect full blooms from all of you whenever my friends come by for a visit, even the Snowd—" she saw the lasses and stopped abruptly, turning from the cowed flowers to face the exhausted Sisters. "Morainn, get home, Kara get into Oak. You didn't finish your chores and your aunt will be here in a shake to fit your gowns for the ball. Where's your sister?" The lasses stood, mute, shocked and confused at the unexpected onslaught.

The elder Rainsong faery cranked it up a notch. "Morainn Dewtickle, you are still here! Go home! You're expected!" She switched her attention to her youngest daughter, neither seeing nor caring if Rainn flew off for home. "Kara! To Oak!" She pointed at the delicate painting on Kara's calf. "And wash that filth off before your aunt sees it. Where…is…Nyla?"

Kara blinked, took a step back out of her mother's sphere of anger, and finally spoke up. "Nyla is on her way to Laughing Elf Lake. A Mist Eater has murdered Torinstag, and Twilly is sick or under a spell, we're not sure."

"That's ridiculous. There're no such things as Mist Eaters. They're just tales we tell children to scare them and make them obey us." She tilted her head back and shouted. "CRAY!" A moment later Kara's brother appeared at their mother's side, his huge bumblebee wings humming. "For some reason, Nyla is on her way to Lady Orlaith's castle. Stop her. Find out what news she is taking to the Lady, send her home, then deliver the news to your father so he can deliver it himself and have someone check the veracity of the report. Make certain to get all of the details from Nyla, including the location. Tell her Kara is home safe, I am sending help for Twilly, and she is to return home immediately to prepare for the Ball. Do you understand it all?"

Cray nodded once, seriously. "Yes, Mother."

"Then go. And when all is done, get yourself back to Oak immediately."

He left in a blur.

Kara took a step back to her mother. "I'm sorry, Mother."

"Sorry? The Midsummer's Eve Ball is *tonight* and you two are wandering far afield getting into who-knows-what trouble, and your aunt has put a great deal of effort into making these gowns for you two."

"But I'm not bonding until *next* year."

"You're still attending, and it's never to soon to make a good impression." She looked Kara up and down, seeing her scuffed knees and unruly hair. "How in the name of the Elder Alder will we ever get the two of you cleaned up and presentable in time, I have no idea." She grabbed her youngest daughter by the elbow and lifted off, forcing Kara to follow suit. They flew up to the entrance landing of the family Oak.

Nyla heard Lady Orlaith's bluebells long before she saw the road winding through the forest to Ten-Oak Castle, the home of her liege at the shore of long, narrow, Laughing Elf Lake. The chimes of the roadway-bordering bluebells were the first welcome to Castle Orlaith. Nyla knew the large iridescent-silver butterflies would be next, to guide travellers to the path and then along it to the castle. No undergrowth grew here, so close to the heart of the Lady's domain, just the seemingly random, thick trunks of stately elms, ash, pines, alders, maples, birches, and... Nyla lost track. There appeared to be some of each species of tree she had ever heard about, let alone seen, and she didn't have time to identify them all as she flew on.

She would have loved to walk through this majestic forest again, to feel the ground beneath her feet, the cool, damp soil, the tiny fir needles, the crunchy leaves, the rough roots and tricky twigs, but right now, as evening approached and her dire news weighed heavily on her, she was ever so thankful for her wings. The distance she'd covered through the air was magnitudes greater than even running would have covered. Weaving between great trunks, trying to plot as straight a course as she could to the bluebells and the roadway, she was caught completely off guard when Cray dropped down in front of her. He hovered directly in her path and she had to fold her wings for a moment and drop nearly to the ground before swooping back up behind him in order to avoid crashing into him. She sped on.

"Nyla! Stop!"

"Can't, Cray! I'm on a mission!" She snapped, worried more bullying was coming her way. She flew faster.

It didn't take her big-winged brother long to catch up, though. He flew above her, just high enough not to interfere with her flight. "I know you are. Kara and Morainn made it home safe. Mother sent me to listen to your stupid message and deliver it to Father so *he* can take it to Lady Orlaith and you can return home where you belong."

Nyla pulled up fast, hovering in place. Cray flipped around and came back to face her. "This is important, Cray. You'll just forget the message or not even bother to deliver it."

"Mother gave me strict instructions. I have no idea what is going on, but she's furious and this is my part to play. No matter what your stupid message is, I *will* deliver it. But I want to know what idiotic thing you did in the woods that could make you actually fly instead of walking around like a useless pixie."

His tone dripped with condescension, so Nyla hit him with the hard facts up front. "Torinstag has been murdered. Slaughtered. Torn apart. We found his head ripped off...and so much blood." She could see the carnage in her mind again and settled down to the ground to hold back the nausea and disgust. Cray followed her to the forest floor.

"You're so full of burrs, Nyla! Torinstag? *Dead?*" He stepped up at her, towering over her. "There's nothing in the duchy that could even lay a paw on Torinstag without his antlers goring it to death."

What Nyla saw more fear than threat in Cray's eyes. Her twin brother cherished rules and order and nothing to change at all—a 'perfect' faery lad. "I'm sorry, Cray. I wouldn't lie about this. I'm going straight to Lady Orlaith to report it. Acacia—*Twilly*—was the first to find him and she snapped. She's sick and is being led back by Fiona and Brigid. Kara and Rainn were supposed to fetch help for Twilly."

"Twilly's hurt?" Of all the Sisterhood, Twilly was the only one Cray had any time for. He'd been sweet on her since they were neighbour babies. Nyla thought it was cute, most of the time.

"Like a spell, or a curse." She didn't have time to mess around with Cray. Too much needed to be done. "Look, I have to deliver this message. Whatever could tear the head off Torinstag is still out there. Mist Eater, troll, or hill giant, it needs to be stopped."

Cray took a deep breath, made a decision, and nodded. "Tell me everything, quickly. I'll take it straight to Father. Sorry to say, but coming from *me*, he'll take the information much more seriously. If *I* believe it, so will he. If he doesn't, then I'll deliver it myself. I have friends in the Royal Guard."

"You're certain?"

"Mother's orders. She is sending help for Twilly, and *you* have to get home to prepare for the ball. Tell me. Quick."

So she did, but only the pertinent details. She made him repeat back the exact location two different ways, to make certain he understood it well enough to explain it clearly. He got it all note-perfect, impressing her. A burr at the best of times, Cray courted the approval of anyone and everyone in a position of authority. Almost every single one of their sibling clashes now came down to her rebelling and him conforming, but now Cray listened to the details of the Sisterhood finding Torinstag, huffing judgmentally only once, in the beginning, when she described walking upon the scene rather than flying.

"And you're certain it was Torinstag himself?"

"I swear." She covered her heart with her right hand

Cray stood tall, accepting her word, and his duty. "I'll go directly to Father and you go to Mother. Fast as you can." He flew off in a blur, so she turned and made her way home.

Chapter Five

Rock-Eye sniffed at the dusk air. His belly should have been full from the elk he'd gorged on, but because he killed and ate out of anger and worried sick about Winsome, the meat sat sideways in his belly. The spring in this cave no more than a trickled along a natural groove in the floor and he yearned for a drink. He lay on his bloated belly, wedged his face down into the groove, and lapped up the meager moisture. It would have to do until he could find the stream he could smell on the late day breeze creeping into the cave to tease him.

He growled to himself, famished, parched, and feeling far too old to be stomping about on faery lands with no real plan for finding his Winsome. He didn't know this duchy a whit and he had no idea where she might be held, but he'd promised his daughter and his granddaughter he would find the baby and bring her home safe. This traipsing about, flailing in anger, was a fine thing when he was a young thumper and the war a recent memory, but his old bones and one remaining eye yearned to be at home, sleeping, farting, and telling Winsome and her brothers about dirt dragons, dwarves with bad attitudes, and the time he wrestled a gryphon in order to get a certain troll-lass' attention.

Rock-Eye sighed. He truly needed an army of his sons and grandsons, to storm this Lady's keep and teach her she couldn't just abduct baby trolls; but an army of trolls would start a war, whereas one, lone, ancient, half-blind former general was hardly a threat, let alone an invasion. If only his liege, Lord Orrin, had known where exactly he could find wee Winsome.

A heavy, tentative knock rattled Nyla's chamber door. She quickly straightened the bow of the pale green ribbon on the front of the gown's bodice. "Come in."

The door swung open slowly and Cray's head appeared. Usually he simply barged in once she'd granted the necessary permission, but since their conversation in the woods earlier, he appeared almost shy, afraid. "Cray, stop being a stump and come in."

He entered, dressed in Rainsong family livery as the coachman and official head of the marmot carriage team assigned to get she and Kara to the Midsummer's Eve Ball in style. He stopped in his tracks when he saw her ensemble. She smiled, knowing full well he wouldn't be the first person to be stunned by the emerald green gown and cape with delicate pinpoints of light dancing around the skirts and playing in her upswept hair. The look was topped off with a woven silver, butterfly-shaped, family-crest-bearing comb given to her by her mother.

"Wow, Nyla, with your wings out and your hair up you almost look like a proper faery."

She curtsied at the backhanded compliment. "Why, thank you, kind sir." Cray didn't say anything further, but he fidgeted, with one hand behind his back and the other tugging at his own, sandy-brown locks. "Speak, Cray, before Mother comes down for her final inspection."

He took a deep breath and held out his closed fist. "I made you a gift, for this evening. You grumble about it, but I know how special this ball is, starting off the bonding season, so I thought you might want to remember it."

She smiled kindly but shook her head as she looked at his closed fist. "That's very sweet, but I can't accept it—" Her brother's expression fell, and she back-peddled. "Cray, I can't accept it unless you open your hand, silly." She held her own hand out, slim and tiny in comparison to his. When did he get so big, she wondered.

Chuckling, Cray opened his hand slowly, revealing a delicate broach with a simple dragonfly etched onto it. Nyla gaped. She accepted the broach when he placed it on her open palm. "It's beautiful, Cray!" And it was. The delicate silver filigree was subtle, but it brought the entire piece to 'life' in her hand.

"I spun a simple 'flytrap' spell into it. It's nothing like what Father can do, but it will trap all of the music and laughter and fun you'll have tonight."

She looked up from the gift to see not joy, but sadness in her brother's expression. "I'm sorry you can't join us, Cray. Twilly would love to get you dancing."

"She'd need a spell-and-a-half to get me traipsing about in silk slippers and a sodding mask. Since the lads all get to come to the Equinox Gala, after you've all bonded, I'm sure I'll be forced to dance then. But maybe you'll let me listen to the trapping after you get home tonight."

"Of course." She hadn't seen her twin's soft side in a very long time. Sharing the trapping could be fun.

Cray tapped the broach once, and six little legs popped out like a tiny Border Beetle, then a second tap made them vanish. "Once you attach it like this, it will stay put until you tap it again, hard. To begin the trapping, simply rub your thumb tip around the edge, widdershins. It will trap a whole day and then stop itself. Last spring Father made me one to trap an entire ten-day—both sight and sound—for my scout quest to Larch Valley." He took it from her palm and clipped it onto her cape, which lay neatly on her bed.

"Thank you, Cray. I'll treasure it." And she did. She caught him off guard with a hug, but he returned a quick return squeeze before she broke it off. "Now, Mother hasn't said more than two soft words to me in hours. I've seen her angry before, but this is something different. Have you heard anything?"

He shook his head. "She's furious, Ny. The day of the most important social event of your life and you not only didn't say where you were going, but you left chores undone, Twilly got hurt, and Lady Orlaith now knows who you are, for all the wrong reasons. I think Mother and Father are trying to decide whether your punishment will be an entire season of pollen collecting and sorting," they both cringed, "or two seasons as a lady-in-waiting at Ten-Oaks Castle. Even though you had nothing to do with Torinstag's murder, Mother feels you've shamed the clan. Rest assured she and the Aunts will be keeping a *very* close eye on you at the ball."

"Oh lovely." Yet another shadow on the biggest social event of the year. For some reason an image of the bloody murder scene flashed in her mind again, and she shivered. "I still see the gore when I close my eyes."

"I'm not surprised. But try to have a least a little fun tonight, and maybe the trapping will be family entertainment for centuries to come."

"I'll try. I think I can avoid embarrassing the family for one blessed evening."

"Hopefully. Just keep Kara out of trouble."

She laughed. "Poor Kara. Most days I think she simply goes along with my silly schemes because *her* friends just want to chase dandelion seeds on morning breezes. In many ways, she's *much* more mature than me. She's the one who should be bonding this year."

"True enough."

"Oi! You're supposed to defend me, tell me I'm wrong, that I'm far more mature than my—*our*—baby sister." She smacked his shoulder.

"I have to do no such thing. I'm your *brother*, not a besotted amore. *My* job is to taunt you and make your life difficult."

"You're such a burr!"

The Rainsong sisters were from a good faery clan with position, power, and access to many of the finer things in the duchy, but when Cray helped them down from the glistening family carriage, Nyla and Kara both stopped cold on the undulating Mulberry-purple pansy carpet, stunned by the sight before them.

More than simply ten large oaks grown cooperatively into one large dwelling, Lady Orlaith's Ten-Oak Castle grew from ten *gargantuan* oaks, each the size of fifty large oaks. The ten Orlaith oaks were intertwined, fused, and melded into a living, ten-spire, monumental palace rivaled only by King Oberon's own, or so the rumours went. Both Rainsong lasses had seen Ten-Oaks before, but Nyla realized it had always been in daylight. Now, with dusk come and gone some shakes before, Ten-Oaks rose and rose and towered and soared above them straight up to the stars themselves, it seemed. On every branch, every surface of the monstrous oaks, white glowing will-o-wisps lounged, frolicked, or flitted about, making their liege's ancestral home appear to be part of the sky's star field itself. Look as hard as she could, Nyla found it impossible to discern where oaks ended and night sky began.

"Oh, my…"

Kara nodded dazedly. "My oh my…"

Nyla leaned in close. "I am so burring terrified I'm going to pee my party panties."

"I know! Me, too!"

Cray interrupted them. "I have to move the carriage." He leaned in and gently ran his thumb around the rim of the trapping broach pinned to Nyla's shimmering, iridescent cape. "There. Now you won't forget. Just remember, both of you, anything said within three arms-lengths of the broach will be trapped, which means…"

"Be wary of our words," Kara finished for him.

Nyla fluttered up and gave Cray a quick kiss on the cheek. "We will. Thank you." She took her sister by the hand and they joined the procession, hovering over the pansies, waiting their turn. She knew most of the lasses ahead of them, but other than polite, gloved finger-waves when she waved at them, no one came back to chat or waved them forward to join them. Torinstag's murder dominated the gossip, but Nyla suspected as much as everyone itched to ask about it, no one wanted to be seen associating with her until the political dust settled. Oh well, why should tonight be any different, she thought.

Between the decorations and the stunning array of gowns and elaborate headpieces, Kara's head turned left and right and back, trying to take it all in, but Nyla's own amazed gaze kept drifting back to where the will-o-wisps and stars met. By the time they arrived at the front of the procession, she *so* wanted to sneak off and fly up for a closer look.

A pair of silver flutes floated above the two identically liveried brownies, livening up the procession with a bouncy minuet. The brownies were announcing the arrival of each and every lass as she arrived, because, like her own parents, the other adults were using the East doors so that on this special night, reserving the main entrance for the lasses soon to bond. An important social event, the rules were quite flexible for lasses, so Kara wasn't the only younger sister in attendance.

"Joyous Midsummer, Lasses!" They had arrived at the brownies.

"Be well come to Ten-Oaks Castle!" The pair alternated, nearly finishing each other's sentences.

"May we know to whom we address this welcome?"

"If you please."

"Nyla Rainsong."

"And Kara Rainsong, of the clan Rainsong."

A delicately flowered space as tall as a hill giant, the main entrance arch of Ten-Oaks formed from two massive roots. Two family carriages could drive between the roots, side by side, and so, when the brownies turned to face into the castle and announced with magically-enhanced volume, "The Sisters Rainsong: Nyla and Kara," for the first time in her life, Nyla felt truly small and insignificant. Each and every face in attendance pivoted around to inspect the youngest lasses of Clan Rainsong, and in that moment Nyla wished she could be at home, reading, or even cleaning. Never before had this richly polished, golden-brown archway so terrified her. Not one to get premonitions, like some of her aunts, the moment she and Kara flew between the entrance roots of Ten-Oaks Castle, though, she got a sour, curdling, tremble deep down in her belly, and a blood-chilling sensation her life would never be the same again.

Chapter Six

"**O**h, Nyla! Look!" Kara gripped her hand and pulled her the last few steps into the Great Hall of Ten-Oaks. The grand hall—nearly as long as Rainsong Grove was wide—was a sensuous riot of sights and sounds and smells. Orchids floated around the space, bearing tall, fluted goblets containing some nectar Nyla could only guess at. She deeply suspected it would be a few levels of expensive above butter-juice. Up near the ceiling, over fifty feet away, it snowed, but as the huge flakes fell, they transformed into fireflies. One of the glowing insects bumped into Nyla and vanished with a 'pop'. Her skin where it had touched her felt like it had just been kissed.

By the light of both the fireflies and scores of floating globes of starlight, she watched the nearest walls ripple and change colour and pattern. After a moment of staring, she realized all of the walls were covered in butterflies beyond counting, and the pattern changes occurred as entire walls of the beauties lifted off and followed some timed rotation, descending on the next wall even as the previous flock took to the air and moved on. It was all seamlessly timed, and wondrously imagined.

Down beneath her slippered feet, the tile floor of the Great Hall had been replaced by an impossibly emerald blue alpine lake, complete with wind-ripples. A snowflake drifted down and landed on her upper lip. Her tongue flicked out and picked it off. "Cream!"

"What?" Kara turned slowly in place, equally enchanted by the marvels all around them.

Nyla laughed. "The snowflakes! They taste like cream!"

Kara reached out, plucked a nearby snowflake in mid tumble, and popped it on her tongue. "Mmmm... with a hint of strawberries."

"Morainn Dewtickle, of Clan Dewtickle," the brownie pair behind them announced to the enormous gathering.

"Azalea!" Nyla pirouetted around just in time to see Rainn flutter into the Hall, looking as lost and overwhelmed as she herself felt. She grabbed Kara's hand and pulled her around, under, and over everyone and everything between them and Rainn. When they finally reached their Sister, she wore a grin bigger than her diamond choker. As Nyla approached, she opened her arms and Rainn threw herself into the embrace.

"This is so wondrous! It's just what I needed after Torinstag."

"It most definitely is." Tall, graceful Fiona joined them, her long snow-white hair in an intricate six-strand braid with tiny red flowers woven in. Rather than have the braid draped over her right shoulder as she usually did, it dropped straight down the centre of her back to the bottom of her gown's indigo-blue bodice. She gave them each quick hugs. "This is *our* night, though according to my mother, we are to eat, dance, and behave like proper ladies, not like 'misfit Sisterhood rabble'."

"Rabble?"

"*Misfit* rabble. Which I suppose is better than 'stumpy humans'. She smiled and winked. "By the way, Twilly is here somewhere with her mother. We never would have made it back in time if your mother hadn't sent a bumblebee lift for us, Nyla, though they seemed more concerned with Twilly being ready for this burring ball, though, than with healing her and breaking her out of whatever has its hold on her."

"That's deplorable!" Nyla flew a little higher and spun slowly, searching but not finding. "Have you seen Hem?"

Fiona shook her head. "She had the furthest to travel, so I expect she'll be fashionably late."

Rainn looked around. "Which won't make Lady Orlaith happy in the least. Speaking of our liege, has anyone seen her?"

"Her Grace? Not a glimmer." Fiona glanced about, but the Sisters were in their own calm little island of space within the maelstrom of the party. "This is so much better than I had ever imagined." All around the four Sisters the adults flitted and floated about, often with a goblet in one hand while the other hand—and sometimes a foot or two—caressed others as they passed or conversed. "No wonder they don't let all the lads attend—we would be too distracted to behave."

"A wise decision on their part. Who knows what mischief we'd be up to if we combined nectar, music, and too many lads." Brigid joined them, looking particularly mischievous in a shoulder-less burgundy gown with gold stitching swirling in and around the bodice like wind currents. From the cameo on her choker hung three layered, pleated silk ruffles, which tumbled down just far enough to cover some of her cleavage. She had opted for her mid-calf leather boots rather the delicate slippers her Sisters and most of the other guests wore. "I say, for one night, we forget that Torinstag is dead and there's a troll loose in the duchy, and just enjoy ourselves. The only pressure is to stay out of serious trouble and not embarrass our clans."

"Look. It's beautiful!" Kara pointed at a perfectly white swan emitting a soft, calming glow as it paddled serenely across the mountain lake that had once been the floor. Celebrants nearest to its path moved quietly out of the way, but Nyla could see many cocking their heads one way or another in confusion.

She whispered. "I expected Lady Orlaith to be riding the swan, somewhere on its back, but it's alone." Kara, too, squinted to see better, confused.

Fiona furtively pointed at the great bird. "No rider, no floating carriage in tow..." She lowered her voice even more. "I suspect our liege has indeed arrived." As if Fiona's hushed words were Lady Orlaith's cue, the swan reared up in the water, stretched her neck out, shook the water off her wings, and transformed down into the perfectly graceful Lady of Ten-Oaks Castle herself, gowned head-to-toe not in swan's white, but in the black of the swan's mask. Their liege spread her own red-gold oak-leaf wings and rose up above the lake, turning slowly as she smiled expansively to all of her guests. Her smile beamed out like pure sunlight and Nyla remembered how much she adored her liege.

"Welcome, my dear friends, to Midsummer's Eve! An especial welcome to your dear daughters on this, the eve of the Bonding Season, when they blossom from lasses into ladies."

Enthusiastic applause and cheers erupted, then the countless butterflies lifted off the walls of the Great Hall in a whirlwind of delicate, whisper-soft wings and furry bodies, converged at what Nyla suspected to be the perfect center of the hall. They spun and flashed and Nyla's head hurt just trying to see individual fliers within the maelstrom. Then, in a blink, there were no individual insects, just one devastatingly handsome faery in a high-collared, purple velvet long-coat, with delicate gold threads reflecting the light in a hundred tiny Celtic knots. Gold spirals, plaits, and interlaced lines drew the eyes in and spellbound them. Gradually, deliberately, he unfolded his wings, revealing the most expansive, perfect, pair of fiery copper, gold, and black Atlas Moth wings.

A hush dropped down over the assembled throng, not because they were all stunned into awed silence, but because a spell drifted down with the snowflakes and the fireflies. Nyla could actually see the air ripple as the spell unfolded from its origin like a heavy drape. She turned to her Sisters and tried to tell them about the ripple, but her voice came out empty as the Great Hall of Ten-Oaks filled with the most sensuous, alluring, heart-stirring voice she'd ever heard.

"*Oíche roimh lár an tsamhraidh beannaithe!* Blessed Midsummer Eve! How delighted I am to finally be able to attend after a century or so of having prior engagements." He nodded in his sister's direction. "I propose a toast." A delicate, ivy-etched flute of bubbling, effervescent nectar appeared in the handsome lord's hand. "Dear sister, may your life and reign fill you with pleasure, love, and moments of enlightenment too numerous for the bards to recount." He raised his glass. "To Orlaith, Lady of Ten-Oaks!"

The silence spell vanished with a soft 'pop' and the toast echoed around the Great Hall. "To Orlaith, our liege and Lady of Ten-Oaks!" Although they weren't drinking, Nyla and her Sisters couldn't help but join the cheer.

Orlaith herself bowed her head in acknowledgement, but even from that distance, Nyla could see their liege fumed. Her smile forced and her eyes hard, Lady Orlaith quickly relaxed a smidgen and the tension in the Great Hall faded. Once the roar subsided back to the musical and conversational rhubarb of noise, Nyla leaned close into her Sisters. "A pretty show and all, but do you get the feeling Lord Orrin wasn't expected? Under our liege's perfect blush I spotted a clenched jaw."

The others nodded, and Fiona added, "I saw it as well. Orrin just upstaged his sister, and as everyone in this duchy knows, our liege does not appreciate last-turn surprises which she herself has not orchestrated. My father told me of a time when one of her elder advisers surprised her with a party on Her Grace's birthday, and she was so angry at being caught off-guard she plucked one of her own waist-length green hairs from beneath her ivy crown and lashed out with it, beheading the elder right there at the feast."

"I heard that story, as well," Brigid whispered. "Then she ate and drank and danced as if nothing whatsoever out of the ordinary had happened."

Nyla's stomach rumbled. "Speaking of feasting, I'm famished. All in favour of seeking out this wondrous repast we've heard tell of for so long?"

"Aye."

"Aye."

"Most definitely 'aye'."

Brigid clapped her hands together for emphasis. "Mother warned me to stay away from the nectar, so we should probably get some food in us before we ignore her warning. It's our party and we'll gorge if we want to."

The five of them found the floating buffet and nibbled and sipped, but too many stares from fellow nibblers and sippers convinced them they'd be better off drifting around the hall together.

If Nyla heard one more lecture from her mother or one of her irritating-as-a-buzzing-mosquito aunts, she was going to scream. Once some nosy magpie of an elder noticed most of the Sisterhood were mingling as a group—Twilly was being kept in a quiet corner where friends and family came by to tell her how lovely she looked and comment on Torinstag's horrible end—all four of their mothers simultaneously descended on the Sisters to split them up, and order them to flit and fly and make happy conversation with as many adults as they possibly could. Lady Orlaith's grand ball was for *them*, and therefore it behooved them to meet as many members of their liege's court as they could, they were told, quite firmly. They also pointed out when it came time to for the upcoming Equinox mixer with the lads, families would be happier if they already knew something about the lasses their sons were meeting.

But to Nyla it seemed every time she started having an interesting conversation with a faery or sprite or pixie *not* connected to the Council in any way, one of her aunts would flutter up and politely but firmly guide her away, and escort her to a more 'acceptable' introduction and conversation. The only problem was that 'acceptable' conversation was burring *boring,* all about lovely hats, or the bountiful buffet, or her first choice for a type of tree for her upcoming bonding, and did she hope to be like her mother and pick a grand oak with fine roots and lineage. Aargh!

She did manage to dance and dance and dance with just about every one of the unmarried lads who were now officially adults though not much older than herself, but almost *every single one* only wanted to talk about the Torinstag tragedy and how the gore. All *she* wanted to do was forget the horror, but again and again she found herself telling the simple, short story of finding the blood and the body. She finally lost count of the times she'd recalled the tale at about the same time she lost track of the last of her Sisters. Fiona, usually the easiest to spot with her height and beautiful white braids sparkling in the soft lights, was nowhere to be seen.

A sprite flew slowly past with a tray full of flutes of the wonderful nectar her aunts were trying to keep her from, so she snatched one off. She chugged it back in a flash and before she could place it back on the server's tray, the glass simply vanished with a soft pop. "Perfect! Easy peasy!" *That* was a spell she could definitely use at home at chore time. She reached for a second flute but a rumble in her stomach stopped her. Oh no. A burp, but not just *any* burp. She could tell by how deep it started and how wide it seemed to be on its slow way up, this was going to be what Cray called a 'Nyla-the-demon' belch. With only a blink of time to spare, Nyla looked frantically for a safe place to release the nectar-flavoured 'demon' rising from her depths.

Chapter Seven

The Great Hall brimming so full of people up, down, and all around, leaving her with nowhere safe. The nearest wall of butterflies separated like a curtain in one corner, and another server entered the celebration. Before the wall closed up again, Nyla darted through the gap as fast as she could. She found herself in a corridor, curving both left and right, with a set of wide, well-worn steps spiralling up and out of sight. No sooner had the wall resealed behind her than the demon burp burst forth with a deep bass vibrato ripping of the very air around her.

The sound echoed horrifically in all directions and somewhere to her right she heard an older female voice exclaim "Oh my word! How truly offensive! Who dares utter such vileness in Ten-Oaks?! That had better not be one of my staff!" Heavy footsteps came pounding Nyla's way.

Oh no! Nyla didn't reply, didn't apologize, she didn't even wait around to meet the offended party — she flew quickly into the stairwell and up the spiral, out of sight. If she got caught here, whatever punishment her mother had planned for her would be doubled, or even tripled. Should she wait a few turns until she felt safe to go back the way she came, or should she risk going up, into the unknown? A second deep down rumble made the decision for her and she flew up the spiral as fast as she possibly could. She passed door after door, but she didn't dare open one. Should it be a private room, she would offend Lady Orlaith herself and then she might as well feed herself to an ogre if that happened. A second demon burp tore through the silence and Nyla knew her only hope of escape was the roof, if there was one.

She kept flying up and up, the wall sconces magically lighting themselves with harmless magical flames as she ascended. The wearing on the steps gradually thinned, until they were glossy and polished and looking absolutely new. If anyone ever went this far, they must be flying, she assumed. Just when she thought her only choice was to return down and try to sneak back out into the ball, she came to a heavy door wooden with wide silver straps and a semi-circle top. It also had a barred window twice the size of her head. Through it she could see either will-o-wisps or stars. It didn't really matter which, because it was the way out. Maybe she could even fly down and re-enter the castle through a side door, and just lie she was getting fresh air, or some such.

Setting down quietly on the landing, Nyla lifted the latch and pushed the door open. Rising warm air from the heart of Ten-Oaks pushed past her, caressing her wings, ruffling her cape, and teasing her hair, as it rose up the stairwell and out into the night. She let it push her forward until she stood on a narrow balcony curving around the trunk in both directions. Once she stood clear of the warm airflow, the fresh, cool midsummer breeze surrounded her.

"My stars, that feels *so* good." She spread her wings fully and held her cape out to the side, letting the revitalizing air embrace her fully. "I could just stand her all night, and let the party go on without me."

"You could, but I'm certain one as lovely as yourself doesn't fly out of a room without leaving a void. I know *I* would miss you."

Nyla spun and looked up to where the alarming voice had come from. Sitting quietly on a thick branch above the balcony was the royal interloper himself, Lord Orrin. "Milord! I am so—" Orrin looked in her eyes and smiled. Her horror evaporated, her words disappeared, and her tongue became so tied she feared she would never be able to speak again. He slipped off the branch and dropped to the balcony, spreading his gorgeous, soft, *huge* moth wings only at the last blink, to soften his landing.

"Please excuse my intrusion on your solitude, milady. I am only taking in a breath of air that doesn't smell of cloying perfume or suffocating politics. It's a shame when a celebration cannot simply be a celebration." He took her hand in his own, bent one knee, bowed respectfully…and kissed the back of her hand before rising to stand at least a head taller than herself. "I am Orrin."

"I know. I mean, of course, Your Grace." She curtsied. The air around them on the balcony was suddenly much cooler on Nyla's skin, or her skin suddenly much warmer.

"Of course you know who I am, after my modest little entrance. I introduce myself simply as a formality, so that *I* may learn *your* name. While I could not possibly have missed seeing your delicate beauty dancing or conversing with those you made shine even brighter by your presence, I could hardly ask anyone your name without arousing their gossipy interest."

"Forgive, me, milord. Nyla Rainsong of Clan Rainsong, at your service." She curtsied her best formal curtsy, which wasn't quite as graceful as she had hoped it would be. She found it a bit harder to breathe than she had two blinks before. If she thought

Lady Orlaith to be the most beautiful faery she had ever seen, she realized now it was only because she had never met Lord Orrin. He stood as tall as her twin, Cray, but while they were both about the same width across the shoulders, Cray was as solid as an elm, while Orrin was more of a lithe, flexible, yet powerful poplar.

She couldn't take her eyes off his hair, though. It appeared silver, then it reflected the will-o-wisp light and seemed to be more coppery, then gold seemed to be the dominant colour. Unlike the current fashion amongst both sexes of wearing their hair long and braided, Orrin's hair chopped off just as it grazed his shoulders. At first it looked to be simply hacked short with a dagger, but the longer she stared, the more she realized it was intentionally styled that way, and in its casual scruffiness it perfectly framed his high cheekbones, firm jaw, and the long, thin scar on his left cheek. His ears were long and tapered to perfect points, which peeked out of his hair. His perfect smile was disarmingly lopsided at the moment, as if he could read Nyla's mind and knew she in that moment, she lost herself and found no word other than 'perfect' to describe him to herself.

"So, how is it that I come to have the honour of your company, so far from the maddening crowd, Lady Nyla?"

"I, um, needed to…burp."

"Burp? As in 'belch'?"

"Yes, milord. I didn't wish to insult Lady Orlaith with such rudeness, so I sought out a more appropriate spot."

"And…?"

"'And', milord?"

"And why else have you left a celebration of which you are a guest of honour? I'm merely an interloper who thought it would be a lark to ruffle my dear sister's emotional feathers."

"Just the burp, milord."

"Truly? You weren't being hounded by elder faeries to behave, to fly the straight line, to bond to a tree just like your father's or your mother's or your great-aunt Miranda, or whatever your great aunt's name is?"

"Well…" How could he know she felt that way? *Did* he have the power to read her mind?

"When I was younger, just after I left 'ladhood' behind for life as a grown-up, I had no end of 'older and wiser' family members and court hangers-on telling me who I could socialize with, which lesser families I should avoid, how to bestow favours in exchange for loyalty, and exactly who was worthy of such favours. If I looked left instead of right while seated at the head table of a formal affair, I was corrected. I had to learn rapier, the weapon of kings, not the bow, the choice of mere hunters and foot soldiers."

He motioned Nyla to a bench off to one side, and she moved to it and sat, numbed by his presence, and completely entranced by every word he uttered. She could listen to his smooth, clear voice all night. He didn't sit beside her, though, as she'd expected and hoped. Instead he fluttered up and over the balcony rail, hovering just out of reach.

"I'm parched. If you promise to wait for my return, I'll bring back enough food and drink for two."

He asked *her* to wait for *him*? Of course she would! "I shall remain rooted to this spot, milord. I won't budge."

With a sloppy salute, Orrin folded his wonderful wings in tight and dropped like a stone. Nyla caught her breath and fought the urge to rush to the rail, but she'd promised not to budge and so she didn't. She hardly wanted to look like an eager country lass, especially since Orrin was a noble, with his own castle and court and stuffy life and rules and regulations and restricting lifestyle—exactly the trappings Nyla and her Sisters wished to avoid. They all wanted to direct their own lives, make their own decisions, and not follow in the footsteps or wing-beats of anyone else's expectations.

She concentrated on thinking of him as simply a gorgeous faery with sparkling gold eyes and a smile to melt a glacier. They would chat over a glass and some nibblies, then she would re-join the celebration and pretend all was as it should be. "Yes. That's exactly what I will do."

"Exactly *what* you will do, milady?" Orrin popped up and over the rail with a tray in each hand; one holding six flutes of nectar, and the other mounded high with chocolate-covered strawberry chunks and a variety of puffy pastries. He deftly set the two trays down on the bench between them. "*What* will you do, Lady Nyla?" He handed her a flute, picked up one for himself, and smiled so wide she nearly swooned.

"Ah, I will, um, enjoy this conversation and hope I don't bore you."

Orrin tipped his tall, slender, delicate glass until it tapped her own and made a clear ringing like a silver bell. "Then that is what *I* shall do as well. Especially the part about not boring you. I'm afraid it has been a terribly long time since I was actually alone with a lass, without some steward or other prompting me or censoring me. I seldom have honest, straightforward conversations with anyone. That, I fear, is the solitary life of a noble." He sipped his nectar politely, not chugging it back, as Nyla did with her first one ages ago back in the hall.

"I hardly think you could bore me, milord. Court life must be so exciting." It wasn't something she wanted for herself, but she *had* heard some of her father's stories about the debates and silliness that took place when self-important faeries gathered and tried to make decisions as a group.

"Court life is *tedious* on the best of days. That's why I avoid it. I love my dear sister, but I wouldn't survive a fortnight in her rule-filled, overly-regimented court of high manners." He sipped again, and seemed to take a long moment to simply enjoy the sensation of the chilled nectar sliding down his throat. "But let's not talk about court life. I would rather hear about life in Clan Rainsong. Your friends, your family, what you like to do when they finally free you from the drudgery of chores and let you have time to yourself..."

"Drudgery is right." He understood! "My mother seems to think life revolves around cleaning this, polishing that, and making certain Oak is in immaculate condition just in case someone important maybe drops in for cream and biscuits."

"My mother was just the same! Of course, it wasn't about cleaning, because we had staff for that, but it was about studies, just in case the King himself dropped by, looking for a young noble lad to take under his wing and mentor personally." He placed the fingertips of his left hand gently on Nyla's arm and lowered his voice conspiratorially. "I spent a lot of time as a lad wishing I were living a simple life in a modest meadow, surrounded by close friends and my family."

"Free of parental 'guidance' and interference," Nyla added, knowing exactly what he meant. Since it was the life she fully expected to have for herself, she actually felt sorry for him.

"Precisely." He picked up a chocolate-fruit treat, but paused to ask the two most amazing questions Nyla had ever been asked. "So, what fills Nyla Rainsong's blinks and turns? What makes you smile and laugh?" He popped the dessert in his mouth and chewed politely while she thought about the question.

Taking a sip to both wet her dry, nervous lips, and to give her a little strength, Nyla answered him as honestly as she dared. She expected there would be the devil to pay for such frankness, but right then and there, she didn't give a flying burr. This was *her* evening, dammit. She told him about her family, and the

Sisterhood, and what it was like to walk by choice and drum like a lad. She told him about how each member of the Sisterhood was renamed after a poisonous plant, and when she expected him to mock the idea, he nodded in agreement and told her about wanting to be called "Badger" when he was younger, before he inherited his own duchy. When she told him how much she loved the smell of smoke, he laughed and said he was always getting lectured by his steward for having the logs of deadfall trees burned in the hearth of his bedchamber.

He listened attentively, asking insightful questions about her views of local politics, life in his sister's duchy, and what she wanted to do once she was bonded. She answered each and every question as honestly as she could, and not once did he laugh *at* her, although he did laugh *with* her, at some of her more outlandish tales about mischief she and her Sisters got into over the years.

"Your Sisters of the Black Dragonfly are important to you, then?"

"They're my life, my family. In the case of Kara, it's doubly true. We do everything together. We're hoping to bond in close proximity to each other." She reached for a glass, but the tray was empty. The last glass was in Orrin's own hand, just touching his own lips. He sipped, and then slowly extended the glass out, straight to Nyla's lips. He didn't take his eyes off of hers for even a blink. She sipped. Then he tilted the glass ever so slightly, and she drank deeply. He pulled the flute back just before she drained it, and then he carefully placed his lips on the exact spot where hers had been and drank the last of the nectar down. The flute vanished with the expected soft pop.

Without saying a single word, Orrin took Nyla's hands in his and stood up. She let him guide her to her feet, and when his wings unfurled, so did hers. Eyes still locked on each other, they lifted up off the balcony and rose higher still, to the far reaches of Ten-Oaks. Soon starlight replaced will-o-wisp light, but she didn't care, one way or another. When Orrin pulled her slowly, gently toward him, the world shrunk down to a little bubble surrounding just the two of them. When their lips touched, nothing else mattered.

The kiss lasted a blink, or a turn, or an entire day... Nyla had no idea. Time was irrelevant. They kissed again—longer, and more certain. He let her take the lead, let her dictate how long and how deep the kiss was. When she hesitated, so did he. When they broke off the kiss, though, it was at his urging, not hers.

"Nyla Rainsong, would you ever consider a life at court?"

Was he *proposing*? "Court? I couldn't leave my sister, or my Sisters."

"I'm not asking you to. They would be welcome to make their lives in my court as well."

"We're not really court ladies spending our days arranging flowers and trying to decide which hat to wear to dinner."

"Or course you're not. If you were, we wouldn't be having this conversation. I'm not looking for a courtly wife, I'm looking for a *partner*, a lass who can challenge me and keep up with me and who thumbs her nose at convention and rules. Someone who can shake things up at my court, and maybe even teach the stuffy old musty-moths how to live and love and have fun again."

Her head spun. They'd known each other for a handful of turns and suddenly the handsomest noble in Faerie was asking for her hand? He *was*, wasn't he? He hadn't actually proposed marriage. She had best clarify it. "Milord—".

"Call me Orrin, please."

"Orrin. What exactly are you asking of me?" It was suddenly *very* warm in the heights of Ten-Oaks, under the stars.

"I'm asking you to be my wife. To complete my life, and start a family of our own. Will you marry me?"

"I…" And she wanted to. She really, *really* wanted to. "Yes. Yes, Orrin, yes!" She laughed, and kissed him long and hard to seal the pact. His strong arms around her reassured her and comforted her and warmed her even more. When they finally came up for air, she got an idea. "We can elope! We'll leave right after the ball. I'll go tell my Sisters right now!" She made to fly off, but Orrin held her firmly, but gently.

"No, my love, I must ask your parents' permission, at your home. Tradition requires me to arrive at sunrise with witnesses— preferably someone from my own family—and knock four times on your family tree, once at each point of the compass. After the fourth knock I'll kneel in complete silence at your door and await your father's invitation to enter."

"We can't just elope?"

"Without your parents' blessing, we would get neither the Elder Alder's nor the King's blessings."

"The King's?"

"Aye. If you are to become my full and true lady and our children have a place at and be accepted in the Royal Court, this is one of the few rules we must obey. After this one thing, though, we make our lives our own."

"If you say so. Can I at least tell my Sisters tonight?"

"Can you trust them not to blab like busy-bees?"

"I trust them with my life."

"Then tell them. I will speak with my sister and arrange to have all of your families to Ten-Oaks for a celebration tomorrow, at High Noon, to celebrate, after I propose on the morrow." He looked up at the stars. "It's late, my love. We both need to return to the celebration, to keep tongues from wagging. Gift me some small favour so I know your heart is true, and I will promise to see you tomorrow at sunrise."

"A favour?"

"Something small and simple, but of personal value. As a promise of your love. I will return it tomorrow, when I ask for your hand."

There wasn't much she could give him. She could hardly part with her cape, and she wasn't wearing much in the way of jewellery. Except for the silver comb! She reached up, slipped it out of her hair, and handed it to Orrin. "I'll get this back? It was a gift from my mother. A family heirloom, I believe."

"You have my word. After I ask for your hand." He smiled warmly.

She closed his strong fingers over the comb. "Until tomorrow, my love." She kissed him quickly and folded her wings in, dropping like a stone. A few blinks from the ground, she opened her wings and landed softly to one side of the main gate. With a serious nod at the guards, she strolled back into the Midsummer's Eve Ball, finally ready to celebrate. She couldn't wait to see the looks on her Sister's faces when she broke the news they were all moving away from the Duchy of Drudgery!

Chapter Eight

Once she was back in the Great Hall, her heart bouncing with joy, Nyla flew straight up and into the snowflake-filled shadows, fluttering over the celebrants, trying to locate her Sisters while evading her mother and aunts.

She found Fiona first, at the center of the dancing with her braids flying as she led a reel in mid-air. Brigid, too, she found dancing, but on the outskirts of the throng and with somewhat less enthusiasm than Fiona. She squinted and saw Twilly remained close by her own mother's side. Rainn and Kara chatted with a group of lads who were no doubt pestering them for all the gruesome details of poor Torinstag's end.

She went to Rainn and Kara first, fluttering quietly down behind the lads, with a finger over her pink lips. Kara looked up and nodded, so Nyla signaled for the two of them to follow her and started off in Brigid's direction, trying to predict where the reel would have taken her within the crowd.

"Look see, if it isn't Nyla Wingbinder herself."

Knowing full well the whiny voice belonged to her own quite dislikeable cousin, Fenella, Nyla ignored the jibe and flew on — she had far more interesting things to do than trade insults with her older cousin in the one place she must behave and stay out of trouble.

But Fenella continued. She flew around in front of Nyla, blocking her way. "Murdered any stags lately, Ny-Ny?"

It had been a long time since Nyla's baby name could get a rise out of her, but Fenella had always been two or three blinks behind everyone else. Even her daffodil gown with flaring, frilly yellow *everywhere* was three seasons out of style. Nyla hovered in place. "We didn't kill Torinstag, Fenella, we simply found his head."

"That's not how the tale is spinning out. You started a fire and used the smoke to lure a Mist Eater there to slay our liege's great stag."

Seriously? "That's ridiculous! I'm sorry Fenella, but I don't have time for frivolous fictions. Besides, why aren't you with Lady Orlaith — I hear she's giving away some of her excess jewellery."

With a squeak of surprise, Fenella flew straight up, spun around until she located Lady Orlaith, and flew off. Kara and Rainn caught up to Nyla. She pointed to the middle of the reeling lines of faeries. "Please fetch Fiona and bring her to where Twilly is. I'll bring Brigid. We have to chat." The lasses nodded and they all went off to round up the rest of the Sisterhood.

As soon as Brigid spied Nyla she broke off from her dance partner and intercepted her. "Where have you been? I've been saddled with dancing with Azalea's clumsy oldest brother because none of the other lads will dance with me after I refused to talk about Torinstag."

"I went out for some fresh air and something magnificent happened. I'll tell you all about it when we're all together. It affects *all* of us." She took Brigid by the hand and led her away from the dance floor, weaving over, under, and around celebrants to Twilly in the Clan Berrycheer corner.

Madame Berrycheer noticed the two Sisters and gently nudged her daughter. Twilly turned and smiled, but Nyla could tell immediately there was something 'off' with her Sister. It wasn't until she landed in front of her she could see Twilly's eyes weren't quite as alert and focused as they usually were, and her smile lacked its usual sparkle.

"Oh, Twilly!" Nyla pulled her in and hugged her fiercely. "What's wrong with you?"

"She'll be fine, dear." The elder Berrycheer put a comforting hand on Nyla's shoulder. "We've given her a simple tonic to help with the shock but will allow her to at least attend the celebration and maybe get some joy from it. Don't expect much conversation from her just yet."

"Madame Berrycheer, we're *so* sorry this happened. We had no idea—"

A gruff cough behind her interrupted Nyla's apology. "You were shirking your responsibilities and playing at your silly walking games in a place you had no business being, lass." Twilly's father—General Berrycheer—stood eye-to-eye with Nyla, but he was twice her width and probably three times her weight. "Trust me when I promise that once my Tuilelaith has bonded, she will be spending *much* less time with you five."

What could she say? Nyla had no smart reply because he was right. "Yes, sir." She gave Twilly a kiss on the cheek and spread her wings to fly away, but Madame Berrycheer intervened.

"Now, Angus, be easy on the lasses. No matter the tales being spun, you know full well they had nothing to do with Torinstag's sad end. What Twilly needs is to heal, and no one is better for that than her friends." She patted her husband's arm then looked at the two Sisters. "Nyla and Brigid, would you be so kind as to take Twilly over to the cream fountain? I think it would do her a world of good."

The General started to object, but his wife held up one finger, silencing him. "Not here. Not now. There are no trolls or Mist Eaters at the ball, Angus, so the lasses will be safe. It's a party, and she should spend at least a few blinks away from her stuffy parents. Besides, husband of mine, you owe me a dance; and if Twilly is feeling better after a visit with the lasses, you owe *her* a dance as well." She gently guided Twilly by the elbow over to Nyla, who took her Sister by the hand.

Quickly and quietly, she and Brigid led Twilly away. She didn't dare say a word or even glance back, but she imagined the General's gaze burning her wings and scorching her back. She kept walking. After a few steps, they were intercepted by Rainn, Kara, and Fiona, the latter of which was flush and disheveled and immediately started babbling on about the music and the food and where had Nyla gotten to. Nyla shook her head firmly and Fiona shut up, one eyebrow raised in question.

Once they were out of earshot of the Berrycheers, Nyla whispered, "The General is *not* happy with us. Madame let Twilly visit for a few turns, but I just wanted to get clear of them. There's enough drama in my own family, and it's going to get worse."

Kara peered closely at her sister. "What's happened? Has mother decided our punishment?"

"Not that I know of. And it won't matter, anyway."

"*Not* matter? You're not even bonded yet and you're going to stand up to Mother?"

"I won't have to."

Brigid looked confused. "You're not making any sense, Ny."

Nyla knew Brigid was right. "How would you all like to live free and clear of the stupid rules? To bond with a tree *you* like, not one your parents choose? How would you like to meet lads you haven't known since before you could fly, ones who aren't distant cousins?"

"It sounds wonderful." Brigid nodded.

"I vote yes!" Kara's enthusiasm made Nyla *very* happy.

"No rules?" Fiona seemed skeptical. "Not *all* of the rules are stupid."

"True, but no matter how well we bond, and marry, and mature to fit in, we will *always* just be their little lasses, living under their thumbs as long as we live here. Our own mother is still terrified of *her* mother."

"Are you suggesting we run away? Mother *and* Grandmother will hunt us down like crazed wolverines."

"Not running away—at least in the usual sense of the word." She took a deep breath, and even Twilly appeared to give Nyla her undivided attention. "I got bored and tired of being hounded by the aunts and started drinking nectar, but I had to flee the Hall because I was going to burp. Then I *did* burp, a real wall-shaker, and almost got caught in the back spaces, so I flew up some stairs, past closed door after closed door, until I finally got to the top and found a balcony between the will-o-wisps and the stars. It was beautiful and amazing and magical."

"Nyla Rainsong!"

Oh no! Mother! Now or never. She whispered quickly, "Lord Orrin was up there, too, and we chatted and chatted, and kissed and kissed, and he asked for my hand and I said yes, but only if I could bring all of you along." She finally stopped talking, just as her mother dropped down into the middle of the group, forcing them all back a few steps. All five of her Sisters stared at Nyla, mute and confused as burrs.

"Young lady, your aunts were unable to find you for far too many turns; and I thought I made myself perfectly clear you six were to split up here at the ball." She glared at each of them.

"Yes, Mother, you did. Because it's such an important evening, I was hoping Rainn, Fiona, Brigid, and Twilly—if her Mother agrees—could stay with Kara and me in Oak tonight. We promise to go our own ways in a blink, but I thought I should ask them if they were interested before I came to you for permission." She paused, and then played her trump card. "We only bond once, and once we do, we'll start to lead our own lives. Can we please have this night? Cray will even be in the next room, so we won't be able to get into any mischief."

"If Twilly is allowed to come, I'll be surprised if your besotted brother will leave her side." She looked closely at each of the lasses, trying to read their true intentions, Nyla suspected. "Yes. Go your own ways from here until the bells end the celebration, then meet at our family carriage. But you must *each* get permission. No lies. Your parents must know exactly where you will be and who you will be with."

They all answered at once. "Of course!"

"Yes!"

"We promise!"

"Thank you!"

"At the carriage, right after the bells!"

"With permission." She wagged a finger at them and Nyla nearly kissed the tip of it, she was so happy.

"Thank you, Mother! I love you, Mother."

"Of course you do, Nyla. Now go mingle. And make certain your aunts don't lose sight of you again. If they can't find *you*, they come find *me*, and I would like to enjoy the party, too, for at least a few blinks."

"Yes. Of course. I promise. I will dance and mingle until the bells toll." She blew them all a big kiss and flew up and away. She knew her Sisters were going crazy with questions, but it couldn't be helped. They had to stay away from each other now so they could get together later. She rose up and above the mass of dancers and searched for Orrin. If she could dance with *him*, she'd never even hear the bells, nor notice the end of the party.

She eventually gave up on trying to find her Love in the crowd, and too nervous to even think about eating, Nyla grabbed a dance partner from the sidelines.

"But I can't dance, Ny!" Mungo was one of Cray's older, more socially-awkward friends, and generally a fun lad to be around.

"Maybe not, Mungo, but you can fly and you can wiggle your feet. Just follow me and in a handful of blinks there'll be a queue of lasses wanting your company, both for dancing, and to find out what 'misfit outcast' Nyla told you about the Torinstag Affair."

"But you haven't told me a thing."

"Dance with me, and I will tell you *everything*, Mungo."

He did, and she did. She told him every little detail Lady Orlaith herself knew. She told him about the gore and the dripping blood and the horrible smell; and while she spun the tale and dragged him through reel after reel, her eyes swept over the crowd for a certain faery lord in a purple doublet.

She discovered Mungo was actually quite well coordinated, but no one had ever taught him a single dance step, so when the enchanted orchestra switched to a waltz, Nyla was forced to give Mungo more of her attention in order to keep the two of them from crashing into other couples. She thought, too, her dance partner was actually fun to chat with, when Mungo suddenly froze in position, lowered his eyes and mumbled. "Good evening, Your Grace."

Doing her best to hide the pounding of her heart and hoping her skin didn't look as flush as it felt, Nyla released Mungo's hand and fluttered around slowly to face Orrin. Knowing all manner of eyes were watching her now, she kept her gaze lowered and executed the absolute best courtly curtsy she could manage. "Good evening, Your Grace. I hope you are enjoying our celebration."

"I am most certainly doing that, milady. Just a few blinks ago I was telling my dear sister about how unexpectedly enjoyable it is, and getting her acquiescence for my plans during the remainder of my visit to her duchy. I was thinking this has been the best ball I've attended in ages. And how about you two?"

Mungo continued to mumble nervously. "Yes, milord. Wonderful, milord."

Nyla raised her eyes up and let slip a hint of a smile. "I, too, am having an unexpectedly wonderful time, finding all of my dreams are coming true in one single night."

Orrin bowed graciously. "Then please continue to enjoy yourselves, and mayhap we will see each other again before I depart for home."

"Yes, milord."

"That would be lovely, milord."

Orrin fluttered over to speak with another young couple, but from what Nyla could hear of the conversation without looking like she was listening to it, it was all just polite small talk, lacking the same subtle hidden meanings. She continued dancing with Mungo, even taking a break for a small glass of nectar and a visit to the desserts array. She saw Orrin twice more, from a distance. The second time he glanced up and smiled, as if he knew she watched. Even from across the huge hall, she could see his gorgeous copper, black, and gold wings.

Somehow, one at a time, each of her beloved Sisters managed to dance past and flash her looks that were a mix of shock, awe, and what-the-burr-are-you-doing. She just smiled and winked at each of them in turn. Her Sisters she could put off chatting with until later—and in fact had been *ordered* to do so—but her aunts were another matter altogether, which she discovered when the most senior and obnoxious of them, Matilda, dropped her scrawny, hook-nosed, chiffon-draped self straight down between she and Mungo.

"What did His Grace want, Nyla? What did you say to him? You better not have offended him and embarrassed the clan, again."

Nyla hovered back from her aunt's accusing finger. "Not at all, Auntie. His Grace was simply making the rounds, being pleasant, and ensuring Mungo and I are enjoying ourselves."

"Is this the truth, Mungo?" She leaned in and glared at the poor lad.

He shrunk back from the assault, but Mungo managed to confirm Nyla's answer. "Yes, yes it is, ma'am. I'm as clumsy as a dwarf and Nyla's grace and poise saved us. His Grace told us how much he was enjoying himself, said maybe we would see him again, and then he flew off."

"Nyla didn't say a word about her stupid Sisterhood?"

"Not a peep, ma'am. She was so charming I thought His Grace was going to cut in and ask her to dance."

Aunt Matilda turned slowly and deliberately from Mungo to Nyla. "*You*, young lass, had best hope His Grace does *not* remember you. Lady Orlaith is already far too aware of who you are after that horrid Torinstag mess. She's fuming over her boorish brother's rude and inconsiderate crashing of her favourite ball, and if she in any way connects the two of you, you will find yourself indentured to her court indefinitely."

"No, Auntie. I mean yes, Auntie." What the burr would Aunt Matilda say when she married Orrin? She'll probably combust, just exploding with fury. Nyla tried not to laugh at the image that popped into her mind, and instead bowed her head to hide her smile. "I promise to avoid both His and Her Graces for the remainder of the celebration."

"See you do. And that goes for your Black Daffodil Sisters as well." With powerful strokes of her monarch butterfly wings, she flew off before Nyla could correct her. She, Mungo, and a few of the nearby faeries watched the crone depart.

Mungo seemed impressed. "Wow, Nyla, you definitely have some eyes on you. I don't think I'd like that too much."

"It's not a lot of fun, Mungo." She held her hand out to him. "So, what do you say we dance and forget the whole silly thing ever happened? I'm quite sure Lord Orrin will come nowhere near us again."

"That's too bad. He *is* quite the eyeful. I nearly burred myself when he arrived."

"I noticed—but I promise not to tell anyone." She winked to reassure him, and then led him back into the dance.

Chapter Nine

Without her Sisters at her side, the remainder of the ball flew past so quickly that before she knew it, the tinkling of the bluebells announced the winding down, then her parents and Kara fluttered along at her side, patiently waiting for the current waltz to end. She smiled at them, and when the final note sounded she curtsied to Mungo, then darted in and kissed him quickly on the cheek.

"It has been a pure joy, Mungo. Thank you *so* much."

Mungo blushed, but managed two perfect courtier's bows, one to Nyla, and one to her family. "The pleasure has been all mine, Nyla. This is a ball I'll not soon forget." He took a deep breath and Nyla had a good idea what came next, so she went there first.

"You should drop by Oak to see Cray sometime, and maybe have tea." She wouldn't be anywhere near there, but even if she were, Mungo would still be welcome.

"I shall. Thank you." Then he flew up and away. He hadn't gone very far when Nyla noticed two lasses and three lads trailing after him. "And so it begins. Good luck, Mungo," she whispered to herself, before turning back to her family. "Home?"

"Home," her father confirmed. "I understand Cray and I will have the blessing of an oak full of excited post-ball lasses."

"We'll be quiet, Father. I promise."

"Make as much noise as you want, Nyla. This is a once-in-a-lifetime night for all of you, and even your Aunt Matilda says you've represented the Clan Rainsong well."

A quick glance at her mother confirmed this news with a smile.

"Thank you Mother, and Father." Reluctant to leave beautiful Ten-Oaks where such wonderful things had happened in such a short time, Nyla took one final slow spin and took it all in. Then she grabbed Kara's hand and led the family toward the main gate and the coach. One by one, Rainn, Fiona, Twilly, and Brigid joined them, each taking a Sister's hand, flying in a joyous formation.

Cray waited with the coach exactly where they expected him to be, and when he saw everyone so happy he raised an eyebrow questioningly. Nyla kissed him lightly on the cheek and he quickly wiped it off with his sleeve, but when Twilly flew up and planted a kiss directly on his lips, she stunned him motionless. He didn't wipe the kiss away, and Nyla spotted a little extra colour in his face. No, this night would not soon be forgotten by *any* of them, she thought as she climbed into the carriage after her mother.

During the long ride back to Rainsong Grove, Nyla could see her Sisters were bursting with questions, but with her parents seated across from her, Nyla deftly steered all conversations back toward mundane topics such as the food and music. When her mother asked about Mungo, Nyla smiled enigmatically and sidestepped the issue with "He's very sweet and has a good heart."

"You certainly spent a great deal of time with him. Should we be speaking with his parents and possibly having them over for tea?"

"You told me to stay out of trouble and avoid my friends, Mother. As I said, Mungo is very sweet, and a complete gentleman. We chatted, danced, and supped, but he's a friend of Cray's, so that almost makes him family."

"Nonsense. Tuilelaith is certainly considered one of our family—as are all you young lasses—but that's not going to keep Cray from pursuing a second kiss."

Once they were back in Oak, Nyla suspected five of the six of them probably set a record for fastest changes from gowns to daily wear. Still a tad sluggish, Twilly needed a bit more help with her buttons and bows, but she still changed quickly. Nyla giggled when she saw Rainn, Twilly, Fiona, and Brigid all dressed in *her* clothes, especially Fiona, whose arms and legs were considerable longer than her own.

Kara planted herself in front of her sister, refusing to budge. "So, tell us all about it! What the burr happened?"

Brigid put up a hand to stall Nyla's answer, and then tapped her ear. Nyla agreed. Her news was best kept for their ears only. She pointed up, then leapt out her bedroom window into the warm, moist, midsummer night air. She popped open her wings and caught the firm breeze. A few blinks later she perched comfortably in the upper reaches of Oak, quickly joined by the others. Kara started in on her before she herself settled in.

"Talk. Now. Or I'll bind your wings and push you off that branch myself."

That earned Kara surprised looks from all of them, but Nyla laughed. "Do you want me to tell you what happened?"

"Of course."

"For burr's sake, *yes*."

"Stupid question."

"I'll help Kara push you if you don't start talking."

Nyla loved stretching it out and adding suspense, but she was busting to tell them everything. She opened her hand and revealed the charm Cray had made for her.

"*Orrin* gave you that?" Brigid was skeptical. "I thought you were wearing it from the beginning."

"She was. *I* gave it to her." Cray hovered in and settled next to Nyla, but not too far from Twilly. "It contains a fly-catcher spell, so whatever has got you five all wound up, it's right there for you to hear."

"You *captured* it?" Fiona was impressed. "Well burr me stupid, but that's brilliant!"

"Hardly brilliant. Cray activated it before we entered Ten-Oaks and, to be completely honest, I completely forgot I was wearing it until I took off my cape when we got home. I have no idea how to work the spell, so maybe you could play it back for us, Cray." She held out the beautiful charm to her twin and he accepted it. With a couple quick taps, he started the trapping.

"*There. Now you won't forget. Just remember, both of you, anything said within three arms-lengths of the broach will be trapped, which means…*"

"*Be wary of our words,*" *Kara finished for him.*

Brigid interrupted. "I'm sure that the entire evening is a wonderfully scintillating listen, but I, personally, *want to hear what happened with Lord Orrin.*"

Cray tapped the charm to stop it. "You met Lord Orrin?"

As an answer, Nyla just smiled. "Cray, is there any way to move ahead through the trapping?"

"I think so. It works like Father's charms. When I tap it to start it, I should be able to move my finger deacil for forward in time, and widdershins to reverse it." He started the trapping again and this time he slid his fingertip around the lip, clockwise. "How far along?" All of the voice and the music sped past at a silly rate, causing them all to snicker and giggle at how they sounded.

She thought about it for a blink. "About halfway through. Listen for my demon burp and its echo, then we'll listen from that point forward."

Cray gaped at her. "You ripped a demon burp in Ten-Oaks and Mother hasn't sold you to an ogre slaver? Burr me!" He kept the trapping advancing.

"In a back passage. The impending burp was why I slipped out of ear shot."

"So no one heard you?"

"I didn't say that. They heard me, but I flew away up the stairs before they set eyes on me." As if intentionally timed, Nyla's burp sounded loud and clear on the trapping, though higher in pitch and shorter in duration than it was in reality. "There! That's it."

Cray lifted his finger and the trapping resumed at normal speed.

"Oh my word! How truly offensive! Who dared utter such vileness in Ten-Oaks?! That had better not be one of my staff!" Heavy footsteps pounded toward Nyla, then fluttering wings and panicked breathing were the only sounds for a number of blinks. A number of smaller, softer burps escaped, but eventually a latch could be heard, and a door opened.

"My stars, that feels so good. I could just stand here all night, and let the party go on without me."

"In this place and in this space your heart will be mine the longer you gaze at my face."

"Wait!" Nyla was confused. That's not what Orrin said. "Who was that?"

"That was Orrin, wasn't it?" Fiona pointed at the charm. "Cray, take it back again, please."

Cray reversed the trapping back to the burp. This time around they heard it at normal speed. "Mother of the Old Ones that was awesome, Ny! It's still echoing!"

"Oh my word! How truly offensive! Who dared utter such vileness in Ten-Oaks?! That had better not be one of my staff!" There were the footsteps, her wings flapping softly, her breathing, the latch lifting and the door opening.

"My stars, that feels so good. I could just stand her all night, and let the party go on without me."

"Starting in this place and in this space your heart will be mine the longer you gaze at my face."

Fiona tapped the charm herself to stop it. "It is definitely Lord Orrin, but there's something strange about his voice. And you don't remember him saying that, Ny?"

"He *didn't* say that. He said something about me being lovely and if I left a room he would miss me." What the burr was going on?

"I think you've been spelled, Nyla."

"No no no! We chatted. He was charming and funny and he understood me. We have so much in common. Play it!" Cray hesitated, so Nyla started the trapping herself.

"You could, but I'm certain one as lovely as yourself doesn't fly out of a room without leaving a void. I know I would miss you."

"Milord! I am so—"

"Please excuse my intrusion on your solitude, milady. I was only taking in a breath of air that doesn't smell of cloying perfume or suffocating politics. It's a shame when a celebration cannot simply be a celebration." There was the sound of a kiss. *"I am Orrin."*

"I know. I mean, of course, Your Grace."

"Of course, you know who I am, after my modest little entrance. I introduce myself simply as a formality, so that I may learn your name. While I could not possibly have missed seeing your delicate beauty dancing or conversing with those you made shine even brighter by your presence, I could hardly ask anyone what your name was without arousing their gossipy interest."

"Forgive, me, milord. Nyla Rainsong of Clan Rainsong, at your service."

"Nyla Rainsong, I bind you to me. Where I goest you will need to find me."

"Oh, burr *me*!" Nyla was devastated. This couldn't be happening. Tears came and she couldn't stop them. Fiona hugged her.

Cray whispered. "Kara, go get Mother and Father. The burr is going to hit the fern, but it can't be helped." Nyla heard rather than saw Kara launch off the branch, but she didn't care. Her life was ruined.

In only a few blinks, Kara returned, but she only brought their father, a robe over his plaid bedclothes.

"Your mother is sleeping, and so should I be. This had best be important."

Nyla couldn't speak through her tears, she could only nod. Cray explained.

"I gave Nyla a charm with a fly-trap to trap her special night. Part way through the evening she stepped out of the celebration to avoid burping in front of everyone."

"That was a wise decision."

"She ended up on a balcony where she met Lord Orrin."

"Orrin? I'm not sure I like where this is going, but continue, Cray."

"I haven't heard the entire conversation, but Nyla says they just chatted."

"That's good."

Nyla pushed back the tears and found her voice. "We talked and laughed and...and...I fell in love with him."

Her father actually laughed. "That doesn't surprise me in the least, Nyla. Every lass does, eventually. He has an inescapable charm about him, does our liege's brother."

"And he fell in love with me."

"Really?"

"He asked me to marry him."

"That's not possible. You must have misinterpreted something he said."

Cray took up Nyla's defense. "It doesn't matter, Father. Just listen to this and tell us what *you* hear, please." He reversed the trapping back to the burp again. Their father snorted with laughter when he heard the belch.

"Oh my word! How truly offensive! Who dared utter such vileness in Ten-Oaks?! That had better not be one of my staff!" There were the footsteps, her wings flapping softly, her breathing, the latch lifting and the door opening.

"My stars, that feels so good. I could just stand her all night, and let the party go on without me."

Softly. *"Starting in this place and in this space your heart will be mine the longer you gaze at my face."*

Normally. *"You could, but I'm certain one as lovely as yourself doesn't fly out of a room without leaving a void. I know I would miss you."*

"Milord! I am so—"

"Please excuse my intrusion on your solitude, milady. I was only taking in a breath of air that doesn't smell of cloying perfume or suffocating politics. It's a shame when a celebration cannot simply be a celebration." There was the sound of a kiss. *"I am Orrin."*

"I know. I mean, of course, Your Grace."

"Of course, you know who I am, after my modest little entrance. I introduce myself simply as a formality, so that I may learn your name. While I could not possibly have missed seeing your delicate beauty dancing or conversing with those you made

shine even brighter by your presence, I could hardly ask anyone what your name was without arousing their gossipy interest."

"Forgive, me, milord. Nyla Rainsong of Clan Rainsong, at your service."

Softly, again. *"Nyla Rainsong, I bind you to me. Where I goest thou wilst need to find me."*

Cray stopped the trapping. Their father was pale. "You heard nothing of the rhymes?"

"No, Father. I swear."

"You've been spelled. Let's hear everything." He tapped the charm and resumed the trapping. They all sat silent, the cool night air filled with cricket songs, bullfrog calls, and the courting of a faery lass by a spell-casting noble.

Nyla blushed at the more intimate moments, but no one gave her any grief over them. Her father did something he hadn't done since she was pre-flight. He hugged her.

"I have no idea what to suggest, Nyla. Part of me wants to wake your mother and play this for her, but part of me wants to spare her this, too. Orrin is coming here tomorrow to ask for your hand, and I expect Lady Orlaith herself will accompany him, being his only relative on this side of the river. You can't say yes, knowing that you've been spelled, but if you say no, there will be darkness to pay."

"But I want to marry him! I want to go away and bring my Sisters with me. He promised I could!"

"You can't. You're under a spell. What you want isn't real." He looked at Nyla's friends. "If we don't break his spell, Nyla will try to run away and follow him. I *have* to wake her mother. We have no choice. You lasses might as well go down to bed, while Nyla and I go see her mother."

"I'm coming, too, Father," Kara insisted.

"Yes. Of course. Cray, can you please fetch the guest bedding for the lasses?"

"Yes sir." He led the four Sisters back to Nyla's bedchamber, and Kara and their father took Nyla down to the Great Room.

"Wait here. I'll go wake your mother. This is not going to go well." He left them and flew up the heartwood path to his own bedchamber. Nyla curled up in a ball and Kara wordlessly hugged her, comforted her.

After so many blinks that Nyla lost count, Father arrived back in the great room.

"I've told your mother only that you've been spelled. After she's broken it, we'll give her the details. Telling her beforehand will just distract her."

"Thank you, Father."

The tell-tale flutter came down the heartwood path.

Chapter Ten

Mother arrived. "A spell? We're certain?"

"Yes, dearest."

"Nyla, what kind of trouble have you gotten yourself into? You went off with some low-meaning lad, didn't you?" She didn't wait for an answer, but instead tilted Nyla's head up so she could see into her eyes. "Look left." Nyla did. "Look right." She did that, too. "Now close your eyes and hold your breath." Nyla did, and felt her Mother's hand on her forehead. It stayed there for a few blinks, and then was lifted. "You can open your eyes, and breathe now. There is definitely strong magic there. Kara, come here. You were at the same party so to make sure this isn't simply some residual magic from all of the spells used for the ball, close your eyes and hold your breath."

Nyla watched her mother put her hand on Kara's forehead, then Mother closed her own eyes and it was as if she was listening to a voice Nyla couldn't hear.

"Not the same. You've been targeted, Nyla. I sense the work of a very powerful spell-caster, but since the spell itself is a fairly simple one, I can unwind it and release you."

"What do you need, my Love?" Nyla's father asked.

"Sage, rosemary, and thyme; plus two fresh belladonna berries. Kara can get the berries from my garden, but use gloves to handle them. The rest should be in the pantry. I'll need my smallest mortar and pestle as well."

Kara and their father left to gather supplies. Her mother placed a fingertip on the end of Nyla's nose. "I expect a complete explanation when this is done, young lady. How is it you attract trouble so easily? The more I think about it, the more I'm inclined to have you spend some time at court, under a watchful eye and strong discipline. I'm sure Lady Orlaith and her staff can keep you out of trouble for a season or two."

Too busy imagining ways she might avoid the disaster due at sunrise, Nyla had no reply for her mother. She couldn't very well go off to marry a lord who would coerce her so blatantly, even though she loved him with all her heart. Of course, to avoid shaming the clan, her mother might just agree to the marriage, spell or not. For her mother there was no crime greater than dishonour and shame. If she tried to run away in the night, both her family and Orrin would hunt her down. Father and Kara returned with the supplies, ending her conjecturing.

"Kara, please grind up the sage, rosemary, and thyme, using half-twists of the pestle in your left hand for ten blinks." She waited while Kara did as she was asked. Kara held out the stone mortar for her mother to inspect the contents. "Yes. Listen closely, and don't do this until everyone has their instructions and I tell you to start. You will add the belladonna berries, but this time don't grind the contents, pound each berry thrice with the pestle, and thrice only. Not twice, for twice is not enough, but thrice, and thrice only. Hold your breath and look away while you do this. You mustn't get any of the juice in your mouth or eyes. When done, hand me the mortar immediately. Nyla, when I hold the mortar under your nose, breathe three short breaths and hold them in. It will sting like nettles, but can't be helped. Do not breathe out again until I say so, and when you do, do so as slowly as you can and don't stop until you feel like you've squeezed out every smidgen of air you can. Do you both understand?"

"Yes, Mother."

"Yes."

"Excellent. Kara, start."

Once, twice, thrice pounding, then once, twice, and thrice on the second berry. Mother received the mortar, keeping it away from her own face, but holding it under Nyla's. Nyla took three short breaths and held them, wondering why her mother was so worried about it stinging. It wasn't so bad. And then it started. The burning, hurtful sting made her eyes water and she desperately needed to get fresh air or she was going to die. Suddenly her mother was waving her hands in front of her face and mumbling some words, but through the tears in her eyes and the pounding of her blood in her ears, Nyla couldn't focus on any of the details. The burning worsened and worsened, and then, suddenly, was gone.

"Breathe out, Nyla. Slow and steady. Get rid of it all."

She breathed it all out, her tongue tingling somewhat as the air flowed over it, but there was none of the sting left. She thought it was all gone and she wanted so much to breathe in, but her mother stopped her.

"More. Squeeze it all out. If you keep any in, you'll die."

Die?! She coughed! "*Mother!*" She breathed in and out, grabbing fresh air as fast as she could.

"It worked. All gone." Nyla saw her Mother ball something dark and amorphous in her hands and shove it into the mortar. "Kara, please get Cray to fly this as high as he can and shake it out into the night. Warn him to hold his breath, close his eyes, and have the breeze at his back when he does this. Go."

"Of course, Mother." She left to find Cray, one gloved hand covering the ugly thing in the mortar.

"Thank you. Now, you two, I want an explanation, right this blink. That was a simple spell, but not lightly cast. The caster will only know it has been dispelled if he gets close to Nyla, which you will not permit. Who is he and what in Faerie brought it on? Who have you angered so much that they would spell you, Nyla?" She sat on the overstuffed milkweed pod.

Nyla held her hand out to her father, who passed over the charm. "You'll never believe my words, so here's a trapping we got of everything in a charm Cray made for me." She tapped the filigree dragonfly and her burp once again filled the room.

"Nyla!"

"Listen, Mother. *Please*." The trapping went on. When it got to the spell, Nyla let it run, but her mother tapped it.

"I know that voice. That's not Mungo, though. Where were you? I don't hear the celebration any longer."

Nyla tapped the charm.

"Milord! I am so—"

"Please excuse my intrusion on your solitude, milady. I was only taking in a breath of air that doesn't smell of cloying perfume or suffocating politics. It's a shame when a celebration cannot simply be a celebration. I am Orrin."

Mother was so stunned she fell off the sitting pod. "Lord *Orrin*?" Nyla would have laughed if things weren't so serious. Father helped Mother back up onto the seat.

"Yes."

"Lord Orrin *himself* spelled you?"

"Yes, Mother." She continued the trapping and the three of them listened. No one interrupted it again until the end.

"We will talk later about your insulting comments, but at this moment I want to confirm you gave him your comb as a favour?"

"I had nothing else. I certainly wasn't going to give him a slipper."

"Yes, that would have been silly. Regardless, he will be returning the comb in the morning."

"You're worried about the comb?"

Her mother ignored the comment. "What His Grace has done is a crime. You are unbonded and therefore without the defensive aid of your own home tree. But he's our liege's brother and a noble in his own right, and so is immune from most laws."

"That's not right, Mother! Noble birth shouldn't give him license to spell *anyone* to marry him." The King couldn't possibly allow it.

"Not officially, but it's done far more often than you think. Your grandmother used to make the best love potions west of Laughing Elf Lake. Usually the spell wears off long before any wedding, and hopefully by then true love has taken hold."

"How could anyone love someone who spelled them to it?"

"The spells fades gradually, so if the speller doesn't tell anyone, no one is the wiser, even the betrothed. You'll go off with His Grace and I expect he'll do his best to make the love real before the wedding."

"That's disgusting."

"He's not the worse choice out there, Nyla. It will be a good life. He even says your friends can go along, too."

"Mother! You're not seriously saying I have to marry the man who spelled me?"

"Of course I am. Now that your head is clear of his spell you can go in with your eyes open and see this as the wonderful opportunity it is. Since His Grace, Lady Orlaith, and likely a retinue of courtly witnesses will be here at first light, I don't know why we are even discussing it. We'll invite him in and grant him permission." She looked at her husband. "Isn't that so, dear?"

"Yes. Certainly." Nyla couldn't believe he was agreeing with Mother! "Nyla, just because there was a spell—"

"Or *two*!"

"Or two, on you, doesn't mean you wouldn't have fallen in love with His Grace anyway. Other than the two castings, everything he said sounded reasonable. His tone certainly sounded kind." He took her by the hands. "Look, your friends are waiting for you. You've been pushing us away and wanting a life away from the Grove and Oak for as long as we remember. Your mother is right that this is a wonderful opportunity. Just get some sleep. It's been a long night and we all need some rest before the day begins with such a momentous event."

She pulled her hands away. "I can't believe you two. You're just doing this to curry favour in the court. You're practically trading me for power and position!"

Her mother lifted quickly and easily off the pod. "We are doing no such thing. You have been accorded an opportunity any other grateful daughter would rejoice at. You will do as your told." She pointed her finger at Nyla and spoke firmly. "Sleep!"

When she opened her eyes, Nyla was lying on her bed, looking up at the ceiling. Brigid's face popped into view, her finger over her lips.

"You're supposed to be asleep," Brigid whispered.

"But I'm not. Why?" She sat up slowly, with Brigid's aid.

"There's a little trick I know where I pinch your baby toes and it snaps the spell. We heard everything through the door, with a little help from Fiona's big-ear spell. What's the plan? Run away?"

Nyla looked at the six worried faces arrayed before her. Even Cray looked concerned. "How far would I run before they hunted me down? Lady Orlaith's Elf Sky Patrols would spot me before I even got out of the Grove." What else could she do? She couldn't kill herself to avoid what *might* be a bad marriage. As a matter of fact, it might even be a good marriage. "When he formally asks me for my hand, I will decline. What's the worse that could happen? I'm a commoner and not subject to the same laws which force royals into marriages for political purposes. I may not have bonded, but I'm of age and no longer under Mother and Father's rule. I'll decline—politely of course—and thank His Grace for considering me worthy."

Fiona sat down on the bed beside her. "Do you honestly think that will work?"

"What choice is there? They can't kill me or even torture me. Besides, I'll bet Lady Orlaith doesn't want someone from her duchy marrying her brother. From everything I've heard, they hate each other."

"You'd better hope she hates him."

"She's smart and reasonable. It won't be a problem. Now, can I please go back to sleep. I'm exhausted."

Kara shook her, gently. "How can you think of sleep? Sunrise is just around the corner."

"I was doing quite fine until you all woke me up. Even a short nap would be better than nothing. There's nothing left for us to do tonight. I'm sure Mother will wake us before sunrise so we can fluff and primp and scrub in order to make a fine impression when company arrives."

"You're delusional, Ny. It's more likely Mother will post guards at the windows and doors to make sure you don't flee, then she'll hand you over to Lord Orrin, and Clan Rainsong will move up a few notches in the social standing."

Fiona sat down on the edge of the bed. "Kara is right. Neither your mother nor His Grace will take 'no' for an answer."

"*Nyla* is right." Cray looked back from where he stood at the window with Twilly. "By our birthday count, Nyla and I are adults, as of two moons ago. Just because she isn't bonded and I haven't been inducted into guard service doesn't mean we're not adults. Father and I were discussing this a ten-day ago. By Faerie Law, it's a very grey area the grown-ups don't want us thinking too much about, but from our Turning Birthday until Bonding Day or Induction Day, we have all the rights and none of the responsibilities of an adult. They can't force Nyla to marry, especially before she has bonded. The bonding is a sacred right and tradition for every lass, older than the King's reign. Three moons ago you would have been fair game, Ny. Not now." He shrugged. "At least that's my interpretation of what Father said, even though we were mostly discussing my own options."

Nyla stared, stunned. Not only was that the most Cray had ever said in front of her friends, it was also the most intelligent. She looked closer and now saw he and Twilly were holding hands, which meant he was no longer her twin ready to snitch on her, but something of a co-conspirator. "Thank you, Cray. As I said, I will politely decline and express my desire to remain close to my family. How can anyone argue that?" They couldn't. Discussion over.

Except that it wasn't. Kara had more to say, lowering her voice even more. "Then you'd best play along with Mother when she comes to wake us, because if she even gets a *whiff* you're going against her wishes, you'll be locked in the root cellar and smuggled out in a sack, to be handed over to Orrin during the dark of the next new moon. This is *Mother* we're talking about. Binding our wings, walking, smelling like smoke, and painting cute patterns on our skin are minor rebellions she mostly lets pass. This... *this* will mean war, and you *know* it."

Nyla looked from her two-blinks-older brother to her younger sister and back. "When did you two get so smart?"

Cray grinned. "We just watch what you do..."

"...and do the opposite." Kara finished for him.

The tension of the past few days popped like a swamp bubble and the seven of them burst out laughing. They laughed so hard they were all rolling on the floor when Nyla's father appeared at the window, startling them.

"I'm glad to hear and see you've changed your mind and are celebrating the big event, but please put a mushmellow in it and try not to awaken your mother. She has to get up well before dawn to prepare. At least she's been forewarned about the visit and the meal at Ten-Oaks. Get some sleep while you can. You will most likely find yourselves up with her, cleaning."

"Yes, Father."

"Yes, sir."

"Yes, Elder Rainsong."

He left.

"I'm not even sure it's worth trying to sleep now. The short night is about to end." As if to confirm Nyla's suspicion, a quick knock tapped at her door. She quickly lay back as if she still slept, and her mother entered a blink later.

"Cray, your father has a list of jobs I need the two of you to do before sunrise." Through half-closed lids, Nyla saw Cray give Twilly's hand a squeeze before he left. "Ladies, you are guests in our home, so asking you to do chores would be crass, but should you feel so inclined as to help Nyla and Kara, the list I have for them won't be nearly as daunting as it first appears." She hovered over Nyla faking sleep, leaned down, and flicked the end of her nose with a fingertip.

"Ouch! Mother!"

"That's what you get for trying to fool me. Don't you think I know when my own spell has been broken?" She pulled a folded parchment from her smock's pocket and dropped it on the bed. "Please start at the top and work your way down the list. You and Kara can decide who does what, but decide quickly." Looking around the chamber, she found Twilly still by the window, where Cray left her. "Tuilelaith, dear, why don't you come give me a hand putting breakfast together and laying out tea for our expected guests."

Unsure, Twilly looked to Nyla, who nodded. "That's a great idea, Twill. You can make sure Cray gets a good meal to start the day."

Twill smiled. "I can do that. I can help with food." She followed her hostess out into the great room and Kara quietly closed the door behind her.

"Now then, let's see this list." She picked it up and unfolded it. "Burr me! This is a week's worth of chores! Crass or not, Ny, this is a list for the entire Sisterhood."

The other three crowded around and read the list. Nyla sighed. "All this work and no one will notice how clean Oak is once the burr hits the fern. Ah, well, most of this was on my chores list anyway. I'll start with the flowerbeds, since it's first on the list. It should be interesting picking weeds by the light of fireflies."

Kara poked the list with a finger. "I'll start with *that*."

One by one, each of the Sisters either picked a task for themselves or joined Nyla or Kara to speed up their work.

When the morning sky began to glow soft lavender and yellow, Rainsong Oak neared readiness for the distinguished visitors. Nyla's mother interrupted her bringing dry laundry in off the spider web line. "We have just enough time to brush and re-braid your hair, splash some colour into your cheeks, and get you into something presentable but not too ostentatious." They both grabbed a plate of fruit from the sideboard and went into Nyla's chamber, where a half-dozen fancy dresses were laid out.

They finally settled on the gold and copper mid-calf dress Nyla's youngest aunt had sewn for Nyla's pre-bonding party. "We can always make another dress, and this one will perfectly match His Grace's wings. You will look beautiful together."

Her mother's excitement almost made Nyla forget she planned to decline the betrothal. Burr it! This should be a happy, fun day with sunrise bringing with it the beginning of her new life with the love of that life; but instead her heart was dark and grey and the lump in her stomach just wouldn't go away. She was terrified, and her mother could see it.

"My dearest one, don't be so nervous."

Dearest one? Mother *never* used such sappy treacle with her, even when Nyla was a baby. She's probably as nervous as I am, Nyla thought, though not for quite the same reason. "It's a big day, Mother. Lady Orlaith hasn't visited our grove in ages, and certainly never on such important business."

"No, never on such—"

Cray appeared at the open portal, interrupting them. "We have company: two Royal bumblebee coaches and a half-dozen archers following a parade of will-o-wisps. And there are silver bells *everywhere*," he added, a bit disgusted. He flew off, and Nyla rushed to the window. She could now hear the approaching bells overlaid on the sound of heavy draft bees. She wanted to vomit.

Her mother spun her around. "A final inspection. No breakfast crumbs, no berry juice stains, your nose is clean, your ears are powdered, and—smile." She peered closely at Nyla's forced grin. "No stuck greens."

Did her own mother just inspect her teeth like a thoroughbred seahorse at auction?! *Now* she wanted to cry. She made her previous crack about being traded for position and power in anger and frustration, but now it seemed she wasn't too far off the mark. Her mother was selling her to a man who would *spell her against her will*, and neither her parents nor Orrin saw anything wrong!

"Perfect, Mother. Thank you for checking. Now, don't you think *you* should be presentable? I'll wait here by the window with bated breath." She tried her best to keep her voice steady and the sarcasm to a minimum, but she seethed.

For once, her mother didn't seem to notice her tone, looking down at her own smock, aghast. "Oh, my!" And out the portal and up the heartwood path she went to change her clothes. She nearly knocked over the Sisters who were gathering in the Great Room.

Brigid smiled, weakly. "You look beautiful, Ny."

"All the better to face the dragons with. I wish there was room in this dress for a dagger. I have no idea how to use one, but I think it would give me a measure of comfort. This off-the-shoulder, fluffy coppery-goldy armour wouldn't stop a mosquito, let alone a royal archer's arrow."

Brigid hugged her. "They're not going to shoot you. You're in the right and we've got your wings. Be polite, respectful, concise, and brief."

"Polite, respectful, concise, and brief." A pair of regal trumpets blasted out a four-note 'All Hail', and Nyla nearly wet herself. "Oh, *burr* me! Trumpets?"

Her Sisters laughed, and Fiona peeked out the window. "Such is the courtly life. Are you absolutely, definitely, without a doubt certain you want to turn it down? Trumpets with supper, trumpets with tea…"

"Trumpets with your crumpets," Rainn added, and snickered. "Sorry. Couldn't resist, I'm nervous, too."

Fiona kept watch at the window, half-hidden by the black curtains. The sound of a hundred or more silver bells got nearer. "Wow. Those are the biggest burring draft bumblebees I have *ever* seen. They're almost as big as your badger! Even the coaches are wondrous, all carved from solid black walnut and polished to a mirrored sheen. They look like giant eggs with elfish carvings of magnificent detail. Wow, and wow." She fanned herself with her hand. "The carriages have been deposited in the grove and one is opening up."

After a blink or two of silent anticipation, Nyla nearly screamed in frustration, but then Fiona gasped. Rainn, Brigid, and Kara rushed to the window and each gasped in turn. The little scene almost made Nyla laugh out loud. Almost. Fiona turned back from the window. "This isn't going to be easy, Ny. He's gorgeous, and if I didn't known what he did to you, he wouldn't need even a single spell to have my heart's undivided attention."

Nyla could no longer resist looking. She had to see him for herself. Rainn stepped aside to let her up to the casement. Dusk approached, the sky still lightening. Though the sun had not yet crested the horizon, she hardly needed sunlight when will-o-wisps now filled the grove. The magical glow bathed their home with unreal beauty—and then she caught sight of Orrin, and her definition of beauty changed forever.

His shaggy locks seemed to dance on his head, like wheat during an electrical storm. He wore no crown nor laurel wreath nor even a silly little hat with a feather in it. With his wings folded back and his head bare, it was a moment of true humility. Except it *wasn't* true. It was all for show. He had *spelled* her. None of it mattered when it had its seed in such tainted actions. His folded wings didn't matter, nor his bare head, his downcast gaze, the simple, dark green waistcoat and breeches, nor the perfectly snow-white linen shirt open at the collar, exposing his throat. He walked, barefoot, to the north side of Oak and knocked. He then repeated the knock at the west and south points. He finally approached the east-facing front door of Rainsong Oak, but *it made no difference to Nyla.* It couldn't. She couldn't allow it to. He had deceived her at the most basic level and now her parents were trading her freedom for favour. She would be no better off than a poor goblin slave, and *that* was all that mattered.

Just as Orrin reached Oak's portal, he looked up in Nyla's direction and smiled. A subtle smile, it turned up one corner of his mouth, like a secret between two lovers, but the smile didn't reach his eyes, which were lit only with power and entitlement. It disgusted Nyla, but before she could even open her mouth to shout something—anything—to stop him, he knocked and dropped to one knee. The door opened, her mother took a step out, and the formalities formally commenced.

"Your Grace, welcome to our humble home. On what occasion do you honour us with a visit?"

Nyla had to stop them, but short of throwing stones, she couldn't do a burring thing. She knew shouting would certainly be ignored. As she ducked back inside she heard Orrin answer quite clearly. "I have come to ask for your daughter Nyla's hand in marriage."

She wanted to rush down and yell at them all to halt this farce, this *joke* of a proposal, but she spun around to find her brother blocking her way. "Cray!"

"No, Ny. Follow protocol. As Father explained it to me, Orrin has asked and so now Mother and Father will serve him tea and hear his proposal. When the time comes, you will be called down and presented with the proposal as they've discussed it."

"You mean the terms of my *sale*." She tried to get around him but he wouldn't budge.

"You have rights, but so does His Grace. He gets to make his proposal and they *must* listen to it. Even before you get summoned Mother and Father can suggest changes or even turn it down. Be patient. Mother should have explained all of this to you."

"She was too worried about whether my slippers matched my panties or some such nonsense." Nyla looked around her small chamber. "Where's Twilly? She's not in *there* with the slaver and the rapist is she?" There was no way she wanted Twilly to have to deal with more stress.

"She wanted a nap so I set her up in Kara's chamber and set Lacey to keep her in there. No one gets past a funnel spider if she doesn't want them to." He nodded toward the window. "Did anyone see Lady Orlaith exit her carriage?"

"No." Brigid moved from the window to the bed. "If I were her, I'd be sound asleep behind carriage curtains, waiting for the silliness to be done. I can't expect she's happy to be dragged out of bed before dawn for some dumb duty involving a brother she despises. With any luck, Ny, she'll be grateful it's not going any further than this and there won't be a wedding."

"Not as grateful as I will be." Nyla stretched and yawned widely, as much from boredom as from exhaustion. "Can't we just skip past today and jump straight to tomorrow? What if I get out there, face-to-face, and can't say 'no? I mean, he's handsome, rich, a rebel, and says I can bring you all along." She paced, from Cray to the window and back, but Kara suddenly stepped in front of her, blocking her way.

"Because you *can't*. If you don't take a stand here, when the proof of his maleficence is so blatant, then you will be telling every lad of every species it's acceptable to use magic to get what you want from an unwilling lass. You will be saying forcing you to serve him is acceptable just so long as he's handsome and rich. You will be saying—"

Nyla held her hand up and stopped her sister's rant. "I understand. I can't. Say no more."

"Good, because I ran out of reasons."

"Those two are big enough. Even if a spells wear off before the wedding, it's unethical."

"Exactly. Now stop pacing. You're making me dizzy."

Her pacing stopped, but a knock on her portal made her jump. Cray opened it, revealing their father. The elder Rainsong looked sad. His usually wide shoulders slouched ever so slightly, and his gaze was downcast.

"Nyla, you have company. Would you join us, please?" He left before hearing her answer, returning to their noble company.

"Of course, Father. It would be my pleasure." She tucked her wings back, stuck her chest out, and lifted her chin, but a hand on her shoulder stopped her from following her father immediately. A second hand landed on her other shoulder. Fiona and Brigid stood on either side of her.

"You can do it. We're right here, ready."

"I know. I love you all."

Nyla knew with certainty she'd followed her father eventually, but later on she didn't remember taking a single step. One blink she was surrounded by the love of her Sisters and Cray, and the next she stood in front of Lord Orrin, performing a curtsy so perfect even her mother smiled with pride.

"Good morning, Your Grace. Welcome to Rainsong Oak. I trust your journey from Ten-Oaks was pleasant."

"It passed in a pre-dawn blur as I could think only of seeing you once again. I'm most certain my dear sister has a beautiful duchy, but I remember little of what I saw before I met you last evening, and certainly will take notice of nothing once I take my leave."

Nyla managed to suppress her laugh into a simple, innocent-looking smile, but it took great effort. Orrin might not notice anything on his journey home, but she would bet a pocketful of sparkly dwarf stones there would be more anger than joy in his heart. Whatever his infatuation with her, she was about to hit it with a lightning strike of disappointment.

"Such kind and flattering words, milord."

"I only speak to the truth in my heart, milady." He bowed his head slightly.

"Then it behooves me to do likewise, milord."

Orrin lifted one eyebrow just a tad. Nyla could see something in his sparkling eyes. Distrust? Confusion? Could he see from across the room that his spells were broken?

A light knock at the door forestalled the impending moment. Being the one closest to it, Nyla opened the door, only to find Lady Orlaith standing on their threshold, resplendent in a blood red travelling skirt with a crimson jacket and matching corset over a white blouse. Nyla curtsied deeply, if awkwardly. "Milady! Please join us. Welcome to Rainsong Oak." She couldn't remember if there was more to the formal greeting, so she looked back at her parents, but they had their eyes downcast, no help whatsoever. Nyla stepped aside to allow her liege entry.

"Thank you, lass. Since I was dragged all this way to be Orrin's family witness to this momentous occasion, I thought the least I could do was actually witness it." She glared at her brother, who smiled back. "I haven't missed it, have I? That would be *so* unfortunate."

Nyla's father stepped forward. "Not at all, Your Grace. Please, be welcome." He motion to his own seat. "Please."

"Offer accepted, Rainsong." She sat, though not before giving the chair's almost new cushion a look of disappointment. Silence reigned as she adjusted her skirts and everyone waited. She finally folded her hands in her lap and looked up expectantly.

Seeming to take that as his cue, Orrin crossed the room, went down on one knee, gently took Nyla's right hand in both of his own, hesitated a blink, and muttered. "Ah. Well, so be it." He whispered something Nyla could barely hear, and then he raised his voice again. "Nyla Rainsong, will you—"

"STOP!" Orlaith was up off the chair, tiny sparks dancing around her brow. "Did you just cast a *spell* on this lass?"

Caught, Orrin shrugged. "Someone broke the ones I cast last night."

"This is all because you *spelled* her?" The brow sparks doubled in size and number and her wings bristled. "If someone broke your spells..." She spun on Nyla's parents and for a moment Nyla actually feared for their lives. "You knew about this, didn't you? You condoned my brother's vile behaviour in *my* duchy, and for *what*? Position and privilege in *my* court?" She lowered her voice to a growl and pointed a sparking finger at her brother. "Go home. You're as reprehensible as these social climbers. Pray to the Old Ones the King never hears of this." She waved the door open with a gesture, and then departed Rainsong Oak with a trail of sparks behind her.

Orrin got slowly to his feet, brushed off his knees, then whispered so low to Nyla she was certain her parents didn't hear it because she wasn't sure if she even heard it herself. "This is not over, unbonded trash, and it will not end well for *you*." He dove out through the open doorway, spread his great wings, and glided to his waiting carriage.

At first Nyla didn't dare look away from the spot on the wall she focussed on, but she couldn't stare at it all day, and she really needed to see the expression on her mother's face. A greater social blow could not have been dealt to Mother, and although it wasn't Nyla's fault, she knew the blame would somehow settle firmly on her head.

Her mother sat, unmoving, the shock so great. Her father, down on one knee, comforted her, whispering softly. He turned to Nyla. "Out. Go to your friends. Now." His voice was firm, a deep sadness in it, but Nyla wasn't sure what the sadness was for. For her, because she was at the centre of it all? For her mother, who was just called a social climber? Or for his family in general, and the price they would all pay because Orrin was a spell-casting letch?

She flew up the heartwood path, to her room, and her waiting friends.

"I should kill that trollop!" Orrin pounded his fist against the carriage cushion, doing no damage whatsoever.

"You cannot, milord." Orrin's steward, Gilroy, poured his liege a glass of wine. "It would be taken as a declaration of war, and you would never get out of this duchy alive."

"True." He accepted the glass and sipped.

"What do you wish me to do, milord? Our choices are few."

"Are we certain I can't kill her?"

"We are. She would be missed, by both her family and by a little group she calls her 'Sisterhood'."

"Yes, she told me of her ridiculous, childish Sisterhood."

"Aye, milord. The wagging tongues at the ball spoke rather

harshly of the 'Sisterhood of the Black Dragonfly'. They're known for being somewhat rebellious lasses. I made a few inquiries after hearing the first whispered rumours. It was they who discovered the bloody ruins of your sister's stag. They're so odd they prefer *walking* to flying."

"Yes, she told me all about it. They even enjoy the scent of wood smoke."

"Not unlike yourself, milord."

"Truly. We actually have quite a bit in common. I rather enjoyed my time alone with her." He smiled thinly. "But that was then and this is now. Use fire."

"Set her on fire, milord?"

"Not *her*. Orlaith's precious forest, and point the blame at this unbonded harlot and her idiotic sisterhood."

"How? Who?"

"You. I trust only you. Wear a forget-me charm, set fire to… to…that stand of great rowans we passed a league east."

"Why would they blame the lasses, milord?"

"Proof." Out of his jacket pocket he pulled the comb the faery trollop had given him as a favour, to be returned at the proposal. "Leave this there, near the fire, but not so near that it will be damaged. Once it is found, her own reputation will hang her and we will be long since home and avenged."

"Consider it done, milord. Might I suggest you take a different route back to the river. I will fly this over to the rowans myself."

"Excellent, Gilroy. Then we can be quit of my sister's domain before she decides the King needs to be informed."

"But the prophecy, milord…"

"*This* was an idiotic idea. I will find a willing bride amongst the poorer faeries in my own duchy." He held the wine glass out for a refill. "Set the fire, frame the lasses, redirect my sister's attention, and we will never set foot in this duchy again without an army at our back."

"As you wish, milord."

Chapter Eleven

"**I** need fresh air." Nyla angrily stripped out of her coppery dress and changed into her hiking clothes.

Kara hopped up on the bed and sat. "What happened? Lady Orlaith and Lord Orrin have both fled the Grove like it was on fire."

"He tried to cast another spell and got caught by his own sister. But instead of ripping *his* head off, she turned on Mother and Father and called them 'social climbers' for allowing this farce to happen."

"Ouch. She's not far off the mark, though, Nyla. Mother *was* trying to marry you up. It's a fairly common occurrence."

"Maybe so, but she wasn't happy. Orlaith kicked Orrin out of the duchy and not so subtly threatened to tell King Oberon." She looked around the room. "Where's Cray?"

"He flew up to check on Twilly," Fiona answered. "What did they say when you declined his marriage proposal."

"I never got the chance. He got caught before I could say a word. For all they know I was going accept."

Brigid clicked her tongue in disapproval. "Why would he risk something so stupid?"

Nyla hung up her dress. "When he took my hand, he must have sensed the original spells were broken and either didn't think anyone would notice a little whispered enchantment, or didn't care if they did."

"At least now you're done with him and we can get back to normal life."

"Hardly, Brig. Just before he left he whispered in my ear, 'This is not over, unbonded trash, and it will not end well for *you*.'"

"Oh my stars!" Kara paled. "Well, Ny, if you're going to have an enemy, it might as well be someone with royal blood."

Nyla stepped over to the window. "Father told me to get out and join you, so I'm joining you as we all go for a fly." She dove out the window and drifted to the ground, needing a great deal of fresh air. Her four Sisters followed.

They circled the grove, flying in the shadows. Nyla heard a soft cough and a rustling in the leaves above them, and stopped.

The others did likewise, hovering in place. She pointed up and after a blink the rustling was repeated, getting closer. She didn't know if it would do any good to hide, so she waited. What was the worst it could be, she thought, Mother coming to yell and ground her? For once, she'd done nothing wrong.

"Why didn't you all come get me?" Twilly fluttered down to join them.

"Twilly, what are you doing? We thought you were sleeping."

"A lass can only sleep for so many turns before she's ready to get back into the world." She hugged Nyla, and then each of the others.

"How did you get past Lacey and Cray?" They continued around the edge of the grove.

"I asked Cray for a cup of cream, and your funnel spider likes her tummy rubbed. He went off to fetch a cup of cream, and Lacey dozed off, purring. I dove out the window and followed you. I hated lying to Cray, though."

Nyla knew what she meant. "I think he's the only one in the family who *isn't* in trouble, and it's best if we keep it that way."

"Where are we off to? Are we running away?"

Brigid laughed. "Hardly. Just off to the hot pool to soak our feet and let the sun bake our worries away."

"Not near Torinstag?" Twilly paled.

"In the opposite direction, Sweetie." She took Twilly's hand. "If we *never* go near there again, I will be happy."

"Me, too." She whispered. "I see his blood in my sleep. It's *everywhere*."

"Me, too," Kara agreed. "I think we all do."

"You do? I thought it was just me, being weak."

"You're not weak, Twill. Sometimes I just close my eyes and it's there…enough blood and more for an entire lifetime of nightmares."

"Then a soak and some sun will be good for all of us." Twilly finally managed a big smile, and Nyla thought her Sister just might pull through this in fine shape.

It was still early, and the sun was low and not too warm when they reached the large pool, but the Sisters shed their boots, hiked up their skirts or rolled up their trousers or tights, and slipped their feet into the healing pool. Not long after, they were joined by an elderly sprite leading a blind dwarf. Nyla had seen the couple around the grove over the seasons, but not in a long time.

"Good morning, James. Hello Maxwell." Nyla finger-waved.

The two squinted in the direction of her voice, but only James saw her. "Is that the Rainsong lass?"

"It is. *Both* of us, actually. How are you gentlemen this fine morning? I haven't seen you about the grove much lately."

Maxwell hacked, and coughed to one side, away from the pristine water. "We don't get out much. Besides, we hear-tell you don't spend nearly as much time in the grove as you used to. Been wandering about, getting yourself into all sorts of mischief. That Torinstag business sounds quite nasty...like something I saw once or twice during the Troll War."

"It was *horrific*." Nyla would rather talk about something else, though. "How is your honey crop this season?"

James waved off her question. "We've handed that over to the younger members of the family. What's truly important is the company you had at Rainsong Oak this sunrise, and why they left in such huffs. *Two* royal bumble-coaches?"

Oh, burr. The whole grove knew, or they would soon. There was no way she wanted to put out a story that didn't match her parents' version. "Ah yes, much excitement. But you must speak to our mother to get the story. I would hate to trump her telling and steal the fun." Nyla now realized that coming to the communal hot pool might not have been the wisest idea. It wouldn't be long before the entire busybody population of the grove made their way there to gossip. She reluctantly pulled her feet out of the soothing heat and dried them on the moss. Her Sisters seemed to understand and followed her example. "I'm sorry, gentlemen, but as lovely as it is to see you again, a lass must attend her chores. You have a pleasant day." She finished lacing up her boots and stood.

"Yes, chores are important." Maxwell smiled a big broken-toothed smile. "You lasses have yourself a wondrously fun day. If we don't see you before, we will see you at your bondings."

"Of course, at our bondings." Burr. In all of the silliness surrounding Orrin, she'd forgotten about her bonding. She'd best start giving some thought to finding a tree-mate. She waved and flew off, trying to be as casual about her escape as possible. She could hear her Sisters say their good-byes and follow along. She waited until they were out of sight of the pool before racing up to the top of the leafy canopy roofing the Forest. She pushed herself hard, flying as fast as she could, needing to burn away frustration and anger and disappointment. Why did Orrin have to be such a burring *ogre*? She probably could have found common ground with the rebellious noble and, really, falling in love with that laugh, those eyes, and his magnificent wings, wouldn't have been all that difficult. But the stump just *had* to go and spell her, take her heart by force.

Her butterfly wings weren't designed for speed, so by the time she fluttered up into the sunlight, she was furious. "Useless wings! Why couldn't I have sparrow wings, or maybe a Nighthawk's?! So slow! *Too* slow! Flutterby silliness!" She found a solid branch and sat, then tucked her accursed wings in and turned her face to the sun, closing her eyes and absorbing the comforting warmth.

Fiona alighted beside her. "It's just the way it is, Ny. Truly, there's very little in our lives requiring speed, at least in the air. I'd never trade my maneuverability for power."

"I could live with hummingbird wings — speed *and* maneuverability." Rainn hovered in the sunlight.

Kara shook her head. "Too noisy. That burring hum would make me crazy. How about you, Brigid?"

Scrunching up her face as she thought about it, Brigid did a slow turn in mid air. "I agree about the hum. It's the same with a bee set, like Cray's."

Twilly sighed. "That's one reason I love Cray — the comforting hum when he's flying nearby."

"Did you just say you *love* my brother?" Nyla's smiled, wide and mischievous.

"No, I *didn't*. I said it's one thing I love *about* him. Like I love your laugh, or I love Fiona's braids."

Lifting up off the branch, Nyla hovered in front of Twilly, first looking into her eyes for some sign of illness, and then feeling her forehead with the back of her hand. "Wrong. You said — and I quote — 'That's one reason I love Cray'."

"I *never*!" She blushed.

"You *did*. But it's all fine, Twill. He can be a stump sometimes —"

"*Sometimes?*" Kara chimed in. "He ratted us out to Mother!"

"He thought he was doing what was right. That's something I've learned about Cray lately — he's not always on your side, but he *is* as honourable and honest as they come."

"I suppose. But he's still a stump."

"But he's the stump who's in love with our Sister, who loves him in return."

Twilly huffed. "I did *not* say that."

"So you're saying you *don't* love my brother? *Our* brother?"

"No, I'm not. I'm saying..." Twilly looked confused.

Nyla realized she maybe pushed Twilly too hard, too soon. She hugged her. "Don't worry. Sometimes it takes the brain a little while to admit what the heart has known all along. *Whatever* you feel for Cray is perfectly fine. Just so you know, he loves you like mad and would travel the length of Faerie for you."

"How do you know that?"

"Because he's my twin, and it's what *I* would do for true love."

"It's what we *all* would do," Fiona added. Brigid, Kara, and Rainn all nodded and smiled in agreement. "And besides," Fiona continued. "You could do worse than Cray. You could be in love with a debonair, bad lad lord."

Nyla bristled. "It's far from love."

"Truly? You can honestly tell us if he hadn't spelled you that you would have found him completely, reprehensibly, unattractive?"

"Honestly?"

"*Honestly.*"

If they wanted the truth, she would give it to them. "In *that* case, given a bit more time than a few turns and a handful of blinks, I might have been tempted to see if those two ginormous wings could have supported the weight of two while I cast *my* spell on *him*."

"Nyla!" Fiona was shocked, exactly as Nyla intended. The others either blushed or giggled.

"Well, you asked." She flew off a short distance, adoring the heat of the sun on her body. She stayed close to the treetops, though, not wanting to temp a passing hawk into snatching up an easy snack. It was a rare occurrence, but it happened often enough that all faeries were trained to be alert for aerial attack. Nearer to the mountains the harpies were more of a concern, but she'd never even seen one in the flesh, so she worried about hawks.

She didn't race ahead, nor did she intentionally fly away from her dear Sisters, so when Kara and Brigid caught up to her she took a hand of each, while Fiona, Rainn, and Twilly joined on the ends. They flew along, greeting butterflies, bluebirds, and the plethora of other life at the top of the Forest. Nyla knew she would have to get back to Oak soon, to attend to her chores, but for now she just needed to fly in the sun.

When she and Kara did finally get back to Oak, there was no sign of either her parents or Cray, so the Rainsong lasses set about doing the remainder of their chores without either haranguing or guilting. All of the cleaning had been done prior to Orrin's disastrous visit, but there were always little projects waiting for spare time. Kara started with rearranging her bedroom, and Nyla took on the arduous task of rubbing honey-oil into Oak's exposed surfaces in her own room. She dug in and put her best effort into the job, somewhat ashamed it usually required arm-twisting and shouting for her mother to get her to do anything around their home. She didn't *hate* Mother or Oak; she just found chores to be boring and a waste of time. For some reason, today, she saw it all in a different light. They had a wonderful home. It wasn't Ten-Oaks or a stone castle, but it was the tree her mother had bonded with and it was wonderfully cozy and warm.

She finally fell asleep facedown on her bed at dusk, exhausted, with still no sign of anyone but Kara.

Chapter Twelve

Angry shouting from beyond her portal woke Nyla long before she had the strength to face the world. She stretched, yawned, and shook off her sleep as best she could. She knuckle-rubbed Lacey's abdomen while she tried to decide what to wear, but her father's raised voice shoved the fashion dilemma aside.

"They have been here all night! They were out for a short time yesterday, but were nowhere near the rowans. It's not possible!"

"With respect, sir, *you* were not here, so you don't know where your daughters were." She had no idea who the voice belonged to.

"I know she was at the hot pool, for I spoke to those who saw her. Later, she was *here* doing chores. You should see the shine on her bedroom floor."

"That doesn't account for all of her time, sir. We have proof. I have my orders from Her Grace, and you know neither you nor I are about to go against Our Liege. If your daughters are innocent, then that will out and they will be returned safely home with speed."

"I'm coming with her."

Nyla's mother piped up. "As am I. My daughters will not be leaving this meadow without me, if for no other reason than to keep them from further mischief." The rock in her mother's voice did not bode well for the man she directed it at.

"You may accompany us in your own carriage. In fact, that may be best. With luck, this is a misunderstanding and you will be able to return home with your daughters by midday."

Fumbling with her bootlaces, Nyla hurried. It *had* to be a misunderstanding. She whispered to the knots to secure them, then stood, brushed the travel dust from her clothes, and exited her bedroom. The main chamber went silent. Nyla looked nervously at the soldier. Kara rushed out of the shadows and into Nyla's arms, weeping dramatically, looking less like her mature self and more like the immature faery everyone expected her to be. Nyla hugged her back.

"Nyla Rainsong?" The soldier fluttered away from the elder Rainsongs and faced Nyla, his hand on the hilt of his sword. He was tall—taller than either her father or Cray, though he wasn't nearly as wide as Cray in the shoulders. The three-layers of miniature maple clusters over his heart indicated officer rank of some sort.

Nyla stood straight, and Kara stepped away, shuffling back to her parents. Nyla knew she had done nothing wrong. Lady Orlaith must finally want details about Torinstag's murder, she assumed. She was glad to do everything she could to help. "Yes, sir. I am Nyla Rainsong. How may I assist you?" She managed a weak, hopefully helpful smile.

The officer did not return the smile, although his eyes looked sad. "I am Captain Tadhg of the Ten-Oaks Guard. Nyla Rainsong—" he looked over his shoulder to Kara, "—and Kara Rainsong—of the Clan Rainsong, you are under arrest for the violation of The Oath, by order of the Elder Alder. You are to be immediately transported to Ten-Oaks Castle to answer for your crimes." He held a thin leather strap out, stretched between his two large hands. "Please extend your arms and place your hands together."

Nyla hesitated, shot a glance at her father who nodded once.

"Please do not resist, lass. This must be done. This *will* be done."

She looked at the strap, and did as asked, in silence. Captain Tadhg placed the leather across her wrists, whispered a word of power that sounded awfully familiar to Nyla, and the leather whipped quickly around her arms, binding her quite securely. The captain turned to Kara and extended a second binding strip. Kara reluctantly shuffled forward and put her arms out. Quickly bound, a small gasp of pain escaping her shut mouth as the leather tightened. Nyla led the way to Oak's main portal and the unusually silent Cray swung it open. He stood tall and brave, but tears coursed down his cheeks.

As the warm breeze caressed Nyla's wings, she briefly considered taking off and flying away. He had bound her hands, but not her wings. Then her eyes adjusted to the now bright morning light, and she spotted a half-dozen archers hovering nearby. She wouldn't even get out of Oak's shadow before they skewered her. She hopped off the sill and landed lightly on her feet. A moment later, Kara stood beside her, and the ring of archers followed. There was a blur to her left and by the time she identified it as Captain Tadhg, he stood beside the rather ugly, heavy carriage being pulled by a massive, well-disciplined wolverine. Tadhg held the door open, like a groom, and the Rainsong sisters walked slowly over to where he waited.

Above and behind her, Nyla heard her mother speak quickly to Cray. "Harness our carriage. Be ready to leave by the time I return from your aunt's." As Nyla ducked her head into the prison carriage, she didn't hear Cray's reply, but she didn't doubt he would do as told. The door clanged shut behind Kara. Captain Tadhg didn't follow them in, so the two of them were alone. A quick tug on her restraints confirmed she couldn't get out of them easily, even if she had an escape plan. But she didn't know what exactly she would be escaping from.

She leaned in close and whispered. "Kara, what the *burr* is happening?"

Kara sniffed back the last of her tears and wiped her runny nose on the back of her hand. "I was across the meadow when they arrived. All I know is that it has something to do with a fire."

"A fire? They think *we* set a fire?"

"I don't know. When I awoke this morning, the smell of smoke was thick in the woods. *Something* has happened and we are in serious burring trouble."

"Why didn't Father stop them?"

"He doesn't dare oppose Lady Orlaith, but he *did* step between a soldier and me when I first arrived. I was afraid he and Cray were going to take them all on."

"And they accuse *us* of being silly. We both know we're innocent, so this is just a misunderstanding. As the Captain said, we'll be back at Oak by nightfall."

"How can you be so calm? We've been *arrested*!"

"Because we've done nothing wrong. Maybe we don't wear bright colours like other faeries, and we often prefer to walk rather than fly, but I never even got a chance to refuse Orrin's proposal. Lady Orlaith caught *him* casting the spell."

"I suppose."

They rode on for a while in silence, accompanied only by the scrape and jingle of the wolverine's harness. Nyla considered trying releasing her bonds with her own word of power but a tap at the bars of the prison wagon stalled her. She leaned around Kara to investigate. A green iridescent hummingbird head popped up.

"Hubert! What's the word?"

Hubert hovered easily outside the wagon as it bounced along the pathway. "Word frommm Crayyy. All siiiiix Sisterhood arrested."

"*What?* Why?"

"Rowannn Grrrrove burnnned to the grounnnd. Soooo mmmany deaths."

"Rowan Grove? *All* of it?"

"Almmmost all. Guards say Sisterhood did this. You broke The Oath."

Nyla stamped her foot. "We did *not!*"

"Mmmother and Father following with Cray. All five fammmilies following. You are not alone."

Kara sobbed and Nyla brushed away a tear of her own. "Tell Father we are well. We are innocent."

"I willll. He knowwwws." Hubert darted away, a blur.

"Orrin." It had to be him. Nyla was certain.

"What about him?"

"He has to be behind this. He just wanted a bride and now he's making us pay for his failure."

"You believe this is all because Orrin wants to wed you?"

"Well, it's not because we started a fire, because we *didn't*."

Lady Orlaith stood lodge-pole-pine-straight on her lush crimson-cushioned seat upon her high dais. Standing before their liege, in a row with her Sisters, Nyla could clearly see the fury behind her liege's sparkling gold eyes, and the dark miniature thunderhead forming behind the dais was for more than effect. She expected lightning to flash out and strike her dead at any moment. She was now, officially, terrified. Her skin goose-bumped, her wings hung low, dejected, and her knees threatened to give out on her. She looked forward to her opportunity to prove their innocence, but was simultaneously mortified she would become tongue-tied and vomitous when her moment came.

"The Oath has been broken! Death has been brought to the Great Woods by faeries, and not just by any faeries, but by *my* faeries. Both the Elder Alder and I are quite satisfied with the proof of guilt. The sentence is as follows—"

"*What?!* NO!" Nyla took a step forward to protest. Orlaith waved her hand and Nyla's braid wrapped around her head and over her mouth, to muzzle her.

"*As I was saying…* the Elder Alder has cast sentence for your crime against the Forest, for your flagrant shattering of The Oath. As for your insults against this Duchy and Ourselves, and your involvement in the death of Torinstag, I will also grant your irritating little Sisterhood your wish." She nodded, and twelve guards stepped up, two to a Sister. The lightly armoured faeries each took hold of a lass' elbow and guided their charges forward. At the base of the dais they turned the six young, unbound faeries to face the gathering.

Nyla now had a clear view of the hundreds who were gathered in the Hall. Every member of her own clan appeared to be in attendance, as were the clans of her Sisters. Beyond the clans were friends and neighbours, then beyond them, the others — sprites, brownies, pixies, gnomes, elves, hobgoblins, some dwarfs, and even a handful of fidgety leprechauns at the back, their bright green attire standing out amongst today's more muted tones of everyone else.

She sensed Lady Orlaith move behind them, but she dared not look. Whatever their punishment was to be, she knew any further act of rebellion would make it ten-fold worse. In the deathly silence of the Hall the sudden plucking of a single violin string filled the great space, followed by the whisper-soft flutter of their liege's wings. Nyla watched nearly everyone's eyes go wide with surprise and fear as the assembled witnesses saw something the Sisters could not. Some began to weep openly. Brigid's father took a step forward, but a rank of archers hovered down from the high ceiling of the Great Hall of Ten-Oaks, and the elder Wigglehop lowered his head and stepped back into his place. His tears cascaded.

Nyla felt a single, cool thread touch down on her wings, one at a time, a hand span from her back, confusing her. Maybe it wasn't a thread. It almost felt like a hair. Looking out at her own family, she raised her eyebrows to ask "What is happening?" Cray shrugged, having no answer. He leaned in to their mother and whispered something. Mother lifted her chin just a smidgen more, her own tears flowing freely, and whispered an answer to Cray. His eye's widened in horror.

"No! Twilly!" He launched himself up and out of the crowd, his large bumblebee wings powering him up and forward. To Nyla it looked like her twin brother attacked Lady Orlaith, which was ridiculous, because Cray would never be so reckless. He was the only one of the three who truly respected the nobles, but twenty bowstrings thrummed, and her big, honest, honourable, Twilly-loving brother tumbled to the floor, arrows bristling from his body, his wings pierced and broken. Stunned, Nyla stared. She didn't understand. It couldn't be real. She just *had* to be dreaming.

Scores of screams echoed through the Hall, but were drowned out in an instant by Lady Orlaith's bellowed "ENOUGH!"

A fraction of a blink later Nyla felt a tug on her wings, followed by fiery, blinding, excruciating pain. She fell forward onto her knees, her scream muffled by her hair. On either side of her, Kara, Fiona, Brigid, Twilly, and Morainn wailed in deafening agony. She turned weakly to Kara, also on her knees, and saw her sister's beautiful butterfly wings lying on the stone behind her. That was impossible. It didn't make sense. She looked further right, then left, and saw five pairs of beautiful faery wings dead and motionless on the stone. She tried flapping her own wings but felt only a naked, cool, breeze on her burning skin. There was no air resistance, no sense of lift, no *nothing*, but coolness and the pain. She was *dewinged*. They were *all* dewinged, and Cray was dead.

She tore free of her guards and crawled toward Cray. He lay bleeding and twitching, the last of his life fading away. She felt the guards' hands once again grip her shoulders, but Orlaith spoke firmly.

"Leave her."

The hands let her be and she reached her brother, cradling his head in her lap. Her hair fell free once again. She wept, and then she lifted her head skyward and screamed long and loud. When she finally ran out of breath, Kara and Twilly were there with her, sobbing side by side. The entire Sisterhood gathered around Cray, holding him, disregarding the blood soaking their garments, forgetting their own personal losses. Their wings were gone, but *Cray was dead*.

"That is *my* sentence, that you should forever walk, never to fly again. As for the Elder Alder's decision, the Clans of Rainsong, Wigglehop, Snowdance, Berrycheer, and Dewtickle are hereby and from this day forward, *Treeless*. All members of the Forests of Faerie are, by the Elder Alder's order, forbidden to shelter, protect, or house any member of these five clans, under penalty of death."

Gasps, cries, wails, and screams of shock, horror, and fear filled the Great Hall with a deafening roar. Kara threw up, Rainn wailed, and Twilly tipped over with a thud, her eyes rolling back in her head. Nyla wanted to die. She yanked an arrow from Cray's side and jabbed it at her own heart, but an unseen force gripped her arm and twisted it, making her drop the shaft.

As soft as a whisper, but clear as a bell even in the tumult, Lady Orlaith laughed. "You will not quit this so easily, Nyla

Rainsong. You will suffer for your crimes. You will live a long and painful life, I promise."

Nyla curled up and sobbed.

Chapter Thirteen

"**N**yla...*Nyla!*" She knew the voice, understood its urgency, but Nyla was lost, empty, and overwhelmed by darkness. "Nyla, I need you to snap to."

She opened her eyes, reluctantly. She was home, in her chamber. "Mother, let me die. This is *all* my fault."

Her mother hovered over her. "There are many things you are responsible for, but, strangely, this is not one of them."

"Cray is dead, my Sisters have lost their wings, *five entire clans are all treeless*, and it's *my* fault. I did this. If I'd just married Orrin. I—"

Her mother gently placed a finger on her lips to shush her. "Child, you are morose, rebellious, and disrespectful, but you... did... not... do... this." She placed her silver comb on the bed. "This was their proof. They returned it to us when they released you."

She sat up slowly. "My comb? I gave that to Orrin as a favour, to return to me when he proposed. That was their proof of our guilt?"

Mother nodded. "But what neither you nor Lord Orrin knew was that your father spun a fly-trap spell into the comb."

"You 'trapped' my evening? Didn't you trust me?" She felt violated, *again*!

"It is simply a trapping identical to the one in your broach."

"But I knew about the one in my broach!"

"Maybe so, but no one else did. If you want to get picky, *your* trapping violated the privacy of everyone you spoke with, just as ours did."

"But..."

"That's not the point, Nyla." A quick knock at the door interrupted them and Nyla's father stepped in. The redness of his eyes made it clear he'd been crying. Nyla opened her arms. He hugged her, careful of the stumps where her wings had once been.

"Have you told her?"

"I was about to. Nyla, the comb's fly-trap spell captured Orrin and his steward planning the entire thing, from the fire in the rowan grove to leaving the comb as damning proof."

That was wonderful news! "Then we must take it to Lady Orlaith immediately! The clans don't have to be treeless!"

"We will do no such thing. We have been shamed. Cast out. If we even approach Ten Oaks we will be executed on the spot. We have until dawn tomorrow to be free of the Grove. The Elder Alder's decision is final. Your dewinging is final. Cray's *death* is final. Get up, get changed, and help Kara pack up. We will be ready to leave as ordered, and we will leave with our heads held high, not bawling like some others are."

"*Mother...*"

Her father sat on the edge of the bed, just as Cray had, only the day before. "We have until sunrise tomorrow to take what we can and flee. The four clans are travelling together to the Creeping Moss Caves."

"Only four?"

"Clan Berrycheer blames us for everything. Twilly collapsed immediately after the pronouncement. Combined with the shock from finding Torinstag, her mind and heart have been badly lashed. They want nothing to do with us or the other three clans. We four will travel together, but in all honesty, we are faeries — without trees we will wither and die."

"I'll speak to the Elder Alder myself! Where is she?"

"The Source Grove."

"The *Source?*"

Her mother stepped in close, and lowered her voice, sounding far too much like Lady Orlaith. "You will *not*. We need every able body to move the elderly and the young. For once in your ungrateful, misspent life, do as you are told." Then she turned and left, silencing any further discussion. Her husband followed. This wasn't the first time Nyla's mother had been furious, but it was the first time she had seen her father speechless and lost.

Her heart gone, torn out, burned, and shot full of arrows, Twilly had nothing inside her except an empty, stunned void. At first her mother kept trying to make her eat and The General kept trying to pour nectar into her, but they had a household to pack up before dawn. They said very little to her or anyone else as they trudged around, doing the necessary tasks. Their anger bristled and radiated, but Twilly didn't give a whit. She was so empty she couldn't even cry. They all tried to comfort her and tell her that wings were overrated, and other stupid burring nonsense, but none of them said a word about Cray. None of them cared that she didn't give a burr about her stupid wings being taken. The pain in her soul was from having Cray dying in her and Nyla's arms. Her one, true love, taken. *Nothing else mattered.* Every able body in the clan rushed about, packing up the household, preparing for the humiliating trek, the leaving of their home as ordered by the Elder Alder... and Twilly couldn't care less. Without Cray, she had no heart, and without a heart, she would never again have a home.

The others were so busy that no one noticed when she climbed out the window of her room and down the vines, with only a few stars peeking through the clouds to light her way. Empty, she just walked. She set her feet on the closest path and let them carry her away and into the Forest.

Dawn remained a long way off when the bumblebee-coach set down in front of her, blocking the path. Twilly's father, The General, jumped out, sword in hand, warily watching the woods around them.

"Hold where you are, damned lass."

Twilly kept walking, going around him, not caring. He could have her shot for all she cared. She would rather die full of arrows like her Love than live without him.

"Tuilelaith Berrycheer, *halt*. That is an *order*, you useless little burr."

She walked on, uncaring about the menacing buzz from the giant bumblebees above her. She had just enough room to squeak past and continue down the path. She definitely wasn't going back to a family who didn't understand the Sisterhood or her love, or really, anything about her. She would just walk until she could no longer walk.

"Tuilelaith! Enough of this burring silliness, you stump. I'm your father and you will return with me to suffer with the clan you have shamed."

He swept her off her feet and carried back to the family carriage. Twilly didn't scream or struggle, but instead, as they flew beneath a hovering bee, she wondered if the bees would still be with them when dawn arrived and the Forest turned away from them? Would Clan Berrycheer leave this gross, ostentatious coach behind in the dust because the bees refused to carry it? What would the bees do at dawn? Would they return to their birth hive? The General dumped her rather rudely into the carriage and followed, folding his wings in and slamming the door behind him. "What about the bees, Father?"

"Worry more about yourself, stupid lass." He pounded on the roof of the carriage with his fist. A moment later the carriage lifted up and settled into a steady flight probably back to Berrycheer Hill before the banishment went into effect.

Rock-Eye started moving the moment sun fell behind the hills. The old troll hated the stench of this place. It smelled horribly fresh and clean. It lacked stink from Dead River and rot from his family carcass hole. Tired, hungry, and more than a little bit cranky, what he needed right at the blink was mutton. A good thick shank of sheep would just about give him the energy to keep hunting. "If only—"

A loud buzzing interrupted his grumbling. He hunkered as low in the shrubbery as he could manage and squinted down the wide trail. Something approached. Something not big, maybe the size of his head. The buzzing grew louder as it approached, flying waist-high above the ground. He cocked his head, trying to remember where he'd heard the sound before, then it came to him like a rockslide—a bumblebee carriage.

In the fast-fading twilight he could make out four draft bees flying in unison, with a sparkly golden carriage hanging beneath their harnesses. A rich pixie or faery's lazy way home. *Maybe it was the baby-taking noble.* Without taking his eye off the prize, he plucked a rock from the pouch on his belt. As soon as the bees were close enough to count them, he flicked his wrist and the rock shot arrow-straight into the carriage's lead steeds. Before the ball-shaped conveyance hit the ground, Rock-Eye bolted out of the shrubbery and attacked. High-pitched screams ripped through the silence, pleasing the troll greatly. Two of the giant bumblebees were dead, one nearly so, and the last one was very much alive and struggling in its harnesses. Rock-Eye put an end to its struggles with the stamp of a thick-soled foot.

He felt a sting in his arm and swatted at it. He found no bee, nor even a stinger. A second pesky bite, on his neck this time, brought him around, squinting to find the source of the irritation. A faery—a coachman by his livery—hovered just out of reach with a bow. He notched a third tiny arrow, staying beyond Rock-Eye's killer grip. The faery laughed as a rock was lobbed slowly in his direction, watching it go past, nowhere near the mark. When his head turned reflexively to follow the first rock, a second, fast as a hummingbird and a hundred times deadlier, shattered his bow, broke his arms, crushed his chest, and snapped his neck. He made a nice thud when the rock crushed him against the elm behind him. It was Rock-Eye's turn to laugh. That felt almost as good as killing baby-stealing Lady Orlaith herself.

The high-pitched screams in the carriage continued, so Rock-Eye moved in to finish them off and maybe have a bite to eat. He picked the carriage up in both hands and twisted in opposite directions, tearing it in half. He heard a thump and a scream, but before he could find the morsel, a flurry of steel flashed before his eye. A very fast faery, with a very sharp pin-pricker of a sword attacked. Rock-Eye closed his good eye to keep from being blinded, and just smashed the two halves of the carriage together in front of his face. He was rewarded with a muffled cry of pain and a squishing sound, followed the delicious smell of faery blood. He opened his eyes and licked at the gore dripping from between the two carriage halves.

A high-pitched tiny scream snatched his attention from his treat. A pixie cowered under a Beech fern. She wept and trembled and he wondered if she would let out a little squeak when he stepped on her. But, though he didn't know much at all about pixies, he guessed this one was quite young. He reached his old, calloused hand down and scooped her up. She screamed, but he just didn't have the heart to crush her. Baby Winsome was a prisoner somewhere, probably as terrified as this little pixie. If he crushed this one, he would be no better than his enemies. He opened his fingers but rather than jumping down, she clung tight to his thick thumb. He lifted her level with his good eye.

"You afraid?" His voice rumbled in the deathly silence of the forest.

She nodded vigorously, but hugged his thumb tighter.

"I not crush you. Will let you go. Trust me?"

She hesitated, then shrugged. She was a quiet one, this one was. He wondered if maybe she was a whistling pixie, like the ones in Compton Down. He never could understand much of what they whistled. He lowered her to the ground.

"No!" She clung tighter to his thumb.

"Not let go?"

She shook her head vigorously.

"Stay with?"

She nodded. He was confused, but even though she was a pixie, she was a child who needed help. She unarmed, she wouldn't be much trouble, he guessed, so he lifted her up and placed her on his shoulder, where she nestled in and got a firm grip on his thinning, wiry hair.

"Hold on, Little One. Meal time." He felt her tighten her grip, so Rock-Eye raised his nose to the air and sniffed the currents, seeking a scent, *any* scent that meant food.

As much as Nyla yearned for it, she found no sleep in the whirlwind of activity leading up to the clan's last dawn in their meadow. By quick consensus, the clans wanted to be quit and clear of their trees before dawn, since no one quite knew what to expect. This was an event without precedent. As Nyla quickly learned, not a single member of the four clans could remember such a widespread execution, *ever*. Because that's exactly what this was, *an execution*. An adult faery without a tree somewhere in the realm was less than half a faery, and not long for the world. Some of the bolder faeries even had a second tree in the human realm, although it was said the forests in the world of the humans were much more subdued. Many believed it was most likely because humans had nothing like The Oath, binding them to protect their world.

Looking around her at the fluttering, flitting, and running faeries of Clan Rainsong, Nyla wept silently. At the core of the matter, it was all *her* fault, but some things cannot be undone, no matter the magic you wield. Her wing stumps both burned and itched.

"Nyla!" The shout snapped her out of her self-indulgent reverie. Rainn waved at her from the far side of the meadow as she brought Starfeather—the Dewtickle family Great Grey owl—in for a landing. Nyla jogged over and threw her arms around her Sister. Her hands bumped the fresh stumps where her wings had been only a day before, and her excitement vanished.

"I'm *so* sorry."

Rainn hugged her back, fiercely. "You did nothing wrong. *We* did nothing wrong." She pulled back and kissed the tip of Nyla's nose. "How long do you think we'll last, without trees?"

"*We* haven't bonded, yet, so we may last longer, but some of the older faeries, like my grandparents, may not have long."

Rainn shook her head. "This is ridiculous. It's as if they were looking for an excuse to banish us."

Fiona joined them. "The Elder just did what's always been done. It's Lady Orlaith I want to have a few sharp words with." She hugged them both, then gently turned Nyla around to examine her stumps. "Clean and smooth. The witch left us stumps just long enough that we can't easily dress over them and will always be reminded of what we once had." She took Nyla by the shoulder and turned her back around to face her, then she turned away to bare her own wing remnants to her Sister.

Nyla gently caressed the smooth ends of what had once been the most beautiful pair of black, red, dark brown, and white Red Admiral butterfly wings. "Oh dear." She kissed her fingertips and touched them to Fiona's flesh. "We can't go with them."

"Our own clans are turning on us?"

"Not yet. But once they starting dying, who knows. No, we have to go to the Elder Alder." She quietly told them about the comb and the second flytrap spell.

Fiona agreed wholeheartedly. "We *have* to go. But we can't tell anyone. I've already heard grumbling and there are members of all the clans who will sell their own mother to get back in the good graces of our liege. If Orlaith finds out we are trying to have the decision reversed, or Orrin finds out we have proof against him, then we will be hunted. We go alone and without aid."

"We may be unaided, but we won't be alone. We have each other, and once we convince the Elder to reverse her decision, I am going to march straight up to Orrin's castle and cut out his stone-cold heart."

Brigid arrived, with a will-o-wisp beside her to light her way. "I love your thinking, Ny. After that we can ride to Ten-Oaks and show *her Grace* that Cray's murder will be neither forgotten nor forgiven."

"Never forgotten." Nyla nodded.

"Never forgiven," Fiona and Rainn added in unison.

The sky began to lighten. Nyla looked around the meadow. "We can't be here at dawn. I want to remember Oak as my home. I'll get Kara and a few supplies. We'll meet you on the west edge of the clover field at sunrise."

"The sooner started, the sooner finished," Fiona wisely pointed out and they all separated, to gather what they could.

Chapter Fourteen

The melodic song of a meadowlark warned of the impending dawn just as Nyla and Kara slipped out of the shadows west of the field of clover. Fiona and Rainn were waiting, but there was no sign of Brigid. Nyla put her pack down on the path. "We have biscuits and nectar. We'll need to find more on the way. Roots, mushrooms, and the like, but we have to be careful of berries—we're not yet sure where the allegiance of shrubs lies. Tree fruit is out of the question." She patted her satchel. "Also, the charmed comb is in a woven silver bag, to shield it from prying magic. We can't open the bag until we reach the Elder Alder or it will act like a beacon for all manner of trouble."

"I'm scared," Rainn whispered.

"Good, because fear will keep you alert. We trust no one. Not faery, beast, nor tree."

Brigid arrived, running awkwardly, with what appeared to be a small carpet roll under her arm. "I've got weapons, but we can look at them later. Our clans are already looking for us. We need to run and we need to run *now*."

With a final look around the clover field, Nyla scooped up her satchel and took off running west. A quick glance over her shoulder showed that her Sisters were right on her heels, and not a dry eye in the group. She settled into a comfortable pace she knew they could all maintain.

She knew the exact blink when the sun crested the horizon and dawn officially struck, because a collective sigh escaped every single tree near them, and even the air seemed different. A low-hanging maple even had the audacity to take a swing at her as she ran beneath the thick branch, but few in the realm were as fast as a faery and she easily dodged the strike.

Behind her, Fiona laughed heartily. "I predict a long journey ahead, Sister-mine. Long indeed."

Nyla laughed and stopped. "We're far enough away, now. Let's divide up the weapons, quickly."

Brigid unrolled the bundle. "I have five slings and silver daggers, each with a belt. I also have my own sword and bow." She gave a sling, dagger, and belt to each of them, strapped on her sword, and slipped the bow and quiver of arrows over her shoulder. Kara quickly rolled the heavy cloth up and strapped it to her own pack. Without a word, Nyla led them off down the trail again. Now that Brigid's cargo was distributed, she increased their pace. They had a long way to go and a short time to get there, and once they arrived, they still had to do the impossible.

The first serious attack came out of the blue, and if the boggart that dropped from a gnarled elm onto Fiona's back had been fully grown or even armed, she wouldn't have a had a chance. But he was barely twice her height and missing all but two dull yellow teeth, so although he knocked her flat onto the trail and gummed her shoulder for a few gross blinks, he didn't do any serious damage before Brigid put two lightning-fast arrows into his back. The four of them quickly rolled the body off Fiona.

Brigid retrieved her arrows just in time, because Fiona jumped up, grabbed a thick stick, and began beating the hairy corpse to a pulp. "Burr! Burr! Burr! Nasty boggie! Nasty! Nasty! Nasty!" Then she spit on the mess and threw her bloody makeshift club as far away as she could. Breathing heavily from the exertion, she grabbed her pack, wiped the boggart drool off her long, beautiful white braid, and marched off down the trail.

Rainn looked at Nyla, at Brigid, and then at Fiona's retreating back, and laughed softly. "Well, who knew she had *that* in her?" She sheathed her own blade and followed Fiona.

"Let's hope we *all* have that in us." Brigid wiped the bloody arrows on a rag hanging from her quiver, then slipped them back into the leather tube. "I'm afraid the boggie is not going to be the last casualty. I think I need to show all of you a few self-defense tricks. When we stop next."

"That sounds like a brilliant idea. When we stop." Nyla smiled and jogged after Fiona, worried their Sister would get too far ahead of them.

"Describe five weapons within two paces of where you stand."

"Five? Um…your bow, Nyla's dagger, my dagger and sling…" Rainn scratched her head, looking and thinking.

Brigid held up one hand to stop her. "Let me rephrase that. You're alone and unarmed. *Now* list five weapons."

"My smile?"

"To a boggart, that spellbinding smile of yours would be taken as a challenge to see who could bite hardest. You would lose and he would eat you, maybe after he cooked you *alive*. Look around you and tell me what you see. Forget about weapons for the nonce."

Rainn turned slowly, and described what she saw within two paces. "Three twigs the length of my arm and one longer, thicker one. Two tiny stones, three pebbles, a boulder as tall as myself, the edge of the thistle patch, and lots of sandy soil beneath my boots."

"Perfect. Pick up two twigs and hold them both like daggers."

She did as she was instructed. Nyla sat quietly on her stump. She'd already guessed what Brigid was trying to achieve with the quietest, most peaceful of the five of them.

"Good. You are now armed for both offence and defence." Brigid picked up the third twig and a fallen leaf, holding one in each hand. "I'm going to try and poke you with this twig, at snail speed. At the same speed, I want you to try to push it away, to keep it from touching you." She pointed the twig at Rainn and slowly walked it forward, as if she were going to skewer her Sister. Rainn easily met the twig with the one in her left hand and pushed it off track so that it missed her.

Brigid beamed. "Brilliant!"

"That was stupid. Any dumb burr could do what I just did."

"True. At *that* speed. But that's just the beginning." She placed the end of her twig on Rainn's chest, between and above her breasts.

Rainn looked down and was about to ask a question when Brigid pushed her with the twig. She stepped back and tripped over the thicker twig still on the ground, landing on her butt. "Ouch! What the burr was that for?"

Brigid extended a hand and helped her to her feet. "Two things. Firstly, your stance. Never face an attacker straight on, with your feet side-by-side. One foot slightly forward, one foot slightly back, so your body is turned to the side, presenting a smaller target and giving you more stability." She demonstrated the stance. "And bend your knees just a little. Now, try to poke me with a twig."

Rainn did as she was told, but Brigid leaned left and the twig missed her. Rainn tried again, anticipating the lean, but Brigid leaned right. Another poke, another dodge. And another, and another. Rainn couldn't get the twig to touch Brigid, and her

Sister hadn't even moved her feet. Eventually Rainn stopped. "I understand."

"Good. This time I won't move out of the way, and I want you to push me over like I did to you."

The point of the twig touched Brigid's left arm and Rainn pushed. Brigid held her ground. Rainn nodded. "Better stability."

"Exactly." She held the leaf up in her left hand and raised the twig in the other. "Now, take that stance. I'll slow-poke you again and this time I want you to push the twig aside with your right one, and then bring it back to tap the leaf. Block across to the left, then backhand to the right, all at snail speed. Ready?"

"Hit me with your best shot."

They all laughed and Brigid made her slow move. Rainn deflected the stick easily, but was a bit off target backhanding the leaf. Nyla suspected it was actually the slower speed Rainn had difficulty with. She made a suggestion. "Good effort, Rainn. Brig, double your speed. I think our little juggler can handle it."

Brigid raised an eyebrow at Rainn and Rainn smiled big and wide. "Burr, yes, Brig! Bring it forth!"

The twig came it quickly and not only did Rainn deflect it easily and tap the leaf with a perfect backhand, but she flipped the twig end-over-end once on the way from the block to the tap. She stuck out her tongue and took a bow. The other three clapped enthusiastically. "Now, what's the second thing I did wrong? My stance was the first."

"It's not quite what *you* did wrong, but what *I* did right. I saw that bigger twig behind you and forced you onto it. I used it as part of my attack. I could just have easily forced you into the thistles or kicked sand up in your face." She demonstrated by flicking sand away from her Sisters with her boot. "In a fight, everything around you can either work *for* you or *against* you." She looked at them one at a time and they each nodded in turn. "So, who wants to find some twigs and have some sparring practice?"

Nyla and Fiona both raised their hands to volunteer. Nyla had one question, though. "Where did you learn all this, and why are we only just now discovering these skills?"

Rainn handed her second twig to Nyla, and Fiona poked around in the grass until she came up with one a bit easier to wield than the club she beat the boggart with. She also found four more leaves and distributed them.

Brigid gave her twig to Kara. "My grandfather taught me, and he strongly suggested I not let it be known I was learning the skills oft restricted to lads. Also, you haven't needed to know until now." She paired Fiona and Kara together, and had Nyla and Rainn face each other and take up the stance. "We'll only spend a few blinks doing this. I just want to make sure you understand the basics before we eat and get back on the move. Agreed?"

"Agreed." Fiona raised her twig.

"As you wish." Rainn brought her own twig and leaf up.

"Whatever you say, Mistress-at-Arms." Nyla smiled and lunged at Rainn, who deflected her blow easily.

Brigid smiled. "I want you to all try it once, slowly. Second time, faster, and then faster the third time. Speed up until one of you can't defend it, and then do repetitions at that speed until you can. No lunging..." She looked directly at Nyla. "...and no showing off, *Rainn.* A boggart doesn't care that you can twirl your blade, only that it leaves your hand for a split second, giving him a chance to strike you dead."

"Sourpuss."

"That's me. Hemlock Sourpuss. Now *start.*"

"Where are we off to *now*, Grandfather? I just got settled in with a nice morning mug." Dillweed nestled further into his fluffy chair, a steaming mug of hot cider cradled in his stubby gnome hands.

"We're off to Court." Torby tucked two pouches of chewable spearmint into his rucksack.

Dillweed jumped up, cider splashing all over. "Court?! We might as well charge into a dragon's den screaming 'Here's breakfast, eat me!'"

"Nonsense, lad. We're going to have to do more casting for our liege, so it's best if we're at Court. Otherwise he'll send someone here to fetch us and they'll discover the women folk have fled. Maybe we'll be at greater risk there, but we do it to protect those dearest to us. That's how life works. Am I understood?"

"Aye. I know what you're saying."

"Good lad. Now wipe up every drop of that spilled cider before it attracts ants, or worse, brownies. Then pack up and meet me at Twisted Maple. I'm going to warn the neighbours to keep their noggins low, and pretend nothing is out of sorts here. There are far too many spies in this duchy for my liking."

"I'll meet you in a handful of blinks. If we're to be at Court, then we'd best pack at least one good, clean jerkin each. Grandmother will never forgive us if we go to court in rags."

"Fair enough, but be quick about it."

"Aye. A handful, no more."

Old Torby went out the door, rucksack over his shoulder, and Dillweed set about cleaning the mess, then searching for the jerkins in question. There weren't too many hidey-holes in the Pondbottom household, so Dillweed turned up the garments in the few blinks he'd promised. He raided the larder for as much cranberry honey cheese, bread, and other essential stuffs as he could carry, then he set off for Twisted Maple at the center of their community's grove.

As he shuffled along, he scooped strawberry mint jelly with two fingers from one of the small pots he'd snatched up with the loaves. Licking his fingers of the cool sweetness, he thought if they were off to their doom, at least they should have full, happy bellies.

The third shot of butter-juice gave Trinnean's mind a wee bit of a fuzzy edge, but he sometimes found his best ideas within the flexible, fuzzy parts of his mind. He tightened the lock-nut in place, gave the whole connection a good shake to ensure its fastness, then he leaned in and started winding the hand crank on the high point between the wings. The spring tightened as he cranked.

At first the crank turned easily, tightening the pair of springs—one in each wing—but as the thin, coiled, and charmed clock springs reached their maximum tension, he needed both hands to turn the crank. When he judged the tension to be perfect, he stopped winding, flipped the crank around on its pin, and locked it into place. Done, he stepped back, smiled, and took a quick sip from his buttercup to celebrate. He swallowed, and reveled in the liquid heat as it coursed down his throat, spreading out through his chest and imbuing him with the confidence to do *anything*.

"Mmm... Your Majesty, ladies and gentlemen of the court, I, Trinn-the-Broken, Trinn-the-Twisted, Trinn-the-Ostracized, am about to amaze and confound you as never before." He spoke confidently to his patient audience—Flutter, a pale-yellow butterfly, three small green-and-black Elm Leaf beetles whose names he could never keep straight, and the house sparrow, Browncap, high above, spying the butterfly for tea. Trinn bowed and scraped as if he were at Lady Orlaith's court, or even King Oberon's itself. He straightened up too quickly, wobbled a bit, then bounded around the glade, addressing the bugs and birds and one or two of the more alert plants. "It is a marvelous day, and I, Trinnean-descended-from-Coll, Birch Faerie of the Third Order, now make this day absolutely, indisputably, more magnificent than any day before it! Or, at least, better than yesterday and one or two before that. This wingless faery will now do the impossible and…maybe…hopefully…*fly.*"

Silence answered his declaration, so he slumped to the grass. "Oh, blue bells! I have no idea if I'll soar or crash." Flutter flitted over to land next to him and kissed the back of his hand with her long tongue. Browncap chirped a loud insult at the butterfly and flew off. Trinn knuckle-rubbed the butterfly gently between her feathery antennae. "Thank you, Flutter." She licked Trinn's hand again. "What I need right at this very moment, though, is food. Breakfast would be nice. Or maybe a nice brunch, with a light cuppa tea. Since I have no idea what time it is, we'll simply have to see what we have at hand, when we get back to Elm."

Browncap dropped to the ground beside Trinn, coming up to his belt in height. "Going to test it, Trinn?"

"Test it?"

"Fly with us."

"After brunch."

Browncap hopped to the edge of the clearing, tossing a sharp insult back over his shoulder. "Scaredy moth."

"I am *not* a scaredy-moth!" Trinn knew he'd had too much butter-juice to be making important decisions, but *no one* called him a scaredy-moth. *Ever.*

"Prove it."

"Fine. I *will* test them. Right this moment!" Flutter suddenly appeared in front of the faery's face, flapping her wings, frantically.

"Get back, Flutter. This is a job for a faery, and I'm just the faery for the job!"

Chapter Fifteen

"It seems the further we get from Laughing Elf Lake and Lady Orlaith, the quieter it is. It's almost as though the edict hasn't been heard out here."

"Or the Forest doesn't recognize us," Fiona countered.

Nyla looked warily about them—left, right, and above. "I'm not so worried about *why* it's so quiet, but about when it will cease to be so. That boggart was a sign of things to come. Dark things. It's been far too easy."

"Nyla," Brigid stepped forward and whispered. "How about we pick up our pace and maybe trot for a few turns?"

Looking at the other three, Nyla received nods. "Fiona, you can still guide us if we make more haste?"

"The trail's well-marked, and I have a rough map. Let's do it. She turned and they were off, keeping a quick, quiet pace. They nibbled and sipped while they ran, making excellent time. Nyla thought she glimpsed a shadow crossing their trail every so often, but when she looked skyward she saw nothing extraordinary.

Fiona slowed and pulled up first. The trail split three ways so she closely examined all three. When she finally turned back to the other four, she didn't look happy. "We have a problem. I've travelled this trail with my family a half dozen times, but I think the forest is deliberately hiding the markings I would usually follow." She unfolded the map, compared it with their surroundings, shook her head and returned it to her satchel.

Brigid stepped up and looked closely at all three trailheads. "This really doesn't come as a surprise. I was actually expecting it to start sooner. Close your eyes, Fiona, and tell me what your heart says."

Fiona closed her eyes and concentrated. Nyla smiled at the furrowed brow, which marred the usually serene face. She waited patiently for her Sister to hear what she needed to. In the meantime, *she* listened to the Forest around them. A chill seemed to be creeping along after them. There was very little birdsong, almost no insect chatter, the trees and other plants were closed up tight to them, and they hadn't seen a single magical being since leaving the meadow. Not even so much as a dryad. Their home had become a very unwelcome place.

Fiona smiled and her brow smoothed out. "I remember now. I hear the river to the right! We go along there for a half a league or so, and then move away from the river. There's a bog in the middle we need to avoid."

Looking back over her shoulder, Nyla thought she saw something dark move in the Forest to one side of the trail. "Good. Happy to hear that, but we need to run...*now!*" She sprinted down the trail to the right. The other four hesitated, but a growl behind them spurred them into motion and they bolted after her. Once they caught up, Nyla slowed her pace somewhat, to one they could maintain over a distance.

"What did you see back there?"

Rainn looked back over her shoulder. "Nothing. I heard a growl, some thumping and branches snapping, but I didn't wait to see what it was. I don't think it followed us."

They ran on in silence, too scared to make much noise.

The tallest of the three naked brownies, Dand, dropped the large branch he'd been banging the elm with and smiled. "Stupid faeries. No outcasts welcome here. Scare you off but good!"

"Good growl, Rab!"

"Not *me*," the shorter brownie replied. "T'was Shug."

Shug shrugged. "Nay me. You sure nay you, Rab?"

"I growl good, but not so good as *that*." He and Shug looked to Dand. "Nay me, nor Shug. Sure nay you, Dand?"

"Stupid question. Why I say 'good growl to you if I know it be m'self?"

Rab scratched his bare butt, confused. His entire family said he was the smartest of the three, to which he usually replied "That says not much." They always laughed, but something was wrong now, and he felt dumb as a stump for not seeing it. Then the pungent scent of unwashed goblin wafted over them and he figured it out.

"Growl not *us*! Growl was goblin!" He was so relieved that he'd solved the puzzle before his brothers did that he was caught completely unawares when the goblin dropped into their midst and cut their throats, one...two...three.

Gilroy waited patiently while Lord Orrin finished licking the warm honey dripping from the strawberry slice. He knew that his liege was aware of his presence, but he also knew even he,

Orrin's chief steward, had to wait on His Grace's pleasure. He didn't have to wait long.

"Good news or ten lashes, Gilroy."

"News, Your Grace, though neither good nor bad at this point."

"So be it." He reached for another strawberry slice and dipped it in the honey bowl as Gilroy spoke.

"One of our hummingbird spies has sent word the Rainsong lass is not travelling with her clan. She, her younger sister, and three others have vanished."

"Vanished? They have no wings and no friends. How can they vanish?"

"'Vanished' is how the spy described it, but I suspect they have simply run off and no one saw where they went."

"Do we still have spies amongst my sister's stupid Sky Patrol?"

"Indeed we do, Your Grace."

"Then get word to them. I don't trust that little harpy. My stupid stump of a sister may be content to let the Forest eliminate Nyla and her burring Sisterhood, but I'm not. I want her found, and I want to know what she's doing. I have no doubt she'll be dead in days, but if she even *hints* at coming in this direction I will send a battalion to head her off and shatter that prophecy into shards. I had no idea what those stupid gnomes were on about at first, but now it's starting to make some sense." He crushed the strawberry piece into a ball, the honey and blood-red juice squirting between his fingers. "Spies. Use them. Use them *all*."

"Yes Your Grace. Immediately." Gilroy handed his liege a towel and departed the chamber to make good on his promise.

Trinn wiggled his deformed wing stumps to ensure the leather sockets of the mechanical wings were well seated, then he cinched the harness tight across his chest. He stood slowly, taking the weight of the wings off of the supporting workbench where he had propped them. They should have been so heavy as to overbalance him and drag him backwards to the ground, but the same charm from the pool that kept him from being poisoned by the nearness of the iron also reduced their weight considerably. They were still a bit heavy, but they weren't completely unwieldy. Slowly, carefully, he stepped away from the workbench to give himself room to stretch. Once clear, he turned around in a circle and stretched the clockwork wings out, then pulled them back in.

"Oh my…that feels…*wondrous!*" He turned his head from side to side and stared as he moved the wings in and out, in and out. "I HAVE WINGS!" He turned back to the workbench, snatched up his mug of butter-juice, and drank it all straight back. The elixir roared down his throat, pumped him full of bravado, and stole away all caution. Without another word, he charged at the open end of the clearing where the top of Gargoyle Bluff waited. He didn't look down or even acknowledge his worried friends as they fluttered above and behind him. Browncap shouted something in alarm, but Trinn, lost in the joy of the moment, couldn't hear him clearly. The edge of Gargoyle Bluff rushed up to him and then he took off, and *flew*.

Except he wasn't flying, he was falling. "Whaaaa….?" Then he remembered. The wings. He had to flap them. Born without wings, he'd never developed the reflex that made him pump them when he was off the ground, but he more than made up for that lack now. With his bone and flesh stumps firmly strapped into the mechanical appendages he pumped and pumped. His arms paralleled the flapping motion as if they could give him lift, but he dropped like a rock, straight down. The base of the bluff rushed up at him without mercy.

"Trinn! Stretch your wings and stop your fall! Lift your head, put your feet together, and feel the air catch. Tilt up your leading edges and aim out over the forest." Browncap swooped past him and spread his own wings out, demonstrating as he shouted, and when the air caught his wings he shot away and across the treetops. Trinn understood immediately and straightened out his new wings. Then he lifted his chin, straightened out his legs, and wished. Even with the butter-juice emboldening him, he scrunched his eyes shut as the ground rushed up. Then the air caught his wings and he abruptly changed direction, soaring out, instead of plummeting down.

"I'm flying! For the first time in my life, I'm *flying!* Woohoo!" He leaned to the right and banked around, passing out over the creek. But he started to lose altitude.

"Flap, Trinn, flap!" Browncap pulled up beside him. "*Flap!*"

The faery flapped. Then he remembered the mechanics of the wings. He reached out with his hands and pulled the pins on the underside of each wing, releasing the power of the wound springs. Then he flapped his wings and his arms and he even kicked his feet like he did when swimming down and through to the humans' realm. The gears turned, the pulleys pulled, and the mechanics of the wings gave him much more power than his mere stumps could ever manage alone. The wings bit into the air, and with every stroke, he gained a little more altitude, found a wee bit more control. With Browncap off his wingtip, he clumsily worked his way back around, and then up toward the top of the plateau.

"Do not try to go straight up, you're too heavy! Go around in a large spiral, work your way up. Try to catch rising air near the cliff face and it will carry you up... but be careful, because it can smash you into the rock."

He did as he was told, without question. If you can't trust a bird to teach you to fly, then what hope was there? He flew a wide spiral, and just as he neared the bluff, he felt the air push him from beneath. "I got it!" Then the air shoved him straight up the bluff's face, in a much tighter spiral.

From up high, Trinn could see Browncap hopping around the plateau, impatient for him to come back to earth. The faery inventor clumsily manoeuvred himself into position for a good landing on the same plateau. He ignored Browncap for the moment, trying to reconcile his distance with his rate of descent and his speed. He squeezed the lever to lock the wings in the glide position, tilted their leading edge up just a mite, then he braced for impact.

The ground rushed up faster than he expected, but when he tried to reverse-flap, he couldn't get the wings to budge. Just as his feet, knees, chest, and chin collided with the plateau at a jarring but not breaking speed, he remembered switching the wings into 'glide'.

"We won't be doing *that* again on landing. *Burr* that hurts." He raised himself up, struggling to stand while wearing the wide wings. "I hope I get better at this sooner rather than later."

Browncap chirped at him. "You need a spell."

"A what?" Trinn released the straps holding the wings in place.

"A spell. Make your wings even lighter. My wings, nice and light."

"A spell..." He should have thought of that himself, but he'd been so caught up in the mechanics that he forgot about the weight in the air.

"Like dandelion seeds, floating on the breeze."

"Or milkweed! The Fluff'n Up spell, the faery standard for

lifting heavy rocks when there's no dwarf handy." He scratched his head. "It has to be cast in moonlight, which is lighter than daylight, it needs one milkweed per casting, and some silver. It should also be a simple spell I can cast with one eye closed."

"Two eyes make a better spell, Trinnean."

"Of course they do, silly sparrow. It's just an expression."

"Ah. Like 'the sound of one wing flapping'."

"'The sound of one wing flapping?' That doesn't make sense."

"Flap, flap, thump. It means to only try half as hard and fail twice as bad."

"I suppose flying with only one wing would spell disaster. I'll get the ingredients together after lunch. I'm thirsty and need a dram of juice to help me think clearly."

"Goblins." Brigid called back over her shoulder as they trotted along.

"What about them?" Rainn caught up with her.

"They sometimes wander down out of the Mushmellow Caves, so we need to be vigilant."

"Are they worse than boggarts? I've never seen one."

"Bigger, meaner, faster, but not so smart. If you can't shoot them with a bow, then you run. If you're close enough to use a blade, you're already dead. They're wiry and strong, and once they get a grip on you, only death—yours or theirs—will break it."

"We have to sleep *sometime*, Brig, and since we don't dare sleep in the trees as usual, what will we do?"

"Nyla may have some thoughts, but I see our best chance here is a small cave with no roots to come after us and catch us unawares. So, solid rock, low roof, and too deep for grabbing goblin arms to pull us out."

"Oh, is *that* all?" Nyla pulled abreast of the two of them, having heard their conversation. She had come to much the same conclusion as Brigid had, but she had no inkling of where or how they would find such a specific cave. "How about we travel a few more turns and then take a break and discuss our choices while we sup?"

The others agreed, so they all drifted back into single file and continued on. The eerie silent rejection by the Forest around them comforted Nyla, but only because she was fully aware their clans were in much more danger than the five of them were.

"I want this troll that butchered Torinstag found, killed and his head sent back to his tribe on a bed of peonies." Orlaith stood by the casement, stroking the wood with the palm of her slender hand. She'd discovered not long after Ten-Oaks Castle was completed that physical contact with her majestic home calmed her like a balm. This particular casement bore smooth, polished evidence much solace had been sought here.

"Double the Elf Sky Patrols over the entire duchy. If anything is not as it should be, I want to be informed immediately. Double the number of airships and double the crews. I want twice the number of keen elf eyes on my duchy. I'll not have Trolls or even Orrin sneaking a ragtag army in under my nose."

"Of course, milady. Immediately." Her steward, Gaell, flew off. She knew he would follow her commands to the rune because he'd stood next to his predecessor when she'd executed him for failing her. Even as his own father's body crumbled to the stone with her favourite silver dagger in his heart, Gaell stepped forward to receive his orders. The transition from father to son was smooth, his devotion complete. Or maybe he obeyed out of fear, she thought. She truly didn't give a whit the reason, so long as he did it without hesitation.

She turned her thoughts back to her stump of a brother. She was certain he had something to do with the butchering of her stag. This whole thing reeked of one of his schemes. Orrin wanted her at war with the bordering trolls again so he could swoop in and pick up the pieces, but she would be ready. Closing her eyes, she stilled her hand on the golden oak and let the life heat enter her body and warm her to the core. Once she finally crushed Orrin like the maggot she knew him to be, she would tear down his cold stone castle and create another oaken wonder-place. She could never have too many castles to call her own.

The slow, almost imperceptible life rhythm of her ten gargantuan oaks slowed her own racing heartbeat and pushed away all the stray thoughts threatening to distract her.

Chapter Sixteen

T rinn spent the remainder of the day gathering everything he needed for the spell. Milkweed pods were not a problem, living as close as he did to the Marsh. It was the silver he had difficulty with. Not because it was difficult to find, but because he loathed using half of his meager hoard on one single project.

This wasn't just any project, though. This was *wings*. He could finally fly, and to perfect them would be worth a thousand times the silver needed for the simple spell. When the moon finally rose, he was ready.

The Sisters had no luck finding a place to sleep and were exhausted. They had long since slowed to a walk. Rainn stumbled over her own feet but Brigid caught her. "Sit. Rest." She guided Rainn to a log and helped her to sit. From there they could see down into the big gully they had just traversed in the moonlight.

Nyla sat right down in the trail, not bothering with a log or even a patch of grass. "I can't go any further."

"Me neither." Fiona sat behind her, leaning against her for support. "We're going to die of exhaustion."

Kara whimpered. "Or hunger. I still smart where that rowan slapped me when I tried to pick those berries."

Nyla saw something large move along the edge of a patch of moonlight on the far side of the gully, not far behind them. She held up a hand for quiet, a signal they'd come to know only too well during the course of the day. She motioned the others to her and whispered. "Whatever it is, it's here. If we can't run, we'll have to fight." She drew her silver dagger, and Fiona and Rainn did likewise.

Brigid, on the other hand, drew her flute from its protective tube. "I'd hoped to avoid this, but we've run out of choices. We journey to save not only our own lives, but those of five entire clans." She looked steadily at each of them. "Do *exactly* what I tell you. Don't hesitate, don't doubt me even for a blink, or we'll all die. I'll gladly explain everything once we're safe."

"But—" Rainn started to ask, but a hard look from Brigid stalled her.

Brigid stood tall, faced a large boulder at the edge of the trail, raised her flute to her lips, and played. A howl of rage answered from across the gully. She tightened her ambiture and blew more firmly, played more confidently. The howl repeated, much closer. Brigid slid the flute's mouthpiece out a smidgen, which dropped the tune down a half-tone, and then she bumped the tempo up.

Nyla's heart swelled as the wonderful, effervescent melody caressed the air around them. She sheathed her blade and listened. The boulder trembled, and then it rolled back as if nudged by a hill giant's hand. A dark hole opened beneath the stone. Brigid played faster, sparks danced in the air, the hole grew, and grunts and snarls came from just around the corner of the trail. "In! Quick! *Now!*"

Nyla pushed Rainn, Kara, and Fiona in, and then dove into the darkness after them as Brigid continued to play. They all tumbled into a sandy, sloped tunnel. Brigid jumped down behind them and abruptly changed the song to a single note. The boulder rolled back into place, cutting off the moonlight. The tunnel glowed of its own accord but Brigid nudged her from behind, urging her on.

"Up! Run! It's not far, but when I say stop, absolutely stop. Not another step further than that."

"Where are we going?" Rainn called back as she ran behind Fiona.

"The realm of humans, I hope."

Nyla stumbled in shock, but recovered quickly and kept up. She took back what she was thinking earlier about not being in danger.

"She's created a gate!" Cathaoir was astounded. Linked Brigid by their bloodline, he knew the instant his granddaughter manifested such powerful magic.

"*Who* did *what?*" George the troll had only been half listening. The two of them were pouring over a map of the duchy.

"My granddaughter."

"No supervision?" George squinted at Cathaoir. "Serious violation of protocol."

"Burr that! There *is* no protocol for an unbonded faery creating her own gate." He flew up to look his friend in the eyes. "There's barely any precedent. My clan has been banished, along with four others, Brigid has had her wings *amputated* out of spite, and she's gone off on her own, against orders, on a quest with four unbonded lasses to try and save hundreds of lives. Every rogue goblin, roving brownie pack, and angry wolverine sees them as a consequence-free meal. There's a troll wandering around this duchy being mistaken for a Mist-Eater, and the latest rumours coming in are telling of a dragon hunter coming down from the hills in search of a trophy kill. I don't care *how* she keeps safe. We'll clean up whatever mess we have to because none of us can make this quest for them." He took a breath and settled back down to the ground.

"Finished rant?" The troll raised a scarred eyebrow.

"Yes, thank you."

"Scared?"

"Terrified."

"Me, too. Dark times, friend."

"Too dark for lasses to be dealing with alone."

"Where she go?"

"I have no idea, and won't until I see her gate for myself."

"Then go."

Cathaoir nodded and left George with the map. Not only did he have no idea into which realm his granddaughter and her friends had gone, but he also suspected *she* didn't know either. Even if she did, though, his biggest concern was whether or not she could find her way back without him to guide her. "Oh, my little Brig, what have you done?"

It was night time on the other side of Brigid's gate, but Nyla knew by the smell they were definitely no longer in Faerie. She had no idea *what* she smelled, but it burned her eyes and nose so badly she had to cover her face with her arms. Fiona and Kara coughed wildly on either side of her, and she thought she heard Rainn retching somewhere behind her.

"Quiet!" Brigid hissed. "Stay here. I'll be back in a blink."

Nyla peeked out from behind her arms, but Brigid was already gone. The acrid air was too much for her eyes to handle so she retreated behind her arms again. Ten blinks later, she felt a tap on her arm and nearly shouted, but caught herself. Brigid stood before her, with a finger over her lips. She leaned in and whispered.

"Quietly. We're in what they call a city, in a park, with a glass-domed hall bigger than Ten-Oaks Palace. I've found us a friendly pair of hares who not only seem completely unaware of the troubles in Faerie, but they were quite pleased to see me. We must move quickly and quietly, though, because there are humans *everywhere*." She stepped out of the passage two steps and pointed to the left. "Hops-With-Grace and Listens-With-a-Twitch are two birches over. They're happy to carry us due west as fast as they can, clear of this city."

Nyla was impressed, but somewhat confused. "Why can't we stay the night and be rested before we move on?"

"Time passes differently between the realms. A night here might be a fortnight back home...or longer. If we tarry, we could be too late when we finally arrive home. We're taking a big chance by not simply going back through the passage. Once we cover some distance I'll take us back and hope the distance we travel will make up for the time we've lost." She led the way out of the shadows of the shrubbery and quickly trotted two birches over.

The others followed closely, finding Brigid already mounted up and tucked in tight behind the long ears of a beautiful, light brown hare when they arrived. "This is Grace, and her sister is Twitch." Fiona climbed up behind Brigid, while Nyla carefully mounted Twitch with Kara and Rainn, the two lightest members of their group. As soon as they were settled in tight, Brigid whispered in Grace's ear and they were off at breakneck speed. Once they bolted out of the shrubbery the park was so bright it astounded Nyla and made her still-stinging eyes water. When she could see, most of the light seemed to be beaming from the glass palace. Tall, slender posts with globes of flickering light stood alongside a hard-packed trail winding through the park.

The does stayed near to the edge of the manicured lawns, close to the shrubs and the shadows, but they were still too much in the light because a deep-chested baying across the lawn startled them all. With only a glance back, Grace nearly doubled her speed and zigzagged as best she could from shadow to shadow. Twitch stayed close behind and Nyla held on for her life. A quick glimpse revealed a pair of huge beasts in heated pursuit.

"Are those wolves?" She'd heard of wolves, but only in tales. There were no wolves in Faerie

"They're hounds—cousins to the wolf," her hare mount called back. "Only half as smart as the stupidest wolf, and they kill for sport, like their human masters. Hold tight." She put her head down and concentrated on eluding the hounds, zigging and zagging, in and out of shrubs and around any and every tree in their path.

Nyla heard frantic, angry shouts directed at them, followed by a piercing whistle, then the hounds abruptly gave up the chase. She peeked, and saw them trotting calmly away, back where they came from. The hares didn't slow even a smidgen, taking them from the brightness of the park into the shadows between the stone towers beyond the greenery. The burning, acrid stench was even worse outside of the park, so Nyla closed her eyes, tucked her head down tight to Twitch's thick, soft fur, and breathed as shallowly as she dared.

Even though he carried a magic lantern as he flew, Cathaoir smelled the ruin of the slaughtered brownies before he saw them. "This doesn't bode well. Faerie beings are slaughtering each other, likely over the chance to be the ones who kill the lasses." With his sword unsheathed and gripped tightly in his hand, he hovered just above the remains of the blood pool that was mostly absorbed by the scavenging life forms of the Forest. He squinted, his old eyes not as good as they once were in moonlight. "Goblin teeth marks, but only one set. He cuts with a blade and smashes with a blunt object. This goblin is faster than three brownies, and armed." He looked closer at odd footprints in the blood. One foot was missing a toe. Cathaoir flew off, following the smell of carnage clinging to the goblin, hoping beyond hope he arrived soon enough to keep young faery blood from being spilled by the goblin's blade.

Without even a warning growl, the new hound burst out of the darkness and slammed into Twitch's shoulder, knocking her and her three passengers into a rancid river of muck running alongside the pathway. Nyla rolled out the other side of the filth and came up on her feet with her blade in hand. Grace leaped straight over the stocky, short-legged, brown-on-brown beast's massive head and bounded a few yards further on, only to stop and turn around.

Twitch recovered quickly, positioning herself between the hound and Nyla. A quick glance showed Rainn wiping the sewage off her face and spitting it out of her mouth. Kara had landed beside her and was covered in muck, but she'd avoided getting it in her face. Nyla crouched down beside her Sisters, afraid to try remounting the hare and possibly impeding Twitch's movement. It was good the three faeries stayed low and out of the way, because the hound lunged, and with a short hop, Twitch met the burly beast's face with the claws of her powerful rear legs.

There was no doubt the hound could tear the hare in two if he got his killer jaws on her, but the claws surprised him and he stumbled back with a yelp. Twitch struck again, yelling at Grace as she did so. "Flee! Meet us at the old park! Go!"

Grace turned and bounded off into the dark of the night, while the hound reeled from the second blow. He shook off the attack and Twitch hunched down. "Mount up! We'll lead him away. My sister is too slow, but I can outpace this one with ease. Up! Quick!"

Nyla cradled her hands together and boosted Rainn up as fast as she could. Rainn somersaulted and landed astride the hare, but the hound charged again and she barely got her fists around Twitch's fur before the hare launched straight up and came down hard on the back of the hound's head. His chin slammed down on the cobblestones but Twitch wasted no time admiring the blow. She landed lightly beside Nyla and Kara, crouched just long enough for them to leap up and grab hold, and then they were away. Deep-chested barking followed them, and when Nyla dared to look back, the hound powered after them as fast as his short legs could carry his barrel-shaped body. Twitch must have seen him, too, because she suddenly veered between two small stone castles and down a lane.

"What about the others?" Nyla called.

"We will meet them after we lead the hound astray," said Twitch, as she slowed enough to make certain the heavy beast didn't lose sight of them. He'd stopped to catch his breath, panting heavily and looking ready to collapse, but once he caught sight of the three of them again, he seemed to summon a reservoir of energy and the chase resumed.

"He is what the humans call a Bull Dog. He is all strength and no speed. Even when he sprints his short little legs tire quickly. He can't really jump or leap so we should be in no danger as long as we keep him in sight and at a bit of distance."

"We can't let the others get too far ahead, Twitch. Time is of the essence."

"This is time well-spent, little one. By keeping the bull here, we give my sister and your friends time to get away." She slowed and let the lumbering hound close some of the distance. Clearly exhausted, the bulldog stumbled on the cobblestones as he approached.

Suddenly Rainn went limp and slid sideways. She would have fallen right off Twitch had Kara not thrown her arms around her. "Mo-*Rainn!*"

"Feel sick. Must sleep. Or vomit. Or both." She leaned back into Kara, who leaned back into Nyla.

"But…" Then Nyla suddenly felt the same way. A bone-deep chill swept over her and bile rose in her throat. Her vision blurred heavily and a mental fog rolled in to her mind. "I don't know…"

The hare must have noticed the shift of weight on her back and turned her head. "What on earth?"

Nyla looked around them, thinking someone must be casting a spell to harm them, but all she could see were bricks and a rickety iron staircase. "*Iron?*"

"Of course. Even the wood is held up with iron. The silly humans love building with it instead of living in nice warm burrows."

"Iron is poison to faeries. We…must be away from here." Her vision was blurred, but she clearly heard the approaching growl.

Twitch tensed beneath the Sisters. "Hold tight!"

Nyla pressed Kara and Rainn hard against Twitch with her own body, and gripped the fur with every ounce of strength she had left, which wasn't much. The hare faked left, then right, then once again leaped up and over the exhausted hound. Nyla's grip slipped a wee bit on the landing, but Twitch's gait leveled off as she picked up speed, so Nyla remained mounted.

From the burning air to the toxic iron, she wondered how anything could possibly live in such a poisonous world. Her head swam and her thoughts kept returning to the idea that if they died here, whether in the jaws of a hound or from the unnaturalness of the environs, their families were truly doomed. "We must find… the others… and return… home."

"On our way, lass! We'll be clear of the worst of the iron soon enough."

"Is that even possible? To be clear of it? I can taste it in the *air.*"

"Aye, we'll soon be upwind of it. Not much farther."

Nyla hadn't the strength to reply, but she was immensely grateful. She closed her eyes and concentrated on keeping the three of them secure. Now, more than ever, she missed her wings.

Chapter Seventeen

Rock-Eye left his rescued pixie sleeping in the cramped cave and went out to find a creek and a cool drink. As he slurped from the shallow pool in the bend of the waterway, anger rose in his belly. This time it was anger with himself. Wandering around with no real idea where he should be searching for Winsome, he felt like a lost cub, not a seasoned warrior. "I be a stump! A burring stump. Faery not allowed command troll. Faery not allowed *steal* troll family. Faery pay!"

"Whooo will pay?" An owl settled on a branch just out of Rock-Eye's considerable reach.

The old troll stared at the Great Horned hunter. "Faery noble pay."

"Ah. *That* whooo. *That* whooo is evil. That whooo hunts *owls*, killing not for food but for fun."

"Evil. Lord say Lady steal troll babies. Rock-Eye now go rescue babies and crush faery Lady."

"Moonclaw will help you."

"Who is Moonclaw?"

"*This* whooo is Moonclaw. You whooo are Rock-Eye?"

"Troll is." Rock-Eye knew he forgot something. He scratched his nearly bald head. Something was missing but he couldn't remember. "Uh...*pixie!*"

"Kill pixie, too?"

"Not kill. *Save* pixie. Bring little miss pixie with." He turned and started back to the cave. Moonclaw glided along, above and to one side.

"Bring a pixie whooo to battle? Is that wise?"

"Pixie miss alone. She safe with Rock-Eye."

"Then she is safest with Rock-Eye *and* Moonclaw. We three whooos will rescue the troll babies and crush the faery Lady-whooo to stop her hunting of us hunters. Where is your troll baby whooo?"

"Um..." Rock-Eye hadn't thought about where his great-granddaughter might be. He assumed she was being kept at the faery Lady's castle, but he didn't know for sure. He plopped down on the trail, causing the ground to shake with his considerable weight. "Rock-Eye not know where she be. Useless troll."

"Not uuuseless, just confuuused. Two whooos will get pixie miss and three whooos start east to Ten-Oaks Castle. We whooos will rescue first, then exterminate the evil whooo."

Rock-Eye levered himself to his feet, his old bones crunching a cracking as he straightened up. "Rescue first, then kill. Good plan."

Old Cathaoir eventually found the boulder beneath which his granddaughter and her friends had escaped, but the goblin was nowhere to be found. He placed his hand on the boulder and concentrated. Each realm gave off its own vibrations, like musical notes, even after the gates were closed. It took but a moment for him to know for certain the lasses had gone to the human realm. He'd been there so many times himself there was no mistaking the signature vibration. He pulled his hand away and wiped it on his vest, although he knew only time would diminish the feeling of wrongness in his palm.

He turned his attention to the boulder itself. There were scratches on it where something had tried desperately to move it, and goblin footprints littered the area, but the footprints eventually continued off down the path. The hunter most likely assumed his prey would reappear somewhere in the direction they were already going, which was pretty smart thinking for a goblin, Cathaoir realized.

There was little he could do now but follow the goblin and keep a close eye on it, just in case it did indeed find the lasses.

Without so much as a whimper, Fiona slid off the back of galloping Grace, taking Brigid with her to the grass. Brigid retained just enough awareness to tuck and roll when she hit the ground, but Fiona bounced like a rag doll, grunting when her tumble ended. Grace skidded to a halt and came back to the two. Brigid pushed herself up into a sit.

"Something is wrong. *I* feel wrong. Sick. Poisoned."

"With what. Lass? Y've not eaten nor drank of our world."

"I feel this in my bones, like iron."

"Iron? Oh, aye. Lots of that here. Glasgow's right full of iron. We just crossed an iron bridge, in fact."

Brigid retched in the grass. "We need to be away from it." She looked around, her sight too fuzzy to see much.

"Away? The middle of this little park, then." She used her teeth to pick up Fiona by her collar and bounded off. Brigid tipped over sideways, away from her retchings. After what seemed like an age, she felt herself picked up and carried with unceremonious, bouncing, urgency. A few blinks later, she was placed gently on the grass beside her Sister.

It wasn't long before she didn't want to throw up, and she soon began to see clearer. She risked a deep breath, and interlaced with the realm's toxins were oak, elm, roses, and clover.

Fiona stirred. "What...?"

"Iron," Brigid explained. "The humans surround themselves with it. This place is better, but we must keep moving." She turned to the hare doe, who crouched low, with her ears flat against her back, alert. "Grace, this place of safety where we are to meet Twitch and our Sisters—is it far?"

"It's a goodly hop, lass, 'specially if we're skirting iron as best we can."

"Then we'd best start out." She helped Fiona to her feet. "Have you still got the map for our Faerie route?"

Fiona patted her vest. "Tucked away, nice and safe, but it won't do us a bit of good here."

"No, but it might help some when I have to take us back." She accepted Grace's offered paw and hopped up, then she reached down and gave Fiona a hand up. They tucked in tight to the hare's front shoulders, having quickly discovered the ride was much smoother away from the powerful hind legs. Brigid leaned forward and kissed the top of Grace's head, between her ears. "All set, Madame Hare."

Hops-With-Grace giggled and they were off and hopping.

Twilly firmly believed chocolate soufflé with butter-juice drizzle was far superior to traditional sixteen-layer elven velvet cake, and she was ready to announce this wondrous discovery to the entire court when someone snapped their fingers like a twig and interrupted her train of thought. She took a deep breath, raised her hand in a way she hope looked imperious and authoritative and... something grabbed her foot.

"Time to go, lass." She recognized the deep voice that interrupted her declaration of dessert superiority, but she was completely unfamiliar with the higher-pitched one that replied.

"This whooo is no pixie. This whooo is a faery."

"Faeries have wings. No wings, means pixie. See—no wings." Twilly was suddenly picked up off her throne and dragged into full wakefulness in their cave. *Their* cave. Her and the troll's. Their *cave*. She sat up and looked directly into a pair of sharp golden eyes leaning over her.

"Those are *wing* stumps, good Sir Troll. This whooo is one the six whooo are punished and banished. We must leave this whooo here or Elder Alder will be in a fury and banish two more whooo.

"No. We *not* leave her."

"No. Please don't." Twilly finally found her voice. "We did none of what they said. We're innocent."

"The Elder Alder is the only whooo whooo decides guilt or innocence. You are dangerous to be near." The Great Horned owl turned his head around to look behind him at the troll. "We must leave this whooo."

Twilly scrambled to cover her back. "No. Please. I will hide my wi—my *stumps*. I will be a pixie."

"Too small for a pixie."

"Then I'll be a *small* pixie. A half-pixie. Please don't leave me."

"Why was this whooo alone in the Forest, Sir Troll?"

The troll hung his head. Twilly knew he had saved her from a slow death of ridicule and pain with her clan. The least she could do was fib a little for him. "I wasn't alone. I was a captive, and Sir Troll, um, saved me and freed me. I owe him my life." She stood up on her rock and curtsied as gracefully as she could. Without her wings, her balance was a bit off, but her rescuer didn't seem to notice. "I, Twilly Berrycheer of the Faerie Clan Berrycheer, thank you, deeply and sincerely from the bottom of my banished heart, Sir—". She realized she didn't even know his name.

"Rock-Eye. Am called Rock-Eye. Was once upon a time Hubert, but have been Rock-Eye for two ages and a bit.

Twilly nodded. "I thank you deeply and sincerely from the bottom of my heart, Sir Hubert-Who-is-Now-Rock-Eye." She finished her curtsy and Rock-Eye returned an awkward bow. Twilly then looked up at the huge owl. "And yooo, Sir Owl. Whooo might yooo be?"

The night hunter blinked slowly, probably trying to decide if this little outcast was worthy of knowing his name. After a moment it was apparent she was. "This whooo is Moonclaw of Larch Valley."

"Larch Valley? Yooo are a long way from home."

"It is no longer a home for this whooo. Whooo's mate was hunted and our home and nestlings destroyed."

Twilly gasped. "Whooo did this?!"

"Twas the royal whoos. Orlaith."

Rock-Eye growled so ferociously Twilly jumped behind the rock for safety.

"Lady Burring Orlaith." He stormed out with no further explanation.

"Where the burr is he going?"

"That whooo is going to rescue whooo's great-granddaughter from not-so-noble Lady Whooo. This whooo is assisting, and avenging whooo's family. Stay or come, pixie-whooo-is-not?"

"Come!" She needed to give Orlaith a piece of her mind, and having a troll with her would make the journey safer. She jogged after Rock-Eye, but Moonclaw dropped down in front of her and crouched low.

"Ride. Much faster. But remember. Whooo is a pixie."

"Burring right, I am. I'm a pixie on the warpath!" She held on tight and Moonclaw hopped out of the cave and took to the night air. She was flying again! Oh, mercy, she missed her wings almost as much as she missed her Love, Cray. The night wind on her face was warm and sweet and blew away her tears as they chased after their lumbering friend.

If Cathaoir hadn't caught wind of the goblin stench in time, the spear that pierced his wing might have lanced his heart. He ignored the pain and threw a handful of charmed olive tree thorns at the advancing hunter. He had no hope they would stop his rancid opponent, but they could slow him enough to give Cathaoir time to draw his blade and circle around to a better position, defensively. The tear in his wing was no small matter, but he'd fought with worse in the Troll War. Of course he'd been ages younger and faster back then.

The thorns all hit their mark, but one in particular struck home, piercing the goblin's left eye. The hunter dropped his club and howled like a banshee. It clawed madly at the wounded eye, and Cathaoir charged in. His sword was small in comparison to the goblin three times his height, but he flew lopsidedly in under the flailing arms and struck hard and true through the goblin's tough hide and into his dark heart. And just to be certain, the old faery spun around and came in from his enemy's recently blinded side where he rammed his blade into the gnarled, crusty ear, right up to the hilt.

The blow to his heart had already killed the goblin, but his sludge-slow brain didn't get the message until it, too, was attacked. He went down onto the grass with a soft thud. A gentle hiss escaped his mouth as his last breath returned to the Forest.

Cathaoir bent down and examined the goblin's feet, but neither was missing a toe. "Just lovely. I don't mind killing goblins when I have to, but I would at least like to kill the *right* one." He sighed and looked off to the west. "Brigid, lass, I certainly hope you've remembered what I taught you about using a blade, because I'm afraid I might not make it in time." He looked to the sky, hoping to sight a passing Sky Patrol airship, but the night sky was airship-lantern-free.

The willow leaned slowly, imperceptibly, over the battle scene. She was certain this old faery was one of the banished clans, so it behooved her to carry out the sentence. She waited until he wiped off and sheathed his sharpy-sharp cutter, then she dropped a dozen tendril-branches right down on top of him. She tightened her grips and he struggled and made an awful noise, but once she closed a branch around his throat, the noise came to a gurgling halt. His thrashing continued for a few more blinks, but eventually those stopped, too. She dropped the punished faery on top of the goblin he had just killed and stood back up straight, proud to have done her part.

Chapter Eighteen

Brigid hopped off Grace, stretched her legs, twisted the kinks out of her back, and flexed the feeling back into her fingers.

"Where are they?" Fiona did a slow back walkover, and the kinks in her own back popped out quite audibly.

"They'll be here. Twitch won't let anything happen to them—will she, Grace?" Brigid worried, though.

Grace sat back on her haunches and regarded Brigid with her big, soft-brown eyes. "If there is a hare I trust m'life to, it's Twitch. Nary a day goes by when I'm not gobsmacked by my much younger sister's speed and instincts. She's a wary fighter, too, and will stand to the death defending your Sisters."

"Let's hope it doesn't come to that."

"Aye."

Grandfather Torby plodded steadily along, single-minded in his desire to get clear of Twisted Maple and arrive at the royal court as quick as could be. Dillweed, on the other hand, struggled the entire way. At first it was will-o-wisps flying along in front of him, nearly blinding him in the dark of the night so he would trip over roots and rocks; then it was sprites dropping spider silks on his face and giggling cruelly when he smashed into trees while slapping and swiping the silks from his eyes. His reputation as a klutz preceded him and throughout Orrin's duchy where cruelty and nastiness were celebrated, he was the brunt of more pranks than any gnome deserved to be.

"She's *what?!*" Orrin threw his rapier at the portal his steward had just closed behind him.

Gilroy didn't even flinch. If he flinched, he knew the dagger on his liege's belt would be the next object thrown in anger, and it would pierce his heart. "Vanished. We were tracking five of the lasses as they ran west, but they have vanished."

Orrin closed his eyes and took a long deep breath, which Gilroy knew meant his own life lay in the balance and the next words out of his mouth determined whether he saw another the coming sunrise. "Your Grace, we believe they have found a means to travel to another realm, that they are no longer in Faerie at all."

"Another realm? Which one?" His eyes opened and Gilroy relaxed just a smidgen.

"We have no way of knowing, sire. The gate was closed by the time our spy reached it. They were fleeing from a goblin."

"They're not even in Faerie?" There was hope in his voice.

"No, sire."

"Do we know what they were running to in the west?"

"They were going in the opposite direction of both your sister and yourself, so most likely they were simply running to some place they think is safe from you both." He retrieved the rapier from the door and walked it back to his liege.

"But now they're gone." He accepted the weapon and slid it back home into its scabbard. "If they can leave, then they can return. Have the spies keep their eyes open." He flew across the large chamber to the stone casement and stared out into the night, dismissing Gilroy.

"Yes, Your Grace." Unseen, he bowed and departed. He suspected their spies were going to earn their payments thrice over before this affair was done.

Nyla didn't need to open her eyes to know they were away from iron. The tightness in her chest was gone, she felt strength in her muscles again, and she could think clearly, without the grey poisonous blanket the iron had thrown over her mind.

Gone, too, was the baying hound, the beast that could likely tear a hobgoblin in half. She took a raggedy breath. The air seemed 'softer', not as harsh. She opened her eyes further, still cautious of the burning. To be stranded in this world wingless, blind, and surrounded by iron—she couldn't imagine a slower, more painful way to die.

As quickly as she could, she got the three of them mounted up, and with a whisper of thanks into the doe's long ear, they were once again on their way. She was so disoriented by this dark, toxic realm, she had no concept of time. The turns and blinks were all blended together into a run-or-die blur. It definitely didn't help she had no way to know how fast time was passing back in Faerie, either. Would this one night be a fortnight back home? Or a *century*? Would they return home only to find Twilly and the five clans were all dead? She tapped the pouch at her hip, hoping the comb and its fly-trap spell would be enough to change the Elder Alder's mind.

Twitch kept them on darker paths, warning them when nearby iron was unavoidable, but the heroic hare ran as if the entire troll army were on her heels. At last she came to a stop in a patch of thistle.

"Almost there, lasses. But the last leg is the most dangerous. We have to cross a bridge."

Kara chuckled. "After all this, I think we can manage one little bridge."

"Oh, this'll be no wee bridge, lass. It's over two hundred bounds long, and there's no cover for hiding. We cross it in the glare of lamps."

"Then we go quickly. Easy peasy."

"It's also nearly solid iron. We run on wood, but nearly everything else is deadly to you. I'll go like the wind, aye, but you must hold fast like your very lives depend on it, which they will, in fact." She pushed aside the thistles to give them a good look at the terror ahead of them.

Nyla dearly hoped Twitch was exaggerating, but upon seeing the stone and iron structure with her own eyes, she had serious doubts. The bridge was *huge*. It could hide a hundred trolls beneath it, and yet she would rather face five-score trolls than the poison before them. "There's no other way?"

"We *must* cross the river, and it's the bridge or fly." Nyla winced at the mention of flight and Twitch bowed her ears. "I'm sorry, lass. That's the simple truth of it. I meant no insult."

Their new friend was hardly to blame for the loss of their wings, so Nyla stroked Twitch's cheek. "None taken. It is what it is, and maybe someday remembering won't hurt so much." She looked at Kara and Rainn, and assessed their condition. They both looked as strong as she felt, maybe stronger. "We can do this, can't we? Together."

Kara took her hand. "Always, big sister."

Rainn smiled. "It's just *one* silly bridge."

"Exactly. One silly bridge, and we can cross it. We *will* cross it."

The Sisters ducked low to keep from being whacked in the head by thistles, and Twitch moved cautiously out from under cover and into the light. It was all quiet. It was now or never. The hare bolted from the lawn and aimed straight for the center of the stone and iron death trap. There was so much metal in the structure Nyla wanted to throw up almost immediately. She knew her Sisters couldn't possibly be feeling any better, so she leaned in close, hugged them tight, and held them in place.

They were a mere handful of bounding leaps from the bridge when a booming shout shattered the relative silence of the night.

"Oy! Leprechauns! Catch 'em Donal!"

So close to the iron, it was all Nyla could do to open one eye to squint in the direction of the voice. An adult human charged at them from shrubs flanking the bridge, fumbling with the front of his britches as he ran. It was all Nyla could do to hold on as Twitch abruptly dodged left, then right, and then leaped onto the bridge. A rock the size of her head whizzed past them and bounced off the iron railings with a deafening 'clang'. Twitch bounded on.

A second shout sounded and at least two pairs of heavy footfalls hammered along the boards behind them. The hare did her best to stay ahead of the pursuit, but she'd been carrying three faeries for quite some time and these humans were much faster than the hound they'd eluded earlier. Another object flew past and shattered on the boards, spreading glass across their path.

"Hang on!" Twitch leaped powerfully over the shards, but twisted on landing and Kara slipped sideways. Nyla leaned over Kara and tightened her grip on the poor hare's fur. Somehow she managed to stop her sister's slide.

"They're leprechauns, Donal! Don't let them get away! They've got *gold!*"

The heavy-booted runner was nearly upon them. The pounding of his feet was so near Nyla expected to be plucked off their steed at any blink. Then they were clear of the bridge and off into the taller grass, which favoured the hare and hopefully hampered pursuit. She didn't dare look back, and had no idea if either of her Sisters was conscious beneath her, so she simply held fast and trusted Twitch.

Jogging from tree to tree on the moonlit grounds, Brigid held her flute firmly in one hand. Any of them would have been sufficient to open a gate, but if she found an ancient beauty with powerful, wide roots, she hoped it would make a stronger and more direct passage. If she were honest with herself, she really had no idea what she was doing. She'd opened the first gate while running solely on fear and instinct.

Near the south end of the park she found a grand yew ages older than anything around her. She sat on one thick, moss-blanketed root and listened. The trees of Faerie were quite chatty—at least they were before the clans were banished—but the trees in this realm seemed to be in a deep sleep, permanent winter dormancy. She could jump up and down and shout at the great beauty, but her grandfather always said the best relationships began with respect. She sat and waited.

With the time restraints they were under, it seemed like an eternity, but it really wasn't long before her patience was rewarded.

"Good evening, Wee One."

"Good evening, Auntie. And how are you enjoying this lovely summer breeze?"

"Fair to middling, lass. It stinks of humans, but it is cool on my slender leaves and berries, and there is the promise of rain soon."

"Rain? Then maybe it will stink less."

"It always, does, for a time. What brings you to my old roots, lass? It has been so long since I've had a visit from any of the Fair Folk."

"That is *unconscionable*, Auntie!" This beautiful tree was old enough to be respected even in Faerie. "I'll speak to my elders when I return home and see if we can perhaps arrange for someone to come by for regular chats."

"That would be lovely. Thank you. Now, how can I help one who is so far from home?"

"Well, Auntie, my Sisters and I are in need of passage home, and I am hoping you might lend us a root or two. I even have a map and a fair idea of where we need to arrive."

"A gate? To Faerie? If you can make one, then it would be my honour to help in any way I can, lass. My roots reach deep and so I have some almost forgotten knowledge of Faerie geography. Between the two of us, I think we can get you close."

Brigid leaped up and clapped her hands gleefully. "That's wonderful! Thank you. There will only be five of us, so nothing too large or strenuous."

"I assume we wait upon your four companions?"

"One Sister, Fiona, is here in the woods, and the others are en route, I hope. I'd best go find out."

"Very well, lass. I'll be here when you need me."

Brigid kissed three fingers and placed them on the yew's nearest root. "I know. I'll return shortly." She sprinted back to the shrub where Grace and Fiona hid, watching for the others to arrive at the park. "I've found us a wonderful grand old yew."

Grace flickered her ears. "The one with mossy roots and a trunk so wide you have to *run* around it? She's sheltered us more than once in foul weather."

"Perfect! You know her, then. Do you two mind waiting here for Twitch to arrive with our Sisters while I go prepare?"

"Not at all. Go, lass. Do what you must and I shall wait for the youngsters. As soon as they hop up, we will be there lickety split."

"Thank you!" She ran, keeping to the deeper shadows.

Chapter Nineteen

Moonclaw and Twilly found Rock-Eye slouched on a boulder in a clearing, with his scarred head in his hands. The owl landed on a branch near the old troll's head. Twilly dismounted and quickly leaped from the branch to Rock-Eye's shoulder.

"What's wrong?"

"Am lost."

"Lost?" She sat down. "Not at all. I know exactly where we are. Laughing Elf Lake and Ten-Oaks is—" She checked the stars overhead. "*That* way. Southeast."

"If you say. Am still lost. Not know where Winsome be. Maybe at castle, maybe in Forest, may be... anywhere. Waste time when time be precious."

"Birds."

"Not birds. Faeries. Faeries steal baby kin."

"No, that's not what I meant. Why not ask the birds. They're *everywhere*. If they haven't seen her, then surely they can find someone who has. Moonclaw?" She looked back up at the owl, who rotated his head around slowly, then cocked it to one side as he thought.

"Little Whooo is correct. I will spread the tweet and chirp." He launched himself off the branch and glided off into the darkness.

The troll sighed and slumped down again. "Take too long. Hate waiting when should be doing. Baby Winsome being tortured while useless Goopa sits in woods."

"Goopa?"

""Goopa—Winsome name for Rock-Eye."

Twilly kissed him on his scarred and twisted ear. "Goopa. I *like* it. It suits you."

"You too nice. I kill faeries and you still nice. Who was it Rock-Eye killed?

She'd tried not to think about the attack, or about *anything* dark and upsetting for that matter. But he had asked, and the truth was always best. "My father. He was a general in Lady Orlaith's army."

"Your kin? Your *father*?" He hung his head. "So, so sorry."

"We were never close, Rock-Eye. He hated my friends and would never have let me marry Cray."

"Cray?"

"My Love, my Heart. The one Lady *Orifice* murdered."

"Ah. Love." He nodded, as if that explained everything.

"My father also fought in the Troll War and killed dozens or more trolls, so don't be sorry or feel pity." Her words seemed to reassure Rock-Eye, but they did little for her. The General had been an angry bully and a butcher who loved proudly recounting the stories of the atrocities he committed during the war, but he was still her father. Part of her heart hurt a little for him, but yet another felt relief, especially for her mother, who rarely smiled when the General was at home.

Moonclaw returned just then, interrupting Twilly's trip down Melancholy Creek.

"Tweets, hoots, and chirps done. This whooo will know soonest."

"Thank you, Moonclaw." She smiled up at him.

"More wait," Rock-Eye huffed.

"Maybe not." Twilly could do nothing, being banished and disguised as a pixie, but maybe Rock-Eye himself could. "Goopa, have you looked to the underworld for help? Maybe dwarfs and spriggans know something."

"No one help from beneath. Trespassing troll get staked out in sun."

"But you're simply looking for Winsome. You've done nothing wrong."

"Nothing but kill General Father."

"Well, there *is* that. But only you and I know, and I promise not to tell."

"Truth?"

"Truth."

He relaxed for a moment, and then suddenly tensed, which she could feel through the muscles in his shoulder. "And killed elk stag."

"*You* killed Torinstag? Then we'd best get underground quickly. Some folks think it was a Mist Eater, but whatever they think, there is a reward for the head of whoever was responsible."

"Mist Eater?" Rock-Eye shivered and Twilly laughed.

"Silly Goopa. You're a *troll*, searching for a kidnapped baby. Mist Eaters should be afraid of *you*. But we still need to get below."

"Caves near here, and tunnel."

"A tunnel would be perfect." She looked up at the owl. "Moonclaw, will you come with us or stay above?"

It was the Great Horned Owl's turn to shiver. "Tunnels? No sky? This whooo needs sky. Sun is good, but stars and moon are best." He blinked. "No tunnels. This whooo will fly above, you whooos hide below."

That made sense to Twilly. She and Rock-Eye truly needed to get out of sight, and Moonclaw could listen for news from the birds. "Agreed. Goopa?"

Rock-Eye smiled. "Agree." He looked up and Twilly followed his gaze. It was getting lighter. "Dawn comes. Time to run, Little One." He flashed Moonclaw a scarred thumbs-up, trotted out of the clearing and back into the dark Forest.

Twilly held tight and, as the two of them went in search of the caves leading to the underworld, she wondered how her Sisters were faring on their pilgrimage with their clans to the Creeping Moss Caves.

Trinn *so* wanted to wear his new wings all the day and night, but after countless turns testing and refining them, both his stunted wing stumps and his arms were exhausted to the point of agony. He had just enough strength to uncork a jug of butter-juice and settle into the mossy cradle between the roots of the grove's lone willow. The stars above danced and shimmied as they always did, but tonight a special sparkle brightened their light; a sparkle brought on less by the potent butter-juice and more by the simple joy of flying.

"I have wings. Did I tell you that? I have marvelous, wonderful, fantabulous wings." No one answered him because his friends were all long ago abed. They'd urged him to do likewise, but he was too full of joy to catch even a single wink, he'd replied.

"Go easy on the butter-juice," Browncap scolded, before he went off to his own nest deep in the White Pine.

Trinn lifted his jug high and poured the distilled juice straight into his mouth. At least, that was his plan. Some of the butter-juice did hit the target, and some even made it into his throat before he started sputtering and wiping it out of his nose and eyes. He soaked up as much as he could with his sleeve, and then he sucked on his sopping sleeve, trying to salvage as much of his cherished elixir as he could.

Once he'd nearly chewed his sleeve off, Trinn washed it all down with a long, controlled, swig from the jug. "No point in risking more spillage", he said to the stars and the few fireflies who dared to come into the mad faery's meadow. "I *am* mad, you know. I'm so mad, I can *fly*. Barmy as a bat. Mad as a marmot.

It was clear gold was a big motivator in the human realm, because as fast as Twitch hopped, the humans stayed close behind. Nyla wished there were something she could shout back to convince the two in pursuit that the three of them weren't leprechauns and had no gold, but it would have been a waste of breath.

"They're makin' for the park, Donal! If they make the park, we'll lose 'em for sure!"

"I'm on it!"

Nyla could hear his heavy, laboured breathing right over her shoulder. She knew he couldn't last much longer before he quit the chase, but so, too, Twitch slowed. The poor hare was exhausted and Nyla still had no idea how much further they had to go.

"Well, bless my hammer if it isn't old One-Eye himself." A long-bearded, barrel-chested dwarf stepped out of a side passage, his huge mining hammer held in front of him both as a shield and as a weapon, or so it seemed to Twilly. "It takes a stone pair to show your ugly face down here. *And* you bring a pet pixie with you."

Rock-Eye bowed his head even further than the low roof required. "Greetings, Giles Fullbeard. Blessing on your house."

"'Bless my house'? Well, if that don't grind the calcite from my wick. I suppose if you're goin' to be all formal then, I'd best do the same. Blessings on your kin, Rock-Eye. Be welcome in my humble home." He shifted his massive hammer and Twilly wondered if the reddish stains on the tool's head were blood. The dwarf definitely looked solid enough to have gone to war and survived. He squinted and leaned a little closer. "What brings you to my door-step, Rock-Eye?"

"Kin."

"You want to be my kin?" He scratched his chin beneath his great beard. "Or are you here to *eat* my kin?"

"Search. For *my* kin." The troll sat suddenly, nearly dislodging Twilly from his shoulder. "Troll baby—great-grandbaby—Winsome, stolen. Orrin say Orlaith to blame."

Giles relaxed a tad and plopped down, facing them. "*Your* liege blames *my* liege for something, and you *believe* his festering little words? That burr of a stump on their family oak hasn't spoken a true word since before he placed his hand on his hollow heart and swore allegiance to King Oberon."

Rock-Eye nodded. "Winsome still missing. Birds searching above."

"Excellent. They're fast and they're *everywhere*. But she's not going to be kept in a tree, so the under-world makes sense. Are you willing to talk to the Council?"

"For Winsome-baby, anything."

"Good." Giles thumped his hammer on the passage floor in a simple, but distinct pattern. "That should get the boulder rolling." He looked directly at Twilly. "We're going deep, Pixie Miss. A long way down from moonlight and the surface."

Twilly was already feeling the rock pressing down around them, but this wasn't about her and her fears. For the first time since she came across Torinstag's bloody carcass, she felt like there was more to life than her own little bubble. A baby was missing, and wings or no wings, Love or no Love, maybe she could help. "Lead on, good Sir Giles. I am honoured to be permitted." As a wingless, tree-less faery, this might just turn out to be the one place where she was welcome.

"Good." He hopped to his feet and started off down the steeply sloped passage. Rock-Eye climbed to his feet and shuffled after their host, careful to avoid bumping his head on the low ceiling. Twilly held on, happy to be doing *something*, rather than marching off into the mountains to die a moping, purposeless death.

Twilly didn't know if Giles intentionally led them on a long, winding, and convoluted route, but after the thirteenth turn, she stopped counting and admitted to herself she was thoroughly lost. She also concluded that a life underground might not be her cup of cream.

She loved roots and soil and plants and insects, but she liked them all with sunshine on her skin and a breeze beneath her wings. Her *wings*…Without warning, reality slammed into her. She sobbed behind her free hand. Even if she found a life with trolls and dwarfs, she would never fly again. She would also never have a tree to call her own, a bonded home full of love and hope. She would never start a family and she would never see her Sisters again. The Sisterhood of the Black Dragonfly was as dead as her former life.

Soon the dirt floor, roughly supported walls, and low roof transitioned into smooth, but unadorned rock walls with a simple vaulted roof tall enough for Rock-Eye to walk upright without banging his head. As they proceeded, the passage evolved. Simple paintings appeared on the columns, and then the columns developed carvings. Eventually the plinths, pilasters, vaults, and columns became so elaborate and the work so masterful Twilly wondered aloud if they were entering a palace.

Giles smiled up at her. "Just the world beneath, missy. While you pixies flitter away your time chasing dandelion seeds or whatever you do, bored dwarfs carve, We even teach trolls, gnomes, and anyone else who has an aversion to daylight and those who dance around in it."

"It's wondrous. Spectacular. I have an uncle who shapes wood, but the wood has to agree with the shape."

"Rock is no different. I might start carving a gryphon, but the stone prefers to be a unicorn. If I don't adapt my work, the stone can split right down the middle and ruin the work completely." He stopped and placed a calloused palm flat on a stunning elaborate relief of dragons in flight, chasing each other around and around the column. "And sometimes it all just works out the way you imagined it before you started."

Even Rock-Eye bent to examine the artistry, and Giles moved his hand so they could both see it clearly. The troll gently brushed his fingertips across the work. "You do good work. Much love in this."

The dwarf's smile was genuine. "Thank you, but I had help." He leaned around his guests. "C'mere, lad."

A young, clean-chinned dwarf scooted around the troll, right beneath Twilly's roost.

"This is m'son, Able. Not even bearded and he has a better eye for stone detail than I *ever* had. Lad, run ahead and gather anyone who's available. Someone has stolen a troll baby and we're going to help Rock-Eye find her."

"Aye, sir!" Able snapped an informal salute and ran down the passage.

"Looks like father."

"Aye, that he does—much to the chagrin of his mother's entire clan." He cocked his head as if he were listening. "Not much further, now."

"Why go to Council?"

"Why? A trio of reasons. One: if anyone has word of missing babies anywhere in the realm, it would be the local underworld council. Two: If anyone can get anywhere they need to and help you rescue her, it'll be your underworld brothers and sisters. And, finally and probably most importantly…if you plan to travel in our tunnels, even on the outskirts where the dirt is fresh and the grubs still know daylight, you'll need permission. You may be a war hero back home, but to many of us you're still an enemy soldier."

"All makes sense. I not trust me, too. But too old, too tired for stupid war. Nobles make war for fun. Is stupid."

"Aye, that it is. I wish all trolls agreed with you."

"Many do. Young and stupid not agree."

"Or old and stupid."

"Some."

They trundled along, going ever and ever deeper. They were silent for quite some time, which was fine with Twilly because now she'd shaken off her shock and malaise and whatever potion her mother had poured down her throat to calm her, she could tackle her heartache head-on. Thinking clearly also made the world look a bit different, too.

Other than some pixies, sprites, and a brownie or two, Twilly's exposure to the other races of Faerie was rather narrow. Her father ran—had run—the clan with an iron fist and unbending opinions, which she now saw were so very racist. She had always believed trolls were dangerous, simple, killing beasts who only ate raw meat, reproduced, and waged war in the dark. But here was Rock-Eye, alone and unarmed, searching for a baby.

She was also taught dwarfs were smelly, dirty, cave dwellers whose lust for gold and gems kept them underground where they lived in holes and wore rusty armour from past glories. It was also said they let vermin live in their disgusting beards and they were once elves who were corrupted and lured away from sunlight by their greed and avarice. Even Twilly's own mother ranted about how nothing good lives underground except slippery, slimy worms.

Just as she was about to swear her allegiance to the misunderstood beings of the world beneath, the passage opened up into a cavern to rival the Great Hall of Ten Oaks Castle. Rock-Eye shuffled to a stop and both he and Twilly stared up in slack-jawed awe.

The circular cavern had to be a hundred yards across and half as tall. It was level upon level of balconies carved straight out of the living rock. Pillars and arches and arches and pillars extending up into the darkness, and there wasn't a smooth, flat surface to be seen. Everywhere Twilly looked, near and far, up and down, were reliefs and carvings and statuary. It was one great, beautiful, soulful, work of art. It was so—

"RUN!" Young Able burst out from under an arch to their left and charged straight at them. "RUN! He isn't welcome! They've gone to the armoury! You...must...*flee!*"

Chapter Twenty

Giles spun around. "Go! Run! I'll slow them down. Maybe they'll listen to reason."

Rock-Eye turned and ran, with Twilly clinging for dear life. Behind them Able shouted. "No, Father! You, as well! Gwynn is calling you a traitor! Go! Go! Go!" Two sets of thumping bootsteps followed close behind them. Rock-Eye turned right at the first intersection, then left, right, left, and left again. They were climbing quickly. The old troll didn't say a word, but plunged into the darkness, stopping and slowing only to sniff the air every so often before making a directional decision. His long legs made up for his ancient years, and so Giles and Able worked hard to keep up.

Eventually they slowed, but Twilly couldn't tell if it was because they were safe or because Rock-Eye was exhausted. He walked two more right turns and a left, and stopped. Her night vision wasn't as keen as the other three, but she could see they were in a tiny cave with a pool and a ceiling low enough Rock-Eye had to both duck and slouch to keep from bonking his head. Even Twilly ducked reflexively, the ceiling was so low.

The old troll raised his hand to his shoulder and Twilly stepped onto it. He placed her gently on the floor, then got down on all fours and sniffed the pool. He dipped a finger in and then licked the drips from his finger. He seemed to swirl the small amount of water around in his mouth, like Twilly's auntie did with nectar.

"Safe. No iron. All drink." He cupped his hands into a gnarled bowl and scooped water up to his mouth.

Flushed from the run, Giles knelt down at the pool's edge, but looked over at Twilly. "He must like you a lot Miss Pixie— trolls usually just dive their head in and drink, not caring what condition they leave the water in for those who come after." He, too, scooped water up and drank.

Twilly moved in and did the same, careful to keep her back away from the dwarfs so her wing stumps weren't quite so obvious. Not having done any of the actual running, her thirst sated quickly. "What happened back there? Is it because he's a troll?" She hoped they didn't find out she was a banished faery.

"Oh, he's not just *a* troll. Our big friend here was an officer in their army in the Troll War and nearly destroyed an entire battalion of dwarfs with a rock-slide trap."

Rock-Eye nodded in agreement, but Twilly didn't think he looked particularly proud of what he'd done. "Was war."

"Aye, it was," Giles agreed. "You aren't the only one with blood on your hands, but much of the blood you have came from this community. It was stupid of me to think we could find peace over the common ground of missing babies."

The troll lifted his head and raised an eyebrow. "Dwarf babies, too?"

Giles looked at Able and nodded. "Tell him what you've heard. I was saving it for the gathering, but this might be as gathered as we get."

"Two dwarf twins, from the clan near the border, on *this* side of the river. Also, four baby pixies from different clans, stretching from the sea to the hills, all along the border."

Twilly was horrified. "Why? Who in Faerie would take babies? Is there a market for fae babies we don't know about?"

"They're not for sale. Able lad thinks they're for power. Threaten to kill his baby, and even a hardened soldier will bow down to an enemy. We think Orrin may be behind it, and that he's manipulating the security of the border, readying for an attack."

Rock-Eye groaned. "Why Winsome? Rock-Eye went to Orrin, not Orrin come to Rock-Eye."

"I wish I knew. Whatever the reason, though, I'll bet a lump of platinum you've been searching in the wrong duchy."

The troll pulled his trouser pockets inside out. "No platinum. No bet."

Giles started to say that he only jested, but Rock-Eye winked at him and they all laughed. Twilly felt some of the tension drain from her body while the laughter echoed off the rock all around them. It felt like forever since she'd last laughed, and she let it loose. She couldn't help herself, though the little voice in her head that sounded a lot like her mother wondered if she should be laughing at all so soon after Cray's death. And then she thought "Burr it!" Cray was a bit dim-witted at times, but he'd always tried to make her smile when they were together. This laugh is for you, my Lost Love! She let the joy roll out, moistened by tears of both joy and sorrow.

She laughed so hard she tipped over onto her side in the sand beside the pool. She only stopped when Rock-Eye gently picked her up and cradled her. Breathing heavily, she wiped her eyes, kissed his thumb, and curled up to sleep.

While they traipsed along forest trails, Torby easily kept ahead of Dillweed, but eventually their local trail joined the duchy's main thoroughfare and they started winding their way up into the mountains. Where Lady Orlaith preferred to live amongst forests, meadows and warm lakes, her cold-hearted brother preferred to surround himself with high-mountain passes, glacial lakes, and rock. "To each their own," Torby muttered, but right at that moment he wished his liege were a lover of gently rolling countryside and maybe even warm beaches.

As the day dawned and they left the Forest for the foothills and then the mountains, Dillweed caught up quickly. Torby noticed the thin lash marks wherever his grandson's skin was exposed. "Do we need to take a break, lad? To tend to the marks of cruelty you bear?"

"That would be lovely, Grandfather." He kept walking, matching his pace to Torby's. "Could we also have some biscuits and jelly, and maybe a mug of mint juice?"

Torby squinted at Dillweed, trying to read the young gnome's expression. "Sarcasm, lad?"

"Yes sir. Sorry. Maybe a little wishful thinking, too. I promise I will only ask this once, but are we there, yet?" He drank from his wineskin, then passed it over.

Torby took a long draught, then belched before answering, to give himself time to calculate. "Near enough to expect a warm lunch, but not so near that breakfast will be eaten at a table."

"That's close enough for me, Grandfather."

"And myself as well. These old feet just don't like to hike like they used to."

Dillweed stopped and pulled Torby's rucksack off his back. He then slipped his arms through the straps and folded his arms under it to support it.

"With a pack on the front and one on your back, you look like a miniature bugbear, lad. I *can* carry my own pack, you know."

"And I can carry two, at least for a short time." He once again started plodding along, the extra weight slowing him somewhat, but not enough Torby would insult him by refusing his aid and taking back his rucksack. To be honest, his old back was grateful for the respite. He caught up with Dillweed and proudly walked beside him on the quiet, early morning road.

Trinn leaned back from the wing's joint, and then stepped back from the workbench where he had the pair secured. He dragged his sleeve across his brow in a third attempt to clear the sweat getting in his eyes while he tightened and tweaked and adjusted. "There. That should increase the torque, give me more control, but not be too unstable. Maybe."

Browncap the sparrow chirped at him from the stump where his tools were laid out. "Fly more, Trinn?"

"Of course. But I need some solid food to soak up some of this butter-juice." He burped, and tasted the effervescent juice again.

"Eat fast. I like flying with you, though you're clumsy like a beetle."

"Gee, thanks." He wiped his hands on the towel he always kept tucked in his vine belt. "I could get used to flying."

"Your own wings are fun, aren't they? Soon you'll fly fast and far." Sparrow preened confidently, having spoken what he considered to be an unavoidable truth.

"Maybe so, but not without food."

"Bugs?" He stopped preening.

"*Mushroom soup*. And maybe some of those biscuits the elves traded for the wire a fortnight past."

"Biscuits? Blech. Bugs or worms. If you want to fly, you must eat like one who flies."

"Hawks fly, and hawks eat sparrows. Should I eat a sparrow?"

"No sparrows! Maybe 'walker' food *is* fine. But *I* am going to find some nice juicy berries." With a powerful down stroke of his wings, he launched off the stump and flapped off for the bushes near the base of the bluff.

Trinn stared after him, realization dawning bright and sunny. "*That's* what I need. A powerful take-off. The first thrust needs to be the strongest." Scrunching his face in thought, he wandered back to his elm for a quick tea.

"We're here! We're here!" Nyla screamed as Twitch passed through the iron gates and into the forested park beyond. She saw Fiona wave from off to the right, but her Sister stood next to Grace, relaxed and off-guard. There was no sign of Brigid. "Mount up and flee! Where's Brigid?!"

Fiona took only a blink to assess the situation, what with the two humans approaching the gates quickly, red-faced and furious. She leapt onto Grace before the doe could crouch down, then they bolted off into the woods. "This way!"

A stone whizzed past Nyla's head and narrowly missed Grace's retreating hind end.

"Don't kill 'em Donal! We want their gold, not their curse!"

Grace led the way and Twitch stayed close on her fluffy tail as they weaved around and through the park's trees and shrubs. Nyla would have preferred a fast, direct route to Brigid, but she understood the hares were doing their best to slow the humans down as much as possible, and maybe even lose the pursuit entirely. What the zig-zaggy course *definitely* did was put a halt to the stone throwing.

They raced around a bed of deep blue hyacinth and bolted back out onto the lawns. Nyla lifted her head just enough to see over Rainn and Kara, and she caught a glimpse of Brigid at the base of a grand yew, with her flute in hand.

"Play, Brigid, play!"

The flute flew to Brigid's lips and her gate-making magic poured forth in crisp, clean notes faster than anything Nyla had ever heard her Sister play before. The gap between two thick roots began to glow, and the closer the four of them got, the brighter it glowed.

"Oy! I see it! Their gold! The pot's a glowin', Donal!" The shout came from the copse of trees behind them; further than it had been, but not far enough.

Grace arrived at the yew and Fiona flipped off to land neatly next to Brigid, her dagger drawn and ready. Grace spun around and put herself between the hunters and her faery friends. As soon as Twitch began to slow, Nyla leaped off, tapping Rainn on the shoulder. "Off! Go!"

Rainn and Kara followed her and all three landed with tumbles and hopped upright next to Fiona. Brigid paused in her magic just long enough to snap, "Nyla and Fiona go! Secure the other end! We're right behind you!" Fearless and furious, Fiona charged down between the roots, through the gate, and into the passage between the realms. Nyla was hot behind her, drawing her own blade as she sprinted into the near darkness. This passage between the realms was much shorter than the previous one for some reason, so the light at the end came up much quicker. With a glimpse back over her shoulder she could still see a bit of the gate glow in the human realm. The wonderful notes of the flute danced after them, down into the damp, rich earth. Nyla turned back and ran.

"Kara, go!" Rainn's command was clear, but Kara shouted "Brigid! Look out!"

The flute music stopped abruptly, the passage went black, and what felt like a hill giant's huge paw shoved Nyla and Fiona out through the gate and back into Faerie. They were back home and the sun was up! Nyla landed with a somersault and popped up to her feet. She spun immediately back to the gate to reach for Kara, but the portal was shut and the covering shrub was settling back down into place. She dove at the roots, digging with both hands.

Chapter Twenty-One

With his belly full of biscuits, cream, and berries, Trinnean wasted no time getting back up in the air. He circled around on a delicious updraft, keeping an eye on Browncap not far below him.

"No! Kara!" Nyla clawed, frantic. How could *she* have made it through but Kara not?!

"Nyla, we have company." Fiona put a hand on Nyla's shoulder and pulled her back from the hole she was digging. A deep growl from down the trail snapped Nyla back to reality. They were home in Faerie, where there were worse things out and about than humans wanting their non-existent gold and hounds wanting their bones for dinner.

Fiona held out Nyla's dagger, which she dropped when she tumbled through.

"Hobgoblin?"

"Well, it's not an incontinent elf."

Heavy footsteps thumped down the thinly worn trail, approaching fast. Nyla urged Fiona into the shrubbery opposite the former gate. "Hide!" She whispered. "Be ready." She ducked back into the undergrowth a few skips down the other side of the trail, and hunkered down with her needle-sharp blade at the ready. Maybe, she hoped, whoever it was would just pass them by and not even notice two inconsequential lasses pretending to be shaky dandelions or thistles.

The footsteps slowed, then around the bend tromped a heavily scarred, nearly naked goblin with a long bone blade in one hand and a short, thick club in the other. He sniffed the air as if he could find his prey by scent alone. Of course, with a nose the size of *his* bent, bulbous snout, Nyla suspected he could find a gnat in a dust storm.

The hunter seemed sure he was in the right place. He stood still and sniffed, then squinted around at the forest then sniffed again and squinted some more. Nyla now noticed he was breathing extremely heavily, as if he'd been running all night. That was when Nyla realized that it was dawn. Or maybe it was dusk. She couldn't be sure. In the meantime, she was about to face a goblin with nothing more than a tiny faery blade. She'd be lucky if it even pierced his hide—provided she could get close enough in the first place.

What was it Brigid had said about if you're close enough to land a blow, you're already dead? By the looks of the scars criss-crossing the hunter's body, many blows had been landed, but he was still very much alive.

Panting, he knelt down at the shrub where the gate had been and took a long, deep sniff. He smiled and nodded to himself, seemingly quite pleased with what he found.

"Strange magics…Faerie magics…*tasty* magics." His nose seemed to catch a trail, so he turned slowly, deliberately, until he was facing the shrubs where Fiona was hiding. "Faerie snacks." He took a step, his bone knife pointed straight ahead, nudging the branches aside in search of his prey. He went down on all fours, crawling in for the kill, and that's when Nyla struck.

She dearly wished she had her wings right now, but even without them she was fast and silent. She broke from cover, darted across the path, then leaped to the goblin's filthy foot and up onto his back. Quick as a bumblebee, she sped along his lumpy spine all the way to his neck, where she reversed her grip on her blade, grabbed it with two hands, and plunged it into the hunter's neck as hard, as fast, and as many times as she could.

The goblin's skin was so thick he didn't even notice he was under attack until the third stab. With a shriek, he stopped prodding the undergrowth, stood up, and swatted at the sting on his neck. His first swat with his club nearly smote Nyla in the head, but she ducked down and kept stabbing frantically. Even if she didn't slice anything vital, she was distracting him from searching for Fiona.

Then, as if on cue, Fiona rushed out of the greenery to their left, screaming, "Sisters forever!!" She ducked under a sloppy swing of the bone blade, and ran right past the goblin's belly, dragging her blade along his flesh as she went.

The stinging on his neck forgotten for the blink, the goblin smashed the club down on Fiona's head, except she wasn't there. Encouraged, Nyla refined her random stabbing into a more directed attack on the hunter's spine, but when he let out a pained yowl and dropped to one knee, she lost her footing and tumbled off.

Even over the wind whistling around the pointed tips of his ears, Trinn heard the goblin roar and what sounded like a lass' scream. He pivoted around on this right wingtip, searching. A second roar ripped up at him from directly beneath him, where the tress arched over the trail.

"Browncap! Down below! Someone is in trouble!" Trinn tucked his wings in and dove for an open portion of the trail, not knowing if the sparrow was following, but hoping with all his heart he was. Whatever was happening, it sounded violent and he was charging in with only the spanner on his belt for a weapon. He popped his wings open, arched his back, pulled out of the dive and skimmed along the trail. He had three blinks at most to see the raging goblin and the stabbing pixie before he zoomed past, just over the larger attacker's head. The goblin looked up, but was too slow to even take a swing before Trinn was past. Trinn looked back over his shoulder and laughed... then he crashed headfirst into a massive lilac bush.

Nyla darted in and stabbed the goblin in the foot with a quick jab-and-back. He roared and turned on her, but Fiona leaped from the bushes again with a terrifying scream of rage and slashed his belly once more. The goblin slammed his club down but Fiona rolled between his legs and came up behind him, covered in gore. Nyla moved out of his immediate reach and shouted for his attention.

"Hey! Puss-Face! Down here, you ugly son of a stump! Come get me, you fat burr!"

The goblin found her quickly enough and cocked his blade arm back, but a flash of metal whizzed past, right over his head, making him hesitate just a blink. Fiona took advantage of the sudden break and slashed the backs of both of the goblin's legs, one-two. He dropped the spear and collapsed to the dirt. His club hand fumbled to hold in his guts while keeping the club, but he was losing on both accounts. Nyla stepped further back, suspecting the evil hunter was nearly done. Fiona had no such thought, apparently, because she appeared on the neck of the writhing enemy, grabbed his thick hair like a rope, then swung down and past, cutting his throat. The goblin sighed out his last breath and Fiona released his hair and landed just out of reach, slipping in the blood and landing on her butt. She burst out laughing, but Nyla couldn't share her joy. They'd almost died.

"Are you *crazy?!* What the burr were you thinking?" Fiona pushed to her feet, wiped the goblin blood from her eyes, and sheathed her blade. "I was thinking that our clans are going to die, our Sisters are trapped in another realm, and I wasn't going to take one more blink of some bully trying to stop us from doing what we must."

"Oh."

"By the way, what did you throw at him to distract him? It was *humongous!*"

"She didn't *throw* anything. That was *me*." The deep voice came from behind them and the Sisters turned to see a strangely winged faery limping toward them with a sparrow hopping along at his side. "It was my awkward attempt to swoop in to the rescue."

Fiona chuckled. "Rescue?"

"Or suicide. I haven't quite decided which story to spin." He bowed awkwardly and the weight of his incredible wings pushed him forward into Fiona, who caught him easily and held him up. "Trinnean, at your service — for whatever it may be worth." He reached up and manually tucked his wings in tighter. "And my mentor of flight and folly here is Browncap." The sparrow bobbed a bow.

Nyla curtsied, feeling a bit odd trading civilities next to the stinking, leaking corpse of a goblin she had just killed. "A pleasure. I'm Nyla and this gory warrior is Fiona." Fiona curtsied even deeper, but she never took her eyes off their would-be rescuer. Though he slouched a bit under the weight of his odd appendages, Nyla could see he stood as tall as Fiona. Beneath his sweaty, unkempt bangs, his eyes were silver, with flecks of green and gold, and those eyes had Fiona's rapt attention. It probably didn't hurt that this Trinnean wasn't in the least put off by the blood drenching Fiona from braid to boot. In fact, he pulled a slightly dirty rag from his belt and wiped the end of her nose.

"Sorry. You had a bit of, um, *goblin* there."

Letting them share whatever silly moment they were having, Nyla curtsied politely to the sparrow and moved around to inspect the lad's wings. They were intricate and amazing and complicated, yet she could see where one toothed wheel meshed with another and how it would turn and affect a spindle and rotate a belt wrapped around another wheel. "This all looks like a dwarf time-teller. You can *fly* with these?"

Attention to his wings broke Trinnean's gaze away from Fiona's, albeit slowly and reluctantly. "Aye. A dwarf taught me the basics. The rest I improvised and created myself. I apprenticed on one of their airships for two summers. I can fly, but if you ask Browncap here, what I do is more like lumbering about in the sky like a drunken June bug."

The sparrow snickered. "But he *is* improving, quickly."

Nyla reached for the wing, astounded. "May I?"

"Of course." Trinnean swung the wing closer.

"What are these made of?" She ran her fingertips carefully over a particularly large toothed wheel. "They almost look like—"

"Metal."

She jerked her hand back *and* took a step back. "Iron?!" He had *iron* in Faerie? "Are you *crazy?!*"

"Probably at least a little, but it's all been spelled. It can't hurt you. I know iron poisoning and *this* is safe." He reached up with both hands and released a catch on each wing, then he opened them both out to their full spread.

Horrified being so close to this much metal, Nyla still couldn't help but be impressed with the workmanship. She leaned back in for a closer look.

"May I inquire where you lasses are bound for? This trail isn't exactly a thoroughfare to Ten Oak's Castle."

A metal-winged pixie could hardly be an agent of their liege, so the truth was probably best—or at least some of it. "We're making for the Source Grove to speak with the Elder Alder on an urgent matter."

"Just the *two* of you? Walking toward troll country to the Source Grove? That's either brave or crazy."

"Says the pixie with the iron wings?"

Without warning, the odd lad brought his wings in fast with a clank and a shudder, and backed away. "I am and always have been a *faery*—a proud Birch Faery of the Third Order. If I were a pixie, I'd be proud to be a pixie, but I'm a faery. Wings don't define a faery."

Nyla now realized he hadn't yet noticed their wing stubs. "So a faery might not have wings and would still be a faery?" He might yet be their best ally.

"That's what I just said. Sometimes by cruel chance, a faery might be born with only...*stubs*. I know it's rare, but *it happens*."

Fiona took a firm step toward him, then turned around and revealed her goblin gore-covered wing stumps. "And sometimes a faery's wings are stolen from her by a cruel, vindictive *stump* who should be banished by the King himself."

It went suddenly very quiet in the Forest, as the bird and the faery lad took in Fiona's stumps. Nyla turned and showed her own wing remnants. Whether he was friend or foe, they would soon discover. After a blink, she turned back around and Fiona did the same, but now her Sister was crying, her tears weaving tracks down her cheeks, through the blood. Nyla reached for her hand, but Trinnean got there first and took Fiona in his arms. Fiona returned the embrace.

After a moment in which Nyla felt much less comfortable than the other two, Trinnean released Fiona and asked, "That's pretty brave, just two of you making the journey."

Nyla plopped down onto a rock, drained both physically and emotionally. "There are five of us, but something happened and the other three are trapped in the human realm and we can't get back. Brigid was the only one who could cast the spell."

"The *human* realm?" Trinnean didn't look doubtful, he looked hopeful.

"The one and only."

"Do you know *where* in their realm? What town or village?"

"It had a huge groomed parkland with a stunning glass palace, and there was *iron* everywhere. And the place reeked. I think it started with a 'G'."

"I've never been anywhere else, but that sounds like Glasgow."

"That was the name! Glasgow. You know this place?"

"I know it exceedingly well."

"Then you can spell a gate open and get us back there to fetch our Sisters!"

"I don't exactly cast a spell, but I *can* take you there."

Nyla and Fiona exchanged glances. They both knew it could mean a long delay or splitting up. "Fiona, you go with Trinnean, and I'll make for the Source Grove. Once you bring the others home you can catch up to me.'

"But…"

"It has to be me and we both know it. Time is too precious for both of us to do all of it. Lives are at stake."

"I know." Fiona turned to Trinnean. "How far away is your passage to the other realm?"

"Only a few turns, even on foot."

Nyla hitched her satchel on her shoulder. "Then it's settled. You two return to Glasgow and I'll hike to The Grove."

"Wouldn't you rather fly?" Trinnean wondered.

She wasn't sure if he was being a burr or just a stump, too dense to know how much his words hurt, but she was too exhausted and frustrated to be polite. "Now why didn't *I* think of flying." She wiggled her stumps madly. "Oh, *that's* why. *I don't have any burring wings!*"

Trinnean didn't seem fazed by her snarkiness. "Then take mine." He started unsnapping the buckles holding his harness across his chest.

"Yours?"

"Of course. You didn't think they were permanent, did you? They should fit onto your stumps nearly as well as they fit mine, and it shouldn't take long for me to show you the basic mechanics. You've been flying all your life, so you're already ages ahead of me in training." He finished with the harness and turned to Fiona. "Fiona, could you hold these while I duck down and out, please?"

Fiona got a firm grip on the harness between the wings and held it tight while Trinnean bent his knees and slipped his wing stumps out of their receivers. He spun around and relieved Fiona of the burden.

"Truly? You would risk your cherished wings with a complete stranger?"

"Well, I can't very well take them where we're going, and if your quest is a life-or-death matter, then of course I can. Here…" He held them out for Nyla to back into, which she did. He snugged them onto her stumps.

At first they burned, but only because her scars were still fresh. After a few blinks, while he tugged on buckles and adjusted laces, they weren't so odd. She reached up and loosened the strap across her breasts. She wasn't endowed like a dwarf maiden, but she wasn't flat, either. It was like when she wore Cray's vest for a costume party. The suddenly memory slapped her heart and she gasped.

"Sorry! Did I pinch you?!"

"Not at all. I just had a memory of my brother, who died recently." She wiggled a bit, to make sure everything was snug. "Fiona, would you mind telling Trinnean our tale while you go? If he's risking his life for us, he should know who were are and what's at stake."

"Of course."

"Risking my life?"

"We were running from two gold-hungry humans who think I'm a leprechaun."

"Two...? *Seriously*? Leprechauns and gold?" He leaned back and laughed. "I think we'll be just fine. We won't go unarmed. You, on the other hand, need a quick lesson in metal wing mechanics."

"Just wind me up and let me loose."

"Don't laugh, because that's not far from the reality of it." He took her hand and guided it gently to a handle. "That's where you hold on. Anywhere else and you could lose a finger or four. There's one on the other side, for your right hand. Now, up here..."

Trinnean slowly went through the parts of the wing, what each of the controls did, and how to rewind it when the clockwork ran down. It all took precious time, but if she as truly going to fly to the Source Grove with these incredible wings, then she needed to know what the burr she was doing.

Chapter Twenty-Two

Torby expressed concern about how they were going to gain entry to Stone Aerie Castle without him having to lie and triggering the spell, but Dillweed stepped up to the faery on sentry duty and took command of the situation.

"Dillweed and Torby Pondbottom reporting as requested by our Lord and Liege, Orrin. We are two of His Grace's seers."

The broad-shouldered faery placed a hand on the pommel of his sword and grunted. "Don't care *who* you are, gnome. If you're stupid enough to use His Grace's name, then it'll be *your* head when he finds you, not mine. Report to the Steward. He'll decide whether it'll be bedding or a beheading you get."

Dillweed looked the armed and armoured sentry directly in the eyes and very calmly countered with "It won't be *my* head rolling into the basket at the end of the day, though I'm not sure a certain insolent sentry should feel so secure. As we are here for the first time on His Grace's *personal* business, we require an escort to the Steward. Make this happen."

The sentry was obviously accustomed to being able to bully anyone who arrived at Commoners' Gate, so a soft, round, gnome lad who pushed back was probably quite unexpected. He looked to be considering his response very carefully when Dillweed made it for him.

"Grandfather, we may be late meeting His Grace, but we'll still do better without this hat-less dunce slowing us down." He picked up both of their satchels and walked through into the courtyard as if he himself was lord of the manor. Torby was as surprised as the sentry, but he followed along, trying to hide his smile.

"No!" The sentry launched up and landed directly in Dillweed's path, but a respectable two paces away. His sword was still sheathed and both hands were palm up, to dissolve any perceived threat. "Please, sirs. I will escort you myself—directly to the Steward. I beg a blink's delay while I order coverage for the gate." He waited, nervous. They all knew Orrin was quite capable of executing a member of his household for a seemingly innocuous offense.

"I'll grant you *two* blinks, but as we're slow walkers, we will start across this vast courtyard ahead of you. Surely your wings will easily catch you up before we reach that portal across the way."

"Yes, sir. Thank you sir." The sentry launched up and flew off, calling to someone named 'Liam' to report immediately. Dillweed continued on and Torby caught up quickly.

"*That*, lad, was *most* impressive. Where in Faerie did you find that voice?"

"I've been bullied my entire life, Grandfather, First by my own sisters and mother, and then by any Faerie resident who thought they could get away with it."

"I'm sorry. I should have noticed."

"*No one* did. I may not wear a red cap, yet, but that truth-or-pain spell was the last straw. We are good people. You did the honourable thing sending word to His Grace about your casting, but we've been bullied and shat on by the very ones we wish to help."

"Truth."

"So, if we're going to continue to be good people, we're going to do it with our heads held high and our backs unbowed."

The sentry abruptly landed on the cobblestones in front to them. He furled his oak-leaf wings and bowed. "Gentle sirs, please follow me to the Steward. Stone Aerie is a maze, but I have confirmed Master Gilroy is inspecting the cellars and so will take you directly to him without further delay." He bowed again and led the way — on foot.

Torby looked over at Dillweed and caught his grandson smiling. The old gnome smiled back. They might meet their doom here, but it was going to be worthy of song.

Twilly forgot Rock-Eye was a great-grandfather until he eventually led them into another cool, dark cave and dropped down across one end, curling up in the sand. "Not young, anymore. Sun is up, so *must* sleep. Not *wanting* sleep, *needing* sleep. Sunshine is two left turns and a right turn, *that* way." He pointed east. "Go see sun, feel warmth, find you food."

The thought of feeling the sun on her face thrilled Twilly, but she as worried about her friend. "Are you sure? Can I bring you anything to eat?"

Rock-Eye chuckled. "Kind offer, but this troll has big appetite and lass has little hands. Will hunt after sleep."

"But no elk."

"No elk. Big promise."

"Good. Get some sleep, then we'll go storm Orrin's castle and save Winsome."

"And maybe eat Orrin."

It was Twilly's turn to chuckle and the two dwarfs joined her. "Yes, maybe."

"How far are we from the Source Grove, then?" Nyla asked.

Trinnean thought about it for a moment. "You should be there by high sun."

"Is it easy to find?" She withdrew her blade and checked it's edge, more for something to keep her hands busy than because it could have gone dull.

"Not so difficult."

Browncap hopped over. "I will take you."

"Thank you!"

"Well, Browncap knows the way, but just stay over this path until it crosses the river at the Silver Bridge, then follow the right-hand path to the mountains. It leads straight into the Grove."

"Over the river at the Silver Bridge and then right?"

"Definitely *right*. The Forest to the left looks friendlier, but it leads to the Troll Hills. As a matter of fact, if you were on foot, you could only cross the bridge in bright daylight, staying in the middle, moving quick and quiet, and ignoring *any* voices you hear as you crossed. The Safe Passage Enchantment is worn thin and the younger trolls like to challenge each other to hide beneath the bridge for as long as they can. Not all trolls are idiots, but the ones who take up the Silver Bridge Challenge are a special kind of stupid, which makes them a special kind of *dangerous,* especially if they catch sight of the wings.

Nyla looked to Fiona, who nodded confidently. "Go, Ny. Make the appeal while we find the others and bring them home." Fiona turned to Trinnean. "Our Sisters are in a landscaped forest away from most of the lights, across an iron bridge with a beautiful, ancient yew on sentinel."

"An *ancient* yew? I've only seen one in all my trips there. It isn't far from, well, from where we emerge. Sally will know for certain."

"Sally?" Fiona's smile stumbled, and Nyla knew then her Sister was smitten.

"The human lass I trade with."

"Ah."

"*What?* She's ten times my size! She's just a friend!"

Fiona darted in and kissed him playfully on the tip of his nose. "Then I should clean up before we go meet your giant friend."

"Oh, that won't be a problem. You'll be clean by the time we arrive."

"How is that possible?"

"Trust me. I hope you can swim."

"Swim? I'm a faery! Of course I can't *swim*."

Needing to get back on track, Nyla interrupted them by hugging them each awkwardly. "How do you suggest I get aloft? I don't dare climb a tree and jump."

"Follow the trail, and in a few turns it drops down into a valley. You'll see the perfect spot when you get there."

"I'll have to take your word for it because I can't wait any longer. Take care of my Sister, Trinnean."

"Of course! We'd best hurry, too, because time passes differently between the realms."

"Then go. See you both soon." She marched off down the trail, trying to keep her balance with the odd wings. Thankfully they weren't as heavy as they looked, but they weren't the membrane-thin beauties she was born with, either.

Browncap hopped along beside her. "I'm starting to hear rumours on the wind about six dewinged faeries and five banished clans, Nyla. Anyone you know?"

Nyla laughed weakly. "My full name is Nyla Rainsong, of the banished Clan Rainsong. If you help or harbour me in any way, you could suffer banishment, too."

"My best friend is an ostracized, wingless faery who drinks too much butter-juice and makes unauthorized trips to the human realm to bring deadly iron back to Faerie—I think we can make this journey together without me getting into too much trouble."

"He *drinks*?" That was something she hadn't guessed.

"Only because he's alone. I would, too, if I only had *me* to talk to."

Kara and Rainn dragged the unconscious and bleeding Brigid under an exposed root of the yew, while Grace placed herself between the faeries and their attackers. Twitch didn't wait for a second attack and instead bounded straight at the closest human.

The man raised his arm to throw another stone, but Twitch was faster and with a perfectly timed leap and twist, hit him in the centre of his chest with her powerful back feet, knocking him over backwards and into the path of his lumbering cohort. She jumped clear just as the two became a cursing jumble of arms and legs.

Before they could untangle themselves, she dove back in, biting and kicking, doing as much damage as she could with tooth and claw. The humans yelped and screamed and each begged the other to get the evil beast off, but she struck quickly and precisely, drawing blood and making pain with each attack. Eventually they both got to their feet and one of them reached for a stone. Twitch made a blink-fast decision and, risking a kick from his heavy boots, she charged again. She dodged a clumsy, swinging foot and crashed sideways with all her weight into his knee. He went down with a scream.

"Donal! Kill it! Kill it!"

Twitch jumped clear of the downed man and pivoted around to face his partner. Exhausted, her legs were weak and sore, but fear of what these two would do to her older sister and the three faeries drove her on. She could see now the second man wasn't going to be as easy to knock down. Even in the wan moonlight, she could see the thick branch he raised like a club as he advanced on her. She backed up, not taking her eyes off the deadly tree limb, while drawing him further from the others.

"Kill it, Donal! It's a faery pooka!"

"Shaddup! It's only a bloody rabbit."

A tiny flash of silver caught the moonlight near the attacker's neck and Twitch thought it was an errant firefly. Then the man slapped at his neck like he'd been stung and she knew it was no firefly. There was a second flash and this time she saw the needle-small arrow jut out of his cheek a moment before he slapped at it and drove it deeper.

"Youch! Bloody hell!" He dropped the branch and grabbed at the tiny arrow, trying to pluck it out. With one final burst of anger and fear, Twitch took advantage of the moment and charged. She tucked her long ears back, leaped, and hit him just where his legs met. He went down with a groan, but she didn't stop to admire her handiwork. With nary a glance back, the doe bolted for where she saw Grace and two of the faery lasses slip into the shrubs. The remaining lass—the one she guessed was the youngest—stood to one side with the bow in hand and an arrow nocked, covering their retreat.

"I was aiming for his backside," she explained with a shrug as she followed Twitch into the thick flowering Fuchsia.

Chapter Twenty-Three

Something in the forest around them had changed for the worse since they'd returned to Faerie, but Nyla didn't know if it was because they'd killed the not-banished-like-them goblin, or simply because they dared to return at all. As she jogged along, she found herself dodging more lashing branches, and sidestepping and dodging more dropped pinecones, acorns, and generally anything the trees could release as she and Browncap passed beneath.

Trinnean was true to his word. After a handful of turns, they stepped out onto a ridge overlooking a gentle valley. It wasn't particularly deep or wide, but she sensed a warm current of air rising from below, and that would make all the difference in the world. She munched on biscuits while she paced the ridge, getting a feel for the Forest below. She offered Browncap a piece of her mother's honey-nut-special biscuit and the sparrow gobbled it up.

"Wonderful! Dry, but flavourful."

"I'm sorry I don't have any nectar to wash it down."

"There's a beautiful spring in the Source Grove, should we survive your appeal."

"*What?*"

"You're making an appeal to the Elder Alder. Should you lose your appeal, you will be a banished faery standing in the Source Grove itself. Beings have been executed for less."

"If I *lose* the appeal, I'm dead anyway without a tree, so it won't matter if I die right then and there. But maybe you shouldn't come all the way, on the off chance mercy is swift and deadly."

"We can decide when we arrive, but to do that we must first take flight. Are you ready?"

"I think so."

"Nervous?"

"Excited. When that witch stole my wings I never thought I would ever fly again, and that's something I've been trying to come to terms with. If this works, and I live to see Trinnean again, I'm going to beg him to make me a pair."

"So let's fly. He explained how everything works, but he forgot to tell you how he gets airborne. Back up down the trail, then run fast, and launch out into the air."

"Just like I've done countless times before."

"Exactly."

Nyla took a final look at the point of the ridge where it dropped off fastest but had the cleanest path leading up to it, then she walked back up the trail until it curved sharply. Turning to face the valley, she flexed her wing stumps, and the wonderful new wings unfurled with soft metallic scrapes and clicks. She reached up and took hold of the handgrips, and by combining arm-power and wing-power, flapped them easily. She was as ready as she as ever going to be and had wasted enough time piddling about when lives were at stake. She was a faery and flying was second nature to her. *She could do this.*

She tucked the wings back and took off running. She ran like an entire hoard of goblins chased her heels. She ran like her life depended on it, which in fact, it did. She focused on the ground in front of her, fearful of tripping and going down in a jumble of metal and faery, ruining everything, but at the edge of the bluff she snapped open the wings, then she was airborne, up and soaring with ease.

She couldn't hover, and manoeuvring was clunky and slow, but she was flying again and *it was wonderful!* She did a quick barrel roll and came back to position easily. Browncap dropped down to fly formation with her.

"I wish Trinnean could see how it should be done. He tries hard, but he needs lessons from a faery."

"Then we'll take care of that when we're all finished this burring quest." She looked down and adjusted her course back over the trail. "How far do we have to go?"

"You see the three almost identical mountains? The Three Sisters?"

"Yes."

"And the foothills directly in front of them?"

"Yes."

"And the single rowan this side of the foothills, standing taller than anything around it?"

"Um…*yes!* I see it."

"*That* is the Source Grove. We will still be there by high sun, though we must get closer to the treetops, Nyla."

"But the sun is out, it's a beautiful day, and we can see *forever*."

"*That* is the problem." He nodded back over his shoulder. "The sun is reflecting off your brass wings and the two Elf Sky Patrol ships behind us will wonder what you are and follow us for a closer look."

"Burr! Down we go, then." She glided down, closer to the treetops. She dipped a bit too close to a tall poplar and got an aggressive branch-flick in her knee before she could pull up. It was fabulous to be flying again, but it was harder than she first expected it to be. Her arms weren't at all used to the exertion her wing muscles took for granted, but she had a long flight ahead so she'd have to fly smarter, glide rather than flap, and catch rising thermals when she dared.

A glance back at the two elf-piloted, dwarf-designed airships showed they were still flying south, perpendicular to her own path, so they hadn't caught sight of the two of them, yet.

Brigid wasn't unconscious for long, but when she awoke she had a whopper of a bruise starting to darken the entire right side of her face. Kara knew that was the least of their problems, though. "Your flute is broken, Brig, so we're not going home unless you know another way to open a gate and a passage."

"I don't. What happened?" She felt her face, wincing as soon as her fingertips brushed the swelling.

"You caught a pebble in the side of your head."

"And *that* broke my flute?"

"Not quite. It knocked the flute out of your hand but you fell on top of it and bent it. I'm sure there's someone back home who can fix it, but we're not home."

Rainn nodded. "And we still have those insane humans to deal with. Twitch slowed them down, but I'm sure they'll be back after us if we don't get somewhere safe. I wish we actually had gold to give them, to distract them.

Lord Orrin's stuffed-shirt steward, Gilroy, recognized Grandfather Torby and Dillweed immediately and waved off their escort without so much as a word of thanks. Dillweed guessed common courtesy wasn't required under Orrin's rule like it was under the gnome's grandmother's. He took a deep breath and stepped up, doing whatever he could to keep his grandfather from lying.

"Sire, we thought it might serve His Grace best if we were here at court to be available for his convenience."

Hovering before them, the steward looked the two simple gnomes up and down before answering. "Yes. Well done. I—" He was interrupted by a chilling, childlike scream from down the corridor and around the corner. He didn't even flinch, as if a screaming child was nothing new to him. He must be a father, Dillweed thought. The faery continued. "You will be housed with the servants. I will introduce you to—". A second scream cut him off, followed by at least a dozen screams, wails, and cries.

Dillweed started to ask if the steward needed to attend to what sounded like a nursery, but his grandfather poked him in the ribs with his finger, out of sight of their liege's major-domo. Dillweed got the hint and swallowed his words. The steward didn't seem to notice or care. The noises continued, so he raised his voice.

"I will introduce you to the cooks so you may eat whenever you wish. It would be best if you didn't stray too far from your quarters, and you are absolutely forbidden to speak with any members of court you may see. That said, should you be *forced* to explain your presence, simply state that you're cobblers."

Grandfather shook his head. "That would be a lie, sir, and we all know I can't lie without triggering a certain spell."

"Then pretend you're a burring mute and let your grandson do the lying. As I was saying, don't stray too far from your quarters so His Grace may find you when *he* wishes." He led Torby away from the nursery, or whatever it was, and Dillweed wisely followed.

They were escorted up a narrow, well-worn, spiral, stone stairway and as they went higher and higher, Dillweed could hear more and more of a busy kitchen that sounded much like their own when his mother and sisters were preparing a large feast. Not long after the sounds caught his ears, the scents of fruit and honey and baking captured his nose and reminded him just how long it had been since he'd had a proper meal.

They reached a landing and the steward led them into the biggest, busiest, gnome-filled kitchen Dillweed had ever seen. There were so many red hats and beards and aprons darting back and forth that he was overwhelmed. The steward shouted something over the cacophony and a heavy-set, gold-hatted gnome separated herself from the mass and waddled over. She looked to be nearly as old as his grandmother, but the twinkle in her eyes and the blush on her cheeks belied her age.

"Kitchen Mistress Marfa, Torby and Dillweed Pondbottom here will be joining the household for a short time, at His Grace's will."

"Yes sir, Master Gilroy. I'll get them set up with—will one chamber be sufficient?"

Dillweed didn't want to be separated from his grandfather. "Yes please. I have my bedroll, so I don't even need a bed."

Mistress Marfa laughed. "That's silly. You'll sleep on a comfortable bed because it would not do to have you ill-rested and cranky when His Grace calls upon you." She turned to the steward. "I will take care of it, sir. They'll be on level two, next to the pantry."

"Perfect." He flew back into the stairwell and was gone in a blink.

Mistress Marfa looked around her kitchen, presumably saw all it would continue to run quite well without her, and motioned for the two of them to follow her. "This way, gentlemen. I'll take you myself. This old gnome needs some cool fresh air." She led them around the outskirts of the kitchen, and every gnome they passed nodded respectfully to her and finger-waved at the two new arrivals.

"This looks like a happy place to work, Mistress."

"It is, for the most part. We gnomes keep to ourselves. It's safer that way, by far. The gnomes who tend the one small garden come by to visit occasionally, but to get here they have to pass two sentries, and even the lower-caste faeries like to toss insults and ridicule." They left the kitchen and entered another stairwell, which only led down. "We're able to keep happy here because we live, work and play far from faery eyes and His Grace's spies. Well, most of them. There are one or two of my team who would sell their own mothers for a chance to be treated as something other than a slave." She stopped suddenly. "My apologies, gentlemen. I didn't mean to speak ill of His Grace's hospitality. We're all lucky to have jobs here." She looked worried she'd just stuck her boot in her mouth with two of Orrin's new favourites.

Grandfather Torby placed his hand on the Mistress' forearm and squeezed. "Lord Orrin is *our* liege, too. We understand completely and nothing you've said will be repeated by either of us."

Mistress Marfa seemed to relax then. She even favoured Torby with a smile. "Let's get you two settled in, then." She led them on and soon stopped in front of a simple green door with a worn wooden knob in the middle. She pushed it open and revealed a spacious chamber with two beds and a thin slot for a window. Dillweed suspected he could shoot an arrow out it, but could never get his thick hand through it.

Torby smiled to the Mistress. "It's perfectly sufficient. We shall remain here in comfort, awaiting His Grace's will."

She returned the smile. "Except to eat. Feel free to wander up to my kitchen any time your belly rumbles. His Grace can't get here without passing through there, so you won't be caught away and incur his displeasure. Drop by, any time." Dillweed realized the two oldsters were flirting. His grandfather was *flirting*! He had to stop it before…well, before *anything*.

"Thank you, Mistress," he interrupted. "We've had a long journey, so we'd best grab a nap before we eat." He shook her hand respectfully, and then tugged his grandfather into the chamber before gently closing the door behind them.

"Grandfather, that was…unsettling. You were flirting!"

"Yes I was, youngster. We're unwanted guests in a strange house bringing with us what will likely be more bad news. We need all the friends we can get here, because a time will come when they are all that keeps us alive."

"Did you see that in the sprite bones?"

"No, I *feel* it in *my* bones." He plunked himself down on the bed. "These are dark times and we two are stuck in the middle."

Dillweed sat on the other bed and let out a gasp when he sank down into it. It was wondrously soft. "Speaking of dark times, Grandfather, why would they have a nursery in the cellars?"

"I wondered that myself, lad. Those babies didn't sound any too happy either."

"Truly an odd thing in an odd place."

"That it is." He slipped off his boots, removed his hat, hung it on the corner of the bed, and lay back. "But it is time for a nap, not for odd wonderings." He closed his eyes and within a handful of blinks he was snoring. Dillweed had always been in awe of the old gnome's ability to sleep in a snap, but this time he was so tired himself, he barely got his own boots off and hat hung up before his eyes were closing and his head nodding.

"Quick! Down into the Forest! Hide!" Browncap darted past Nyla down through a gap in the treetops, and vanished. The old, silly Nyla might have wondered what all of the fuss was about and wasted time looking around for the cause of the sparrow's concern. That was the *old* Nyla, the one who fancied herself a rebel because she walked everywhere and dressed in black; not the one who watched her twin brother be murdered and then herself was dewinged, banished, chased by hounds and humans, and fought and killed a goblin. *This* Nyla tucked in her borrowed metal wings and dropped down beneath the canopy in a blink, without question or doubt.

Chapter Twenty-Four

Just before she collided with the narrow path, Nyla snapped the wings open and, with the added strength of her arms on the handles, executed a tight fast glide with a sudden scoop up and reverse back, resulting in a nearly perfect standing landing. That was the easy part, she feared. Now that she was back amongst them, every tree and shrub leaned toward her, reaching, yearning to punish the crippled outcast.

"Over here!"

She spun about, seeking Browncap, and finally spied him poking his head out of a hollow log just off the trail. She sprinted over, retracting the wings as she went. When she arrived, Browncap hopped out and let her pass, into the log.

"Quick! Into the back! Sky Patrol!"

"Elf ships? How in Faerie did they sneak up on us?" She pulled the wings in as tight as she could and worked her way as far back in the rotten log as she could get.

"They flew high, hiding in the sun. It's a trick hawks use every day, and now I suppose elves in airships on Her Grace's missions do as well."

"Will hiding do us any good? Won't they just use magic to find us?"

"They have to know what or who they're looking for, so unless they know it is you and those are metal wings, they will sweep the area with their eyes and ears only. At least, I *think* that's what will happen. I've learned a lot from Trinn, but not having any magic of my own, it's all just guesswork."

"Well, *I* have magic, and your guesses sound pretty good. I just hope they don't dawdle but do a quick sweep and leave. We can't afford much of a delay."

"I'll go take a look. You stay here, where it's safe, for a few blinks, anyway. That elm above us looked like it wants to crush this log with you in it, and probably will as soon as she can free a root big enough. I'll be quick."

"Excellent idea."

Browncap flew off, and although Nyla suspected the Sky Patrols weren't looking for a sparrow, she worried about her friend's safety. She didn't want anyone else getting hurt because of her. She thought she heard the sound of soil being overturned and the creak of wood moving, so she soft-stepped to the mouth of the log and peeked out. Sure enough, the elm was tearing one of its own roots up from the ground. The root, probably stiff from age, trembled and shuffled along unwillingly rather than reaching over and simply crushing Nyla's hiding place. Nyla looked skyward, but saw neither Browncap nor any sign of elf ships, so she darted out onto the trail, out of reach of the elm.

Something flashed by her ear, nearly taking her head off, and she saw a sharp, green pinecone bounce down the trail. Burr! She couldn't wait for the sparrow. If she stayed there, it wouldn't matter if the Sky Patrol caught her or not because she would already be dead. She ran. Another pinecone flashed past her, but nowhere as close as the first one was. The yew shrubs ahead of her started to crowd the trail. She was going to get blocked in and then the pinecones and acorns and whatever else would come faster and harder. She had to get airborne, but there was no bluff to launch herself off. She couldn't even climb a tree and jump, because every tree was an enemy. She opened the wings fully, grabbed hold of the handles, and then...then she remembered the springs! She hadn't needed them, yet, but they were wound tight and ready to go, she hoped.

The hedge closed up fast, so she did the unexpected and turned back. There was more open trail back where she'd just come from and she needed all she could get. She tucked her chin down tight, clenched her teeth, and ran as fast as her legs would go. She flapped the wings as hard as she could, but she got no lift whatsoever. Another pinecone skipped off the trail and she leaped over it just as she released the springs. The brass and iron wings flapped at a speed she could never achieve with muscle alone and she was up...then she was down, her feet still running. She kept her hands clear of the flashing metal but her wing stumps were able to keep up. This was what they were for! She adjusted her leading edge and suddenly she was up and flying. She swerved around and flew straight down the trail, right over the reaching hedge. She didn't look for Browncap, she didn't glance back for the Sky Patrol, she just flew as fast as she could.

Branches flapped at her half-heartedly and birds chirped at her as she passed, but she suspected the sight of the flashing, deadly metal wings was enough to keep them from doing anything more than make noise and token efforts to stop her. By the time the spring ran down, she flew unassisted.

Sleep didn't visit Dillweed for very long. He felt like he'd been down for only a few turns when the thoughts tumbling around in his head dragged him from the mossy-soft bed, past his snoring-like-a-rock-giant grandfather, out into the corridor, and up the two sets of steps to the kitchen. It wasn't so much that he was hungry—he was *always* hungry—it was a matter of worry. Ever since he heard the cries of the babies in the castle's cellars, he couldn't stop thinking about the one-eyed troll searching for his little great-granddaughter.

Lord Orrin had told Stone-Eye or One-Eye or… *Rock-Eye*! That was it! Orrin told Rock-Eye that many babies were missing from different tribes, and Lady Orlaith was responsible. But what *if*, Dillweed asked himself, what *if* Orrin himself was the culprit? What *if* their liege had some twisted reason for having a rogue troll smashing around his sister's duchy? Dillweed knew first hand how cruel Orrin could be, so what was stopping the fancy-winged faery from stealing babies? And if he was willing to torture a dumb gnome lad with a truth-or-pain spell just to get some burring bone-casting, what was going to stop the faery lord stump from *killing* the babies when he'd achieved whatever goal he had?

Again he heard the kitchen long before he reached the top of the steps. He rounded the corner and almost bumped into Marfa, who was squeezing decorative icing on to a cake using a canvas bag with a hole on one end. When she saw him, she put the icing tube down and folded her arms across her generous chest.

"I thought it might be you wandering up this way. Somehow I suspected your appetite would get the better of you." She unfolded her arms and flashed her fingers at him. *Something is on your mind, youngster, and I think I know what it might be.* She kept her body between her hands and most of her staff, who jogged around the kitchen on one task or another.

"I'd love a mushroom salad if you have any, Mistress." *The babies. I think Lord Orrin has stolen them.* He watched around them, trying to see if anyone in particular was watching him with more than a passing interest.

Stolen? "One mushroom salad with a cucumber dressing, coming up. The honey beer is in the jug behind you, next to the mugs. Why not pour us both a swallow?" *How can you be sure?*

He uncorked the jug and filled two mugs. He handed Marfa one, sipped from his own, and then set it down, to free both hands. *We met a troll—well, 'met' is the wrong word. Lord Orrin threatened to feed our fingers and toes to the old troll if we disobeyed His Grace. The troll went to Orrin for help in finding his missing great-granddaughter, and Orrin told him Orlaith had taken her, along with others.*

Marfa set about making a huge salad with one hand while easily signing with the other. *Nonsense. Orlaith's not a fool and would never risk the wrath of King Oberon by stealing babies from another duchy. Her brother's no fool, either, but he thinks all of the non-flying races are stupid. I agree with you. Those babies have been taken from their families and are not the orphans we were told they are.*

Dillweed took another sip. The brew was delicious. *This is all guessing. I need to speak with the gnomes caring for them. If the little ones are truly orphans, then we'll do what we came to do and return home when it's all done. But if they've been stolen, then… then I have no idea. Two days ago I was a cowardly idiot younger brother. I'm not going to turn into a hero knight overnight.*

Heroes aren't made, Dillweed, they're born. And I do not see any sign of idiot or coward in you. If you're going to be a hero, you won't be alone. We gnomes have a network of friends that help us pass in and out of the castle. When staff here get injured, they used to have fatal accidents soon after. Now if someone is hurt or sick, we sneak them out and replace them before the steward notices. He's just like Orrin in that he believes if we don't have wings, we're nothing more than beasts. I'm probably the only one he can identify by sight. "Here. Enjoy." She placed the mammoth bowl in front of Dillweed.

He couldn't help but drool. He had never seen so many different types of mushrooms in all his life. And the cucumber dressing smelled splendiferous. "Thank you, Mistress. This looks wonderful." He dug in, thoughts of the stolen babies put aside for a few blinks.

"You're welcome." She drained her beer and walked the mug over to the wash area. "While you're eating, I'd best finish with this cake." *Then we'll go down and check on the babies. There's nothing we can do for them today, but we can start preparations to make everything ready when the moment is upon us.* "Don't bother saving any for your grandfather. I'll make him one of his own." With that, she left Dillweed alone with his feast and turned her attention back to decorating the cake.

The Forest was slow to react to her fleeting presence, so Nyla flew quickly down the trail mostly unmolested. She would rather have been *above* the trees, where it was safer and flying with the awkward wings was easier, but the threat of an attack by a sky patrol frightened her more than a pinecone in the head did. When they'd ducked down out of sight of the Sky Patrol, she saw they were almost at the Source Grove. Somewhere just ahead was the river and Silver Bridge, which also meant there were trolls, and probably enough open space for her to easily be spotted from the air.

She was so close to the end of the journey, but she could only think of her Sisters and the danger she'd left them all in. She wouldn't trade places with any of them right now, because she wasn't sure hers wasn't the worst of the three situations, but she did wish that she could do it all herself, and keep them all safe. She'd lost Cray, and couldn't bear it if she lost anyone else. This was *her* responsibility and hers alone. She flew on.

Marfa motioned to Dillweed to follow her and silently led him down the steps, shuffling and hopping her way down, past the level where Torby slept, and down all the way to the cellars. Before she stepped out into the corridor, she listened. Dillweed could hear a few cries and a muffled conversation, but nothing in the vicinity of the steps. The Mistress of the Kitchens moved quickly and quietly down the corridor and around a corner, stopping at an unassuming door with a thick wooden bar across it. She lifted the bar and silently leaned it against the wall, then, using both fists, she knocked a complicated pattern and stepped back. They waited. The conversation in the room stopped suddenly but a high-pitched baby started crying again.

After a moment there was a return knock pattern, though it was shorter and softer. The door swung inward. Marfa led the way, Dillweed close on her heels. The smell was horrendous. He was nearly knocked over by the thick, stable-like stench that assaulted his senses when he stepped inside. Two pale, exhausted gnome ladies his mother's age nodded wordlessly at Dillweed. He nodded back, afraid to open his mouth to breathe, let alone greet them.

"Dillweed, this is Peony and Lily, my nieces. Lasses, Dillweed here thinks your charges here may not be orphans at all, but have been stolen by His Grace for political purposes."

Peony scratched her head and though about it. "They're babies. No way to tell, one way or another, because they only know a few words." She closed a small door and threw a bar across it. "Sorry for the smell. We were just changing the bedding. The whole place will stink for a few turns until we can wash it all."

Dillweed took a slow breath though his nose, doing his best not to gag. The smell lessened after a few blinks. "There may be a way to find out, about the babies. Do you have a troll baby here?"

"We have three. All lasses." Lily shuffled over to a doorway off the main chamber.

"You don't know their names, do you?"

"No. They're too young to talk, and even if they did, our trollish is a bit decayed."

"But *I* know one of their names. We crossed paths with an old one-eyed troll looking for his great-granddaughter. These lasses may not be able to tell you their names, but I'd wager they *know* their own names. If she answers to it, we can be pretty sure she's the stolen baby, and that means all of the others must be as well."

Peony shrugged. "It can't hurt to try. I've always wondered why orphans were being kept locked away from potential parents." She walked them down to a thick door at the end of the main room.

"How many are here?"

"An even dozen."

"A *dozen* babies?" Dillweed was stunned. "Other than trolls…"

"Dwarves, gnomes, and brownies." She unbarred the door. The chamber within was dark. "The lasses sleep mostly during the day."

Dillweed shook his head in disgust and followed her in. He wasn't sure what he expected, but the smell in the smaller chamber was much more pleasant than the outer one. The sounds of three different tones of snoring greeted them. Lily brought in a charmed lantern and lit the room up just a bit, while Peony went to each of the big cradles and roused the three babies. One by one she awkwardly placed the big sleepy lasses on a heavy canvas in the middle of the floor. All three looked up, blinking themselves awake, but none of them made a peep.

"They were fed just before bed, so they'll be quiet a bit longer. Once they get hungry, they make it known quite loudly.

They're very sweet, though, and love to cuddle. Go ahead." Peony motioned Dillweed to the floor.

Two of the babies were almost as big as he, but the third was twice his size. He sat down on the canvas, leaving some distance between himself and them. They could probably crush him without much effort. "Hello, wee ones." The three just looked at him, still blinking awake. He stuck his tongue out at them and blew a dwarf raspberry. Two of them giggled, but the biggest lass just smiled. He stuck his fingers in his ears and wiggled them at her, then blew another raspberry, but still was only rewarded with a smile.

The other three gnomes waited patiently behind him. "Hello Tiddleywink." No reply from any of them other than smiles. Then one of them farted and everyone in the chamber giggled. "Hello Stinkybutt." Just blank stares and smiles. "Hello Winsome." The biggest troll stopped picking her nose and looked closely at him. "That's you, isn't it? Hi Winsome. Wanna come give me a hug?"

She moved from a sitting position to a crawling one, though didn't get any closer. But she listened to every word.

"Hello beautiful Winsome." Winsome giggled. "I'm a friend of your great-grampa, Rock-Eye." That's all it took. She crawled across the space and climbed onto Dillweed's lap, nearly crushing him. "Hello, Beautiful. I don't know how we're going to do it, but we're going to get you home. I promise." He shifted his position a bit so she wasn't crushing as much of him, and she cuddled in close, not letting him go. He stroked her wiry hair and hummed softly to her the song his own grandmother calmed him with, once upon a time. He heard a sniffle behind him and looked back over his shoulder to see Marfa, tears tracking down the baking flour on her cheeks.

"What in the name of His Grace is going on here?! Why is this door open?!" The high voice bellowed from the main chamber and all three troll babies scurried behind their cradles, obviously terrified. Dillweed jumped up. So much for being a hero, he thought—they were already caught. The three gnome ladies gasped and rushed out into the main chamber.

"Master Gilroy, sir, we were just airing the place out."

"You lie. And why is the troll cave open? The little beasts should be sleeping."

The sweet scent of baby still on his clothes, Dillweed charged straight out of the dark chamber as fast as he had ever run, and grabbed the hovering royal steward by the neck. His hands weren't big, but Dillweed could easily hold a faery by the neck with one hand. The steward reached for the blade on his belt, but Dillweed slapped his hand away, then plucked the sword from its scabbard and tossed it out of reach. "Try that again, Master Gilroy, and His Grace will be needing a new steward." The young gnome smiled. He sounded so much braver than he felt. He'd just signed his own execution papers by even *touching* Gilroy, but he had no idea what do with him. He couldn't very well kill him, because then Lord Orrin would execute everyone in the Pondbottom family. He also couldn't let him go, because the babies needed saving.

"In here." Peony stood by the stinky chamber, holding the door open. "He won't get out of here until we let him out."

Gilroy struggled to twist around and see what she was talking about, but Dillweed tightened his grip and pulled the faery around to look him in the eye. "Sir, I don't want to hurt you, but His Grace has been stealing babies, and that's just wrong, and seeing as how you're his steward, you're probably the one passing the orders on and know more about what's happening here than anyone else. For that alone, I should just kill you and dump you down a drain." Gilroy's eyes went wide. "Or I could take you to Rock-Eye and let him pluck your legs off like a goblin lad would to a spider, but I'm not going to stoop to your level. The bones have been cast and His Grace is finished. Somehow, somewhen, he will vanish from Faerie. Unless you want to go before him…"

The steward spat in Dillweed's face, and the ages of being bullied by anyone and everyone boiled up inside the young gnome until it was ready to burst out. He drew back his free fist and slammed it fast and hard at the steward's face. But he stopped his fist just before it made contact, then unclenched it, walked over to where Peony was holding the door open, and tossed Gilroy on top of the rancid, baby-mess-covered bedding. He slammed the door and threw the bar across it.

"I sure hope you're right about him not being able to get out of there, at least for a day."

Peony and Lily both hugged him. Marfa kissed him on the cheek. "Why didn't you kill him? It's only what he deserves."

"That's not my place. If we were both armed and it were a fair fight, then I would do what had to be done. Of course, I've never even lifted a sword, so I probably wouldn't stand a chance in a fair fight. But, most of all, no matter what he has done, I couldn't kill an unarmed faery and ever look my grandfather in the eyes again. He would be ashamed of me and he would be right."

"I have never been ashamed of you, son." Grandfather Torby stood in the doorway leading to the corridor. "And right at this moment, I have never been prouder." He nodded to Marfa. "It looks like my grandson here has been stirring up a nest of harpies. Do you have a plan?"

She nodded, slowly. "It's a loose one, but we do. We were expecting to have more time to put it into place, though. As I told our young hero, we have a gnome network that can help. We need to wait until nightfall, though, because we need the cover of dark. We also can't travel with troll babies in sunlight."

"The steward will be missed sooner rather than later, but maybe if we make everything look normal, we can stall until nightfall while everything is put in place. You'd best return to the kitchens and these lovely ladies should probably get the babies ready to travel—how many do you have?"

"A dozen."

"Well then, I hope you have quite a few bodies to help, and a way out of the castle without getting caught."

"We do. I'll send word as soon as I return to work, and it will all be ready. I'll also get word out through the non-magical creatures that these babies have been found and they can meet us in a certain easily defended grove. Believe it or not, getting them all out of the castle will be simple-ish." She rubbed her knuckles on Dillweed's head, like most older gnomes do to their children. "You two need to return to your rooms and be ready for when His Grace summons you. Gilroy is Orrin's major domo, but he's not the only one on his staff. Don't unpack your belongings, and I will send someone for you after dark."

"Of course. In the meantime, could this old gnome get a bite to eat, and maybe a pint of something to wash it down?"

They all laughed, then Peony and Lily went about their tasks, while Marfa led the Pondbottoms back upstairs.

Hops-With-Grace and Twitch led the three Sisters to an old tree that had good ground-level access and then an easy climb up inside the rotted trunk.

Kara hugged Grace. "This is wonderful. Thank you. But what happens when my sister comes looking for us?"

Brigid sighed. "That'll be next to impossible. There's no way for them to open a gate themselves and they don't know anyone who can. *I* do, but I'm in the wrong realm. We're just going to have to figure it out ourselves. I've heard that in this human realm a faery ring can open a gate between the realms."

"*A faery ring?*" Rainn looked doubtful. "With buttercups and mushrooms and silly dancing?"

"No sillier than what *we* do when we're bored. Besides, I've just heard the tales; I wouldn't even know where to begin, except maybe to find a nice quiet glade in the moonlight."

"And as soon as we start dancing and singing, Dumb-Donal will show up and stone us to death for our imaginary pot of gold."

"I know." Rainn had a good point. Brigid sat down heavily on the dead tree's root. She pulled her flute out of her satchel and examined it closely. Seeing the damage nearly broke her heart. "This will take some serious talent to fix. It was a gift from my grandfather, so I don't even want to try straightening it out myself." She held it to her lips and tried a note. It blew flat and sour. "If I try to open a gate with notes like that we'll end up in the fiery realm of Djinns, or worse."

"What's worse than fire?" Kara asked.

"I don't know; I'm just saying." She was frustrated and angry and more than a little bit scared. She suspected they were trapped here forever. Only Nyla and Fiona knew where they were, and *they* were on a quest that would likely end in their deaths, which meant no one at all would know where they were. "Burr my life. *Our* lives."

Kara and Rainn hugged her, and the hares snuggled in, too. It was going to be a long night.

Chapter Twenty-Five

The knock on the massive maple door was light and tentative, but Orrin had no time for fear and trepidation. He'd just started reviewing long-term plans with his senior-most general, Filkster, and Gilroy was uncharacteristically late in joining them. The knock came again and he'd had enough. "WHAT?! Who has the death wish this morning?!"

The door pushed open and a young faery lad in House livery fluttered in. His bare head was bowed and he stayed just above the floor, which was the proper entry. Orrin held off beheading him, for a few blinks.

"Speak."

"Pardon Your Grace, I usually deliver spy reports to Master Gilroy, but he's nowhere to be found."

"Keep looking and don't bother me again. If you're to report to Gilroy, then you report to *Gilroy.*"

"Yes, m'lord." The lad remained where he was, though. He trembled, but he didn't depart, even though it was obvious he'd been dismissed.

Orrin took a deep breath. He was furious, but he wasn't an idiot. If this lad was willing to face Orrin's fury, then he probably needed to be heard sooner, rather than later. "Deliver you report. What's the word from our spies?"

"M'lord, a hummingbird just arrived from one of Lady Orlaith's Sky Patrols. Nyla Rainsong has been spotted. She is approaching the Source Grove, alone. She should arrive just past high sun."

What? Why? "The Source Grove?! She was banished by the Elder Alder herself. Entering the Grove would be suicide."

General Filkster cleared his throat and joined the conversation. "Is she a stupid lass, sire?"

"Not at all. She's truly an exceptionally bright lass."

"Then she's gone to the Grove with a purpose. If you were her, what would drive you to the Grove and almost certain death?"

"To prove her innocence?"

"Could she?"

"How should I know? I was long gone from that burring duchy before it all came to a head."

"Well, sire, from what you've told me, she either has a death wish or proof."

Orrin's heart skipped a beat. If that wingless tramp is granted an audience with the Elder, she might tell a convincing tale. She obviously broke the spells he'd cast on her, so who knew what else she was capable of. "Leave me!"

The messenger was gone in a blur, but the General hesitated. "Anything I can help with, Your Grace?"

"Not unless you can get me to the far side of my sister's duchy in a blink."

"Not quite that fast, but one of our Harpy war eagles would have you there before high sun."

That would be brilliant! "Make it so. And on your way out, tell the door guard to find Gilroy, immediately." He started to make a mental list of the few things he would need to take. His bow, his rapier, and a dirk. Food and a wine skin.

General Filkster saluted. "Immediately, m'lord. The eagle will be saddled and in the courtyard when you're ready." He left without awaiting a reply.

Orrin respected a man of action. He also respected a salute between officers more than any obsequious bowing and scraping. His dirk hung on his belt, while both his bow and rapier were in his personal armoury, next to his wardrobe chamber, on the way to the kitchens. He would wear his ox-blood hunting leathers and a long coat, for the cooler air at the elevation the eagle would fly. He hadn't been out on a war eagle in ages, so this could actually be fun. Of course, killing that tramp commoner before she reached the Grove would be the icing on the cake. He should have done that when he first met her. Should have taken her right there on the balcony and then just tossed her over the parapet. It would have eliminated oh so many headaches. Ah well, better late than never.

Fiona crouched behind the bench in the tiny garden, soaking wet and trying to quietly blow pond water out of her nose. As the chill night wrapped around her, she shivered, thankful she wore her heavy vest and not just the thin blouse beneath it. Soaking wet, it would hide few of her body's secrets from Trinnean. She grabbed her long braid and wrung it out as best she could.

When he had told her what they were about to do, she'd laughed at him, not thinking he could possibly be serious. Then he'd leaned in and kissed her on the nose and said, "I wouldn't joke about your life or your friends'." He stole her heart with the kiss on the nose, but his words still echoed in her head and warmed her more than any heat charm would. Now she waited in this Sally person's garden while Trinn did his best to convince the human lass to help.

"Are you a pixie?"

Fiona jumped up with a squeak. "*Who?*"

A human lad stepped up to the edge of the pond, holding a half-shuttered lantern in his hand. He was still in his blue striped nightclothes. "I'm Colm. You're Trinnean's friend, aren't you? Are you a pixie?"

"No, I'm a faery." She peeked out from behind the bench, wondering where Trinnean was.

"But you don't have wings, silly. Faeries have wings." He sat on the stone wall across the pond, apparently content to chat from a respectful distance.

"That's true, but someone evil took my wings."

"Is that what happened to Trinnean?"

"I don't believe so. He said he was born that way." ·

"That's too bad. I was hoping to see a flying faery. It would be beautiful."

"It is. It *was*. We just had a ball and there were so many faeries in the air at once that it made my eyes go buggy."

"Trinnean says you need our help, or at least, Sally's help."

"We do. My Sisters are stuck here and can't get home. Trinnean has a way we can get them home, but we aren't sure where they are. He *thinks* he knows, but we're hoping Sally can help us get there. Two faeries running through Glasgow shouting the names of our friends would draw a wee bit of attention."

"Aye, just a wee bit. Where do you think they are?"

"Do you know this city well?"

"Not at all. I'm only eight."

There was a scuffle by the garden door of the house and Fiona looked up. A lass stood there in trousers, a dark jacket, and scuffed, brown, knee-high boots. Trinnean was perched on her shoulder.

"Quick! Time to go!"

Colm jumped up. "I'm coming, too! I want to rescue faeries!"

Sally raised a finger to her lips. "Shut yer gob, Colm!" She whispered.

A light came on in an upstairs window, and then there was a shout in the house. "Oy! Who the hell is up at this hour?!"

"Auntie!" Young Colm rushed through the garden with the lantern jangling, and Fiona raced after him. Sally stepped fully into the garden and quietly closed the door behind her, but she was too late. Fiona could see through the full-length windows of the door, and an older woman, a full head shorter than Sally, clomped down the stairs in nightclothes, with a riding crop clutched tight in her hand.

Sally gently but quickly placed Trinnean down behind a potted cedar, and then turned to face her aunt. Colm ran to his sister's side and Fiona darted over behind the cedar with Trinnean, who looked much calmer than everyone else. He climbed up into the pot and then reached a hand down to Fiona. She took it and he pulled her up. Once she was beside him, he didn't let go of her hand, and she was perfectly fine with that. They peeked around the small tree, fearing for their friend.

The door burst open and without so much as a warning, Auntie charged straight at Sally, raised the crop, and brought it down on Sally's shoulder. Sally and Colm both flinched, but Sally stood tall and took the blow. And then the oddest thing happened. Although the blow landed hard and fast on Sally's shoulder, it was her aunt who cried out in pain and grabbed her own shoulder. Growling, she swung the crop in a vicious backhand, striking Sally in the upper arm, but once again Sally stood strong and unyielding while her aunt cowered from the blow.

"You little witch! You'll be casting no spells on me!"

"I cast nothing, Auntie. The Lord Jesus Christ himself defends both Colm and me. We prayed for His protection and now whatever you rain down upon us shall instead be delivered unto you. I believe that when Father returns from his trip to Edinburgh tomorrow, we'll sit him down and explain that as lovely as it is to have you come and visit, I'll be taking responsibility for myself and Malcolm from here on out."

"You'll do no such thing!" She swung the crop directly at Sally's face, but the blow knocked her own self off her feet. The riding crop fell to the side and Sally snatched it up. Auntie made a crossing motion with one hand across the front of her body.

"Thank you, Auntie. I'll be needing this. We have to go out. We're taking your one-horse shay, but we will return it soon, in the same condition in which it leaves. Our friends need us. I don't think you'll be staying past breakfast tomorrow. " Sally sniffed the air and smiled. "I can smell a storm coming, so I expect you will want an early breakfast so you can make it home to Falkirk before the storm hits. Your beautiful shay with its big, thin wheels wouldn't do well in the mud, I imagine."

"But—" The older woman struggled to her feet, but stayed clear of the crop in Sally's hand.

"No 'buts' Auntie. You leave tomorrow. It is the Lord's will." She took a step toward her aunt, but didn't raise the crop or make any other threatening gesture. Her low, steady voice was threat enough, Fiona suspected.

"Aye! Of course!" Auntie fled back into the house.

Sally turned and marched toward the back of the tiny garden, with Colm, Fiona, and Trinnean close behind. "It will only take a few minutes to harness up Butternut, then we'll be on our way." She looked at Colm. "Will you be warm enough?"

"Aye. There's a blanket in the shay if I need it."

"Then let's get to the park and rescue some faeries!"

With the huge war eagle saddled and waiting as promised, Orrin got airborne and on his way so fast that whatever the falconer shouted to him was lost to the winds. The largest of the eagles in Faerie, the Harpy eagle was powerful and swift, and should they be attacked by actual harpies, the eagle was more than capable of defending itself. Orrin held tight to the reins, and tucked his own wings in close, in order to keep from getting blown out of the ornate saddle. "We're bound for the Source Grove. Do you know where it is?"

The war eagle looked back at the faery lord and lifted a feathered brow. "Aye, Your Grace. I think I might just be able to find the centre of all authority in Faerie."

"Excellent." Was the damned beast being sarcastic? Orrin promised himself he would speak to the falconer when they returned. Sarcasm was *his* weapon, not that of lesser beasts.

The Forest passed beneath them at a blurring speed that Orrin himself couldn't have managed. They would easily reach the Source Grove before the sun peaked.

The dwarfs—Giles and Able—approached while Twilly soaked up the sun on a rock just out of reach of an angry cedar.

"We'll be parting from you here, lass." Giles bowed his head a bit. "We didn't mind helping to find a missing baby, but we're nearly at the border and *this* is our home duchy. We'll make our way back quietly and hope the hotheads have cooled off enough for us to assure them you two are out of the duchy."

Twilly stood up on the rock so she could look the kind-hearted dwarf in the eyes, as was proper. "You've been very generous of your time, sir. I will keep the big lunk moving east. Once the sun sets, we'll get across the river and, well, I guess we'll see."

Able stepped up his hat in his hand. "Will you be safe? He *is* General Rock-Eye, Butcher of the Troll Wars."

"Not any more. He's Rock-Eye, the great-grandfather who just wants to spend his nights with his loved ones. We have a friend who is asking the birds for us. With luck, he'll have some news at dusk, before we cross the river. I'm hoping he'll at least point us in the right direction; otherwise I'm afraid a certain old troll will just knock down the gates with his head.

"Well, I've not seen the gates in question, but I've seen the head, and I'll place my bet on Rock-Eye, but let's hope it doesn't come to that."

"Let's hope." She kissed Able on the cheek and saw him blush as he turned away and tucked his hat on. The two dwarfs jogged off toward the tunnels, leaving Twilly her rock and her sunshine. She sat back down, closed her eyes, and lifted her face to another warm, sparkling day in Faerie.

"Are the twooo whooos gone, Pixie whooo?"

Twilly jumped up so fast it made her head spin. "Moonclaw!" She looked around, but couldn't see him until he glided out of the dense Forest and landed silently beside the rock.

"Dwarf whooos do not like troll whooos, so *this* whooo worried that hurt was being done to Rock-Eye."

She laughed. "Not at all. Giles and Able were trying to help us. They say Winsome isn't the only missing baby."

"Truuue. The word from the birds is more than ten babies, and not just trolls."

"Do they know where they are, and are they safe?"

"Next duchy. But birds of this duchy not know more. We three whooos must cross the river to learn more."

"That's what I thought. Are we far?"

"Close by air, near by ground, some few turns by tunnel."

"Brilliant!" And it was. "Rock-Eye is sleeping. The poor dear is exhausted." She hopped down off the rock. "I'll go keep him company. Keep guard. He has a lot of enemies."

"Troll whooos outside The Hills *always* have enemies." He looked round the little glade. "Did youuu whooo eat?"

"I…no. Nothing but water." Now that the idea was in her head, Twilly realized she was *famished*. "I'm fine," she lied. "I can't go wandering off looking for berries and nectar anymore. I'll wait until we reach the river." She blew Moonclaw a kiss and skipped off back to the tunnels. The past few days weighed heavily on her, but the sunshine did wonders, if only for a few blinks. She would just find a quiet corner near Rock-Eye and have a nap of her own.

Nyla had a clear view of the river and the bridge through the trees when she touched down on the trail for a ten-blink break. Six blinks into the break, her mistake dawned on her.

"Oh, *burr* me! I'm such a stump!" Without the springs to give her the extra power she needed to take off, there was no way she was getting airborne again. "Burr! Burr! Burr!" If she'd only flown over the river first, before she'd taken her break, it wouldn't be all that serious. An acorn bounced off her right wing with a distinct 'clang', and she looked back to see the Forest once again closing in over the trail.

"Break's over!" Tucking the wings in tight, she took off running. She hoped she was small enough and light enough to get across the bridge unseen, at least by the trolls. Once the sunlight hit the brass on the wings, though, the Sky Patrol would be after her again.

The trail widened, so she stopped. The bridge was just ahead. All she had to do was wind the spring up again, but to do that she'd have to remove the wings. She could do that easily enough, but she wasn't so sure about getting them back on. Even if she *could,* it would take all the time she was sure she didn't have.

Nyla squinted at the bridge, then up into the sky, and then back to the bridge one last time. She could see only one solution — remove the wings and *run*. She would be faster, more agile, and less visible. Something moved in the shadows beneath the bridge and she was pretty sure it wasn't nesting swallows. "Burr!" she whispered. She sat down on the trail and leaned back so the bottom tips of the wings touched the ground. Watching and listening for any kind of attack from any direction, she unbuckled the straps holding the harness in place, and then she carefully leaned forward and wiggled her wing stumps. They slid free of the rig and as soon as the breeze brushed them, the pain hit, and she realized how worn raw they were.

Wiggling and stretching out the knots in her muscles, she stood and nudged the wings gently into the underbrush until they were hidden from above. It wouldn't do to lose such wonderful devices. With or without the protective spell, she was pretty sure no one in Faerie would risk touching the metal.

She reached down and confirmed her comb with its trapping was safe in her satchel, then she took a deep breath and ran for the bridge. As she approached, she stayed in the middle of the trail, running as quietly as she could in her boots. The bridge, only as wide as a dwarf cart, was a solidly built stone span with no railings, just a stone lip on each side, not even as tall as her. She would find no protection here but what she carried with her.

Nyla slipped her silver dagger from its sheath, tightened her other hand's grip on her satchel, and picked up speed. Exhausted, ravenous, and running headfirst onto a troll-occupied bridge, she knew one way or another it would be over soon. She reached the bridge in silence, her boots making little noise on the path, but once she stepped foot on the bridge, even her tiny feet made so much noise she almost turned back. She suspected some kind of spell was responsible for magnifying her footsteps, but she surged ahead, senses alert and blade ready.

The whispers began when she was a third of the way across. The words were indistinct, but they sounded eerily like children calling for help. She nearly veered over to the side to investigate, to find the poor thing drowning in the river, or stranded on the riverbank, but she fought the urge. She knew full well it was a troll, trying to lure her to the edge, where it could lash her with a whip or a willow switch or something, and pull her into the shadows where they could safely eat her out of reach of the sun, but that knowledge still didn't make it any easier to resist.

By the time she was halfway across, the voices were louder, more insistent, and she could make out individual words like "Help me! I'm drowning!" She stumbled, but kept running. Her boots echoed on the stone, her heart pounded in her ears, and just when she was sure she was going to make it safely across, the voices got angry and the shouting mixed with growling from at least two sources. She was only a few blinks from reaching the far bank of the river when a heavily cloaked shape flipped up onto the bridge, blocking her way. The troll was so fully covered it could move clumsily about in daylight and snare its meal without risk; but Nyla didn't give a burr. She didn't care about some stupid adolescent troll dare or some dark-hearted stump looking to ruin her day. She charged straight at it, ran past its covered feet, and stabbed out with her blade without slowing even slightly. She must have hit a tender part of his foot because the troll let out a deafening howl and flung back the cloak's cowl in rage.

Still running, Nyla heard the scream cut off suddenly and risked a glance back over her shoulder. The sun hit the stupid troll square in the head and he'd been turned to stone in an instant. She guessed the troll's friends beneath the bridge knew exactly what happened because at least three different voices screamed trollish obscenities at her as she reached the end of the bridge and leaped to safe ground. The trail split into two and she took the right branch, as Trinnean had instructed. The left trail looked nice and wide and clear of roots and weeds, with a dappling of shimmering gold sunshine smiling on the flowers on each side, but Nyla stuck with the dingy, overgrown trail, running as fast as she could away from the bridge, the trolls, and the airship patrol she knew flew in the sky somewhere above her. There was no sign of pursuit, but she kept up as quick a pace as she could, doing her best to keep within the shadows without stirring up the ire of the Forest. A few blinks earlier she wished she'd been barefoot as she clomped across the bridge, but now, with burrs and thorns and stones littering the Source Grove path, her boots were a blessing.

Orrin could clearly see the giant rowan of the Source Grove towering above the rest of the Forest and nearly adjusted the eagle's course, but the eagle did it himself and even ventured a huff and scowl in his regal direction. The faerie lord couldn't care less what the massive beast of burden thought. Although it was named after the twisted, evil Harpies to the northwest because of its size, the eagle was not a faery and had no magic. Its ability to fly faster and farther than he could alone made it tolerable; and possibly, at some point in the inevitable war with his sister, this beast and its kin would come in handy in battle.

As they neared the Grove, Orrin also spotted the dwarf airship patrolling far beneath them. With his own spies on board he hardly worried about being attacked, and as long as he stayed above them, this was simply a big eagle, flying across the duchy. There was no army, no attack, and no danger to Orlaith's lands or subjects, with one exception. "Eagle, without alerting the patrol below, we need to find a wingless faery on her way to the Source Grove. Do you think you can do that?"

The war eagle sighed. "Aye, m'lord. Those were my orders. I am hunting with my eyes in the Forest, and staying in the sun, where it is harder to see us." The raptor adjusted his course slightly. "Shall we go to where the path enters the Grove? She will need to pass that way."

"Yes. Excellent. But still keep a watch. If we can head her off before she ever reaches the Grove, it'll save us a great deal of effort and reduce our risk."

"Aye, Your Grace."

Nyla was able to maintain a moderate running pace, even as rough as the trail was. Most of the obstacles were intended to slow and discourage larger feet clomping along to the Source Grove, so she was easily able to run under or around most everything in her way. She wasn't even sure if flying would have been easier because vines, webs, and branches hung over the trail. This trail, in fact, was nearly perfect for her. She couldn't be seen from above and any ambushers would face the same obstacles, she did.

Then the Forest itself reacted to her presence. In the space of two blinks she went from dodging ground-thistles to being frozen mid-step, facing a wall of impenetrable thorns as long as her arm. She'd been expecting something like this and had been rehearsing her words in her head as she ran. Very carefully, not wanting to even rub up against the stinger-sharp thorns, she went down on one knee, her hands open, empty, and held away from her body. The barrier moved closer, tightening the trap. She bowed her head, took a slow, cautious breath, and spoke.

"I am Nyla Rainsong, of the banished Clan Rainsong." A ripple of alarm moved through the Forest, which made her suspect she was initially stopped just because of *where* she was, not because of *who* or *what* she was. "I seek an audience with the Grace and Wisdom of the Elder Alder." Another ripple, and the thorns moved so close she could smell the ichor dripping from the poison ones. She raised her voice, but tried to keep from sounding panicky. "I seek an audience with the Elder Alder, *as is my right*! The right of appeal belongs to *all* faeries. I come bearing proof of my innocence, and evidence of the party responsible for destruction of the cherished rowans."

The thorns retreated just a smidgen, so Nyla risked a deeper breath. She was *so* close. It was time to do her best impression of her mother. "I am exercising my right of appeal. You *will* let me pass. I am Nyla Rainsong of the Clan Rainsong, and *I will be heard!*" The thorns withdrew. It was going to work, she just *knew* it; she was so certain, that when the vines dropped down and wrapped themselves around her wrists and ankles, she was too stunned to struggle. She managed a quick "Oy!", though, before she found herself being whisked off through the Forest. She was passed from vine to vine with such blurring speed that her head spun. She tumbled and spun and tossed, and for once, she was glad she didn't have wings, because they would have been broken and shredded. Of course, if she had wings, none of this would have been necessary.

Only a few turns and some blinks passed before the vines quite gently placed her on her feet in what had to be the most wondrous place in all of Faerie. She hadn't seen all of Faerie by any means, but she couldn't imagine any place coming close to the grandeur and majesty of the Source Grove. Lady Orlaith's Ten Oaks Castle was breathtaking and stunning, but it was a twig hut when compared to here. On one hand, it was just like every part of the Forest, full of trees and life, but on the other hand, it was incredibly massive as if this was the source of all the life, which spread across Faerie.

And then it dawned on her. This was *the Source Grove*. This *was* where it all emanated from. Every young sapling or seed descended from the gargantuan trees here. Every kind of tree imaginable towered straight up from the valley floor, except in the centre, where the trees were crowded out by flowers. Nyla saw now she stood in a valley, which was why from outside the Grove the level of the treetops changed very little, when in fact every tree here soared straight up to the canopy. The giant rowan they had seen from a distance stood up on the far rim of the valley, sentinel to the Grove.

The oaks, yews, maples, cedars, elms, birches, apples, spruces, cherries, rowans...*all* of them were *ages* old, a direct contrast to the raw, random, visual symphony of flowers, and flowering shrubs, and insects of every colour imaginable. The heady perfumes of the blossoms tickled her nose in an almost sensuous manner, while the rich, welcoming smells of everything from the cedar boughs to the apple blossoms created a scented background, like stars in the night sky were the background to the fireflies and other night beings. She smiled, she laughed, and finally, she cried. The days of stress that felt like a fortnight and more bubbled to the surface of her soul and poured out in tears. Her heart ached, her body was exhausted to the point of trembling, and she could barely think straight, here in the heart of the Forest.

"Nyla Rainsong. Your end is upon you." The voice was warm and smooth and disturbing, all at the same time. Nyla just wanted to curl up in it and cry away her pain. "You have come a long way, Child. You should *not* have. You should have remained with your clan, as I ordered."

Nyla swiped at her tears and managed to dry her eyes enough that she could get a blurry view of the owner of the voice. The Elder Alder stood grandly amongst the flowers, a visual symphony of butterflies and moths dancing in and out of her serrated leaves, and caressing her grey, fissured bark. "We are innocent", Nyla choked out. She used her sleeves to clean herself up, and dry the tears and snot.

"Your comb with your family crest was found at the site of the murder. Your fire destroyed an entire family of rowans, and others too numerous to count. You were judged and found guilty. The crime of fire by a faery is heinous, and so all five of your clans will pay the price."

"But why everyone? Why not just the six of us?"

"Your liege felt an example needed to be set. It was her suggestion, and I agree."

Nyla could now see the Elder Alder's face, and nearly smiled at the kind eyes watching her. Instead, she got back to her feet and reached into her satchel. Ivy whipped up from within the flowers and caught her wrist.

"What evil have you brought to this sacred place?"

She struggled to free her wrist, but couldn't. "It's just the comb. It's my proof!"

The Elder seemed to consider for a moment, then she waved a branch and the ivy slipped away. Nyla pulled the comb out and unwrapped it carefully.

"Your right to appeal is granted. Bring it here. Show me this proof of yours."

Nyla got two steps before she heard a soft whistle of wood and feather on the breeze, and then an excruciating pain erupted from both her back and chest. Just before she fell face first into the daisies, she noticed an amethyst arrowhead on the end of a finely wrought shaft protruding from below her left breast.

Chapter Twenty-Six

The eagle, true to its word, managed to elude the sky patrol while getting Orrin to the grove in record time. As they approached the great rowan dominating the canopy, the Forest dropped away and revealed a wide valley with a flower-filled meadow surrounded by an ancient grove.

"I see the Elder Alder, m'Lord, and there appears to be a wingless faery with her."

"You can see that far?!" Orrin was astounded. He had perfect hunter's sight, but even he couldn't yet see the stump of a faery. "Take us in!"

The eagle dove and Orrin held tight to the saddle with his legs while he notched an arrow and waited for a clear target. "Faster, you damned bird, faster!" The bird folded his wings in tight and they dropped from the sky like a stone. A lesser faery might have been terrified, but Orrin revelled in the thrill of the hunt. A testament to his skill, the eagle kept them upright, which enabled Orrin to eventually spot the damned faery lass and take aim. He had no idea what she planned to say to the Elder, or what she might have already said, but because of her banishment, there was a death mark on her and he was within his rights to kill her. He drew the bowstring back, sighted, held his breath, and released the arrow a blink before the eagle snapped open its wings and brought them to a perfect landing in the meadow, his massive black claws digging deep into the Forest floor.

Orrin leaped from the eagle's saddle and opened his own wings to glide down next to the bleeding body of the wingless tart. He took a step, thinking he should probably slip his dagger between her ribs and secure their little secret, but a single, thick vine of ivy stretched across to bar his way without actually touching him. It didn't dare. This might be the Elder Alder's little domain, but *he* was still a distant cousin of the king and above reproach.

"You have brought Death to the Grove, faery lord."

He resisted the urge to laugh in the face of the tree and instead lowered his eyes. He could fake humility and respect better even than his sister. "Her life was forfeit. You yourself banished her from our lands. Having heard she was on her way here to do you harm, I raced to intervene. If she could burn down sacred rowans, then bringing fire to the Grove would be next."

He kept his head bowed, quite pleased with how easy it was to spin a tale for the tree.

The Alder sighed. "We here are not mere saplings, unable to protect ourselves."

"I sought only to serve, Your Grace."

"You have flown far from your home duchy simply to give aide to those who neither requested nor need it. Will more faeries be arriving on war eagles to 'aide' us?"

Out of the corner of his eye, Orrin saw the cowardly eagle take a step back, away from him. He'd deal with the bird later. "I have come alone, Elder." The lass at his feet groaned. She still lived? He shot another arrow into her back to finish her off. She stopped groaning, but he reached for another arrow, thinking how much she was starting to look like a pincushion. The ivy snaked around his wrist, holding it tight.

"How dare you!" He dropped his bow, drew his sword, and cut off the offending plant. He'd had enough of this game.

"How dare *we?!* How dare *you*, you whelp!" The ivy grabbed at him from all directions, pinning his arms, legs, and wings, and wrapping around his throat before he could cast a spell or even blink. He struggled, but was held fast. Wisely, he opened his fist and let his rapier fall next to his bow. The ivy near the lass' outstretched hand picked something from the flowers and carried it to the Alder. At first Orrin couldn't see what the object was, but when sunlight struck it he recognized the cheap comb she'd given him as a favour. He smiled. It was only the evidence against the Rainsong stump. It could do nothing but *help* his cause.

The Alder accepted the trinket and examined it closely. "This was the proof of their guilt, but I think now I was rash and should have examined it closer when it was initially presented. If I had, I might have noticed the spell." She tapped a gem on the comb and the centre of Grove was filled with the voices of the ball.

Orrin nearly screamed, but held off, hoping the arrogant plant would think the trapping was just party nonsense. He bit down on the inside of his cheek, tasting blood, and it calmed him. The Elder Alder touched a twig to the comb and sped the trapping up until it was barely comprehensible. Orrin relaxed, and, a blink later, so did the ivy holding him. While the trapping went on and on, Orrin slowly edged one hand down toward his dagger on his belt. At the rate the Alder was playing back the trapping, Orrin guessed he only had a turn or two to free himself before the truth came out. There was a high-pitched burp in the trapping and the tree slowed it back down to regular speed. Orrin knew what was coming, so he concentrated on reaching his blade.

The trapping reached the point when Nyla gave him the comb as a favour, and he'd tucked it into his belt, and then the sound was muffled. The muffling went on and on, with occasional snippets of music or conversation becoming clearer when the comb shifted position briefly. The Elder once again sped up the trapping. Orrin was surprised his spell casting didn't upset the tree, and he fervently hoped the Elder got bored by the long silence that preceded the next morning's fiasco in Rainsong Meadow. He worked his right arm down, slowly, carefully. His fingers were so close he was sure he could feel the coolness of the silver pommel, just out of reach.

The Elder Alder sighed, probably bored, as Orrin hoped she would be. The ivy, too, found the whole thing quite tedious, and finally loosened up enough that Orrin's hand slipped out of the green grip and landed right on the pommel of his weapon. He had the dagger out in a blink, slashing and cutting himself free. If he could just get airborne, he could flee the damned Grove and get back to the comfort and safety of Stone Aerie.

As fast as he was, though, and as sharp as his blade was, Orrin discovered the ivy was faster. As rapidly as he cut, more vines reached for him. He spun and slashed and kicked and ducked down for his sword, knowing that with two blades he would have a fighting chance. What he really needed, though, was help. "Eagle! Come to my aide! Help your liege! I command—" The pain was excruciating! *What in Faerie was happening?* His sword was knocked out of reach, but he didn't care because he couldn't see past the pain in his belly. He looked down, but was confused. There was a branch sticking out of his gut that hadn't been there before. "I…"

The Elder Alder leaned over him and twisted her branch, so Orrin couldn't stop the scream that tore out of him. A vine picked up his sword but moved so quickly he only saw a flash of silver as it passed over his head. Then he forgot the agony in his belly because his own sword severed his wings. His beautiful Emperor Moth wings, unequalled in all of Faerie, fell to the ground, dead. He had no time to mourn their lost magnificence, though, because the vines grew tenfold in number and they pulled. They pulled like he was a spider and they were a bored brownie.

His left arm tore off a blink before his right one did; but before either of his legs went away, the Elder Alder slashed out with a branch and Orrin felt a wet burning sensation in his throat. He begged for it all to stop, for forgiveness, but all that came out of his mouth was a bubbling sound. He was done. That old gnome was—.

Dillweed first heard the news in the kitchens, just after lunch. He heard it again later, from one of the sentries. Lord Orrin had flown off on a Harpy war eagle and no one had any idea when he would return. Dillweed scurried back to their room, where he found Grandfather sitting cross-legged on his bed, his back against the wall and his bone-casting bowl on his lap. "Lord Orrin has left the castle on a war eagle! I wish we knew how long he will be away."

Torby squinted at the tiny bones in the bowl. The lantern on the wall cast only a dim, wavering light, but Dillweed could see enough when he leaned in to see the casting. "Is that—?" There's no way it could be. He pointed at a particular set of three bones lying across each other.

"The Gryphon's Triangle? Yes. Good eye, Dill. He's gone."

"I know. He flew off." But he knew what 'gone' really meant.

"Lord Orrin is no longer in Faerie. The bones say he has vanished from our world."

"How is that possible?" He took a breath. "Tell a lie, please."

"No, lad, I couldn't do that to you a—oh. I see what you're suggesting. Loathe as I am to cause you any hurt, you're right. We need to know." He squinted at Dillweed. "Ready? My hat is pink."

Dillweed flinched in anticipation of the coming agony, but there was nothing. "That seals it. The spell is broken but only death or a stronger faery could do that, and we've not seen any friendly faeries in an age. Maybe it would be best if you told Mistress Marfa of His Grace's passing. We may not be able to wait until nightfall."

"Yes sir. I suppose once the news reaches here, the search for the steward will intensify." He left his grandfather and made his way back up to the kitchen.

With the steward missing and their liege absent, confusion started to spread amongst the staff. It took Dillweed a few blinks to locate Marfa's gold hat bobby along, and then a few more to make his way through the milling staff who surrounded her, firing confused questions at her.

"So, are we preparing a banquet or not?"

"Is His Grace returning for the evening meal or not?"

"Are we brazing the tubers or boiling them?"

Just as Dillweed wiggled between the last of the kitchen staff between himself and Marfa, she erupted. "ENOUGH! We will prepare the meals that were last ordered by Master Gilroy's office. Both he and His Grace have left Stone Aerie before and we managed to do just fine without them. We will survive and thrive. We all have jobs to do, so get to them. We have people to feed!" She wiped her sweaty brow with the small towel tucked in her apron, then smiled at Dillweed. Her staff all hustled off to their tasks.

"You're hungry again, lad?"

His hands close to his body, his fingers flashed quickly. *I have urgent news.* "Of course, Mistress. I'm a growing lad. And my grandfather would like me to bring him another bowl of that delicious soup. It turns out the mountain air makes us extra hungry."

"Then follow me and we'll see what we can round up for our out-of-town guests." She nodded toward the stairwell. "I'm sure we have something in the pantry to fill your aching belly." She led the way back across the kitchen and into the stairwell. As soon as they were out of sight, she turned to face him and raised her hands. *What news? Good, I hope.*

For some, maybe. For many, maybe not. Lord Orrin is dead. Gone from Faerie, never to return.

You jest! It's not possible for you to know such a thing sitting in your chamber in the Aerie.

Grandfather saw it. He's been casting the bones while we waited for nightfall and says what the bones first predicted has come to pass. It is earlier than the bones predicted, but something must have happened between his last casting and now to change the future. Orrin is gone. The word will spread, the King will investigate, and on the second full moon from now, His Majesty will deed our liege's lands and holdings to Orlaith, as the closest living relative.

Mistress sat heavily. *Unbelievable.*

Maybe so, but the dark sprite bones are never wrong, and my Grandfather cannot lie without me knowing it. We have to find a way to leave as soon as possible, or they will find the steward and we will never get those babies home to their families.

He paused and shook out his fingers. He hadn't had to sign this much in his entire life.

Marfa nodded. *Agreed. For the babies. You're certain?*

As certain as you are standing before me.

"Then so be it. She started to stand and he helped her up. *Give me two-score turns and meet me at the nursery. Be ready to travel.*

Two-score. See you then. Be careful.

She rubbed his head affectionately. *You, too. There are curious eyes all about the Aerie, so be vigilant.*

Of course. If I don't get Grandfather home safely, my Grandmother will cook me alive. He smiled to reassure her and jogged back down the stairs, his heart pounding in his chest from both fear and excitement.

It became apparent after they visited two parks that Trinnean's human friend, Sally, did *not* know exactly which park they were looking for. Both parks had low, iron fences and gates that didn't look anything like what Fiona remembered. There was enough iron in the structure of the carriage to give her a small headache, but she took comfort in Trinnean's nearness.

"The fences were iron, but the pillars holding up the huge gates were stone, and half as wide as your steed."

Sally looked down at the two faeries on the bench beside her. "Stone? You're sure, lass? Then we're almost there." She snapped the reins and Butternut increased her pace.

Moonlight lit their way, or else they would have been blundering along in complete darkness. The carriage hit a small bump and shifted them on the bench. Trinnean's fingers brushed Fiona's and a blink later he took her hand in his, warm in the cool night, both strong and reassuring. Fiona laced her fingers in Trinn's, gently caressed his thumb with her own. He smiled at her, raised their entwined hands to his mouth, and kissed the ticklish back of her hand. She felt a blush warm her face and squeezed his hand, hoping he couldn't see her inexperienced, embarrassed flush.

"Och, this should be it, Miss Fiona." Sally reined in the carriage and they came to a stop facing a gate.

Fiona let go of Trinnean's hand and jumped up. "This *is* it!" She squinted through the gates into the dark park. "There is an old yew in the middle, where our gate to Faerie was and where we were attacked. We should start there, but carefully, because the two men are dangerous."

Sally gently snapped the reins, clicked twice with her tongue, and Butternut started forward again, slowly, as if he, too, knew the risks. The narrow wheels crunched on the stone pathway like an ogre on bones, and Fiona was certain the whole world could hear them coming. All four of them stared into the dark and Fiona hoped at least one of them could see well enough to find her Sisters. They came to a fork in the path and Sally stopped the carriage.

"Which way, Miss?"

Further along the left path, Fiona could see the yew lit by strands of moonlight cutting through the clouds, but then she heard a faint, familiar shout off to the right. She knew it was the leprechaun-hunting humans. "Right. But slowly, because we're getting close." Colm grabbed his sister's arm tightly and that's when the scope of the danger they were in hit Fiona. Colm and Sally were just children, compared to those men who would attack faeries. She could move undetected almost anywhere in the park, but the same wasn't true for her new human friends. "I'll go alone from here. Turn your carriage around and wait for me outside the gates, facing your home, please."

Colm protested first. "You can't! They'll kill you!"

"I can hide easier than either of you. With luck, they won't even see me. I'll follow them from a distance."

"*We* will follow them, from a distance." Trinnean took her hand again.

"*We*, then." She gave him a smile, strengthened in her resolve simply by his presence. She looked up at Colm and Sally. "You can't leave the carriage, and the carriage is too loud, so we two have to go alone, on foot. If we know where you are and that you're safe, we can concentrate on what needs to be done." She released Trinnean's hand, hopped down to the carriage's footrest, then leaped to the grass. She landed a bit awkwardly, not having her wings for balance and loft, but she recovered quickly and stepped to one side as Trinnean landed beside her.

Sally gave them a thumbs-up and whispered. "We'll be out by the gate, around to the left. If we're not there, cross the bridge and take the second laneway."

"What's down there?" She wasn't too keen on crossing the bridge on foot.

"I haven't a clue, but I thought it better than the first laneway, which seems obvious."

"That makes sense. See you soon." She drew her dagger and ran toward the voices to the right. A quick glance behind her showed Sally turning the carriage around slowly while Colm waved goodbye.

Fiona stayed on the path, but beside the right-hand verge, if she had to slip into the grass to hide. Trinnean mimicked her every step, probably letting her be the warrior princess he thought she was but she didn't much feel like.

Chapter Twenty-Seven

Peeking through the shrub's foliage, Brigid smiled. The two humans had just passed the Sisters' hiding spot, but although they were out of sight, she could still hear their boots shuffling on the gravel path and an occasional mumbled curse. They were moving slowly, but they were moving away, and that's what mattered most. She thought they might be soon be able to sneak back to the yew, and then Kara screamed like her arm was being ripped off.

Brigid's heart jumped into her throat. She spun to see Kara on her knees with Rainn and the hares looking as terrified as *she* felt. Rainn looked up, eyes wide. "No one touched her! She just screamed."

"Oy! Donal! Back this way!" The shout was some distance off.

Without looking up, Kara managed to mutter words that tore out Brigid's own heart. "Nyla is dead. I felt it. She's…she's… *gone.*"

"Start checking all the bushes! They're near, I just knows it!" the one human ordered the other.

Whatever comfort Kara needed had to wait. Pushing past her own shock and growing grief, Brigid pulled her Sister to her feet, boosted her up onto Grace's back and nodded to Rainn, whose own pale expression was discomfiting. "You, too! Up! Go! Twitch and I will lead them away. Get back to the yew and hide nearby." Rainn hesitated, so Brigid gave her a quick shake. "Now! Or we're *all* dead!"

Rainn swallowed, nodded, and quickly climbed up behind Kara. She barely had time to get a firm grip before Grace bolted from the shrubbery. Brigid leaped onto Twitch, Grabbed her scruff, and they leaped out into the open, towards the humans.

"BRIGID!"

She twisted around, looking for Grace and her Sisters, but there was no sign of them. They were long gone. Then she saw Fiona jumping up and down and waving madly at her from the grass! *Fiona?*

"There they are, Donal! They're riding the damned rabbit again!"

Fiona pointed to her right. "Follow the fence to the gate! Meet us there!" She sprinted away, toward the fence, with what looked like a pixie lad at her side. Brigid was thoroughly confused.

Twitch deked to the left and Brigid nearly fell off. She righted herself and leaned in as Twitch took them across the lawn in the wrong direction. "Twitch, we need to get to the fence and back to the gates."

"Aye, I heard, but we can't lead these ruffians there. We'll take them a little deeper into the park and circle around, again."

A pebble the size of Brigid's head bounced silently past them so she looked back quickly to ensure both of the vile monsters followed them and had not split up. They were both there. "Let's do this, missy!" She shifted her satchel around to protect her back and crouched low as Twitch bolted.

The hare zigzagged so quickly and randomly that each time Brigid's thoughts strayed to what Kara had said about Nyla, she was jerked back to reality and forced to give her attention to simply staying on and staying alive. They entered a much darker part of the park where the overhanging trees blocked out the little moonlight that remained. They slowed and stopped.

"I'm just making certain they see us, miss."

Brigid kissed the top of Twitch's head. "Of course you are. I trust you to know what you're doing. It feels like we've been running, dodging and hiding for an age. I don't trust much else right now, but I trust *you*."

Heavy grunting, panting, and shuffling announced the approach of the human predators, but they still hadn't spotted her and Twitch. She waved and shouted. "Oy! Slowpokes!"

The bigger of the two saw her and pointed, but was too busy trying to catch his breath to say anything. He stumbled after them and his mate followed. Twitch backed up slowly, but when both men cocked an arm back to throw something, she fled. Two rocks crashed into the branches around them but came nowhere near them. The hare looked back and whispered, "Hang on. It's time we leave these two behind and get you lasses clear of the park."

Brigid grabbed as tight as she dared and Twitch cut around a tree to the right, bolted behind a low hedge, then reversed course and began to finally circle around. Brigid was tired of the dangerous game they were playing and if Fiona was back here, then she had a way to get them home. But if Fiona was here, then Nyla had been alone when she died. Brigid sobbed and buried her face into the fur, but there was no way Kara could have felt what she said she did, all the way over in this realm of no magic. She just had to be wrong. Fiona would tell them everything was fine and Nyla was safe. *How in Faerie did Fiona get here, though?* None of it made sense!

Fiona easily spotted Grace leaping free of the shrubs with Rainn and Kara on board. Frantic waving of her arms quickly caught the hare's attention. One bound brought them face-to-face.

"Go that way to the fence, follow it to the gates. Look for a one-horse carriage outside — it's our way home. Go!"

Grace sped off, gone in a flash. A blink later, Twitch and Brigid burst into sight just as one of the humans came around the curve of the path. But her Sister went the wrong way, racing toward the humans!

"BRIGID!" Fiona jumped up and down, frantic to get her attention.

Her Sister turned. Fiona pointed to her right. "Follow the fence to the gate! Meet us there!" Before the humans could spy her she ran as fast as she could through the short grass, into the shrubs, and all the way to the fence, with Trinnean at her side. As she neared the park's perimeter she slammed into a wall of nausea — the fence was iron! A quick look confirmed Trinnean could feel it, too. He was pale and unsteady on his feet. She took his arm to steady him, wishing someone would steady *her*.

A twig snapped to their right and she caught a glimpse of Grace racing along beside the fence, toward the park's gate. She pulled Trinnean back far enough from the iron posts that the nausea was merely a nuisance and no longer debilitating. "Can you run, Trinn?"

"Aye. I suppose."

"Then keep up." She took off at a jog, the proximity of the toxic metal sapping her energy quickly. She angled a bit further from the fence and soon she was able to run, Trinnean stumbled along behind her, but he kept up. Before long she spotted Grace and stopped, facing the fence. When they caught up to her, Fiona immediately understood why — Sally stood on the other side of the deadly black posts and rails, encouraging them.

"Quick! Slip through! You're all wee and the gaps are huge!"

Fiona saw the simplicity of the plan. They didn't have to go all the way to the gate and then back. Even the hares could fit through, though with a bit of a squeeze. She waved for the others to come along and walked through the bars. Or at least she *tried* to. She managed three steps before the poison knocked her to her knees. She threw up in the grass twice before Trinn reached her and dragged her back to safety.

Sally looked confused. "Is there a spell on it?"

Fiona shook her head, slowly. "No spell, but iron kills faeries."

"Is it deadly to rabbits?"

"Not in the same way, no."

"Then climb on them and let them carry you through. Hurry!"

Hands helped Fiona to her feet, but it wasn't Trinnean, it was Brigid. She and Twitch had arrived! The Sisters hugged quickly. "You're soaking wet! However you got through and whatever is your plan, we have to get away from here first! Climb up." She boosted Fiona up onto Twitch, and then helped Rainn get Kara mounted on Grace. Fiona reached down and pulled Trinnean up behind her. Quickly and nimbly, Brigid hopped behind Rainn and urged Grace forward. "Everyone lift your legs up! Don't let them touch the iron.

Twitch went first. Fiona closed her eyes, pulled her legs up, and held on for dear life. Even though the hare moved steadily and quickly, the iron was too much and Fiona began to slip, unable to stop herself. Then Trinn wrapped his arms around her, pressed hard against her back, and held her in place. Her mind thickened and she could barely think straight, but she could hear her hero sobbing behind her.

Suddenly they were through. Twitch got them two steps onto the roadway before Trinn released his hold and they both slid off, only to be caught by Sally and lifted up. Fiona shook her head. "Please, I need to speak to Twitch." Sally gently put them down. Grace and the remaining three faeries slipped between the bars so Sally moved over to help them. Fiona hugged Twitch around her neck, burying herself in her new friend's luxurious brown fur.

After a moment she stepped back and looked her in the eye. "Sweet, sweet lady, if we were going back through a tunnel in a tree or under a rock, I would take you with us because you have more than earned escape from this poisonous world. Maybe, if we can find a way back like that..." She left the offer hanging. It broke her heart to abandon two beautiful ladies.

But Twitch nuzzled her nose into Fiona's shoulder. "There is more to this world than this iron-and-smoke-filled place of humans. We have family on a farm. They say there is food a-plenty and humans are few and far between, at least compared to *this* place. We will have to be wary of foxes and maybe even wolves, but my farm kin live long, happy lives, so we will hope for the same.

"But *you*—Fiona—you return to a world where nature Herself has turned Her back on you and your families. I know you journey to save them, but if that fails, know you'll have a home here with us. We have great forests and ancient woods, and…" Twitch sniffled back tears, so Fiona hugged her again. When the two finally separated, Twitch added, "We will be north of this city. The human name for the place is Mugdock. Just ask for the Long-Foot warren."

"The Long-Foot warren?" She repeated it back, to make sure she had it correct. They were whispering and Twitch's accent made it sound like she'd said 'Wrong-Food'.

"One and the same. Give us some time to get there, though, lass. It's a long hop and my sister is going to need a few days of rest before we start off."

"It *has* been an adventurous night, hasn't it?"

"I wouldn't have missed it for the world."

"They're in the bushes! The damned leprechauns are in the *bushes*, Donal!"

The men were close! Time was up! Fiona kissed Twitch on the end of her nose. "I love you, big Sister. Be safe."

"And *you,* little Sister."

 The other lasses skipped over to Twitch to say goodbye, so Fiona jumped over to Grace and smothered her with hugs and kisses. "You, dear lady, are a life saver. Twitch told me where you will be off to, and considering what we're going *back* to, we may see you sooner than later. Be safe, Sister. I love you."

As she hugged the elder doe, Grace whispered in her ear. "I love you, too, Sister, and I am so sorry about Nyla. Go avenge her and with luck we will meet—" She was interrupted by a loud crashing of branches as one of the men blundered through the shrubs. Faeries, hares, and human helpers all jumped, startled.

"Got 'em! They're t'other side of the fence! Go 'round the gate and I'll climb over here!"

In one expert motion, Brigid notched, drew, and shot an arrow between the fence posts, hitting the man in the knee. He stumbled, tripped, and fell head first into the fence with a heavy thump and a clang. He slid to the ground and lay face down, unconscious, still breathing. Brigid spit at him and growled. "That's for breaking my flute, you *stump*!"

As quickly as she could, Sally boosted them all up and onto the bench, two at a time, and then she joined them, snatching up the reins once she was settled. "Hang on!" With a snap of the leather, Butternut was off. Fiona grabbed Trinn on her right and Kara on her left. Kara clung tight to her arm and burying her face in Fiona's shoulder. Her Sister's pain was tremendous and Fiona finally let her tears flow. They still had a long way to go and no idea what they were going back to. A knot deep in her stomach told her Nyla might not be the last of the Sisterhood to die this night.

Old Torby spent what remained of the day sitting on a stump in a lesser garden, cleaning his finger nails slowly and methodically with an old porcupine quill, and listening to the chatter of servants and soldiers alike as they came and went in their duties in the cold stone castle. The tension in Stone Aerie was building. He could taste it on the air like an incontinent skunk.

When Mistress Marfa appeared in a doorway and nodded almost imperceptibly, he hopped down onto the cobblestone path and strolled back inside as casually as he could. He was determined to take his sweet time because no one noticed one more gnome in a garden unless he was running. Besides, he thought, after the long hike from home, his old muscles were too tired and stiff to run anywhere. A handful of blinks later, he wandered past one of the kitchen staff and into their chamber near the pantry. He shut the door firmly. When he finally turned around, Dillweed was butt-hopping on his bed, hands flashing.

What news, Grandfather?!

We need to go, lad. They're searching madly for the steward, so it's only a matter of time. Go tell Mistress, but don't let your guard down. That skinny pastry cook is hanging about near the pantry. I've never met a skinny gnome I could trust.

I don't know if being skinny has anything to do with it, but Mistress warned me about that *particular gnome.*

Then we shall be vigilante in our caution.

Do you think we have a hope of succeeding, Grandfather?

Before our little visit from Lord Orrin, I would have laughed at the thought of the likes of we two doing anything resembling daring-do, but these are babies, he's no longer our liege, and it has *to be done. Besides, your grandmother would cut us both hats from our own hides if we* didn't *do this.*

And Mother would hold us down while Gram did it. Well, when all is said and done, I hope somebody is still alive to sing a rousing ballad to us.

If they find the steward before we are clear of the castle and back down in the foothills, they'll be singing a funeral dirge, not a ballad.

Aye, point made. I've packed our things, I'll go start the pebble rolling. He pointed at the two packs leaning against the end of his bed.

Have you got road snacks in there? We have no idea how long it'll be before we get home again.

There are biscuits and jam. I was waiting for you to return so I could skip up to the kitchens and maybe put together something tasty for us both. I'll do that lickety-split when I see Mistress.

I'll go down and tell the sisters. I have no idea how we're going to move all these babies, especially the troll lasses.

Mistress Marfa seems confident we can do it, so let's trust her.

Aye. Trust her with our lives.

As she and the others are trusting us. He left quietly and Torby wondered when his grandson had suddenly grown up.

The grey sky over the city called 'Glasgow' was slowly lightening when Sally, unhitched beautiful Butternut, slipped off the gigantic horse's harness, and walked her into her stall. Brigid itched to get back to Faerie and prove Kara's premonition about Nyla to be fully false. It couldn't possibly the true.

According to Fiona and Trinnean—Fiona's new *love*—Nyla was outfitted with a pair of fully functional mechanical wings and was accompanied by Browncap, a faithful and trustworthy sparrow. Nyla supposedly had one troll-occupied bridge to fly over before she reached the Source Grove, and that was the only hazard.

When they'd driven off, away from the park and the two leprechaun hunters, she'd peppered Fiona with questions, but it was the younger human—the lad, Colm—who answered enthusiastically from his corner of the carriage. He deluged them with all the details of how Trinnean travelled between the two worlds through the pond, holding his breath for 'hours and hours', the types of things Trinnean and Sally traded, and finally, a blow-by-blow account of Trinnean's charm making their Auntie hurt herself instead of Sally. They arrived at the humans' home just as young Colm ran out of breath. When he finished, Brigid not only knew how they were going to return to Faerie, but also why Fiona was smitten so quickly with this faery lad with the stunted wings. Her Sister had found someone as smart, funny, and imaginative as she herself, and none of them had ever thought that would be possible.

Sally latched the stall and led them out of the small stable. She'd insisted on personally escorting them to the pond. "Between Auntie and Bobby, it's too dangerous."

"But we can handle danger," Brigid reassured her.

"Aye, maybe so, Miss Brigid, but the pond is in a wee walled garden and if Bobby is out—he's so fast he can catch a squirrel— then there will be nowhere for you to run." She picked up a large woven basket by the door. "It smells of sausage and bread from today's trip to the market, but if you don't mind, it'd be safer if I carried you all. I mean, if it doesn't insult you. I don't intend to imply that you can't...that you...that you have to be carried... like babies."

Rainn laughed and waved the basket down to the ground. "Miss Sally, I am so exhausted you're welcome to dress me in a bonnet and carry me around like a doll if you wish." Brigid grabbed the rim of the basket at a level with her head and flipped up and inside, then she reached back and took Kara's hand from Rainn, pulling her up and in. The rest of them quickly hopped aboard and sat out of sight. Sally scooped up the basket and they were off and across the garden. There was single, muffled bark from somewhere nearby, but when she craned her neck the only windows of the home she could see were still dark. The five of them must have been unbearably heavy in the basket, but Sally carried them with quick ease, setting down only a few blinks after entering the garden.

Brigid reached for Kara's hand to help her Sister up and out, but Kara smiled and shook her head. "It's all good. I have to shake this off. Whatever in Faerie has happened to Nyla, she wouldn't want me drowning on my way back home to avenge her and Cray." She vaulted over the basket's rim and onto the flagstones. Brigid followed her, unsuccessfully hiding her smile. If Kara could suffer all of this and still hold her head up, then the rest of them could do no less.

Trinnean stood with his boot on a cord running out of the little pond. Their end of the cord was anchored by a stone. "We're here. This isn't easy, but I believe you can—"

Fiona interrupted him. "It's not as far as it feels. Don't panic, follow the cord, and once you surface at the other end, let go of the cord immediately or you'll get dragged into his machine. Then get out of the pool and clear because it's small and there's no room to mill about. We're faeries, not mermaids—we can't swim, but we *can* hold our breath. If you find yourself confused or overwhelmed, simply pull yourself along the cord hand-over-hand. Once the last one is in the water, the cord will be moving, too, so trust it." She looked at each of them in turn. "I was terrified when Trinn explained this to me." She took his hand. "But I trusted him and you'll have to trust me. I'll go first and Trinnean will go last, to make sure we all get through. Your heads will get a bit wobbly as we pass from this world into Faerie, but ignore it. You're not drowning, you're going home."

"I'll go first. I'm the Betweener." Brigid knew that simple admission would get her into trouble with her grandfather when she got home, but if they were passing between realms, she really should go first, and they all needed to know why. "Even without my flute, this is what I'm trained to do."

Trinnean handed her a charm on a string. "You'll need this to keep the gate open."

"I suppose. Thank you."

"A Betweener?" Rainn asked. They all looked confused.

"I'll explain later. We have clans to save." She looked up at Sally and Colm who sat quietly attentive on the stone bench. "You have been wonderful. You have most truly saved our lives. We are in your debt and will find a way to repay you both." She blew them both kisses, secured her bow across her body, and dove into the pond. The frigid darkness wrapped around her and threatened to punch the very air out of her chest, but she found the cord with her hands and started pulling herself along. After a few blinks, her eyes adjusted to the dark and she saw the lining of the passage illuminated by glowing plankton. It was lovely and peaceful, but she also knew it was deadly. She pulled and kicked and hurried along. A quick look back behind her showed someone close on her heels, but although in the low light it looked like Fiona, it could have been any of her four Sisters.

She passed through into Faerie in a blink and knew it immediately. There was simply something different about the water around her. It wasn't warmer, it just seemed more *alive*.

The glowing plankton now waved back at her, but she was running out of air and panic seeped in. Then the cord jerked and it was all she could do to hold tight as it dragged her along.

Mistress Marfa must have expected Dillweed to pop up soon because the moment he stepped into the kitchen she strode over, handed him a large basket weighing heavy with what felt like a feast for ten. "Here you go, young sir. As you requested. I'm sorry your grandfather isn't feeling well. Hopefully this will perk him up while you await His Grace's return.

Dillweed took the basket and Mistress switched to quick hand signs. Everyone in the kitchen was most likely fluent, so she kept her hands close to her body, using her girth to shield the conversation. *You have to leave. I'm just coming to fetch you both. They should be ready in the nursery. Go. Quickly. I will stay here to deflect attention. Be safe. And tell that handsome grandfather of yours he's welcome to visit any time he sees fit.* She winked at him, straightened the cloth covering the contents of the basket, and returned to her work.

Even though he knew what was required and the plans were well laid, it was a bit of a shock to Dillweed for it all to actually be set into motion. He clutched the basket tightly and trotted back down the steps, around the corner, and down the next steps, all the way to the nursery. He went as silently as he could. Lord Orrin might be gone, but the steward yet lived so they were a long way from danger, yet.

He obviously wasn't as quiet as he thought he was, because the thick door of the nursery swung open before he arrived, and Peony poked her head out.

"Good lad! If you've got the basket, then you've spoken with my aunt and it's all in motion." She held the door for him and ushered him into the chamber, though he could only take two steps in before running up against a crowd of gnomes. The nursery buzzed with activity, with wheelbarrows everywhere and adults gently laying quilt-wrapped babies into them. There were some cries and some giggles, but each of the wee ones appeared to have a damp cloth to gum on and distract them.

A sturdy gnome about twice Dillweed's age, relieved him of the basket with quick thanks, then whipped off the cloth, revealing the feast within. No wonder it was so heavy! It was filled with bone knives! "The young feller has brought the blades.

Everyone who requested one, come get. There's also zucchini bread and goat cheese—nothing but the best for this lot." The elder dispensed blades as a half dozen gnomes approached him. The other eight or nine folk seemed to have some sort of weapon strapped to their belts or slung over their shoulders.

Torby stepped up, accepted two sheathed blades, and handed Dillweed one. "Hope we don't need them, but at least we're prepared." He slid his own blade out of the leather, ran his thumb across the nicked bone blade for sharpness, and nodded. "Sharp enough. These are all old blades no one'll miss. Now, there's been a wee bit of a change of plans."

"We're leaving earlier than planned." Dillweed knew that.

"Well, yes, lad, but we're also going to have to move a little faster than originally planned. Especially you. It turns out the fumes in that dirty bedding closet weren't just nasty, they were deadly. When the Logjaw brothers there," he pointed at the gnome with the basket and another who did indeed look like the first. "When they arrived, they drew their blades and opened the closet to check on the steward. He was dead. All purple and swollen. Something in baby troll scat must have disagreed with him."

Dillweed's knees went weak, and he sat down before he fell down. "I killed him."

"There's no simple way to put it. Aye. Not directly, but his death is yours. The good news is, his body has already been well and truly disposed of. They weren't told who is responsible for the death and they wouldn't tell me where they stuffed him, that way fewer tongues can wag and unravel this nasty business." He reached down and took Dillweed's hand, helping him up.

"I'm sorry grandfather. I've taken a life."

"You have, but you did it to save many others. Lift your head with pride that you were acting in the best interests of all. Many would have tortured him and then snapped his neck. You had mercy, at least in your heart. But enough chatter. I've already fetched our packs. They're in the corner. We have just one thing left to do."

The gnomes all shifted away from the centre of the room, where Peony and Lily were now bound, back-to-back on a pair of sturdy chairs. The two Logjaw brothers each faced a women, the older one shaking his head. "You're sure, cousin?"

Lily nodded. "It's for the best. Blacken my eye, break my nose, drop the hood over my head, and when Mistress finds us in the morning we'll be worse for wear but alive and with a plausible tale to tell to the guards. That'll be more than enough time for you to all get clear."

"And Peony, you're fine with this?"

"Aye. If we're not here, then the whole clan will be suspect and it'll be a death sentence for all. If you're going to break my nose, though, could you break it to the left? It needs fixing that way." Her laugh was cut short by two quick punches to her face. Lily received two similar blows. Dillweed was stunned at the suddenness, but understood the necessity. Tears in their own eyes, the two men each kissed a cousin on their forehead and slipped black cloth sacks over their heads.

"Can you breathe okay? We don't need any more accidental deaths." He winked at Dillweed, who blushed.

"Just fine."

"All good here. Now flee, you fools."

That seemed to be the cue they were all waiting for. Hands quickly grabbed packs and blanket rolls, and hoisted up wheelbarrows, moving with precision out into the corridor. Torby moved over to the remaining wheelbarrow. "This one is ours, lad. Lily and Peony insisted." The blanket suddenly flung up and Winsome stuck her sleepy head out. She saw Dillweed and giggled. Dillweed took up the barrow's handles, made a dwarf raspberry back at her, and they were off. She was a big lass, but gnome wheelbarrows were designed for one person to carry many times their own weight, so he turned it around and started off, only to stop beside the hooded sisters.

"Thank you. Be safe. We'll get them home. You know where to find us if you find yourself in need of a roof away from the castle."

"Thank *you*, Dillweed. Safe travels, hero."

"Safe travels to you both. See you soon."

Torby held the door, Dillweed wheeled out into the corridor and to the left, away from the populated parts of the castle. Both of the Pondbottom men had tears in their eyes as they trotted along, although the happy gurgling sounds from Winsome under the blanket quickly pushed his sadness aside. It was time to get these babies home.

The gnome network was so efficient and well organized Dillweed didn't have time to worry or fuss. He trotted along at the end of the long line of barrows, the light of the half-dozen lanterns showing them the way. They passed side openings without slowing, and took a left branching followed by a right without even a slight hesitation to consider whether they were going the correct way, which is what *he* would have had to do. He didn't even bother to try and keep track of the turns and twists. He trusted his fellow gnomes to know where they were going.

Just as his arms began to feel a bit of ache, they came to a quiet halt. The barrows were gently set down, the babies were each fed and cuddled. One wee brownie lad up near the front started to wail, but was quickly scooped up and hugged. Words were murmured, then he was placed silently back in his mobile cradle. The gnome lady ahead of Dillweed leaned back and whispered "Bubble of silence. A last resort, but necessary as we are passing a surface vent."

Chapter Twenty-Eight

Two gnomes made their way down the line, each with a pot of liniment and a cloth. They stopped at each barrow-porter and worked the liniment into their arms from shoulders to fingertips. Soft sighs of relief were audible as the soothing heat worked into the tired muscles. Dillweed pulled his sleeves up and held his arms out, recognizing the comforting scents of lemongrass with peppermint. The gnomes were quick, their fingertips strong, and the effect was almost immediate. Dillweed let out a sigh of his own.

He heard a scuffle and a noise at the front of the line, then a whispered conversation. The first barrow was lifted and the break was over. A few turns later, the whispered update made its way back to them.

"The word went out far and wide, but only with the non-magical creatures we can trust. We just heard back that a solitary, hidden meadow is being guarded and awaiting our arrival. We're almost out of the tunnels and will still have some distance to travel, but by then we will have an armed escort."

They continued to move forward, babies being attended to as need arose, but without breaking stride. Winsome and the other two troll lasses were surprisingly docile, all more than happy to lie back in their barrows and smile at the tunnel roof. "They're awfully quiet, Grandfather. I mean, for trolls."

"Well, the sun is still up, and I'm sure their bodies know that, so they're dozy. When night falls, they may be a bit more active. *That's* when it will get interesting.

In the darkness of the tunnels, Dillweed had no idea when the sun set, but apparently the troll lasses did, because Winsome burped, farted, growled, and climbed up out of the barrow and into Dillweed's arms, knocking him to the ground. She slathered him with licks and kisses, giggling and mewling.

"Maybe you can get her to walk, lad. That'll keep her occupied. I can manage the barrow."

"Thank you. Can't hurt to give it a try." He pulled himself out from under the wiggly troll and stood up. He reached for her hand and she grabbed it immediately. "Come on Sweetie. Let's walk, shall we." He tugged gently at her hand, and taking the cue, she crawled along beside him, though awkwardly, with him holding one hand. Seeing this, he let go of her hand so she could use it to crawl. He took a few steps and she followed, keeping up as best she could. "Keep going, Grandfather. We'll be along behind you. She moves pretty quickly—" She took his hand again but when he turned, she stood above him, walking. Clumsy and unsteady, but holding onto his hand, Winsome took tentative steps. "Good girl!" he whispered. "But we have to move a bit faster, so maybe you should climb back in the barrow and I'll carry you that way. We can't afford to get lost in this place."

He was certain she couldn't understand gnomish, but she definitely understood the urgency in his words, because she sped up her steps. The accompanying torches were getting further and further away, but Dillweed could still clearly see that with very step, the troll lass got steadier and steadier. "Wow. You're learning as fast as a unicorn foal, sweetie. All right, then, let's see if you can keep up." He urged her to go a bit faster, and she did, as if the combination of the solid rock under her feet and the setting of the sun gave her more confidence and coordination.

They didn't catch up quickly, but they were able to close the distance eventually, and by the time they reached the night air at the end of the tunnel, Winsome and Dillweed were only a few blinks behind Torby and the barrow. The convoy milled about the area in front of the tunnels, and their numbers seemed to have swollen. Dillweed squinted in the moonlight and saw the new members of the group carried shields, spears, and swords— their armed escort, as promised.

He led Winsome out to join them, but when her foot went from rock to soil, she pulled it back and wailed loud enough to wake a wight. The entire gathering jumped and turned.

"Shut her up!"

Two of the ladies rushed over to help him, but once he walked her back onto the rock floor of the tunnel, she settled down, though her grip on his hand threatened to crush his fingers. He hugged her, then whispered very softly, "It's okay, Winsome. It's safe. That's moonlight, not sunlight. It can't hurt you. We have all these big, tough soldiers to keep us safe while we go find Grampa Rock-Eye."

Her eyes widened at the mention of her grandfather's name. Dillweed pointed at the gathering. "He's out there, and I've brought all these friends to help us find him." A rounder-than-usual gnome waddled up and growled at Winsome. Then he muttered and spit, and growled some more in what Dillweed hoped was a translation of what he'd just said.

Winsome smiled and replied with a single trollish word Dillweed thought might be the word for 'yes'.

The translator smiled at Dillweed. "She seems to understand, at least on a basic level. She knows you'll keep her safe and we will all keep *you* safe. We can continue." He growl-spit to Winsome again and this time she nodded, then walked over to the barrow and climbed in. "I told her we have to hurry and her Grampa would be so impressed she'd learned to ride like a big lass." He chuckled. "I have wee ones of my own, so I know what works."

"So we're set?" One of the Logjaw brothers asked. Dillweed nodded, as did most of the party. "Good. We have plenty of bodies now, so if any barrow pushers get tired, call for relief. Word in the Forest is that something is amiss up at Stone Aerie and patrols will increase at dawn. These babies need to be home to their families before then so we can all get safely home to ours." He jogged off down the trail and everyone fell in behind him.

Dillweed took over with the barrow once more, and Torby plodded along beside him, looking a wee bit tired. "Grandfather, we have enough people to take care of this. You don't have to keep up. Rest and I'll come back for you, or make for home and I'll see you there."

The old gnome shook his head. "Lad, I can count the numbers of adventures in my life on one hand. I am not quitting or slowing down or walking away from this one. I am at your side, as a Pondbottom should be. Surprisingly, I've not had this much energy in an age or two. Tis a good pace."

"It *is*, sir. I'm glad to have you by my side."

They trotted on in silence, both wary of the night, and conservative of their breaths.

The moment the sun dropped down over the mountains and the sky gave over to the moon, Rock-Eye snapped out of his slumber, sat up and stretched. Twilly rolled her shoulders and wiggled the stiffness out of her hips while her big friend popped the joints of his neck, then loosened up his knuckles, and swung the stiffness out of his arms.

"We go." He lowered his hand and Twilly hopped on. She settled in on his shoulder like it was a place she'd been born to inhabit. It felt safe and comfortable. Rock-Eye sniffed the air, then strode out of the cave and into the tunnels. It wasn't long before they reached the surface. "Moon is up. We travel faster."

"Which is exactly what troll whooo should dooo." Moonclaw waited for them, preening on an elm branch just above Rock-Eye's eye level. "This whooo has news."

Rock-Eye stood, hands on his hips, waiting. "News?"

"A group of gnome whooos has rescued a group of babies from the evil whooos of Stone Aerie castle. Many babies, many races, but no word if any baby-whooos are troll babies."

"Winsome!" Rock-Eye charged off into the forest but stopped. "Where?"

"A meadow well west of castle. That is all this whooo knows. Travel east and I will hunt for more details and find you two whooos with more news."

"East."

"East." He flew off into the moonlight, this time a silent hunter for information. Twilly strained to hear even the slightest sound from his flight, but once again, she heard nothing.

"East. To Winsome." Rock-Eye sounded almost happy. She wasn't sure what a happy troll sounded like, but there seemed to be a thread of joy in his voice.

"Soon, Rock-Eye. Soon."

The meadow was quiet. Eight families had come and been ecstatically, unbelievably, tearfully reunited with their stolen children. One dwarf lad and the three troll lasses remained, and they played in the moonlight while the gnomes stood guard in shifts. They all promised to stay until sunrise, so with only four infants remaining, the custodians and guards were able to take turns sleeping.

Dillweed handed his grandfather a bedroll and pointed to a bed of ferns. "Sleep. You'll be safe in there but not so far away that you can't jump up to defend the realm if needed."

"I can't argue with you, lad. I'm now exhausted and probably will be for days. Keep our little girl safe, and wake me if any of her family arrive." He untied the bedroll. "Agreed?"

"Yes sir. Sleep as long as you need to. I'll wake you only if someone arrives or if I can't keep my eyes open."

"Good lad. Now, I strongly suggest you get those children fed before they start calling for a teet you don't have." He hobbled over to the ferns and Dillweed noticed his grandfather's limp. He considered asking him if he was hurt, but his Old Torby removed his boots and massaged his feet, so Dillweed let him be.

Eventually Winsome got bored or tired, and wobbled over to sit with Dillweed. She plunked herself down, stuck her thumb in her mouth, and curled up with her big head in his lap. Dillweed had very little experience with children, so he simply rubbed her brow and hummed his way through the six songs he could remember. The little troll lass purred and hummed along, seemingly content.

The moon sat directly overhead when a commotion disrupted the silence of the Forest east of the group's position. The last dwarf infant was claimed not long before, but the three troll babies remained. Winsome now sat across from Dillweed, catching pinecones he tossed to her and trying heroically but unsuccessfully to throw them back. The cones went every which way and she giggled and clapped when a cone hit anything at all.

When the commotion broke out, Winsome's wobbly ears perked up and Dillweed reached for his blade. The two of them pushed their way to their feet and the gnome placed himself between his charge and the threat. Within two blinks everyone in the meadow stood at the alert, brandishing a weapon of one sort or another. Someone called out a name and the roly-poly translator made his way over to the trailhead. He slipped into the Forest, brandishing his own long blade.

A hushed conversation drifted out of the trees, but Dillweed couldn't make out any individual words. Torby stepped up beside him, rubbing his eyes awake. "What befalls, lad? It doesn't sound like we're under attack."

"I haven't a clue, sir. I think someone approached the perimeter guard. Maybe you could keep an eye behind us, just so we can avoid surprises."

"Aye." Torby turned to watch their rear approach, drawing his own blade.

The Forest seemed to come alive across the meadow, and many of the guards converged on the trailhead. The foliage grew thick there, so the moonlight only illuminated a few patches, but it didn't take much light for Dillweed to see a huge troll moving down the trail, within a corral of blades. When it reached the meadow and stood fully in the moonlight Dillweed was so relieved he almost cried out, but a better idea occurred to him.

He turned to Winsome. "Sweetie. Grampa Rock-Eye is here. Go! Run to Grampa! Show him what a big lass you are." As he spoke he moved aside and pointed across at the old warrior. Winsome looked where he pointed, blinked slowly while her young mind connected the dots, and with her best baby troll roar, she raced across the clearing. She tripped, rolled, came up a bit dizzy, got her bearings again, and kept going. Dillweed and Torby followed along, smiling.

Rock-Eye squinted at the charging trollette, rubbed his good eye to clear it, then roared out, "WINSOME!" He managed two long strides before she reached him. He scooped her up and tossed the wiggling, laughing baby high in the air above his head. Gnomes around the meadow gasped and Dillweed nearly attacked with his meager blade, but Rock-Eye easily caught his great-granddaughter and collapsed to the grass with her in his arms. He wept as she covered him with sloppy kisses.

The other two troll babies crawled up and climbed on Rock-Eye's lap just as Dillweed arrived, and that's when he noticed the pixie lass sitting on Rock-Eye's shoulder, clinging to his hair, trying not to get crushed in the excitement. She wept, and yet had the most wonderful smile.

Winsome pulled out of Rock-Eye's embrace and came to Dillweed. She took both him and Torby by the hands and led them back to the old troll. She climbed back up into his lap and pulled the reluctant gnomes with her.

Rock-Eye looked down at Dillweed, then at Torby. "*Bone caster? You* find Winsome baby?"

Torby removed his hat and nodded in greeting. "Aye, I am the bone caster, but the hero is my grandson. He found the babies and learned she's your Winsome."

Rock-Eye wiped away tears from his good eye. "Life debt I owe, gnomes. Life debt." One of the other troll lasses pulled on his nose to get his attention. "Yes. Rock-Eye take babies home. Safer for troll in troll caves. Keep them safe with my life."

The Logjaw brothers looked around the group for any opposition to the idea, then the older one stepped forward and offered his hand to the troll. "Agreed. You will take full responsibility for these babies, getting them home safely, soonest?"

Rock-Eye shook the tiny gnome hand with his massive troll paw. "Agreed. Winsome home, then these two. Safe and sound."

"Just be warned Lord Orrin's guards will be looking for you."

The troll spat on the ground beside him. "Then they die."

"That is entirely your choice. Just don't start a war. We're still recovering from the last one."

"No. No war. Maybe best hide. Avoid fight." Winsome licked his cheek and giggled. He sighed. "Too old for fights." He gently lifted Dillweed and Toby off his lap then stood. His long arms easily held the three babies safe. He looked at the little pixie on his shoulder. "Your choice. Go with gnomes or stay with Rock-Eye and trolls."

The sweet little lass laughed like silver bells and kissed the big man on his ear. "Silly Goopa! You're my family now. I'll go with you, if you'll have me."

"Family. Come then." He swept his gaze across the gathered gnomes. "My thanks. Be safe." Then with three troll babies in his arms and a lovely wee pixie on his shoulder, General Rock-Eye the troll crossed the meadow and disappeared into the Forest.

A few blinks passed before anyone said a word and it was the translator who broke the silence. "I have never, in all my years, *ever* seen anything like that. Telling this tale is going to earn us all a few pints in the ages to come, that's for sure."

"Then I say we all get home, to pints and families, and safety," The elder Logjaw brother suggested. "All agreed?"

"Agreed."

"Agreed."

"Rightly done."

"On our way."

Within a handful of blinks, Torby and Dillweed were alone in the meadow. Dillweed crossed back over to where they'd left their bedrolls and packs. Torby looked up at the sky. "I don't think we're all that far from home, now, lad. Shall we get ourselves back to our own beds?"

"That would be bloody brilliant, Grandfather. Do we have to tell anyone about this?"

"I thought you wanted songs to be sung in our honour."

"I think I prefer a quiet life. If we become famous, peace and quiet will vanish. Also, even if we tell only those we trust, at some point someone will tell wiggling ears with a wagging tongue and the tale will be told to the wrong audience. As I killed a member of a royal household, I think the rest of my life should be spent keeping my head *down* so I can keep it *on*."

"Well put. Then home it is, and this little adventure never happened."

"Never." He hoisted his pack onto his back and lifted his grandfather's up so the older gnome could wiggle into it. "If it gets too heavy, speak up and we'll rest."

"That I will, son. I'm not the hero here."

"Oh hush, old man."

"Old? I'll show you *old*." Torby settled his pack into place and took off down a wide trail at a quick jog.

Dillweed followed. "Last one home pours the pints!"

Just when she felt her breath ending, Brigid's head broke the surface of the pool and she could breathe again. She let go of the cord and gulped for air, grabbing for the side of the small pool in Trinnean's cave. The noise in the small space was deafening. There was a clanking and hissing and banging, and she was sure they were being ambushed by goblins or trolls or whatever creature made that kind of cacophony. She clung to the side of the pool, certain if she lifted her head too high something horrible would bite it off.

Chapter Twenty-Nine

Brigid looked around the cave in the soft glow of a spelled lantern and realized the enclosure was far too small for anything she couldn't fight off with her blade. A blink later, Fiona came rushing up on the cord and bumped into her. Brigid quickly climbed up and out of the way, then grabbed hold of Fiona's reaching hand and pulled her up and out. Kara and Rainn came along in a snap and they were both lifted clear, then Brigid led them away from the pool, both of them still gulping air.

Kara leaned on Brigid and the cave suddenly went silent. "I thought…I was going…to die. I know sprites…and pixies who do that for…*fun*! They must be…crazy!"

"You get used to it." Trinnean stood next to what looked like a winch without crank handles. His hand rested lightly on a lever. "Fiona knows the way. There's a supply of drying moss just outside."

Fiona led them outside, and that's when Brigid realized the low light wasn't the dawn they just left in Glasgow, but was dusk. The sun was setting in Faerie. Oh goodness, how long had they been gone? A few turns? A fortnight? Was there anything left of their clans to save? What of Nyla? Or even what of Twilly and her clan, stubbornly off on their own?

They dried off quickly, the magical moss making quick work of the job, but Brigid began to panic. "How long have we been gone?"

Trinnean shook the water from his shaggy hair. "Not long. We've missed one or two sunsets at the most. The time passes differently in both worlds, but it's not consistent. The longer you stay in one realm, the faster time moves in the other. Or not. That's the problem with magic and the realms. I can tell it hasn't been long because my ladies are still in full bloom." He pointed at the large patch of buttercups, which were just closing up for the night. "But you're right. We still need to move quickly. The Source Grove is at least a half night's journey on foot, in what has become extremely hostile territory."

"Not as hostile as it once was." A large sparrow hopped down off a branch.

"Browncap!" Trinnean rushed over and hugged the handsome bird, who nuzzled his beak gently into his neck. "You're safe. But you were with Nyla."

"We had to separate. We were being followed by a Sky Patrol. We went down into the Forest to avoid them. When I went back up to see if it was safe, she continued on. I searched for her and found the wings. She removed them and tucked them off to the side of the trail, near the bridge and the trolls."

Kara gasped. "The trolls got her?!"

"Not at all. What happened to your friend—"

"My *sister,*" she corrected with a whisper.

"Your sister succeeded in her quest, somehow. I flew above the trail, all the way to the Source Grove. I had to hide briefly from a war eagle, but snuck along in its wake. I saw Nyla address the Elder Alder for a brief moment before the war eagle swooped in and a faery I hadn't seen from below shot her. In the back."

All four of the Sisters collapsed to the ground like someone had cut their strings. Brigid felt worse than when Lady Witch-Face sliced off their wings and mutilated them. She felt like an iron rod had been speared through her heart. She wept and wanted to die.

Browncap continued, but Brigid barely registered his words. "The eagle landed and a fancy-dressed faery with huge Emperor moth wings landed beside Nyla. He shot her once again in the back, poor thing. I couldn't hear what was said—I didn't dare get too close to the Elder Alder, a Harpy war eagle, and a faery with a bow—but ivy seized the fancy faery and held him. Then he was *executed.* The Forest tore him apart and the very ground opened up and swallowed all of the gory pieces. I nearly threw up into my beak.

"The Elder Alder then lifted Nyla up, looked directly at me, fluttering high above her, and shook her foliage to warn me off, I suspect. She carried your sister off into the Grove and I didn't dare follow them. But a few blinks later, I could feel a dizzying ripple of power flow out from the Source Grove. I landed and chatted with a couple of birches by the river. They were as surprised as I was, but they confirmed the banishment of your clans is reversed." He stepped up to Kara and bowed his head. "It cost brave Nyla her life, but the Forest is once again your home."

Brigid leaned over and took Kara's hand in a firm grip. She had no words for her, though. As much as she knew she needed to comfort her Sister, she, too, needed comfort. Nyla was gone. She was a hero, but she was a *dead* hero. They could go home, but without Nyla, it just wouldn't be the same. The clans would all know instantly the banishment was lifted, so they would already be making their way back. They didn't need their outcast daughters to find them and tell them what they would know by now. She wanted to tell them what regaining their meadows and ponds and groves cost, but she was sure the eldest members of the five clans—including Nyla's own parents—would say one faery lass' life was a worthwhile price, especially as it was all *her* fault in the first place.

She made her decision. "I want to see where Nyla died. I want to go to the Source Grove. It was *all* of our quest. We started out to reach there together. We came all this way and I'm not going to stop this close. Maybe we no longer have a quest, but I need to see it. I'm not ready to go home, yet. She saved us all…and…and I failed her." She *had* failed Nyla. She was the one who took them into another realm without a clue what she was doing, and she was the one who got half of the Sisterhood trapped away from Faerie, leaving Nyla to do it alone.

"I'm coming with you." Fiona whispered. "I left her alone. I should never have left her. Even if we'd had to walk the whole way, I should have stayed with her and been her shield. It was *my* task. I promised."

Trinnean coughed softly. "I will come with you. I have to retrieve the wings, anyway, so let's do it together. The three of us."

"Four," Kara added.

"Five," Rainn confirmed.

Browncap chirped up. "Six. I will go, too. I am the one who failed her in the end. You all had to do what you did. But my task was to keep her safe. I am the one who failed to keep my promise."

Brigid stood. "Then we'll go together."

There was a soft thump and the sound of metal sliding on metal. "Where are we going? Home, I hope."

They all turned to face the new voice in the little glade. Nyla stepped out of the shadows with what looked to Brigid like a pair of metal wings, tucked under her arm. Their dead Sister bent down and gently placed the wings next to Trinnean, ignoring everyone's stares. "Thank you. They worked wonderfully." She stood up just in time to intercept Kara leaping into her arms.

"The Elder Alder says I wasn't quite dead, though it was too close to measure, even in blinks. She drew me in and gave all her magic over to healing me, and in doing so, we bonded. She also reversed the exile."

Kara shook her head. "You're bonded? As in '*bonded* bonded'? Oh burr, Mother is going to be livid she had no say in the matter. Rainsong lasses simply do *not* bond with a tree of their choosing."

"Mother can go burr herself. She wouldn't even have a tree to come back to if it wasn't for what we all did."

"And you'll tell her that to her face no doubt, when we get back to the meadow?"

"I'm not planning to go back. We have a new home, granted to the Sisterhood in perpetuity, beyond the authority of liege lady or king."

Trinnean tossed a berry to Browncap. "Beyond the *King's* authority? Is this place in this realm?"

"The stand of sacred rowans we were accused of burning down."

Brigid coughed on her drink. "You've been 'given' Her Grace's sacred, favourite spot in all her domain? She'd rather kill you than let you have that."

"That's between her and the Alder. Even King Oberon dares not cross the Alder. The Realm is his, but the Forest is hers."

"And you're *bonded* with her?"

"It wasn't her intention but she's actually quite pleased. All these ages and she's never bonded."

"What about us? We can't very well bond to the ashes of murdered rowans."

"There are a dozen great rowans still standing. They were all hurt in some way by the fire, so they need help to heal. I can do it alone if I have to, but I'd rather not have to."

"Isn't your bond tree your new home?" Fiona wondered.

"Usually, yes. But because she's connected to *everything*, I have been asked to make my home amongst the rowans. Will any of you join me?"

Rainn jumped up. "You're asking if we'll bond with ancient rowans? No commoner *ever* gets to bond with a rowan, ancient or otherwise. Burr *yes!*" She skipped a little jig around Trinnean's meadow.

Brigid placed her mug at her side. "I'm with you, though I will also have other responsibilities, if they'll still have me."

"They who?" Fiona leaned in.

"If I tell you, you swear to lifelong secrecy. Everyone,

including Trinn and Browncap."

They all swore on their hearts.

"I'm a Betweener, a member of a secret organization whose job it is to patrol and control the portals between the many realms. The fabric between the worlds weakens every so often and people and things occasionally pass through to the other side. It's our job to clean up the mess. We're also known as Mist Eaters."

"*Mist Eaters?*"

"A myth my predecessors made up to keep the curious away from portals. Of course, they could toss me out on my butt because I opened those unauthorized portals."

"Maybe they don't know."

"They *always* know. It's what they do. So if the Elder will allow me to be a Betweener first, I will dedicate the rest of my time to the rowans."

Nyla asked her bond-tree silently, in her head, and the answer was immediate. "Of course. Who else? Fiona?"

Fiona squeezed Trinnean's hand. "I'm in, but I'll need a tree big enough for two."

"No surprise there. Rainn is in. Kara?"

Kara stared at the ground between her feet, her shoulders slumped, her voice grey. "I don't bond until next year."

"You bond when the Alder says you bond, and you've more than proven yourself mature enough. Will you come, little sister?"

"In a heartbeat!"

"Excellent! Then at first light we'll start out. That includes Trinnean, of course."

He kissed the back of Fiona's hand. "I'll make the journey with you, but I will have to return home for a time so I can build you six sets of wings."

"You would do that for us?"

"Nyla, I'd give you the set Browncap says you've apparently already mastered, but I'll need them pattern the others after. On the hike to your new home, though, I'd love to hear what improvements you'd suggest."

"Of course. In the meantime, though, I think we need more butter-juice."

"Coming right up," and he hopped up to fetch another bottle. They had a lot to celebrate.

Dillweed got two steps through the door before he dropped the packsacks on the floor in front of him and fell face-first onto them. He was exhausted. For the last however many turns, he'd carried both packs. He didn't mind and had in fact insisted on it after his grandfather casually commented he felt light headed and like he'd been punched in the chest. A few turns later, Torby shuffled in after him and shut the door.

"I built you a bed for a reason, lad, but if you wish to sleep with a cook pot poking you in the ribs, so be it."

"I'm just catching a few wee winks before I start off to fetch the ladies."

"That can wait. I think we have both earned a quiet night or two in our own beds, with our own kitchen and no nagging."

Dillweed lifted his head just a smidgen. "Then if you wouldn't mind giving me a hand up, that bed sounds perfect." He felt his grandfather's strong hand grab the back of his vest and lift. He added what little strength he could muster and between the two of them he made it to his feet. "Do you mind if I leave the packs here until morning?"

"I'd mind if you didn't. There's nothing we need in there for a good sleep tonight." He opened his arms for a hug and Torby gladly stepped into it. "I'm proud of you, lad. Even though the tale will go untold, you have shown the world the Pondbottoms at their best." They held the embrace, both exhausted and supportive.

"I couldn't have done it without you, Grandfather. I just did what I thought needed to be done."

They broke free of the hug and Torby patted Dillweed's cheek affectionately. "Then you thought well. The adventure is over. Get some sleep."

"Yes sir. You, too."

"Count on it, lad. Count on it."

There had been an odd vibration throughout Ten Oaks for quite some time, but Orlaith was too distracted by an odd sensation there was something wrong with her brother. They were the opposite of close, but they were still blood. When she finally poured herself a glass of wine and sat back in her high tower to gaze out over her domain, the vibration moved up from the polished floor, through the chair, and the Elder Alder spoke directly to her, through the Forest and the Ten Oaks themselves.

"Greetings, Your Grace. Your brother has forfeited his life. He brought death to my Grove. He is also responsible for the murder of the rowans we both hold so dear."

"Orrin is gone?" She wasn't sure how she felt about that.

"He is. You punished the wrong faeries."

"As was my prerogative. That lass was still responsible for the mess which started this."

"That lass was spelled by your brother. She did nothing wrong. Her friends did nothing wrong. Their clans have been re-instated. I was hasty."

"And I still have a grove of ruined, murdered rowans."

"Not at all. I have granted that grove and the surrounding rowans to Nyla Rainsong and her Sisterhood. Forever."

"*What?* "You can't!"

"I have. It is done. Your King has been notified, their clans are on their way back to their homes, and the lasses will be settling in and bonding as soon as they arrive there. I have decided. I have spoken. They are still your subjects, but she is my bond and I will protect her life before all else."

"You *bonded…?*"

The connection broke. The vibration stopped. The Elder Alder had just—she threw her glass out the window and screamed in fury.

Epilogue

Nyla gently brushed the ashes of the murdered rowans aside, then patted down the smoothed patch of scorched soil with her hand. When the spot looked big enough, she sat, snuggled her butt down firmly, crossed her legs, and placed her hands palms-down, her fingers clutching the dark earth. She had no idea what she was doing, but it seemed like a reasonable start. Her Sisters and Trinnean watched from a short distance off, sitting on stumps, logs, or the ground. Their mothers would all be scandalized, but not one of her friends worried about the ashes and their clothes. They were the least of their concerns.

Nyla closed her eyes and felt the energy of everything around her tickling her skin, the ebb and flow of all life in Faerie. Strongest of all, she felt her bond with the Elder Alder, undiminished by the distance even though they were now in the remains of the rowan grove. She pictured Twilly in her ball gown, all lace and frills, looking as lovely as any faery ever has, she was sure. In her mind, Twilly danced and smiled and finger-waved while Nyla felt Faerie's energy flow up and into her.

She got a sense of Twilly, but it didn't come from the direction the Berrycheer clan had marched off, alone. It seemed to be coming from the east, a long way off. She caught hold of that feeling and let it pull her along. A bizarre experience, it felt like bobbing along on a river in a barrel, up and down, round and round. She lost the dancing image for a moment and the magic energy thinned and slowed. She concentrated harder, and her connection—or whatever it was—with her wayward Sister strengthened. Then there Twilly sat, on a bright green and yellow-spotted toadstool, smiling up at the sun with her eyes closed. Twilly's eyes snapped opened and she turned left and right, searching the little clearing she was in.

"*Nyla?*"

"Twilly! Where in Faerie *are* you?"

"Just outside our cave, sunning while everyone else sleeps."

"Sleeping on a sunny day?"

"Trolls do that, Silly."

"*Trolls*? You've been captured?"

"Not at all. I've been saved. You five all went with your clans and I was forbidden allowed to go along. With Cray dead, you all gone, and the Forest trying to kill us, somehow I ended up here."

"Where is 'here'?"

"Well, I'm not entirely sure, but we're somewhere in the

mountains in Lord Orrin's domain."

"Orrin is dead."

"Truly?"

"It's a long story. Are you coming home?"

"What home? The Forest has orders to kill us."

"Not any more. That's all part of the story."

"I hope it includes how in the burr you're talking to me through the toadstool under my butt."

"It does. Do you need us to come fetch you, or can you get the trolls to get you here?"

"Rock-Eye and Winsome will be sad, but I'm sure they'll take me back home. I miss the meadow."

"You have—we *all* have—a new home, if you want. Have them bring you to the rowan grove we were supposed to have burned down."

"That's part of this story?"

"It is."

"Then I can't wait to hear it. We have Winsome's birthday party during the new moon, so we'll start out after that."

"It sounds like you have your own story to share, Twill."

"You know it, Sister. See you soon. Love you."

"Soon. Love you back."

Nyla released her hold on the earth energy and opened her eyes. She shook off the fuzziness clinging to her thoughts, and smiled.

The two humans stood next to the grand old yew in the park's centre, the older one awkwardly rubbing a lump on his head from where it hit the fence, and his knee where he'd been shot with an arrow.

"Can you walk?"

"Aye. Slow, but sure I can make it."

"Good. Then let's get ourselves gone from this place. I never want to hear the words 'gold' or 'leprechaun' come from your mouth again."

"But it was the lads at the pub who first told me about them."

"I don't care if it was God hisself. We're shut of the idea, and will not speak to a soul about this night. *Ever.*"

"Aye. Not ever." He limped down the path and out the gates, back to their rooming house. Donal walked along at his side.

The giant rhododendron across the path from the yew shimmied and wiggled a bit down near the ground, and two green-hatted heads popped out. The shorter leprechaun scratched his bearded chin and sighed. "I thought they'd *never* leave, Shamus."

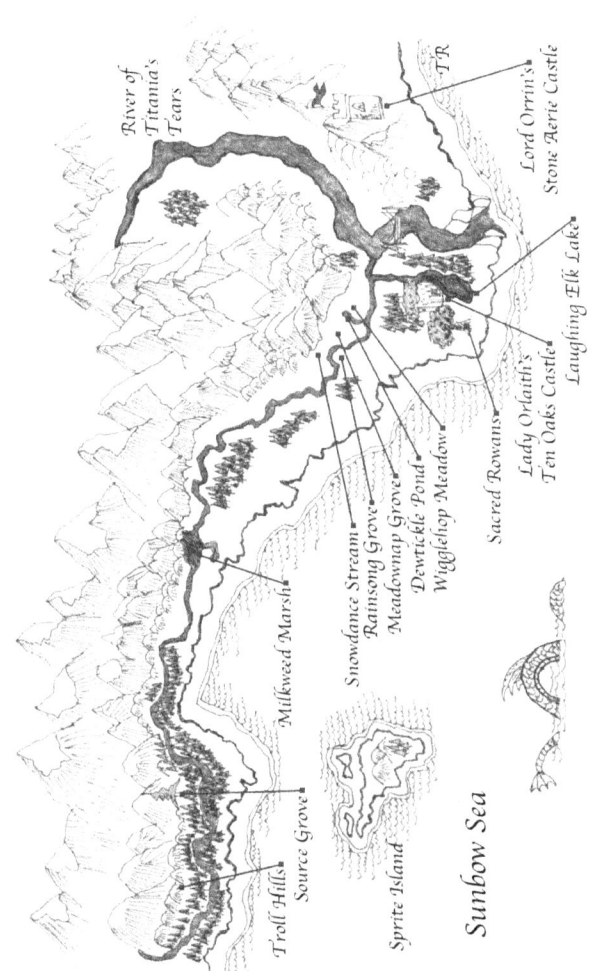

River of Titania's Tears

Lord Orrin's Stone Aerie Castle

TR

Laughing Elk Lake

Lady Orlaith's Ten Oaks Castle

Sacred Rowans

Wigglehop Meadow

Dewtrickle Pond

Meadownap Grove

Rainsong Grove

Snowdance Stream

Milkweed Marsh

Source Grove

Troll Hills

Sprite Island

Sunbow Sea

From The Sisterhood of the Black Dragonfly by Timothy Reynolds

About the Author

"Canada's modern-day Aesop." ~ CBC Radio

Tim Reynolds grew up in Toronto, Ontario, but has called Calgary, Alberta home since 1999. He lives a quiet, peaceful, cluttered life with his dog, Sedona, two cats, Kerouac and Calliope, and a collection of musical instruments he has neither the talent nor the self-discipline to play.

An internationally-published writer/photographer/artist he writes his stories "from the character on up".

The Sisterhood of the Black Dragonfly is his third published novel. He also has a self-help book, a collection of short stories, and writes a quarterly humour column for SEARCH Magazine out of California.

Long-Listed: *2017 Alberta Readers' Choice Award*
Finalist: *2016 Baen Fantasy Adventure Award*
A Winner: *Kobo Writing Life's Jeffrey Archer*
Short Story Challenge
Two Honourable Mentions: *Writers of the Future Contest*
Honourable Mention: *Illustrators of the Future Contest*
Winner: *The First Great Canadian Fable Contest*

www.ingramcontent.com/pod-product-compliance
Lightning Source LLC
Chambersburg PA
CBHW071131200626
46817CB00018B/2671